The Free Negress Elisabeth

CYNTHIA MC LEOD is the daughter of Dr Johann Ferrier, the last governor and first president of Suriname. She invested twelve years of historical research in writing *The Free Negress Elisabeth*, and is widely regarded as one of the leading authorities on Surinamese history. Her first novel, *The High Price of Sugar*, published in Suriname in 1978, remains a bestseller.

BRIAN DOYLE is a part-time professor at the Katholieke Universiteit Leuven, and he has also translated a wide variety of academic works from Dutch/Flemish into English. His translation of Pieter Waterdrinker's *German Wedding* is to be published by Atlantic Grove in 2008 and his translation of Jef Geeraerts' *The PG* by Bitter Lemon in early 2009.

The Free Negress Elisabeth

Cynthia Mc Leod

Translated from the Dutch by Brian Doyle

Arcadia Books Ltd
15–16 Nassau Street
London W1W 7AB

www.arcadiabooks.co.uk

First published in the United Kingdom by BlackAmber
an imprint of Arcadia Books 2008
Originally published by Uitgeverij Conserve 2000
Copyright © Cynthia Mc Leod 2000

The English translation from the Dutch
Copyright © Brian Doyle 2008

Cynthia Mc Leod has asserted her moral right to be identified as the author of this work in accordance with the Copyright, Designs and Patents Act, 1988

A catalogue record for this book is available from the British Library.

ISBN 978-1-905147-83-0

Typeset in Minion by MacGuru Ltd
Printed in Finland by WS Bookwell

This translation has been published with financial support from the Foundation for the Production and Translation of Dutch Literature.

Arcadia Books supports English PEN, the fellowship of writers who work together to promote literature and its understanding. English PEN upholds writers' freedoms in Britain and around the world, challenging political and cultural limits on free expression. To find out more, visit www. englishpen.org or contact
English PEN, 6-8 Amwell Street, London EC1R 1UQ

Arcadia Books distributors are as follows:

in the UK and elsewhere in Europe:
Turnaround Publishers Services
Unit 3, Olympia Trading Estate
Coburg Road
London N22 6TZ

in the US and Canada:
Independent Publishers Group
814 N. Franklin Street
Chicago, IL 60610

in Australia:
Tower Books
PO Box 213
Brookvale, NSW 2100

in New Zealand:
Addenda
PO Box 78224
Grey Lynn
Auckland

in South Africa:
Quartet Sales and Marketing
PO Box 1218
Northcliffe
Johannesburg 2115

Arcadia Books is the *Sunday Times* Small Publisher of the Year

Introduction

Elisabeth Samson's name crops up in just about every historical work on Suriname because she is said to have been the first negress to have aspired to marry a white man. Her ambitions caused considerable commotion in eighteenth-century Suriname, since the Commissioners for Marital Affairs were of the opinion that marriage between whites and blacks had been forbidden by an edict dating back to the time of Governor Van Aerssen Van Sommelsdijck (1683–1688). The Commissioners referred her to the Police Council, which wrote in turn to the Directors of the Suriname Society in the Netherlands. In the meantime, however, Elisabeth had already petitioned the Heren xvii – the Directors of the Suriname Society – via her business representative in Amsterdam to grant her request.

The Police Council, which represented the sentiments of the white community in Suriname, entered into an elaborate correspondence with the Directors of the Society. They explained why such a marriage would be a serious mistake, although there were arguments that favoured approval in Elisabeth's case. Their main justification was the belief that the wealth acquired by the young bridegroom would 'ultimately find its way into the white community, which is not a bad thing. Much evil is to be feared of free folk among the negroes who had acquired too much power, since it gives our slaves the idea that they can rise above their station and be like us'.

After a lengthy correspondence, which lasted the best part of three years, a decision was made by the States General (the legislative assembly of the day), who informed the Directors of the Society that Dutch law did not prohibit marriage between whites and blacks. The Directors of the Society left the final judgement in the case to the Police Council in Suriname, although they advised them to grant permission. By the time the message arrived in Suriname, however, the bridegroom-to-be had passed away. Elisabeth Samson then married another white man, 22 years her younger.

Reference is made to this fact in the works of J.J. Hartsinck, J.G. Stedman, J. Wolbers, R.A.J. Van Lier, Lichtveld and Voorhoeve, among others:

J.G. Stedman: 'One free negress named Elisabeth Samson married a European. She had inherited more than one hundred thousand pounds sterling from someone whose slave she had once been.' (From: *Narrative of a Five Years Expedition…*)

J. Wolbers: 'The Court had difficulty granting permission because the description of Suriname published in 1718 by J.D. Herlein states that such marriages were said to have been prohibited by decree under Governor Van Sommelsdijck...' (From: *Geschiedenis van Suriname*)

R.A.J. Van Lier: 'Elisabeth Samson, a free negress, had acquired a considerable fortune. A memorandum ascribed to [Governor] Nepveu indicates that she had an income of between eighty and one hundred thousand guilders from her plantation. The source of her wealth remains unknown, although her name suggests it came from her Jewish owner, who had granted her freedom and left her his fortune.' (From: *Samenleving in een grensgebied*)

U. Lichtveld and J. Voorhoeve: 'Schouten married a coloured woman, Suzanna Johanna Hanssen by name, in 1772. She was a niece of the free and wealthy Nanette Samson, who was the first to enter into a legal marriage with a white man in 1776.' (From: *Spiegel der Vaderlandse Kooplieden*)

Although the references are not identical, the historians in question agree nevertheless that Elisabeth had inherited her wealth from a white man. It was her passionate desire to be allowed to marry, however, that made the matter interesting and worthy of mention.

When my husband became ambassador for the second time in Belgium and the then EEC, I took the opportunity to do further research into the figure of Elisabeth Samson in an effort to find out who she was, where she had acquired her wealth and why she had been so determined to marry.

I was able to gather information on who she was, the source of her wealth, whether the expectation that her riches 'would eventually find their way into the white community' had been fulfilled, and whether the separation of blacks and whites in Suriname was as strict as most historians suggest. In addition to the Office of Public Records (OPR) in The Hague, which provided the most important documents, the Municipal Archives of the city of Amsterdam and the Royal Tropical Institute in the same city also provided large amounts of information. I was likewise able to gather useful material from the Municipal Archives of the city of Rotterdam as well as archives in Germany (Emmerich and Sonsbeek) and Suriname (e.g. the Estates Office).

The enthusiasm required to begin such a mammoth task and, in particular, to maintain and complete it, was sustained in essence by my fascination for the figure of Elisabeth Samson. She struck me as a decidedly self-assured black woman, unwilling to comply with the negative response she had received to her request to marry the person of her choice. As a free negress without rights, she succeeded in taking action against discrimination on the basis of race, in spite of the prejudices of the white community. As my research progressed and bore fruit, I was able to demonstrate that Elisabeth Samson had been responsible to a considerable degree for her own wealth and that the sense of white supremacy among the Dutch had apparently been subordinate to money. Elisabeth Samson must have been a striking individual in Suriname, a reality that the present volume together with my earlier study set out to prove.

My search for information on Elisabeth Samson felt initially like searching for a needle in a haystack. The OPR in The Hague had preserved thousands of books containing information about Suriname. Each book contained 600 or more handwritten folios and hundreds of books were related to the period between 1740 and 1773. To complicate matters, none of the books had been classified according to content. The search for sources is far from simple and is certainly not a question of paying a visit to the local archives, calling up this or that document and discovering what one was looking for in a matter of minutes. The present study is the result of years of research and weeks on end spent knee deep in documents at the OPR.

I started my research with the intention of writing a novel about Elisabeth Samson, but as I focused in on this striking figure, I came to realise that a novel alone would not do her justice. It became clear quite early on that the historians had been mistaken. Indeed, the presupposition that this eighteenth-century black woman had inherited her wealth from a white man turned out to be a prime example of 'machismo and sentiments of white supremacy'.

The reality surrounding this remarkable figure was so interesting that I felt obliged to share it with the Surinamese community. At the same time, it had to be made clear that I had gathered and organised my material in an academically warranted manner. For this reason, the first edition of this book was published in October 1993 by the Department of Cultural Anthropology of the University of Utrecht, edited by Dr W. Hoogbergen.[1] Public demand for a novel persisted, nevertheless. After the document's publication, my research continued and I devoted the following years to the formation of a picture of the mid-eighteenth century social circumstances in which Elisabeth's motivation and the behaviour of the people surrounding her might be better understood.

The characters in *The Free Negress Elisabeth* are based on real men and women and many of the statements they make are authentic. Where appropriate, therefore, I have included a reference to specific sources. Most of the facts and events described in the book are likewise based on historical facts and events. My own imagination has been limited to developing the novel's various characters and their emotions.

It would appear that twentieth and twenty-first century men and women

3

still react to the fact that Elisabeth wanted to marry a white man, focusing their attention on the significance of the concept 'white'. In my opinion, however, the whiteness of the man Elisabeth wanted to marry was not the point. Relationships between free negresses or mulattos and white men were nothing unusual in Elisabeth's Suriname. While things were undoubtedly different in the United States or British West Indies, virtually all free negresses and coloured women had such a relationship in Suriname at the time, because there were fifteen times as many white men in the colony as there were white women. Elisabeth lived with Carl Otto Creutz for at least fifteen years, but they were unable to marry because she was 100 per cent negress.

In their book *Spiegel der Vaderlandse Kooplieden* (*The Face of Dutch Merchant Traders*), Lichtveld and Voorhoeve write that Nanette Samson married in 1767 and that she was of mixed race. This, however, is a source of confusion. Nanette lived at least twenty years longer than her sister, but never married. Lichtveld and Voorhoeve make no distinction between 'coloured' and 'negro'. People raised in a society in which the colour of a person's skin had an important role to play generally understand such distinctions. Indeed, many more distinctions were made in Elisabeth's day and different shades of colour acquired different designations.

'Coloured' is a collective term for people of mixed black-white blood. Marriage between a white man and a coloured woman was never prohibited by ordinance in Suriname. The prohibition was only valid for black people, which in eighteenth-century Suriname meant 100 per cent negroes. An abundance of examples exists of mulattos and other coloured people entering into licit marriages quite early on in the history of slavery. It is evident from Elisabeth's case that the colonial authorities maintained the prohibition to the letter, yet they were likewise critical of black or coloured women who lived with a man out of wedlock, describing them as 'whores' living 'iniquitous' lives 'in sin'. Such inconsistent duplicity must have irritated Elisabeth tremendously. She was extremely wealthy, had everything money could buy, but the status of married woman eluded her and she was prepared to do everything in her power to realise her desire.

Some will disapprove of Elisabeth Samson's conduct in this matter and they are free to do so. I am likewise unable to argue that she should be treated as a role model for contemporary Surinamese woman. It is important to realise, nevertheless, that one cannot judge the conduct of eighteenth-century Suriname against today's standards. Slavery was not like the Second World War, a five-year episode in history. Slavery lasted 300 years. Generations of black men and women were born in slavery and died as slaves. Black people were obliged to find a way to live with their fate and only a small portion of the hundreds of thousands of slaves brought to Suriname were capable of escaping their bonds and joining the rebellious Maroons.

Elisabeth lived at a time in which 300 years of slavery had reached their peak. In the year 1750, no one was calling for the abolition of slavery. Indeed, the most one could expect to find was an appeal for the proper treatment of black people. A relationship with a white man was one of the means adopted by black women to ensure that their children would be born free and enjoy a better life.

Elisabeth Samson's life reveals that a black woman with daring and courage, intelligence and culture, lacking fear and subservience, had the capacity to acquire an important financial position within a society based on slavery, in spite of opposition and the racist prejudices of the day. She did not wait until someone else took up her cause; she decided rather to be master of her own destiny.

Notes

ARA/OPR: *Algemeen Rijks Archief*/Office of Public Records
GS/GO: *Gouvernements Secretarie*/Government Office
OAS: Old Archive Suriname
ONAS: Old Notarial Archive Suriname
SS: Suriname Society

A. The Court of Police and Criminal Justice administered the colony of Suriname. It consisted of the governor and (mostly) fourteen members. The governor was appointed from the Netherlands, the members were elected.
B. Under the sovereignty of the States General, the Chartered Society of Amsterdam exercised authority over Suriname (see Van Lier 1977: 15–16).
C. Office of Public Records, The Hague, letter from the members of the Court of Police to the Suriname Society. For more detailed information, the reader should consult chapter 8 of my study on Elisabeth Samson (Conserve, 1996).

PART ONE

The Court Case

December 1733
Paramaribo, Suriname

Elisabeth stood at one of the windows of the big house on Waterkant and looked outside at the broad Suriname River, but could not quite make out what was going on. Large and small sailing ships were moored at a jetty a little further upriver. The tide was on its way out and a couple of covered tent boats had made their way onto the river. Rowed by six black slaves, they were heading towards the plantations near the estuary of the Suriname, or the banks of the Commewijne or the Cottica. A few sailing boats had arrived with a cargo of slaves. Two ships had already been in port for a couple of days. In addition to the red bricks that served as ballast, they had brought provisions and other merchandise from Holland. All the boats were obliged to return to Europe fully loaded with sugar and other local produce.

The street was a hive of activity. Waterkant was one of the busiest neighbourhoods in Paramaribo. Two substantial wooden mansions flanked the beginning of the street, while the buildings closer to the jetty served as warehouses. The place was always busy at midmorning, with white masters and mistresses followed by one or more slaves. A few white men had gathered for a chat. Heavily laden carts vied for space with horse-drawn buggies and the occasional single horseman.

'Ho!' someone shouted.

Elisabeth was shaken from her reverie with a start and she turned her attention to the scene taking place in front of her. A white man was shouting and waving a cane beside a cart laden with chests and casks. One of the chests had fallen to the ground and one of its sides had come undone. A couple of pitchers had fallen out of the chest and smashed to pieces on the street, their contents spilling onto the sand. Two black youngsters wearing nothing but loincloths, did their utmost to save the other cask from the same fate. The black coachman leapt from his seat, heaved the chest from the ground and tried to fasten it shut. He then returned it to the cart as the white man struck one of the broken pitchers with his cane. The coachmen tried to squeeze the chest between the others on the cart. The white man indicated with his cane that the smallest of the youngsters was to sit on the cart and secure the chests.

In the meantime, a young futuboi had crouched down beside the broken pitchers. He checked to see if anyone was watching him, grabbed the base of one of the broken pitchers, looked inside and swigged at its contents. As he was drinking, he suddenly realised that Elisabeth was watching him. He seemed startled for a moment, but he quickly got hold of himself and grinned back at her. He licked his lips in what appeared to be a gesture of conspiracy and rubbed his bare belly with his hand.

Elisabeth smiled. He'll be drunk before long, she thought. She was well aware that the pitchers had contained Dutch Jenever. Her brother-in-law, Frederik Bosse, the owner of the house on Waterkant in which she also lived, had pitchers of Jenever brought over from Holland often enough.

'Elisabeth,' someone called from behind. Elisabeth turned. Her sister Nanette, five years her elder, was standing in the doorway.

'Nanette,' said Elisabeth. 'Have you been standing there long? I was at the window but I didn't see you come in.'

'I, well… I used the negerpoort,' she replied, hesitantly.

'The negerpoort?' Elisabeth erupted. 'Yet again? How many times do I have to tell you to use the front door? Why do you still behave like a slave? If it's so hard to get rid of that slave behaviour, then Charlo shouldn't have wasted so much effort purchasing your freedom. You know how much he had to pay! Your behaviour betrays a lack of gratitude!'

'Our brother was a good man, God rest him, who was prepared to do whatever it took to ensure our freedom and we are more than grateful,' Nanette answered. 'I used the negerpoort because I saw nene go in and I wanted to talk to her.'

'I don't care what you were doing. You are a free woman and free women do not use the negerpoort. Remember that once and for all.'

'You're right, you're right,' said Nanette contritely. She was a little nervous of her younger sister, who never missed an opportunity to speak her mind if she disapproved of something.

Elisabeth sat down on one of the settees. Nanette remained standing and announced: 'Mina gave birth to a daughter yesterday.'

'Really?' said Elisabeth. 'And is she alright?'

'Yes, they're both fine. A healthy baby girl,' Nanette responded. 'Jacki's with her.'

'You mean Izaak,' Elisabeth snapped.

'Yes, Izaak, yes,' Nanette quickly corrected herself. This was yet another source of irritation for Elisabeth. Her liberated brothers and sisters seemed to be unable to get used to the new names they had taken after emancipation two years earlier.

'You know Izaak,' Nanette continued. 'His daughters are named after his sisters. Cato and I have already been taken, and now he wants to know if you would allow him to use your name.'

At first, Elisabeth did not answer. She looked at her sister, who was standing close to the door, and thought to herself: in spite of your pretty clothes and the shoes on your feet, you still look like a slave. 'Tell Izaak he can call his daughter Liesbeth.'

'Liesbeth?' asked Nanette. 'But your name is Elisabeth?'

'That's true,' said her sister, 'absolutely true. My name is Elisabeth and the child can take Liesbeth or perhaps Bettie.'

She just wants to avoid there being two Elisabeths, Nanette thought. Lucky the child is free at least. Her sister would definitely have had problems giving her name to a slave child.

'Where is Sisa Maria?' Nanette asked, not because she wanted to know the whereabouts of her oldest sister, but because she didn't know what to say next.

'I think she's upstairs,' said Elisabeth, and she got to her feet and returned to the window.

Nanette left the room and slowly climbed the stairs.

She thought about their half-brother Charlo Jansz who had purchased their freedom two years earlier: Jacki, Kwakoe, Nanno and Cato.[2] Jacki and Kwakoe, however, still had children who were slaves.

Her youngest sister Elisabeth had never been a slave because she was born after her mother had gained her freedom. Their half-brother Charlo and half-sister Maria had acquired their freedom twenty years earlier together with their mother Nanno. The father of Charlo and Maria, who was a white man, had indicated in his will that his widow was to purchase the freedom of his two mulatto children together with their mother, the slave Nanno. And that is precisely what she did. Charlo and Maria, who were thirteen and fourteen years old at the time, acquired their freedom and were given the surname Jansz after their father Jan Van Susteren. Since then, their mother was spoken of as 'the free negress Mariana'. Her other children, all of them negroes, remained slaves.

Mariana gave birth to yet another child two years later and named her Elisabeth. Since her mother was free, Elisabeth was also free. In the meantime, Maria had married a wealthy husband of Swiss origin named Pierre Mevila. Mother Mariana lived with Charlo on Keizerstraat, while the other children lived in the slave houses on the property of the widow of Jan Van Susteren. Fortunately, their white mistress enjoyed a particularly good relationship with the mulatto son of her deceased husband and she had promised him permission to purchase the freedom of his brothers and sisters.

Little free Elisabeth was taken in by her older half-sister Maria who had no children of her own. She spoiled her mother's youngest child shamefully. Maria's husband Mevila was a rich planter who owned a substantial sugar

THE FREE NEGRESS ELISABETH

plantation and a couple of handsome mansion houses along Waterkant. But he was fated not to enjoy his wealth into old age, and passed away before his tenth wedding anniversary. Two years later Maria married Frederik Coenraad Bosse, an army captain. Bosse took enormous pleasure in quick-witted little Elisabeth. He taught her everything: writing, arithmetic, chess; and when the Bosses received visitors, Elisabeth was always asked to demonstrate her skills.

If you had never been a slave and had always lived in a big house as a spoiled little girl dealing out the orders right and left, then you are unlikely to have developed the manners of a slave, even if you were a negress and black as pitch, thought Nanette as she climbed the stairs to her sister's room.

Maria, a handsome brown-skinned woman with black hair tied in a bun at the neck, was standing in front of the open wardrobe. A slave woman sat beside her on the floor folding sheets.

'Hello Sisa Maria,' said Nanette. 'Izaak sends his regards. His Mina has just given birth to a daughter.'

'A daughter? How wonderful!' said Maria. 'Everything as it should be, I hope? What's the child's name?'

'Well, that's the big question,' said Nanette. 'Izaak sent me to Elisabeth to ask if he could name his child after her, but our sister insists that the child be called Liesbeth or Bettie.'

Maria laughed for a moment. 'Typical Elisabeth,' she said, 'but where's the problem? Liesbeth is also a fine name.' She turned to the slave woman: 'Throw that sheet away. Can't you see it's torn? Come, Nanette,' she continued, 'let's go downstairs. I'll give you a couple of bottles of wine to take to Mina.'

When they descended the stairs, Maria sent one of the slaves to the basement to fetch three bottles of wine and a dish of butter, which she arranged in a basket with some eggs. A moment or two later and Nanette was on her way, a little futuboi behind her carrying the basket.

Nanette was tempted to leave by the back door and the negerpoort, but she remembered her sister's angry words just in time and hurried to the front room and the front door. Elisabeth was seated at her writing desk.

'Bye, Elisabeth, I'm just going out,' said Nanette

'Bye. See you later,' Elisabeth responded without looking up from her papers.

Poor Charlo, Nanette thought as she made her way onto the street. He had died a year earlier, after an illness that had lasted a painful six months. One more week and he would have celebrated his thirty-fifth birthday. Fortunately, he had lived to see the emancipation and had even been able to hand over the documents in person. Charlo and Maria were a truly wonderful brother and sister. Nanette knew of mulattos with brothers and sisters who were still slaves.

They often paid little if any attention to negroes and didn't treat them as family. Mulattos like that weren't likely to offer up their savings to purchase their negro family's freedom as Charlo had done. He had dedicated his life to it.

We will always be grateful to him, thought Nanette. Elisabeth could make such a fuss. That was one of her specialities. What a scene she had made about names at the emancipation! Elisabeth had insisted that Jacki was to be referred to henceforth as Izaak, Cato as Catharina, she herself as Nanette instead of Nanno, and Kwakoe as Jan. Elisabeth had argued that their old names were slave names and were inappropriate for free people. She herself had obeyed her younger sister together with Jacki and Cato, but Kwakoe had stood his ground.

'My name is Kwakoe and that's the way it stays,' he had said. 'You can forget about Jan.' He even went as far as to name his son Kwakoe.

Everyone did whatever Elisabeth wanted. It was almost as if they were a little afraid of her, in spite of the fact that she was the youngest. Even Maria, who was all of sixteen years older than Elisabeth and had raised her as if she were her own child, was afraid of Elisabeth's sharp tongue and often devastating opinions. Her brothers and sisters wondered on occasion what life would be like if Elisabeth had been a mulatta instead of a negress. She would have bossed us around even more than now, they concluded. There was only one person who dared to disagree with Elisabeth, and that was Frederik Bosse, the husband of their sister Maria. But Frederik was so taken by his youngest sister-in-law that they rarely if ever disagreed. Hardly surprising when you consider he had raised her and spoiled her as if she were his daughter. He was proud of her because she was so clever.

Nanette was well aware that Elisabeth's brightness and intelligence were the subject of local conversation and that her name had found its way into many a white person's drawing room. There had even been reports that the governor and his entourage had talked about her. She was indeed extremely intelligent.

Frederik Bosse had given Elisabeth a Bible when she was only eight years old and she spent hours reading it. She was baptised in the Reformed Church when she was ten. Frederik Bosse still related with considerable pleasure how the little negro girl had surprised the elders and church council members with her knowledge of the gospel during the Christening ceremony. She could recite Psalms by heart and whole portions of the Bible one after the other. When one of the church council members asked her to explain something, her response was flawless and included all sorts of difficult words that the men themselves had never heard before. This turned out to be the main topic of conversation in the entire colony for weeks on end and Frederik Bosse was aglow with pride. Nanette also knew that Bosse had entrusted a large part of his business affairs to Elisabeth for several years. She decided what was necessary for his dealings in the colony, ordered all sorts of things from Holland in writing, and kept a close eye on Saltzhallen, the colossal plantation that once belonged to Mevila. Masra Frederik always said that thanks to Elisabeth none of the plantation directors had ever been able to make a fool of him. But she still makes us feel like stupid negroes, newly emancipated, Nanette thought. I wonder what kind of husband she'll find, now that she's turned eighteen. He'll have to be strong, otherwise he'll be henpecked!

Nanette felt at home in Keizerstraat where she lived with her mother, her mother's friend, the free negro Harder and her sister Catharina. Charlo had lived in the house next door with his wife Johanna. Izaak lived with his new wife Mina in Wagenwegstraat. Nanette thought it best to head directly to Izaak and Mina's house, but she decided to pay a quick visit to her sister Catharina on the way, to tell her about their youngest sister's reaction when she heard that Izaak wanted to name his daughter Elisabeth.

'If Mina had been a slave, even Liesbeth would have been out of the question,' said Nanette, having informed her sister about Elisabeth's reaction.

'Nanno!' mother Mariana called from the back of the house. She was sitting on a bench on the rear gallery where Cato, Izaak's oldest daughter, was braiding her grandmother's hair.

'Are you going to see Mina?' Mariana asked in nengre English. She couldn't speak a word of Dutch and always spoke nengre or English because she had been born and raised in Saint Christopher.

'Yes. I have a basket with me from Maria,' Nanette answered, and she took the basket from the futuboi to show its contents to her mother.

'Sammy, fetch some bita from nene,' Mariana instructed her grandson, 'and Cato, wash your hands. You're both going with your aunt to see your new sister.' Her eleven-year-old granddaughter immediately put down the wooden comb, raced to the well where she plunged her hands into a bucket and splashed her face with water. She then disappeared into one of the little houses at the back of the property only to emerge a few moments later dressed in a skirt and blouse instead of the pagni she had been wearing earlier. She was not wearing shoes, however, because Izaak's daughter was still a slave, as were her sister and two brothers. Their mother had once been Mariana's slave. She had been dead for more than five years and the children lived with their grandmother.

Before long Nanette was on her way to Izaak's house with Cato and Sammy a couple of steps behind, barely able to carry the basket between them because Mariana had stuffed it to the brim with all sorts of goodies.

Elisabeth was still at her writing desk in the front room where she had been working when Nanette left the house. Through the front door, thank goodness, and not the negerpoort, thought Elisabeth with a sigh. The things her brothers and sister did sometimes angered her so. How fortunate she had been to be born a free woman. The very idea of being born a slave hardly bore thinking about. She was black and well aware of it, but she was not a slave. In truth, she was more cultivated than many a white person.

Elisabeth rummaged among the papers and produced a goose feather, which she transformed into a quill with a sharp knife and began to write. She wanted to finish the requisitions before her brother-in-law Frederik arrived home and she planned to write the accompanying letters later in the week.

She finished her work in less than an hour, moved over to the harpsichord and started to play.

A young blond-haired gentleman stood outside on the street staring at the house. It was a substantial wood-built residence with three floors, a redbrick path leading to the front door. Green painted wooden window frames lay open on either side. This had to be the home of Frederik Bosse, thought Carl Otto Creutz, cadet in the army of the Suriname Society and a new arrival in Paramaribo. When his ship turned into the River Suriname the day before on the final leg of its journey, he had spotted the houses on Waterkant. A pleasant sight, he had thought, like oversized building blocks. The temperature was bearable. He had heard that the heat could soar to such a degree that people had difficulty breathing, but it wasn't as bad as he had expected. The sun was blazing, but the refreshing wind blowing in from the river made everything appear crisp and clear. All quite manageable, he thought.

One of the officers had disembarked them the previous afternoon, after they had said their personal farewells to Captain Jan Smit and his ship the *New Clarenbeek*. The short journey from the ship to Fort Zeelandia was a feast for the eyes and Creutz tried to take in as much as he could. The new officers and cadets were billeted with other officers, while the soldiers spent the night in an enormous hangar. The new officers were expected to pay their respects to the governor that morning, and senior servicemen who had already been resident in the colony for some time were also present for the occasion, among them Captain Frederik Coenraad Bosse. Bosse was delighted to hear that he and Carl Otto Creutz came from the same region of Germany. When it turned out that Creutz was still in search of a place to stay in Paramaribo, Bosse insisted that anyone hailing from the duchy of Cleve was more than welcome in his home and that the young cadet should collect his belongings and make his way to the Bosse residence on Waterkant without further ado. One of his fellow cadets, who had found lodgings with another family, informed Carl Otto that Bosse was not only a captain in the army but also a wealthy merchant and plantation owner.

Carl Otto made his way to the Bosse residence as agreed, but he did not know if his future host was at home and found arriving on the doorstep unannounced a little strange. What if Captain Bosse's family knew nothing about him? What would he say?

He suddenly heard music wafting through an open window. Someone was playing the harpsichord and Carl Otto Creutz was familiar with the melody.

The music strengthened his reserve. He climbed the eight steps to the doorway and peered through the louvered shutters on one of the ground-floor windows. He saw a woman at the harpsichord. She was wearing a dress made of floral cotton and a lace bonnet. He could not see her face or her hands as they moved across the keys. Must be Bosse's daughter, thought Creutz, perhaps even his wife. He signalled his presence with the heavy brass doorknocker. The music stopped and he heard a chair being pushed aside. After a moment's wait, the door was opened. Not by the woman he had seen playing the harpsichord through the shutters but by a small black futuboi wearing short trousers and naked from the waist up.

'Mister Frederik Bosse,' said Creutz. 'Masra?'

The boy stepped to one side, nodded, and gestured towards a settee. 'Masra, sidon,' he said and disappeared.

Carl Otto looked around the room with interest. The windows were draped with magnificent curtains. A china cabinet graced one of the corners, with a drinks cabinet full of bottles and a selection of Jenevers gracing another. A writing desk lay open against the wall as if someone had just been using it.

The furniture was exactly the same as the tables, chairs and settees one could find in the houses of well-to-do people at home. The walls were decorated with paintings and candelabras and a large crystal chandelier dangled from the ceiling.

A door gently opened and the little black boy entered the room again, this time holding a large fan, which he placed on the settee at Creutz's side. He then sat on his heels, unlaced Creutz's boots, removed them and placed a cushion under his feet. That finished, he took his place at Carl Otto's side and wafted him with the fan. The door opened once again and a little black girl entered the room. She was not dressed according to European norms, but was wearing nothing more than a short skirt and her small round breasts were exposed. She was carrying a tray with a carafe and a glass, which she set down on a table at Creutz's side, muttering quietly, 'Odi, masra'. She then filled the glass and left the room.

Local custom, Carl Otto thought. Not bad, and he took a hearty mouthful of the refreshing bittersweet drink. Who was playing the harpsichord just then? he asked himself.

A moment later, he heard footsteps on the porch outside. The little futuboi at his side opened the door and Mr Bosse entered the room. 'Aha, so you found the place, eh?' said Bosse cheerfully.

'Good afternoon, Captain Bosse,' said Carl Otto as he got to his feet, a little embarrassed about the situation. Here he was sitting in the front room of a man he barely knew as if he belonged there. 'Is the offer of lodgings still open?' he inquired.

'Well of course, my dear fellow,' said Bosse. 'That's how we do things around here. We're much in need of new servicemen these days, with the runaways causing so much trouble. Did you bring your things?'

'No, my chest is still at the fort,' Creutz answered.

'Let me send a boy to collect it on the double,' said Bosse.

'Have you met my wife?' asked the master of the house, loosening his collar and handing his hat to the futuboi.

'No, not yet, just a slave girl and the boy here,' Carl Otto answered. Bosse took a seat and said to the futuboi: 'Go fetch misi.' Moments later a woman entered the room.

Was this Bosse's wife? Creutz asked himself. She was European from top to toe, but her face and hands were brown. She was not black, but she was clearly not white. How unusual!

'This is Mrs Bosse,' Frederik announced. He then turned to his wife and said: 'You have a lodger. Cadet Creutz will be staying with us. He arrived only yesterday.'

The woman smiled kindly and said: 'Welcome, young man. And what is your Christian name?'

'Carl Otto,' he said, and politely shook her hand. He was still not quite sure what to do with himself, embarrassed to be standing barefoot in the drawing room of people he barely knew.

'Where is Elisabeth?' asked Bosse, and his wife answered: 'Upstairs, I think.'

'Go fetch Misi Elisabeth,' said Bosse to the futuboi.

Carl Otto was thinking that Elisabeth had to be their daughter, the woman at the harpsichord, but his host said, 'Elisabeth is my wife's sister. So, how was your journey?'

'Could have been better,' Creutz answered, and he related how they had left in September to avoid autumn storms in the North Sea, but had been delayed by damage near one of the British Isles and had ended up sailing through three storms. 'During one of the heavier storms,' he continued, 'I was certain I would meet a watery grave and never set sight on Suriname.' He cut short his story and stared in surprise at the woman who had entered the room. Surely this was the woman at the harpsichord, he thought. He could tell by the clothes she was wearing. She was black, black as pitch!

'This is my sister-in-law Elisabeth,' said Bosse. 'If I'm not mistaken, you're both the same age.'

'I'll be nineteen in a couple of weeks,' said Carl Otto after shaking the woman's hand.

'That makes you eighteen now, same as Elisabeth,' said Bosse, and turning to Elisabeth: 'So what do you think of having company your own age in the house?'

She smiled briefly but did not answer. 'The requisitions are ready,' and she gestured towards the writing desk.

'Excellent, my girl,' said Bosse. 'We can despatch them within the week.' He turned to Creutz and said: 'Elisabeth does all the paperwork for my business affairs, or should I say, our business affairs.'

In the meantime, Mrs Bosse had left the room and Elisabeth had disappeared into an adjoining parlour.

Creutz was at a loss for words. He had been told that slaves did the work in Suriname, ignorant slaves brought over from Africa because of their physical strength. He had been given to understand that black people and white people were not the same and that blacks were more like animals. But Bosse, a white man, was married to a brown woman, and he had claimed that a black woman took care of all the paperwork for his business affairs.

'Apollo,' Bosse grunted, and the daydreaming futuboi, whose name was evidently Apollo, jumped to attention, rushed to the drinks cabinet and poured two large glasses.

Bosse talked about life in the colony and offered the young Carl Otto all sorts of advice. He would be granted his own futuboi who would stay with him at all times and see to his every need. 'Never do anything yourself,' he advised. 'Always let the futuboi do it. If you do things yourself, the slaves will lose respect for you and there'll be trouble. Servicemen in particular have to keep them under the thumb. Apollo, go fetch Rufus.'

Apollo disappeared and returned a moment later followed by Rufus, a lanky negro boy, who held his hands behind his back and stood in front of Bosse with downcast eyes.

'How old are you, Rufus? Fourteen?' asked Captain Bosse.

'Yes, masra,' the boy mumbled.

'This is Masra Creutz. From now on you'll be his futuboi. And don't be getting up to any nonsense or you'll spend the rest of your days on the plantation.' The boy glanced at Creutz for a second and said: 'Yes, masra. Thank you, masra.'

'Take the barrow and fetch Masra Creutz's chest from the fort. Get Amos to help you. When you get back, make sure Masra Creutz's room is ready upstairs.'

'Yes, masra,' said the boy, and he left the room without turning his back.

Mrs Bosse came back into the room.

'Mina has just given birth to a daughter,' she said. 'Nanette brought the news and came to ask Elisabeth's permission to give the child her name, but Elisabeth found Liesbeth better for her new little niece.'

'And right she is,' laughed Bosse. 'One Elisabeth is more than enough.' He turned to Creutz: 'Our Elisabeth has a mind of her own.' The young girl with the naked breasts appeared at the door and announced without looking up: 'Misi, the table is ready.'

'Come, young man, it's time to eat,' said Bosse and they walked into an adjoining room in which a table had been lavishly set with a variety of steaming dishes: game, greens and root vegetables. To Creutz's surprise, the women did not join them at the table. He ate alone with his host, while a futuboi stood behind them cooling the air with a large fan.

After dinner, the men returned to the drawing room to smoke a cigar and Captain Bosse continued his account of life in the colony. Half an hour later he said: 'Now it's time for a rest. That's the custom here. Apollo! Is Rufus back yet?'

'Don't know, masra,' the boy answered.

'Go and find out,' ordered the captain, and the boy left the room only to return a moment later with Rufus.

'Rufus, take Masra Creutz to his room. Is the hammock ready?'

'Yes, masra,' Rufus answered and he followed behind his new master as he climbed the two flights of stairs. Carl Otto looked around the spacious room. There was a hammock on one side and a table with two chairs on the other. Two windows looked out to the rear of the house and there was a basin and ewer on a stand between them. His chest had been set down in a corner.

Carl Otto undressed and lay down in the hammock in his underwear. He had fallen out of the hammock at the fort a couple of times the night before and was particularly careful.

He looked around, his hands behind his head. The windows had been fitted with green gauze. Excellent, he thought, no mosquitoes! And with that he fell asleep.

Around five in the afternoon he freshened up and made his way downstairs. Mrs Bosse and her sister Elisabeth were relaxing on the rear gallery. Mrs Bosse asked if he liked tamarind syrup. He wasn't exactly sure what tamarind syrup was, but when the slave brought a glass he realised it was the same bitter-sweet drink he had tasted earlier. Not wanting to disturb the ladies, he excused himself and went outside onto the street.

Maria was busy embroidering a large white piece of cloth. Amarante and Fenisi sat beside her on the floor, each unravelling a ball of tangled thread and winding in onto a bobbin of wood.

'Were you expecting him, Sisa Maria?' asked Elisabeth.

'Who? That young cadet? No. Masra Frederik met him only this morning, and when it turned out he had no address in the city he immediately invited him to stay with us. You know what Frederik is like with that sort of thing,' said Maria. 'He has family in Suriname apparently. Misi Bellier of Plantation Vieux Roeland on the River Commewijne is his cousin. That's what gave him the idea of coming to Suriname. He plans to visit her while he is here. What did you think of him?'

'We've only just met! How can I tell you what I think of him?' said Elisabeth, and she stood and made her way into the dining room.

What a stupid question, she thought. He seemed like a decent young man, but what did he think about blacks?

Her brother-in-law was the type of person who treated free negroes and whites as equals, but the majority of white people in the colony were a high and mighty bunch who considered all negroes to be stupid and lazy.

If Carl Otto Creutz was among them, then he would learn soon enough that she was different.

Creutz had found his way in the meantime to a café close to the main square, to which the new cadets had been introduced the previous afternoon by Reserve Officer Helling. The place was for junior and senior officers only. The ordinary soldiers frequented a café on Saramacca Street.

He recognised a few of the men from the day before. Helling was among them and he greeted Carl Otto with a smile: 'I hear you're lodging with Captain Bosse. Not bad, man, not bad at all.'

'Do you know the Bosse family?' asked Creutz.

Helling burst out laughing and roared: 'Do I know his family? Well of course! Everybody in Suriname knows the Bosse family. And what about that young Elisabeth? Quite the little lady, eh?' He explicitly said 'lady'.

'Have you met?' asked Carl Otto.

'Not personally. A pleasure I've yet to savour. But everyone here knows all about Elisabeth, the black girl who fancies herself white because she can read and write.'

'And play the harpsichord,' Carl Otto added.

'That too?' Helling bellowed. 'Well who knows? Perhaps we'll be treated to a concert by a black woman one of these days? What're you drinking, man?'

Someone thrust a beer into Creutz's hand and the conversation shifted away from the Bosse family. He returned to his new lodgings later that evening, a little the worse for wear, emptied his bladder against a tree before climbing the stairs to the front door and going straight to his room.

Carl Otto woke the following morning with a start. He did not know where he was at first and he glanced furtively around the room in a groggy haze. He had grown accustomed to the tiny, cramped berth on the ship where he had slept for weeks, but suddenly he found himself in spacious accommodation, lying in a hammock. It had taken time and effort to find a comfortable position the night before. He remembered the events of the previous day, finally realised he was in Paramaribo and that he had slept in a room on the second floor of a large house on Waterkant. He rubbed his neck and scratched his head. What was life going to be like in this new land? I should write to my brothers, he thought. They would surely be wondering how he had fared. He pictured his home and wondered what the weather might be like. Cold, for sure, perhaps even snow.

A long drawn-out shriek interrupted his musings. It must have woken him.

What was going on? Where was that dreadful noise coming from?

Another desperate squeal, followed by wailing, weeping and loud voices shattered the silence.

Carl Otto jumped from his hammock and hurried to the window, which gave out onto Bosse's property and that of the neighbouring houses. An almost naked young black boy had been roped to a couple of wooden poles in the middle of the property. A well-built black man stood beside him, lashing his back with a rod tipped with strips of leather. Another black boy was crouched at the bottom of one of the poles, his naked back scored with blood.

What a dreadful sight, thought Carl Otto. But he continued to watch as the lashing progressed. He had been told that it was better to get used to such matters, since whippings and other punishments were used regularly to keep the slaves under control.

He looked onto the neighbouring properties, which appeared to be more or less the same as that of his host. There was a courtyard in the middle with a well and an extended shed towards the back with windows and doors. The many blacks walking in and out of the shed gave him to understand that it had to be their living quarters. To the left of Bosse's property there were stables and a coach house, and a building near the front with smoke billowing from its chimney. He could see people at work through the open windows. Must be the kitchen, he thought.

He heard the faint shuffle of feet at his door and he opened it to reveal his futuboi Rufus standing at the ready, water jug in hand.

Carl Otto washed, dressed and made his way downstairs. Mr and Mrs Bosse were drinking coffee on the rear gallery. It did not take long before he too was sipping at a cup of steaming hot coffee. His host inquired with interest if he had slept well in his hammock.

Carl Otto reported for duty an hour later at Fort Zeelandia and had to wait in a small room together with three other new cadets for the commanding officer to arrive. Another officer entered the room while they were waiting and announced: 'Seven blacks for the "seven corners". Bring along the new cadets. The sooner they witness the seven corners the better.'

The cadets made their way outside where a group of soldiers had roped together a party of negroes. Two of the soldiers were holding whips with tiny chunks of lead fastened to the leather thongs.

The group set off, the soldiers flanking the blacks on either side, the four cadets bringing up the rear. They headed along a short, tree-lined avenue at the side of the government building and stopped at the corner of Gravenstraat. One of the blacks was thrown into the middle of the circle and a soldier started to whip him. The other slaves followed, each receiving ten lashes from a different soldier. And so it continued, the soldiers taking turns until each of the slaves had received ten lashes.

Two of the slaves groaned and another screamed aloud, but three of them were resolute and unperturbed.

They turned into Gravenstraat, which was still relatively free of passers-by. At the corner of Watermolenstraat, the soldier in front shouted: 'Halt!' Once again, the slaves were treated to a lashing. They then made their way to the corner of Klipstenenstraat where it was much busier. Three whites stopped to watch the whipping, making loud comments for all to hear.

'Quite right. The scum deserve what's coming to them,' said one of the men, and the other asked: 'Whose slaves are they?'

The soldiers ignored the questions and calmly continued whipping.

A white woman with two slave girls passed by. The slave girls wanted to stop and watch but the woman commanded, 'Keep moving!'

Carl Otto had wondered at first what the seven corners might be, but now he understood that slaves were to be given ten lashes on seven street corners.

The fourth stop was on the corner of Keizerstraat and Klipstenenstraat. In the meantime, a couple of naked black children had rushed from their master's yard and joined the procession. The fifth stop was on the corner of

Quateroliestraat, which was awash with people. A sizeable circle quickly formed, including whites, a few coloureds and several blacks. Carl Otto was unable to understand their intermittent shouts, but he guessed from the tone that they must have been terms of abuse. Some of the black bystanders muttered to themselves with their eyes closed while others mumbled what appeared to be curses and maledictions accompanied by unusual gestures. Carl Otto was appalled by the entire process but the other soldiers talked among themselves as if there was nothing wrong. The children shouted to one another from time to time and grinned with their hands covering their mouths. The back and thighs of each of the black slaves were now covered with bloody scores and welts. One of the men had an open wound, which was bleeding heavily. Sweat and tears ran down his cheeks, but he did not make a sound.

An elderly black woman emerged from a negerpoort with a moist cloth. Without even glancing at the soldiers and the other bystanders, she started to bathe a wound on the back of one of the men. She glared at the children and shouted at them. Carl Otto did not catch her words but he understood what she meant. She pointed towards Keizerstraat and the children stopped grinning, hung their heads, and headed back in the direction they had come.

The woman disappeared through the negerpoort only to reappear on the corner of Keizerstraat and Waterkant, where the procession had stopped for the sixth lashing. This time she was accompanied by two other women, one with a pail of water, the other with a calabash full of ointment.

The seventh stop was on the corner of Waterkant and the main square. Two of the slaves passed out, and all of them were covered with blood. When the soldiers were finished they tossed their whips to the ground, rubbed their hands and stretched their fingers.

'Not exactly fun,' said one, and another agreed: 'You're telling me!'

Two of the slaves leaned against the wall of a house and two rested on the steps. The women set about washing their backs. Some of the occupants of the yard behind the house emerged from the negerpoort and looked on with compassion. More buckets of water and cloths were brought until each of the slaves had a woman tending to him, washing his back, and rubbing ointment from the calabash into his wounds.

A couple of the men groaned gently, one gritting his teeth with a dogged stare, the other with tears in his eyes, puffing and panting, his chest heaving up and down. An elderly man emerged from the negerpoort with a small calabash and gave the men something to drink.

The women mumbled to the men as they tended them. Probably words of comfort, thought Carl Otto.

After a brief respite, one of the soldiers yelled: 'Enough. Move along!'

The women and the old man stepped timidly to one side and the slaves hobbled off towards the fort.

When they arrived, the soldiers took the slaves to their shack. Creutz and the other cadets made their way to the house of one of the officers, where they waited until he came outside and told them they could go home. They were to report for further instructions at eight o'clock the following morning. Nothing further was said of the slaves, leading Carl Otto to presume that the seven corners and suchlike were a matter of routine.

He noticed Helling leave one of the houses, raised his arm and ran to join him. They left the fort together and made their way towards Waterkant.

Helling asked how Creutz was getting on and whether he had settled in. Creutz told him he had never witnessed a seven corners before and that he had found it hard to appreciate.

'Wait until you're on a jungle expedition,' said Helling. 'Bloody runaways! You'll be hacking their heads off with pleasure before you know it.'

Carl Otto shivered at the thought, and Helling responded: 'Come on, man, none of that girlish stuff. Hacking off heads is child's play. The governor is a hard man when it comes to that scum. If we're lucky enough to catch a couple in the woods, they'll be hung up with a hook between their ribs. Some of them are burned alive and others quartered.'

'I thought we were supposed to catch them and return them to the plantations for work,' said Carl Otto.

'Not a bit of it. Wouldn't work anyway. They'd run off again at the first opportunity and sow unrest among the other plantation slaves in the meantime. A good hiding is what the governor recommends, then the plantation slaves won't be so keen to escape. Not that Governor De Cheusses is any less strict with whites when they misbehave. A couple of years ago we had Mathias de Goyer here, son of a former governor. A strange chap altogether. In fact he wasn't really a chap, if you get my drift!'

Carl Otto had no idea what Helling was talking about: 'No, I don't.'

'You know, a chap who prefers other chaps, a molly… they caught him red-handed.' Creutz finally got the message: 'Ah! A sodomite!'

'Exactly, a sodomite,' Helling continued. 'Before the court had the chance to pass down a verdict, the governor already knew what the punishment was to be and it was fitting, make no mistake. De Goyer was first half throttled, then scorched alive, and then his corpse was tossed into the sea in a sack weighted down with stones.'

Creutz pointed out that sodomy was subject to severe punishment in his own part of the world, but nothing as cruel and awful as they dealt out here.

With the story of De Goyer still in his mind, he climbed the steps to the front door of his lodgings. Elisabeth was at the harpsichord and stopped playing when Carl Otto entered the room: 'Please, miss, please play on.'

'No one calls me miss,' she responded. 'My name is Elisabeth. And why should I play on?'

'Because your music is a million times more beautiful than the lashes of the whip I have been forced to listen to all morning,' said Carl Otto. 'I'll be happy to call you Elisabeth if it pleases you, but then you must call me Carl Otto.'

'What kind of whiplashes did you hear this morning?' Elisabeth inquired, turning on her stool to look at Carl Otto.

'Early this morning, here behind the house. They woke me up. Then a seven corners out on the street.'

'Surely the seven corners didn't involve any of our slaves?' asked Elisabeth.

'Your slaves? I've no idea,' said Carl Otto. He wanted to say that blacks all looked the same to him, but changed his mind. 'Were they part of it?'

'No. We don't send our slaves to the fort,' said Elisabeth. 'If they deserve a beating, we do it ourselves.'

'That's what I saw this morning at the back of the house, then. Not a pretty sight,' said Carl Otto.

'Sultan and Fortuin got what was coming to them,' said Elisabeth calmly. 'They were supposed to cut hay for the horses three days ago and only arrived back last evening, claiming they had lost their way.'

'Could they have been telling the truth?'

'Of course not,' Elisabeth laughed. 'They know the roads around here inside out. They were probably skulking with the renegades and only came home because they were hungry.'

'Renegades? What do you mean?' asked Carl Otto.

'Renegade slaves, runaways who hide in the woods around the city instead of escaping to the interior. Sometimes they come back of their own accord, sometimes they're caught, but they always have one or other excuse about losing their way, being robbed by the Maroons, beguiled by an evil spirit or bitten by a snake. Naturally, no one believes their tales of woe. A good hiding is enough to convince them not to get up to the same mischief in the future,' said Elisabeth, and she turned and continued to play.

Carl Otto remained silent and gazed at the upright posture of the girl at the harpsichord. He wasn't quite sure where to place her in the hierarchy of things. She was black but not a slave. Anyone who heard her speak without seeing her would probably think she was a white woman. How did she manage to be a free woman and a negress at the same time? He didn't dare to ask her such a direct question, certainly since she behaved as if being a free woman and not a slave was the most natural thing in the world. She also appeared to think it normal that slaves should be subject to whippings. Carl Otto wondered if it ever crossed her mind that she too could have been a slave. He realised that he still had a great deal to learn about the colony of Suriname.

1 January 1734

'Take a look at my train, Elisabeth. Make sure it's straight all the way round. Catharina, the lace on the bonnet needs to be a little higher on this side, like that…' Elisabeth and Catharina fluttered round their sister Maria in the spacious dining room. Nanette stood in front of her, holding the mirror with its heavy gilded frame so that her sister could see herself from head to toe.

Catharina, Nanette and Elisabeth had spent the best part of an hour getting their sister ready for the governor's New Year reception.

On Catharina's instructions, a slave girl sitting on the floor tugged at the hem on the right side of the dress, which flowed into a broad train. The dress itself was made of blue velvet, adorned with gold brocade and golden buttons.

Elisabeth dusted her sister's face with white powder.

'Don't fan so hard,' she said to the slave girl fanning her sister.

'Leave her be. It's so warm in here,' Maria groaned.

'But then she'll blow off all the powder,' Elisabeth answered. 'Be patient, Sisa Maria, you're almost ready.'

Maria submitted to Elisabeth's powder, while Catharina walked around her to be sure her train was even on all sides. Nanette inspected her sister's face to see if the powder had been smoothly applied. The slave girl on the floor ran her hand over the train while the slave girl with the fan wafted carefully up and down. This was the scene Frederik Bosse encountered when he descended the stairs and entered the dining room.

'Come, woman, it's time to go. You're pretty enough!' said Bosse, himself neatly dressed in the uniform of a lieutenant-captain in the forces of the Society.'

'Is the reception in Government House?' asked Elisabeth.

'Where else would it be?' asked Nanette, surprised.

'Government House is still being refurbished,' Elisabeth retorted.

'The ground floor is ready,' said Bosse. 'The governor took it upon himself to make sure everything would be ready for the New Year reception.' He turned to his futuboi: 'Apollo, tell Bruno we're ready.'

Frederik Bosse and his wife Maria left the house. Maria carefully descended the steep stairs, the slave girl behind her holding up her train. A coach was awaiting them by the door. Bruno the coachman was wearing red trousers and a white jacket, and even little Apollo, who ran beside the coach, was dressed for the occasion in trousers and a jacket.

The sisters stood at the top of the steps and watched as the coach disappeared into Oranjestraat, heading for Government House. 'When will I get the chance to attend one of the governor's receptions,' Elisabeth sighed as she and her sister went back into the house.

'Never, mi gudu, eh eh,' Catharina replied. 'Such things are not for negroes. We might be free but we're still negroes. And no matter how intelligent you might be, you are and remain a negress, and negresses are not invited to Government House.

'Maybe I'll marry a white man one day, then they'll have to invite me,' said Elisabeth.

'But that would be impossible,' said Nanette taken aback. Catharina shook her head: 'Stop that nonsense, girl, stop it!'

Elisabeth said nothing. She bit her lip stubbornly and thought to herself: Think what you like, but I'll show you different. One day I'll be invited to Government House.

Elisabeth was well aware of social arrangements in Suriname. A negress would never be invited to Government House. Negresses lived with whites and even had their children, but white men were forbidden by law from marrying black women. Countless negresses lived out of wedlock with their white partners, but only whites were invited to receptions. The women were regarded as 'housekeepers' and never as 'wives'. Even the mulattas who lived unmarried with their white partners were left uninvited. Maria was invited because she was one of the few mulattas who was actually married.

How did Maria feel at such an event, Elisabeth asked herself. She had an acquaintance or two among the whites, women she visited from time to time or invited to join her at home, but how would they behave towards the mulattas in the company of other whites who treated coloured people as worthless.

Nanette returned the mirror to its place in the front room and Elisabeth told a slave girl to clean up the whitening powder from the floor with a damp cloth.

The unexpected sound of footsteps running up the front stairs was immediately followed by an out of breath Carl Otto Creutz bursting into the room.

'What are you doing here?' asked Elisabeth.

Creutz's face was flushed and red. 'I was almost at the palace when I bumped into Landsknegt. He kindly pointed out that I had forgotten my sword.' He rushed up the two flights of stairs and returned moments later in as much of a hurry, this time with his sword in hand. He was about to dash outside when Elisabeth shouted: 'Wait a second.' She then turned to Fenisi, a slave girl, and ordered her to bring a clean damp cloth.

'Hold still for an instant,' she told Carl Otto, 'take a moment to fasten your sword.'

She took the damp cloth from the slave girl and wiped the face of the man in front of her saying: 'With a face as red and flushed as that, everyone will think you've been drinking.' She blew over his face a couple of times and said: 'There's plenty of time for you to walk to Government House calmly and slowly.'

How nice of her, thought Carl Otto as he made his way to the reception. She had been right, of course. More than a few people were still heading towards the reception. Oh well, he admitted to himself, there was a first time for everything.

The reception was well underway an hour later. The guests amused themselves in two large halls and on the rear terrace of the recently renovated Government House. The women were dressed in magnificent outfits, draped with jewels, while the majority of the men were in uniform. Baron De Cheusses and his wife mixed and chatted with the guests. Carl Otto stood with the other cadets, taking in as much as he could of the new experience.

'Baroness De Cheusses was Governor Temming's first wife,' said Reserve Officer Helling. 'She stayed at the palace after her husband died. When the new governor arrived, he not only took possession of his predecessor's residence he also took possession of his widow.'

Carl Otto almost choked on his drink from laughing. He looked over at the Bosses. Captain Bosse was talking to a couple of gentlemen, while Mrs Bosse kept company with two women, all three of them staring at a circle of women – gathered around Baroness De Cheusses – who did nothing but laugh and chatter at the tops of their voices. Carl Otto had the impression that Mrs Bosse and her companions did not dare approach the other circle of women. When he looked closely, he realised that Maria's companions were also coloured.

Creutz was introduced to a variety of plantation owners who had all made a special effort to come to the city for the New Year reception. He even met his own cousin, Miss Bellier. He did not know her personally, because she had lived in the colony for sixteen years and he could no longer remember her. She remembered him as a child though, and introduced him to his cousin by marriage who immediately invited him to lodge with them on their plantation.

It occurred to Carl Otto that conversations repeatedly turned to Reverend and Mrs Kals. 'She's under house arrest,' he heard someone say. He decided to ask Helling what was going on with the minister and his wife.

Helling informed him that Reverend Kals had been the cause of a great deal of commotion. From the moment he had arrived in Suriname, he had preached his theory on the equality of negroes and whites. In his book *Debauched Morality*, he had written that the colonial authorities had promoted the sinful life by prohibiting marriage between whites and negroes. He had been in the colony for barely a year and had fought with just about everyone, especially the other ministers. After being banned from preaching, he became so angry that the colonial authorities had to send him back to the Netherlands. His wife had remained in Suriname, however, because the reverend was convinced he would return. In the meantime, she continued to distribute her husband's pamphlets. When she was called to task for these activities, she insulted the legislative councillor. This upset the colonial authorities to such a degree that they placed her under house arrest until her departure. 'Women, they're beyond my comprehension,' Helling concluded with a laugh. 'Do you know what the other ministers use as an argument against Kals? His never-ending arguments with his wife! Apparently, they cursed each other openly and everyone around them was forced to share in their conflicts; first in the city and then at the church on the Commewijne to which they were later banished. She still seemed to believe in him. Distributing his pamphlets could cost her a prison sentence!'

'Perhaps it's true love?' said Creutz

'What about you?' inquired Helling. 'Fallen for the charms of the beautiful Elisabeth yet?'

'Elisabeth, of course not,' Creutz laughed. 'A plucky lass, I'll give you that, but she's not interested in the likes of me.'

'And a good thing too,' said Helling. 'Those negroes are a dangerous bunch.' He snatched a glass from a passing tray and made his way to the other side of the hall. Carl Otto stood alone for a while, taking in the scene.

Neatly dressed slaves passed among the guests with trays of drinks and dishes containing a variety of pastries. The voices and laughter got louder and louder. Around twelve o'clock, coaches lined up on the street outside and the guests started to leave. The governor and the baroness stood by the door, politely shaking hands.

As he ambled in the direction of his lodgings, Carl Otto thought to himself that life in the colony was quite tolerable after all and hoped that there would be more such receptions.

He climbed the stairs to his room, unfastened his sword and relaxed in his hammock He didn't even notice his futuboi Rufus carefully remove his boots and close the curtains.

Creutz woke around four in the afternoon to an irritating itch over his entire body. When he scratched his arms the itch got worse on his legs, and when he scratched his legs it got worse on his belly and then moved to his back. He turned, twisted and scratched in his hammock for a while, but when he got up and looked at himself, he could barely suppress his horror. His body was covered from head to toe with little red spots.

'Rufus, come here! Look!' Creutz yelled when he heard a shuffle outside in the corridor some moments later. Rufus came into the room: 'Yes masra, krasi-krasi,' he said calmly.

Creutz got dressed and went downstairs where he found Mrs Bosse in the dining room.

'I'm itching all over,' he said. 'Look, it's terrible!' and he showed her his arms and his legs.

'Heavens, you've got a bad case of scarlatina,' said Mrs Bosse. 'It looks worse than it is. I've something for it. Best not to scratch!'

The captain came down from his room at that point, examined Creutz's arms and said: 'Scarlatina and no mistake. All the new arrivals get it. They say it's a sign of a good constitution if you get over it unscathed. Don't worry, my wife has a remedy, you'll be fine. Have a drink and then Rufus will look after you.'

After fifteen minutes, Carl Otto returned to his room followed by Rufus, calabash in hand. Carl Otto undressed and Rufus rubbed his entire body with a cloth soaked in lime juice. It stung his skin and he wanted to scream every now and then, but it was clearly working and the itch gradually disappeared. Rufus repeated the treatment three times that day and the day after. By then it had passed.

'Mark my words: this is a sign of a good constitution,' laughed Captain Bosse. I hope you're right, Creutz thought to himself.

On 27 January 1734, four weeks after the New Year reception, yet another function was organised at Government House, not a party this time but a funeral. After an illness that lasted four days, Governor De Cheusses had passed away. All the noteworthy people in Suriname were present and members of the Police Council flanked each side of the bier at the request of his widow. Drummers thrumming muffled drums headed the procession. After the ceremony, the Police Council and various senior functionaries, lieutenants and officers were expected at Government House for a funeral reception presided over by the commandant, the highest authority in the country in the absence of a governor.

A few days later, the deceased governor's widow, now Dowager De Cheusses, despatched a letter edged in black to the Directors of the Society in Amsterdam, informing them that she had become a governor's widow for the second time. She asked permission to remain in residence at the palace with her two daughters and reminded them how much her deceased husband had dedicated himself to improving the building.

In the same week, the colony was shaken by the news that Maroons had attacked Plantations Espérance and Marseille on the River Cottica and

Breukelerwaard in Upper Commewijne. The slaves at Plantation Espérance had immediately sided with the attackers. They took provisions and useful implements with them and set fire to the buildings. The sentries had opened fire at Plantation Marseille and had even managed to force the attackers into retreat, but not before having to surrender a considerable number of slaves and other material goods. The slaves put up a fight at Breukelerwaard, but the Maroons were armed. One slave and a blankofficier were shot dead, and a badly wounded plantation director had to be brought to the city by his neighbours shortly after the attack. The buildings had survived, but the cane fields had been destroyed by fire.

The attacks were the talk of the town in Paramaribo.

'It's time to put a stop to this,' the planters complained at an emergency gathering. Horrified reactions to the dreadful events were issued by the Police Council and the governor, together for their weekly meeting. 'Why don't the soldiers do something about this satanic vermin?' the council members lamented. The very same afternoon, the decision was made to despatch the new soldiers and cadets on a jungle expedition at the first possible opportunity.

Six weeks later, on March 15th, twelve open vessels set out from Fort Zeelandia, six of them pondos, the remainder large dugout canoes, fully loaded with supplies and troops for transportation to the Upper Commewijne and the Cottica region. Captain Smidt commanded the expedition, which included Lieutenant Laveaux, two officers, four reserve officers, Helling among them, six cadets, Carl Otto among them, two chirurgians, a gunsmith, two drummers, sixty soldiers, a negro guide, and one hundred and forty slaves as porters and rowers.

Canons roared and the fort and the ships in the harbour were decorated with flags. Carl Otto and the other newcomers could hardly believe their eyes. It was like a party. Hordes of people stood beside the fort and along Waterkant waving and shouting, as if all of Paramaribo had turned out to wish them well.

Captain Bosse was not part of the expedition on this occasion, but Creutz had received an entire chest full of provisions as a gift from the family: twelve bottles of wine, two bottles of Jenever, ham, butter, flour and sugar. He was surprised at first, but had presumed it was the way things were done and had said nothing. Immediately before their departure, they had received a great deal more at the fort. The wives and daughters of the colonists had come to say their farewells. Slaves and futubois stood beside their mistresses and passed out the contents of enormous baskets: wine, liqueur, pastries, preserved fruit. Carl Otto had no idea where to stow it all.

'Not bad, eh?' he said to Landsknegt, a fellow cadet, just managing to avoid a collision.

'Not bad at all,' Landskneght chuckled. 'We can look forward to a party or two. Watch out, Maroons, here we come!'

They received their instructions the day before departure. They were to sail up the River Commewijne and split into two groups at Plantation Schoonoord, one destined for the Upper Commewijne, the other for the River Cottica. A station with storage facilities for provisions, gunpowder and firearms was to be set up on the banks of the Cottica, and permanently manned from then on. The station was to serve as a base for rooting out runaway settlements, while the group heading to Upper Commewijne was to do the same in its part of the country. The time had come to settle with the runaways once and for all!

Their orders were clear: find settlements, kill the negroes, burn their houses. Wherever they encountered patches of kostgrond, they had orders to dig them up and destroy them. Strategically located settlements with abundant kostgrond were to be confiscated for later use as military forts. No one was to be spared except the women and children, who might be useful later on when returned to their respective plantations.

The expedition first made its way to Fort Nieuw Amsterdam, which was still under construction, where they waited for high tide to allow them to sail up the Commewijne.

Carl Otto Creutz sat in one of the dugout canoes and watched as twelve strong negroes rowed and sung in unison. What a magnificent sight, he thought. The rhythm of the song helped them keep up the pace as huge beads of sweat glistened on their black skin.

They passed plantations on both sides of the river, some with enormous mansions and outbuildings, a few with smaller, less ostentatious residences, and the occasional little church beside the main house. The pondo with provisions had been overloaded. The rowers had to bail out water with all the energy they could muster, but were unable to prevent it reaching some of the gunpowder and stocks of food, much to the captain's annoyance. When the tide turned they tied up at Plantation Mon Trésor. The rowers jumped into the water at the first opportunity, swam around, disappeared under the surface, splashed each other, laughed, shouted, and had no end of fun. They seemed to have energy to burn. Lieutenant Laveaux turned to Creutz. 'Look at them,' he said. 'They're like dolphins. They don't feel things as we do. They may look like humans but their intelligence is limited. That's why we have to look after them and try to teach them what we can.'

The captain and the lieutenants were invited to stay at the owner's residence, while the officers were allowed to spend the night at the plantation supervisor's house. The reserve officers and cadets had a large shed placed at their disposal and the ordinary soldiers were free to hang up their hammocks between the trees.

The vessels continued upstream the following day, making slow but steady progress. That evening, they spent the night at Plantation Hecht-en-Sterk on the other side of the Commewijne, which was now much narrower than at the estuary. They expected to arrive at Plantation Schoonoord after a third day on the river. Plantation Vieux Roeland was a short distance downriver from Schoonoord and Creutz asked permission to go ashore and visit his family. Reserve Officer Helling and Cadet Landsknegt were allowed to join him, as long as all three promised to rejoin the group the following morning at Schoonoord.

Jacques and Helena Bellier were pleased to see their cousin and heartily welcomed their guests. Carl Otto was introduced to his twelve- and eight-year-old second cousins. Helena told him that she and her husband had brought five children into the world, but a son and a daughter had died when they were only two years of age and another son had died two years ago at the age of eight. 'Raising children in this place can be difficult,' his cousin lamented. 'There are so many diseases, terrible tropical maladies. Your child can fall ill and die before you know it.'

After an elaborate dinner, the men settled down to a smoke and Jacques Bellier told them about his plantation. He had good supervisors, who had already managed to fend off a Maroon attack no less than three times, but on the last occasion, the runaways had captured ten of his slaves. 'Sometimes they're after women, because they don't have enough,' he said. 'During the last attack, they made off with four of them.'

'Perhaps we'll find them and bring them back,' said Carl Otto. Bellier shook his head.

'Don't build up your expectations,' he said. 'You should be content if you capture two or three runaways. It's a hopeless business. They're invisible. They'll be watching you but you won't see them.'

'But if we destroy their kostgrond, they'll have to come looking for food,' Landsknegt argued.

Bellier laughed sarcastically. 'Did you say kostgrond? Don't let them fool you! They lay out small patches to dupe the soldiers, but their real kostgrond is elsewhere, much bigger, and impossible to find. They're a shrewd bunch, let me tell you.'

'But the lieutenant says they're simple souls, almost animals. He compared our rowers with dolphins,' Creutz interjected.

'That's what the authorities in the city think, but we know better. We have to face their cunning on a regular basis. Be careful, friends, and realise what you're about to do is far from easy. The place you're going is unhealthy to start with, marshland, biri-biri, and alive with mosquitoes. Do your hammocks have nets?'

Helena Bellier joined them and the conversation took a different turn. She wanted to know all about the city. Was Creutz comfortable with the Bosse family? Creutz laughed. 'Very comfortable. Very fine people. I'm a lucky man!'

Jacques Bellier puffed at his pipe and Helena inquired hesitatingly: 'What's it like having blacks in the house? I hear the black family of the lady of the house participate in everything.'

'Do you mean Elisabeth? You're right. She helps her brother-in-law with his business affairs and he is most content with her. Understandable, really, considering she's so good at it,' said Creutz.

'It sounds as if she's also good with you,' said Bellier.

'She's extremely pleasant and well educated. We talk a great deal,' said Creutz.

'And before you know it she'll have you round her little finger. That's the way they work,' Bellier interrupted. 'Look around you, friend. There might not be many unmarried white women in town, but there are quite a few young widows. Don't waste yourself on a black.'

'I already warned him,' said Helling. 'A little fun with a black is one thing, that's what the bitches are for after all, but don't let it get serious!'

'I know what I'm doing, thank you very much,' Carl Otto asserted and they changed the subject.

Unable to sleep, Carl Otto listened to Helling and Landsknegt snoring in their hammocks and his thoughts turned to Elisabeth.

In the three months he had been on shore, he had been constantly confronted with the rumours that the Bosse family were set on pairing him with Elisabeth, that black women used witchcraft to charm white men, and that this was precisely what Elisabeth was up to. All of this was news to Carl Otto. Elisabeth was an agreeable woman, nothing more, someone he could talk with and share a laugh. But there was nothing, absolutely nothing to suggest that she had any romantic feelings for him. Did he have feelings for her? Of course not! Whites and blacks together? Out of the question in Suriname. He was certainly not going to start something that would lead nowhere. Elisabeth was pleasant company and he missed her, there was no doubting it. He wished he were with her at that moment.

The following morning, Bellier brought his guests to the neighbouring plantation in the tent boat. The entire expedition was hard at work readying the vessels for departure at high tide. The negroes had caught and roasted a number of large fish. The company was divided in two parts.

'If I'm not mistaken there are fewer rowers on board,' said Carl Otto to Helling.

'You're not mistaken, man. A dozen of them disappeared in the night. And where do you think they went? The runaway camp, of course. Treacherous bunch!' said Helling.

Five soldiers had fallen ill. Two of them were in such a state that they could no longer walk and they were obliged to remain on the plantation.

'Lucky buggers,' said Helling. 'Anyone who gets sick from now on will be left to his own devices in the jungle.'

They sailed the Cottica upstream for a full day. The jungle between the plantations became more and more dense. They set ashore beyond a small plantation, where the permanent station and storage facilities were to be built.

After a couple of weeks, they had constructed two simple buildings with pinadaks. A group of negroes had felled a couple of trees and cut them into planks, while another group had woven the roofs from pina leaves. One of the buildings was to be used for storage. The other was immediately put to use as a hospital to house the eight soldiers, one officer and one cadet who had by this time fallen ill. A couple of them had fever, a couple diarrhoea, another a rash. The chirurgian did his best. He gave Jenever to the men with fever and asked the dresneger to boil bita for the men with diarrhoea. In some cases the treatment helped, in others it was too late. Two of the men were buried a few days later.

Under Lieutenant Laveaux's command, a group of thirty soldiers, two officers and two non-commissioned officers set off through the forest towards the Upper Commewijne. Forty carriers accompanied them. This was Carl Otto's group. Fortunately, he had not fallen ill but he didn't exactly feel fit either. He hoped they would catch some runaways, but to his surprise they didn't find a single one, only an abandoned village with ten huts and a piece of kostgrond. They dug up the cassavas for their own use and set fire to the huts.

Every day a couple of the carriers disappeared. The soldiers were given orders to keep a better eye on them and to shoot them if it became clear they were planning to escape.

One day they came across a small hut with an elderly negro and a woman, both of whom immediately pleaded for mercy. Lieutenant Laveaux promised to spare them if they cooperated and told his men where to find runaways. The elderly man babbled something Creutz could barely understand. The woman also piped up, pointed in a certain direction and said that there were runaways on the other side of the marsh.

The soldiers headed off in the direction she had shown them, with two negroes up front to clear the way. After a couple of hours, they arrived at the marsh. 'How do we cross?' asked Creutz quietly to the man beside him.

'We go through it,' the lieutenant announced. 'Boots off, laces tied and hang them round your neck. Rifles hoisted to keep them dry. Make plenty of noise to scare off the caimans and abomas.'

Carl Otto was scared out of his wits but didn't dare to let it show. He waded warily behind a couple of soldiers. Halfway across, a sudden commotion from the other side stopped them in their tracks. At least thirty Maroons emerged from behind the trees and bushes, a few with rifles, others with bows and arrows. They fired. Dead and wounded fell right and left. The soldiers in the marsh were unable to return fire. They screamed and tried to run faster but without success. Five minutes later the Maroons were nowhere to be seen. The old man and the woman who had kept out of the way at first had also disappeared.

By the time they reached the other side of the marsh, one officer and three soldiers had died, five soldiers and Lieutenant Laveaux had been wounded and six carriers had disappeared.

They met up with the other group five days later. They had encountered a similar fate: sickness, death, Maroon ambush with fatalities and wounded. Neither group had managed to capture a single runaway.

Ten weeks after leaving Paramaribo, the expedition started on its return journey. They had managed to surprise three runaways after all and had shot them on the spot, hacking off their heads as trophies to bring back to the city. But the expedition was far from triumphant. Twelve soldiers, two officers and a non-commissioned officer had been left to rot in the jungle and only half of the carriers and rowers remained. Only two of the slaves had died. The remainder had joined the runaways with considerable pleasure.

January 1735

Elisabeth was at the table in her room in front of an open ledger. Her room was spacious with a large four-poster bed on one side, two mahogany cupboards on the other and a round table with two chairs in the middle. A cabinet with a mirror graced one of the corners together with a smaller table with a washbasin and ewer.

A slave girl sat beside the cabinet on the floor with part of the contents of one of the mahogany cupboards piled up on a sheet beside her. Elisabeth studied her ledger with a furrowed forehead and counted. She then walked over to the cupboard, counting aloud and pointing with her finger: 'Thirty yards of velvet, twenty yards of dress silk, ten yards of English chintz, fifteen yards of bias binding, thirty yards of linen lining, eight yards of gold braid... But where is the black silk and the ordinary linen, and what about all the bonnet lace?'

'Put everything back in the cupboard, Amarante,' Elisabeth ordered, and she placed a heavy silver inkpot on the open ledger to prevent the pages from fluttering in the wind from the wide-open window.

When Amarante was ready with the piles of cloth, Elisabeth said: 'Run along and make me a glass of lemonade. I'll be downstairs shortly.'

She stood and crossed to the window. Where might Carl Otto be, she wondered. What might he be doing? Was he thinking as much of her as she of him? She missed him. Every day he wasn't there she missed him. When he was at home, she had to force herself not to reveal her feelings for him. She tried her best to appear as normal as possible. She suspected that he had feelings for her also. He always looked for her when he got home. She had never allowed him into her bedroom. Intentionally! It would be inappropriate, she thought. They could spend hours talking and laughing in the front room, the dining room, the rear gallery. He was so kind, so interested in everything she did.

He was often invited for dinners and card games by other families, where naturally he would meet any number of white women. He would tell such amusing stories about them and she would laugh heartily at his remarks. 'They tried to pair me off with widow Gantz yesterday evening,' he once told her.

'Did it work?' Elisabeth inquired with as much indifference as she could muster.

He burst out laughing: 'My dear, have you ever seen widow Gantz? She's twice my age and has an enormous wart on her chin. Not on your life!'

A short while ago he had told her about Caroline Planteau of Plantation Beaulieu. 'The poor child is cross-eyed and so terribly thick. I really feel sorry for her.'

'Perhaps she's sweet and would make someone a wonderful wife,' Elisabeth had answered. 'I'm sure of it,' Carl Otto replied, 'but for someone else, not for me.'

One day he'll fall for a white woman, Elisabeth thought wearily, and then he'll marry and leave Suriname. They would never see each other again and her hopes would be dashed. He would never choose her to be his wife.

Perhaps he would take her as his mistress or concubine. Many white men had a legal wife at home in the city or on the plantation and a black or coloured concubine housed elsewhere, with whom they would spend most of their time. Concubines or mistresses generally spoiled 'their masra' and in recognition, he would provide lodgings and maintenance for her and her children. But Elisabeth would never consent to such a life. Some black women considered the life of a concubine or mistress an honour, but not her. For Elisabeth it was all or nothing!

She wanted marriage, legal marriage, with a magnificent wedding that would have the colonists talking for weeks on end. Everyone told her such a thing was impossible, but she was determined. So many impossibilities turn out to be possible after all. Wasn't she herself the perfect example? She knew no other negro or negress in the colony who had been born free. Indeed, she sometimes took her extraordinary position for granted.

When she was a child, no more than an infant, she would play with the other black children at the back of her house. She barely noticed that they were naked while she was dressed. At mealtimes she sat on the ground like the others and stuffed pieces of cassava and banana in her mouth with her hands from the calabash between her legs.

At the age of five, she heard Nene Kwasiba say something that changed her perception of life forever. Nene Kwasiba was an elderly woman, more like Nanno's foster mother, who treated Nanno's children as a grandmother would. Kwasiba, Nanno and other slaves had been brought to Suriname by their master Jan Van Susteren. Both of them had arrived from Africa at the same time and had met each other on the Dutch slave ship. Kwasiba was a young woman and Nanno still a girl. They had wept and wailed in each other's arms and survived the terrible journey together. They were sold on St Christopher, and ended up by coincidence with the same master, Jan Van Susteren. Kwasiba was twenty-three years of age at the time and had taken the young Nanno under her wing. When Nanno was fifteen, the master took her into his home and they had two children together, Maria and Charlo. On Nanno's request, Kwasiba became a house slave. In the meantime, she had given birth to three children of her own, and buried two of them.

Jan Van Susteren owned two plantations in Suriname, but he preferred to live the life of a businessman in Paramaribo. He married a white woman, Prijna Rubens. Nanno and Kwasiba continued as house slaves. Nanno gave birth to six more children, fathered by different slaves. When Jan Van Susteren died, he gave orders in his last will and testament that his two mulatto children, Maria and Charlo, and their mother Nanno were to be granted their freedom. The free mulatta Maria was fourteen at the time and she married the wealthy widower Pierre Mevila less than a year later. Van Susteren's widow sold Kwasiba to Maria for two hundred guilders. She was later to cherish and look after little Elisabeth together with her own grandchildren, Amarante and Daniel, the children of her only daughter Jana, who had died shortly after the birth of her son.

Elisabeth played with Daniel, Amarante and other children at the back of her mother's house. Daniel was a year older than Elisabeth and Kwasiba's favourite. She would let him do whatever he wanted, always gave him the tastiest titbits and the biggest piece of fish, and rarely scolded him. Elisabeth admired Daniel. He was big and strong, thought up games, was always raring to go. Elisabeth followed suit until one day they got into a fight. Daniel had given her a thrashing and was holding her under his arm as he pinched her cheek. Elisabeth roared and Nene Kwasiba ordered them to stop, pulling Daniel away. Much to the other children's surprise, she gave him a clout about the ears and a good shaking. When he started to cry, she pulled him towards her and said: 'There, there, my boy, but you mustn't hit her. That's the way the world is. When she's older she can have you whipped. You are a slave, but she is not.'

That evening, Elisabeth asked Sisa Maria what 'slave' meant. Maria explained and added that she was different from the other children and should get used to the fact.

Everything changed completely when Masra Pierre Mevila passed away and Captain Frederik Bosse made his appearance, first as a guest and then as a lodger. After a couple of weeks he married Maria. He was immediately drawn to the eight-year-old free negress and her inquiring mind. He taught her reading, writing and arithmetic and gave her a Bible and other books. Whenever Masra Frederik was not at work, he would give her a lesson every morning and an assignment that kept her busy throughout the day.

Daniel was still her best friend and she told him everything she had learned. Now he was the one who admired her, especially after she started to take harpsichord lessons from a white music teacher. Pierre Mevila's first wife had owned a harpsichord and it was still in the front room of the house. On the request of the governor and the Police Council, a dance teacher had been brought to the colony to teach the young white folk to make music and dance. The man in question, Monsieur Beaumonde, was not only a lover of music, however, he also enjoyed his drink. Before long he found himself in serious debt to Captain Bosse, who imported and retailed alcohol. As the debt increased, Bosse came to realise that the man would never be able to repay it from his meagre salary.

Bosse suggested that Beaumonde give Elisabeth music lessons. Beaumonde was delighted to be able to rid himself of his debt in this manner. He set about the music lessons without much expectation, but ultimately took great pleasure in the progress the little negress made when compared with his white pupils. Elisabeth was well aware of the uniqueness of her position in those days. Everyone in the house confirmed it and Masra Frederik boasted about her to his friends. He would sometimes ask her to play the harpsichord when he had visitors. Then he would laugh and exclaim: 'What do you think of that, eh? Don't tell me negroes are dumb; they only pretend to be dumb to make a fool of the whites.'

Elisabeth had learned all about her background by this time. She knew that her mother was the free negress Mariana, who had once been a slave by the name of Nanno. She knew she had six brothers and sisters, all of whom were slaves to her half-brother Charlo, who had bought them from his father's widow. She didn't get to see her family very often. Sisa Maria only allowed her to visit her mother for an hour every week.

One day Misi Talbot came to visit with her ten-year-old daughter Charlotte. Elisabeth was eleven at the time, and the two played together the entire day. Elisabeth's gifts and skills surprised Charlotte.

'Such a shame you're black,' she said when it was time to go home. 'If you hadn't been black we could have been friends.'

'And can't we be friends?' Elisabeth asked.

'Of course not,' said Charlotte. 'Blacks are inferior to whites. How could we be friends?'

Elisabeth protested to Daniel about it later: 'Why do whites have to be superior?' Daniel answered: 'They don't have to be, but they are. And do you know why? Because they have rifles and cannons, and they use them to crush everybody and make themselves rich.'

'I wish I was white,' Elisabeth said and Daniel immediately turned on her: 'Don't be so stupid! You're black and will never be white. Mark my words. One day the whites are going to lose, and then the blacks will be superior. Then we'll teach them. The blacks in Africa are powerful people. They have kingdoms, weapons, everything. And the Maroons in the jungle are also a force to be reckoned with. I hope they hurry to attack all the plantations and chase out the whites. Then the blacks will be superior.'

'That's unlikely to happen,' Elisabeth interrupted. 'Before the Maroons reach the city, the soldiers will kill them. Masra Frederik says they're about to take harsh action against all the runaways.'

Sisa Maria started to disapprove of Elisabeth's friendship with Daniel all of a sudden and often told her that it was inappropriate to be whispering all the time with a mere futuboi. She was eleven and Daniel twelve when she missed him one morning and noticed that eight-year-old Pierlala had taken over as Masra Frederik's futuboi.

'Where is Daniel?' she asked Maria.

'Sent to the plantation,' Maria snapped. 'And he's not coming back.'

'What did he do?' Elisabeth asked, knowing that being sent to the plantation often served as a punishment for negroes in the city who had done something wrong.

'Nothing, but he's better off on the plantation,' Sisa Maria replied.

'But why? It's not fair! Why should Daniel have to go to the plantation if he's done nothing wrong?' Elisabeth complained, but Sisa Maria took her firmly by the shoulders and told her to her face: 'He's done nothing wrong. You're the reason. You were getting too close to him. You have to learn to keep yourself decent and respectable. You are a free woman, a freeborn woman no less. Do you want to throw that away by getting involved with a slave? You have to stay pure, spotless. White men are always after a pretty young black girl, but they won't be interested in used property, especially if a black man's had his hands all over it. Get that into your head once and for all! Kwasiba will never forgive me for sending her darling boy away,' she added softly. 'But I did it for you. You have to make something of your life!'

Nene Kwasiba died a month later. Old age, everyone said, but Elisabeth knew it was grief that killed her.

As she reminisced about her early years, Elisabeth realised that she had heard nothing more about Daniel since his departure. What had become of him, she wondered. She had visited Plantation Saltzhallen often enough, but had always stayed at the big house and rarely if ever visited the slave village. She had neither seen him nor heard from him in all that time. Was he at Saltzhallen? If so, what was his job? Was he a field negro and did he have to work hard all day long? Had he become a carpenter or a boat negro? Had he ever been lashed by a basya on the orders of one or other white supervisor? Perhaps he had run away and joined the Maroons. Her questions remained unanswered.

As far as her own future was concerned, however, she was resolutely determined to marry a white man, in a real marriage, and not just as a housekeeper or a concubine. She wanted to marry in the church, to have a wedding with all the trimmings, the likes of which the colony had never seen before. Then everyone would talk about the free negress Elisabeth who had married the man of her choice. All the rest might think it impossible, but she was going to prove them wrong. How? With money, of course. Money worked wonders. Even the colonial government was keen on money, and all the whites thought of nothing else. Fine, if that's how it must be! She had money and expected to have a lot more in the future. She would marry the man she loved. She would marry Carl Otto Creutz!

Maria was entertaining visitors on the rear gallery, her sisters Nanette and Catharina together with Mina, the wife of her brother Izaak. Cato, Izaak's eldest daughter, sat at the bottom of the stairs leading down from the gallery. The women were watching a little girl chasing chickens in the adjacent yard and shouting: 'Come, titi, come.'

'A strapping young girl,' said Maria. She turned and saw Elisabeth coming down the stairs. 'Come, Liesbeth, your aunt Elisabeth is here, your namesake.'

'We call her Bettie,' said Mina shyly, knowing full well that Izaak had wanted to name her Elisabeth after her aunt but had been forced to settle for Liesbeth.

'Hello Bettie,' said Elisabeth, as Cato took her sister's hand and they climbed the stairs to the gallery. The child looked up and smiled. 'Goodness,' said Elisabeth, 'she has a full set of teeth.'

'Well, of course, she's almost two,' Maria chuckled. 'She's already learning to talk. Come, Bettie, what do we say to the chickens?'

'Come, titi, come, titi,' the child shouted, clenching her little fists and rubbing her fingers with her thumbs. The women laughed.

Elisabeth joined Mina and the sisters but did not participate in the conversation. Her thoughts were elsewhere.

She had been ordering goods from Holland for more than two years. The firm with which her brother-in-law Frederik did business also supplied her with various sorts of fabric, lace, buttons and other accessories, which she sold in Paramaribo. The wives of several plantation owners and civil servants were among her clientele and she earned a pretty penny fulfilling their insatiable desire for new clothes. The young businesswoman also sold on credit as long as she received her money before the end of the year. But now fifteen yards of black silk, ten yards of linen, several yards of bonnet lace and a dozen silver buttons had gone missing.

A tray with a carafe and glasses graced the table. A while later, Appolonia, one of the slaves, appeared with a fresh carafe filled with lemonade. Elisabeth sipped from her glass but the others refrained. Another slave announced that dinner was ready. The sisters stood and made their way to the table but Elisabeth remained seated.

'Don't you want to join us for dinner?' asked Nanette.

'Yes, of course, but there's something on my mind and it's sure to ruin my appetite,' Elisabeth replied.

'What's worrying you so, little sister?' asked Maria as she passed Liesbeth to Catharina.

'Something's not right with my ledger,' said Elisabeth. 'I seem to have misplaced fifteen yards of black silk, ten yards of linen, a length of bonnet lace and a dozen silver buttons.'

'Isn't that the silk and linen I gave to Misi Peltzer when Governor De Cheusses died?' asked Maria. 'You remember, don't you? You had gone to Saltzhallen with Masra Frederik that day, but Mrs Peltzer couldn't wait until you returned because her mourning outfit had to be put together in a hurry. When she insisted, I fetched the silk from the cupboard and gave it to her. And then she asked for bonnet linen and those buttons. I told you all about it but you must have forgotten to write it down.'

'That's it, of course,' Elisabeth exclaimed, 'how could I have forgotten.' She quickly got to her feet and raced up the stairs. 'Hasn't she paid her account yet?' Maria shouted, but Elisabeth was already in her room scribbling in her ledger and could no longer hear her. I should pay Misi Peltzer a visit, she thought. It's been at least a year. If I forgot about it, then perhaps she did too. And she still owes me for gold braid, lace and silk she bought for her daughter's Christening outfit. So, now that that was settled she could get on with noting the new requisitions in her ledger.

She would send Bruno and Amos the following morning to collect the new consignment. Captain Schouten had sent Bosse a message that his ship was in harbour and that their orders were ready for delivery.

The following day, Bruno and Amos fetched the new consignment from the harbour by horse and cart. They left the trunks of cloth on the rear gallery and stored the casks of butter, sacks of flour and crates of drink in the cellar. Elisabeth spent the entire morning running back and forth, checking the delivery and writing everything down in her ledger. She made sure to finish her brother-in-law's business before moving on to her own.

Elisabeth took a rest after lunch and continued work until around four in the afternoon. The female slaves Amarante and Fenisi opened the trunks and unpacked the cloth, while Elisabeth checked it carefully for any damage that may have been incurred on the journey. They were hard at work when they heard the front door open and a thumping noise in the front room.

'Who's there?' Elisabeth shouted.

A clearly exhausted Carl Otto staggered onto the rear gallery and groaned as he collapsed in a chair still wearing his sword. At that point, his eyes appeared to roll upwards in their sockets and he slipped from the chair onto the floor.

'Mi Gado,' Amarante exclaimed, raising her hand to her mouth.

'Heavens,' yelped Fenisi, 'is masra going to die?'

Elisabeth was already kneeling at Carl Otto's side.

'He's fainted,' she said. 'Quickly, Amarante, fetch water. Fenisi, find Plato.'

Amarante returned a moment later with water. Plato, the negro charged with the health of the household, immediately loosened Carl Otto's clothing and washed his face. 'Masra's on fire with fever,' said Plato. 'Look how thin he has become.'

'But where is Rufus?' said Elisabeth. 'Fetch Rufus!'

At that moment, Carl Otto opened his eyes and gently murmured: 'Let Rufus be. He's also tired and sick, so tired…'

'Masra should eat something. Can misi have someone bring soup?' Plato asked and ordered Fenisi to take off his shoes.

Carl Otto groaned as Plato tried to remove his uniform trousers, which turned out to be caked to a gaping wound on his leg. Plato carefully cut the trousers free and set about washing the wound. He then sponged Carl Otto's entire body and asked for a sheet to cover him.

In the meantime, Fenisi had brought a bowl of soup from the kitchen and

Elisabeth held it to Carl Otto's mouth to allow him to drink it slowly. When the soup was finished, he looked Elisabeth in the eye for a second and said: 'Thank you… tired… so tired.' He then fell asleep.

'Shouldn't we bring masra upstairs, misi?' asked Plato, but Maria, who had joined them on the rear gallery, said: 'Bring him to the dining room and let him rest on the settee. Bringing him upstairs would be too tiring.'

Carl Otto was brought to the settee in the dining room where he slept until the following morning.

Plato arrived to nurse his wound and told him what he had heard from Rufus. Apparently, the patrol had lost its way in the jungle, had survived without food for four days, and had finally found its way back. Eighteen of the thirty soldiers had died of fever and exhaustion. They hadn't found a single runaway.

By noon, Carl Otto was feeling much better.

'A good thing too,' said Elisabeth. 'We have to get you to your room.'

'And just when I was getting used to the settee,' Carl Otto laughed, 'and all the women taking such good care of me.'

'We're expecting visitors this evening and the last thing they would expect is a naked soldier in the dining room,' Elisabeth answered.

'Oh yes? Who are we expecting?' Carl Otto inquired.

'Just my brother-in-law's card friends. But this time for dinner. Now that my brother-in-law has resigned his commission, he has all the time in the world for receptions. He enjoys it. This evening's in honour of someone special.'

'And who might that someone be?' asked Carl Otto.

'Don't ask me,' said Elisabeth.

'If that someone is the new governor, then the festivities will have to be cancelled. He's seriously ill. He might even be dead by now.'

'Is that right?' asked Elisabeth.

'Yes. I heard about it yesterday when we returned to the fort,' Creutz replied.

'But he's only been here a couple of months!' Elisabeth exclaimed. 'Didn't the last governor die only a year ago? And weren't they brothers? Such a strange thing!'

'He was appointed to replace his brother. I'm told they're grandchildren of Van Aerssen Van Sommelsdijck, who more or less founded the colony,' said Creutz. 'But sickness and death are no respecters of persons. Governors are no exception.'

'Oh well, I'm sure they'll send another,' was Elisabeth's laconic response.

'And a widow looking for a husband. In fact he'll have two widows De Cheusses to choose from,' said Creutz.

'Perhaps he'll bring his own wife,' said Elisabeth. 'Listen to us! The governor might not even be dead!'

'From what I heard he wasn't far from it,' Creutz asserted.

'Imagine. Yet another governor's funeral and I still haven't been paid for the cloth I sold to make a mourning outfit for the last. I'll have to pay a visit to Mrs Peltzer or I'll never see my money,' said Elisabeth.

'Dead governors are good for business, eh?' Carl Otto observed as he smiled at the young woman in front of him and caressed her hand.

'Nonsense! But good cloth doesn't grow on trees,' Elisabeth scolded. 'And now upstairs with you! There are women expected this evening.'

'I know how it works,' said Carl Otto. 'After dinner the men retire to the front room for a game of cards and the women make their way to the rear gallery or stay in the dining room to chat and gossip. Sometimes they spend the rest of the evening walking round the house, approving and disapproving of what they see.'

'You've clearly settled in,' Elisabeth chuckled. 'You know exactly *what* to expect, but do you know *who* to expect?'

'Strube, I imagine, Van Harlingen, Van Daale, the Du Peijrons, De Vrieses, Planteaus, Coudercs, Wiltens. Am I close?' Creutz inquired.

'Very close! My brother-in-law can't abide some of them but he wouldn't dare leave them out.'

'If you ask me, it won't be long before Frederik Coenraad Bosse, former captain in the Society's army, is nominated for a function on the Police Council,' said Carl Otto.

'Masra Frederik would make an excellent council member,' said Elisabeth.

'Do I really have to be there this evening?' Creutz asked.

'I'm afraid you're expected,' said Elisabeth, 'but if you still feel unwell you can stay upstairs. Masra Frederik will offer your apologies to the guests.'

'Will you keep me company?' Carl Otto asked with a smile.

'Of course not. I have to be here to keep an eye on the servants. Sisa Maria's counting on me,' Elisabeth replied.

'Let's wait and see, eh? Time for me to go upstairs,' said Carl Otto as he tried to stand up but fell back immediately into his chair. 'I'm so dizzy.'

'Should I call for help,' asked Elisabeth.

'No, no. I'll be fine,' Carl Otto answered and he got to his feet, tied the sheet in a large knot around his waist and headed for the door. After three short steps, however, he was forced to hold onto the doorpost to keep himself upright.

Elisabeth rushed to his side.

'Come, let me help you.' She gave him her arm for support and the pair slowly climbed the stairs.

'Wait a second,' said Carl Otto as they stood on the first landing. Elisabeth looked up at him and said with a smile: 'Where's the burly cadet I once knew? Did you ever imagine you would have to lean on a woman for support? Never entered your mind, eh?' and she tickled him teasingly in the side.

'Don't! Otherwise I'll never make it upstairs,' said Carl Otto, and he groaned as they climbed the second flight: 'And don't think you can take advantage of the situation, because I feel a lot better than I did earlier.'

At the top of the stairs he said: 'Do you want to see how much better?' and before Elisabeth had the chance to answer, he took her in his arms and kissed her on the lips.

Elisabeth let him have his way and a second kiss followed the first. He took a couple of steps, went into his room, and pulled her with him. They kissed again and collapsed on the bed.

'Stop! Don't! I'm expected downstairs,' said Elisabeth when Carl Otto kissed her yet again and started to undo the buttons on her bodice.

'Stay with me, please,' said Carl Otto, but she stood and fastened the buttons of her dress.

'You should sleep. Then you'll be fit for this evening,' she said with a smile as she rushed to the door.

'You'll see just how fit I am!' he said. 'I'll be down in a minute to show the men I'm still alive, although it was a close shave.'

'How many runaways did you actually capture,' asked Elisabeth before leaving the room.

'Not one. We came across three abandoned villages but there was no one to be seen. They must have fled in a hurry because they left their chickens behind and we ate them. They're experts at hiding, those people. They know we're coming long before we know they're there. We'll have to prepare ourselves better next time.

'I'm off downstairs. Sleep for a while and you can have dinner later. Bye.'

She was gone. Carl Otto turned and sighed. A few moments later he was asleep.

The guests arrived later in the evening, on foot preceded by a slave holding a lamp, or in carriages with a futuboi on the block next to the coachman carrying a burning torch. The lavishly dressed couples ascended the steep front stairs, while the slaves made their way to the rear of the property via the negerpoort. A recently arrived colonist and his wife made the acquaintance of the hostess and her little sister in the front room, a mulatta and a negress, as they had already been informed.

Nicolas Gabion and his wife Pauline were accompanied by their fifteen-year-old daughter. The family had only been in the colony for six weeks and were lodging with the Drouillet family at Plantation Bergerac, while their own plantation house was being readied for their arrival. The Gabions were the new owners of Plantation L'Embarras on the Commewijne. They were on a brief visit to the city and were staying with the Cellier family on Gravenstraat.

Frederik Bosse always invited newcomers. Sometimes they would stop coming after a couple of visits because they had made friends of their own who wanted nothing to do with people who had black relatives. Bosse made sure that none of the male members of his wife's family were present when he invited couples. It was an unwritten rule that coloured men, slaves excepted, were considered *persona non grata* in the presence of white women.

After the meal, which neither Elisabeth nor Carl Otto attended, two violinists provided the guests with musical entertainment. According to custom, the guests wandered through the house, stopping here and there to chat. The men quickly found their way to the front room to enjoy a game a cards, while the women relaxed on the rear gallery, and a couple stood in the dining room next to an open window.

Carl Otto had remained in his room after all. A slave girl had brought a tray with food and after eating he had fallen asleep. He heard all sorts of noises from downstairs and wondered whether he should get dressed and join the guests.

Lucie Gabion sat beside her mother and Mrs Van Meel. Her mother complained about the heat. It was stifling. Her husband and daughter were also finding it difficult, but her ten-year-old and eight-year-old sons seemed to be taking it in their stride. They wanted to wear as little as possible, of course, but their entire bodies were covered with red blisters and their arms and legs with scratched-open mosquito bites. Madame Gabion heaved a sigh. Heavens, it was warm. And is it true what they say? That it's like this the whole year round?

Mrs Van Meel confirmed her suspicions: 'Yes, it's always warm, frequently much warmer than this.' She also found it difficult to bear. That was why she had a futuboi and a young slave girl at home whose sole job was to waft cool air in Misi Van Meel's direction with an enormous fan.

'But weren't you born here?' Pauline asked, knowing that Constance Van Meel's maiden name was Pichot and that she had her roots in a group of French Huguenots, who had lived in the colony for a couple of generations.

'Yes, I was born here and I've lived here all my life,' Mrs Van Meel answered, 'but that doesn't mean that I'm immune to the climate. We white folk have a more delicate constitution, you know. We're not made for the tropics. Take our children, for example. So few make it through their first year. I've already lost two children myself.'

Pauline Gabion nodded. She had heard about the high mortality rate. She and her family had set out from Amsterdam four months ago. Her father-in-law, who had only told them about the positive side of life in the colony, especially the money they could earn as plantation owners, had more or less insisted that they come. She had seen that planters lived a life of affluence, but the tropical diseases and other dangers – such as being attacked by runaway slaves – didn't make it easy. To be honest, she felt listless and tired all the time. Fortunately, there were slaves everywhere to do the work. Imagine having to do it all by yourself? It didn't bear thinking about. Even walking was an effort.

Her daughter Lucie found the whole thing boring and tedious. Was this all she had to look forward to? She had already been to an assortment of parties and receptions, often organised to welcome her family to the colony, but was this all there was to do in Suriname? She had wanted to stay in Holland, but her parents had insisted that the change would do her good. She would have the chance to meet the sons of wealthy plantation owners. In truth, she had yet to meet an attractive young man. It was different in Amsterdam where she had been good friends with the baker's son, but her parents didn't want her getting involved with an ordinary middle-class boy. Her mother had had a serious talk with her before they left and told her to prepare herself for a fine and prosperous marriage. Who was she going to marry? she asked herself. Surely not one of these old fogies! Imagine!

They've been harping on all day about the acting governor who's on his deathbed, so they say. Lucie looked at her mother and wondered whether she was really listening to Mrs Van Meel's chatter and how she hadn't felt her best recently with the constant fevers and the ever increasing pain in her legs. Mummy appeared to be listening. At least she nodded now and then. Lucie had heard such stories before. Countless people, especially women, complained of terrible fevers and legs so badly swollen they could barely walk. Lucie carefully felt her legs through her skirt, as if she were afraid they had started to swell. The last thing she wanted was to fall ill or have bulging legs. She hated the heat and detested the miserable colony. If it were up to her, she would go back to Holland in the morning.

Lucie looked at her father who was standing next to a couple of gentlemen and listening to their animated story about importing horses from America. She was trying to follow the conversation when she suddenly caught sight of a handsome young man entering the front room: blond, tall, broad-shouldered. Well, well, she thought, this was a step in the right direction. Where did he come from? The young man shook hands with a couple of gentleman who patted him on the back and asked him how he was getting on.

Lucie was unable to understand what he was saying, but she followed his every move and hoped he would make his way to the dining room and they would be introduced. And that is precisely what happened. She watched him come into the room and say something to Mrs Bosse who then brought him over to their table.

'Carl Otto Creutz,' said the young man, as he offered Mrs Van Meel, Mrs Gabion and Lucie a polite kiss of the hand. Lucie smiled radiantly, but his attention seemed to be drawn to someone sitting on the rear gallery and she noticed his face light up. He hurried past her and when she turned she saw the beautifully dressed negress standing in the doorway. How strange, she thought.

Their host, and the owner of this magnificent house, was a German, married to a mulatta. She may have been a beautiful woman, but it still wasn't right. A mulatta! His wife's sister also stayed with them and she was a genuine negress. A common-or-garden negress, just like the slaves. But she was a free negress, and she was always around when the Bosses received guests. Lucie had heard that she could read and write and that she had her own business. She imported cloth from Holland, America, and even France.

There she was, a common negress, standing in the doorway as if she were one of them, and the only decent-looking man in the place had gone directly to her. Who knows, perhaps she had snared him with her witchcraft, thought Lucie. She had heard from other women that negroes were dangerous, but negresses were even worse, and that they used all sorts of sinister trickery to entice men into their beds before they knew what was happening to them. The slave women were said to be so good at leading white men astray that some completely forgot their white wives and moved in with their black mistresses.

Mrs Van Meel said something to Lucie, but she had not been part of the conversation and had no idea what she was talking about. Fortunately, she was saved from having to answer by a slave girl who appeared in front of them with a tray of hot chocolate and she simply nodded at Mrs Van Meel as she sipped at her cup. She followed the blond-headed man and the negress nervously as they stepped onto the rear terrace. Lucie put down her cup, got to her feet, hurried to the rear terrace and positioned herself in such a way that she could see the cadet and the negress clearly. She watched as they chatted with one another. The man reached out and took hold of the necklace the negress was wearing in his open hand and said something to her. She smiled and said something in response.

Those two obviously knew one another, that was clear.

A voice echoed from the front room: 'Creutz!'

It was their host, Frederik Bosse.

Creutz shouted back, 'I'm here', said something to the black woman, turned and went inside. Lucie was about to make her way back to the dining room when she saw Mr Van Meel walking towards the negress.

He spoke to her, but the look on her face was not exactly friendly when she replied. He then took hold of her necklace as Creutz had done and whispered something in her ear. The woman seemed to get even angrier. Lucie was too far away to follow the conversation but she saw how Van Meel tried to caress the woman's chest with the necklace in his hand. The woman stepped back and pulled the necklace from his hand. With a lecherous look in his eye, he said something else to her and she shouted: 'Never!' as she turned her back to him. Van Meel took hold of her dress from behind. She turned, wrenched her dress free and ran to the dining room.

Van Meel laughed mockingly. Then he noticed Lucie and made his way over to her. 'Well, young lady, beginning to settle down?' he said. 'I suppose so,' she replied. 'It's just this heat!'

'Yes, my dear, only to be expected in the tropics.' With that, he smiled and walked past her towards a group of gentlemen in the front room.

Elisabeth kept close to Maria in the dining room. She was furious! She had been so happy to see that Carl Otto had come downstairs after all. When he noticed her standing in the doorway, he had joined her immediately and admired her pretty necklace as they stood on the rear terrace. Then Masra Frederik called him over and before she knew it Van Meel was standing in front of her.

'When do I get my turn?' he had asked.

'What do you mean?' she replied, his proximity forcing her to step backwards. Then he took hold of her necklace, as Carl Otto had done a few minutes earlier, and said: 'Come, come, my dear, I think you know what I mean. It's common knowledge that you sleep with your brother-in-law and with Creutz. So when do I get my turn?'

She was furious. The man was a scoundrel. If she'd had the chance she would have slapped his face, but she was well aware that a black woman would never do such a thing to a white man, and that is why she had taken a step backwards. When it became clear that he also wanted to caress her breasts, she tugged the necklace from his hand and turned her back to him. At that moment he tried to grab her hand and whispered in her ear: 'I'll get what's coming to me.'

'Never!' she had yelled. He grabbed her skirt as she hurried towards the dining room and she spontaneously yanked it away from him.

'Will you take a look at the cake trays, Elisabeth?' asked Maria, who was chatting with Reverend Visser's wife.

Elisabeth hurried to the rear gallery and checked to see if the cake trays were correctly arranged. When the slave brought them inside, she quickly made her way upstairs. Van Meel! What a despicable scoundrel!

Lucie was hoping the blond-haired young man would come over and talk to her, but he lingered with the men in the front room from which hails of raucous laughter emerged every now and then.

'Who was that young man we met just a moment ago?' she asked Mrs Van Meel.

'Who, indeed. Ah, now I remember. Creutz, one of the cadets. He arrived a short while ago and recently returned from an important jungle expedition. They said he was seriously ill, but he seems hale and hearty to me.'

'Does he live here?' Lucie inquired.

'Yes, he does,' Mrs Van Meel answered. 'He and Bosse both hail from the duchy of Cleve. Just like the French, it's not uncommon for people from the same part of the world to lodge with one another.' She then continued to whisper to Lucie's mother: 'But they're not the same as we French, you know. Look at Bosse, for example, married to a mulatta who was first married to someone else. Swiss, I believe, same language I suppose. And what about the newcomer, Creutz. They say he's fond of the negress.'

Lucie wondered to herself if Mrs Van Meel had any idea that her own husband had been talking to the same negress moments ago, but she said nothing. She listened as Constance Van Meel explained to her mother that they were fortunate to have an edict in the colony that forbade marriages between blacks and whites. It was acceptable for a mulatta to marry a white man but not a regular black, not a negress.

'How fortunate,' her mother sighed. Fortunate indeed, thought Lucie, realising that the negress was out of the running.

The evening came to an end and the guests took their leave in a flurry of handshakes by the door.

When Lucie held out her hand to Carl Otto she said: 'I hear you've just returned from a jungle expedition. Are you alright?'

'Well, I survived,' said Creutz with a smile, 'but only just.'

'I hope we can expect a visit from you soon. What do you think, mummy?' asked Lucie and her mother hastily replied: 'But of course. We'll set a date as soon as our house is ready. We plan to live on Plantation L'Embarras on the Commewijne, but you don't have to wait that long. We'll be at the Celliers' place on Gravenstraat for the next three weeks.'

'Thank you. I would be happy to accept your invitation,' Creutz replied as he accompanied the ladies to their coach.

Elisabeth had remained in her room upstairs, thinking about the events of the evening. What angered her most was the remark about her brother-in-law. She knew that many of the whites indulged in shameful gossip about relationships between whites and blacks, but the thought that such things were being said about her brother-in-law was simply unbearable. He was like a father to her. She decided to stay in her room. All those puffed up colonists can whistle for all I care.

Shortly afterwards she heard a gentle knock at the door and Carl Otto peered through the opening.

'I was looking for you everywhere, but you had disappeared,' he said. 'Do you mind if I come in?'

'No, not at all,' said Elisabeth. 'I'm not planning to go back downstairs.'

'What's the matter? Did something happen?' asked Carl Otto.

'That scoundrel Van Meel. I could have slapped his face,' said Elisabeth, seething with anger.

'What did he do?' asked Carl Otto.

'He's nothing but a conniving scoundrel,' Elisabeth barked.

'That's nothing new,' Carl Otto replied. Bosse had already told him that Van Meel was a slippery character and that he often spread lies about others if he thought he might profit.

'What did he do?' asked Carl Otto a second time.

'Oh, just leave it alone,' said Elisabeth, staring at her hands.

'No. I won't hear of it. Did the man insult you?'

'Yes, he certainly did,' Elisabeth spluttered. 'But that doesn't count, seeing I'm a negress and it's alright to insult a negress, isn't it? But he also insulted my brother-in-law, here in his own house no less, and…'

'Your sister?' Carl Otto interrupted.

'No, not my sister. You!' said Elisabeth shyly.

'Me!' Creutz thundered. 'Should I get ready for a duel? What did he say?'

'Leave it alone. The scoundrel isn't worth it,' she whispered unable to look him in the eye.

'Tell me. I want to know.' Carl Otto lifted her chin and looked at her. 'Tell me. What did he say?'

'He insinuated that I was sleeping with my brother-in-law. Masra Frederik doesn't deserve such an insult. He has always been like a father to me. I never knew my own father and don't even know who he is, but I couldn't have asked for a better father than my brother-in-law. But if you believe Van Meel and his like, white men are only interested in getting negresses into bed.'

Carlo Otto gazed at the young black woman in front of him and said: 'And that's what they think about us? About you and me?'

'Of course. They're convinced of it,' said Elisabeth indignantly.

'But my dear Elisabeth,' said Carl Otto, taking her hands in his. 'That's not an insult. You know there's so much more between us: friendship, trust, love

I hope, and yes… I would warmly welcome that other aspect. I don't mind if you're mad at Van Meel, the rogue, but not at me!'

He pulled her close and kissed her. She responded to his kisses, but when they became more intense and he started to caress her body with his hands she pushed him away.

'Come on, Elisabeth. What's the matter? You know I love you,' Carl Otto whispered passionately, pulling her towards the bed.

'No. I don't want this. I refuse to prove those wretches right. I might be black, but I'm not the sort of black that jumps into bed with any old man,' Elisabeth protested.

'Any old man? Is that what I mean to you?' asked Carl Otto.

'No, no, you're special, very special. But this is not what I want. Don't you understand?' She pushed him away and took a couple of steps backwards.

Creutz stretched out his arm and pulled her back into his embrace. 'Come, Elisabeth. I'm not like Van Meel and his cronies. I love you. I really love you. You must have noticed by now. You're the only one that I want. I don't care what they say,' and he tried to kiss her again but she turned her face.

'Do I mean so little to you,' asked Carl Otto insistently.

'You mean a great deal to me, but…' said Elisabeth gently.

'Come then, my darling, no excuses,' whispered Carl Otto against her cheeks and into her neck, and his hands once more caressed her breasts.

'No. This is not what I want. Not this!' said Elisabeth categorically. 'Don't you understand?' she insisted. 'I want to marry. I want it all: a real wedding, a proper wedding night. I don't want to do this without a reason. I want to save it for my man, my future husband. Just like… like…'

'Like official weddings? Like white women? But my dearest, don't let them fool you. Many of them have sampled the pleasures of the bed long before their wedding night,' he chuckled. But then he looked her straight in the face and saw a teardrop glisten in her eye. He had never seen Elisabeth crying before.

'If that's what you want, mein Mädchen, mein Babetchen, then that's what you'll have. A wedding with all the trimmings and a proper wedding night. Believe me! As long as I can be the groom. If it means so much to you, then let's stop now, let's wait. But say it again, please, say you love me.'

'I love you, but I'm black, and blacks are not allowed to marry whites. You know that, don't you?' said Elisabeth softly.

'We'll find a way,' said Creutz beaming with confidence. 'You'll see. Before you know it, your brother-in-law will be a member of the Police Council. He'll bring the other councillors round, don't you think?'

'I'm sure he'll do his best,' said Elisabeth.

'Come, my sweet, give me a final kiss and I'll go back to my room like a respectable and decent young man,' said Creutz, and he took her in his arms. She laughed and pursed her lips.

In the slave quarters at the back of the house, Amarante said to Fenisi: 'She'll have her way, that Misi Elisabeth.'

'What do you mean?' asked Fenisi.

'Masra Carl Otto. I saw him in her room,' Amarante replied.

'Finally! I thought it would never happen,' chortled Fenisi, and she edged her little boy to one side and lay down next to him on the floor.

Amarante sighed. She couldn't sleep. She could hear Fenisi snoring gently by her side and the smack of her child's lips as he sucked at his mother's breast. Appolonia, Sylvia and her daughter Amimba lay sleeping on the other side. Sylvia used to be the wife of Elisabeth's brother Kwakoe and Amimba was his child. But they were slaves, just like Amarante. Life was strange, she thought, full of twists and turns. Nanno and Kwasiba, both abducted in Africa, both sent to America on a slave ship. And yet a number of years later Nanno was free and Kwasiba's grandchildren were slaves to Nanno's descendents. She thought about her brother Daniel, who had been sent to the plantation on Elisabeth's account, and who was probably hard at work. And Elisabeth always gets what she wants, Amarante thought. Poor slaves that we are. Why? Why?

July 1736
Paramaribo

The new governor Johan Raye, who had arrived in Suriname in December 1735 and set about his task with great enthusiasm, clearly did not share the ideas of his predecessors Temming and the brothers De Cheusses. Although the governor endeavoured to be friendly with one and all and often visited plantations and accepted invitations to card evenings in the city, many of the colonists did not like him and several claimed that his new ideas did not promote the advancement of the colony. Governor Raye believed himself to be acting in the best interests of Suriname, and argued that 'laziness and debt' were predominant among some of the colony's inhabitants.

The man had only been in service for four months when he found himself in a serious conflict with the Police Council. Raye was of the opinion that slave owners were not at liberty to do whatever they wanted with their slaves. Plantation owner George Hendrik Sieffaart had had a young slave tortured to death and the governor wanted to see Sieffaart punished, and not with a fine, which would have been tolerable, but with the rack. Sieffaart was taken into custody, but continued to deny that he had tortured the slave. Raye believed it his duty to uphold Dutch law in the colony. The marks of torture on the slave's body were more than enough evidence, and to top it all there were other slaves who were witness to Sieffaart's misconduct.

The councillors, planters and slave owners had never heard the like of it. The new governor had violated every rule in the colony's books. After all, slaves were not allowed to testify against their masters. Such a thing had never happened and should never be allowed to happen. Raye insisted that the councillors show him the resolutions in which it was stated that slaves were not allowed to serve as witnesses. The councillors retorted that they were not obliged to prove themselves. It had never been the practice in the colony and that was enough. The governor wrote to the Directors of the Society in Holland. When they heard about the governor's letter, the councillors decided that they and as many planters and colonists as possible should also write to the Directors to inform them of their side of the dispute.

Messrs Lemmers, Jurans, Talbot, Van Sandick, Braum, Pater, Lippert and company had already written and were in search of other colonists willing to inform the Directors in Amsterdam of their opinion in the matter. Talbot paid a visit to his friend Bosse, insisting that the captain should also write. The more letters the better.

Frederik Coenraad Bosse had just recovered from a week in bed. He agreed to write a letter to the Directors of the Society, but it did not refer to the testimony of the slaves. After fifteen years service in the Society's army, he felt that it was time to retire. He resigned his commission to concentrate on his business affairs and look after Plantation Saltzhallen. Bosse told his friend Planteau that he thought the governor was right. It was unnecessary to send slaves to their death in such a cruel manner, and he could see no reason why a slave should not be allowed to testify against his master if the latter had done something terrible.

Bosse's opinion in the matter cost him several friends, all of whom claimed he was motivated by his own self-interest. After all, he lived with a mulatta and had been foolish enough to take his wife's black family as his own. Planteau was also an interested party. Everyone knew he had children by a black woman whose freedom he had purchased at their birth. From that moment on, many former friends avoided both Bosse and Pierre Planteau, but the governor appreciated them for their standpoint. As was often the case with clashes between colonists, the Directors did not respond to the letters from the governor or to those from the slave owners who had complained about the governor's behaviour. After a while, Sieffaart was allowed to go home unpunished and nothing more was said about the murdered slave.

Governor Raye was choosy when it came to his friends and he no longer visited all the colonists at home as before. The Bosses, however, continued to be a regular port of call, for an afternoon chat or a game of cards in the evening. The first time Governor Raye ascended the stairs in front of Bosse's house on Waterkant he heard harpsichord music. There was no need to knock on the door as a little futuboi who had seen him coming had already opened it. Raye took a seat without making a sound and the woman at the harpsichord continued to play, unaware that she had an audience. When the melody came to an end, Raye shouted, 'Bravo!' Elisabeth turned around and stared into the governor's face.

She stammered in surprise: 'O Excellency, forgive me. I did not know you were there.'

'And a good thing too. Otherwise I would not have been able to enjoy your delightful music,' said Raye with a smile.

'I'll let Masra Frederik know you're here,' said Elisabeth, but the governor interrupted: 'Your futuboi has already done so, I'm sure. Please sit down and keep me company,' and he pointed to a chair.

Elisabeth sat down with some hesitation. The governor wanted to put her at ease and asked: 'Have you been playing long?'

'I started lessons when I was ten years old and continued until I was twelve. My brother-in-law then ordered books to allow me to practise further by myself,' said Elisabeth, not knowing what to do with herself and hoping fervently that Bosse would hurry.

'Your efforts have born fruit, I hear. Please play something else,' said Raye, but fortunately Masra Frederik entered the front room just in time.

'Excellency, welcome!' he exclaimed. 'Sorry to have kept you waiting!'

'No need,' said Raye. 'Your sister-in-law's music has been a most pleasant distraction.'

'Yes. Our Elisabeth is quite accomplished,' said Bosse smiling proudly. Elisabeth curtsied and muttered, 'Excellency,' as she scurried out of the room.

A week later, Elisabeth made her way to the Peltzers' house for the umpteenth time, hoping to collect her dues. She visited a couple of other clients on the way who had ordered bonnet lace and a new wig. She then followed Heerenstraat and Watermolenstraat towards Gravenstraat where the Peltzers lived. Paramaribo was growing, she thought. New houses had been built and orange blossom trees planted along the streets. Elisabeth wondered what other cities looked like, such as Amsterdam or Emmerich where Carl Otto used to live, with their tall stone buildings in contrast to Paramaribo's wooden constructions.

She knocked at the door of the Peltzers' house in Gravenstraat.

Mrs Peltzer was extremely kind. Elisabeth was welcomed in and invited to take a seat in the dining room where she was offered fruit juice and biscuits while the lady of the house babbled on nineteen to the dozen about everything and nothing. Her main concern was Bellaard, who rented two rooms above the storehouse on her property and had not paid his rent for all of four months. 'He hasn't enough to pay his rent but he has plenty to spend in the café every day,' she said. 'I want him out of my house. Then I can rent the rooms to a lodger who pays.'

Elisabeth nodded. She didn't know Bellaard and wasn't interested in such affairs. She realised later that the woman was preparing her for what was to come next, namely that she had no money to pay Elisabeth the twelve guilders she owed her. 'I'll give you the entire sum next week. You have my word,' said Mrs Peltzer after Elisabeth remarked that she had been waiting such a long time to be paid for the goods she had already supplied.

'Next week. If you can't be here to collect it, I'll send someone. Thank you for your patience and regards to your sister and brother-in-law,' said Mrs Peltzer as she saw Elisabeth to the door.

That afternoon, Mrs Peltzer paid her respects to the governor. She had considered waiting a couple of days until the weekly reception organised for all the colonists, but had decided it would be better to speak to the governor in private. She had often heard Raye speak his mind about debtors, and Bellaard owed her money. Of course, she would say nothing about her own debts. When she arrived at the palace, she asked the orderly to announce her arrival and a moment or two later she was sitting in the governor's study telling him about Bellaard who lived on her property but hadn't paid rent for four months. She asked for him to be evicted from her house as soon as possible. Even if the man were to pay his entire debt this moment, she still wished to be rid of him. He was simply unreliable and prone to debt. The governor promised to have him evicted, agreeing that four months' arrears for someone who received a monthly salary was an outrage.

A couple of days later, Mrs Peltzer stormed up to Governor Raye during his lunchtime reception and asked him if he had forgotten his promise to have Bellaard evicted from her house.

The governor was irritated, particularly by the tone with which the woman had addressed him. He reacted disgruntled: 'Wench, do you think I have nothing else to do? I promised I would do it and I will keep my promise.'[3]

Now it was Mrs Peltzer's turn to be angry. Her husband was also annoyed that the governor had shouted, 'Wench, do you think I have nothing else to do?' for all to hear.

'How dare the man scream at me like that,' she bellowed as she left the room. 'Wench, indeed! I don't care if he addresses the hussy who shares his bed in the palace with such language, but I refuse to put up with it.'

The governor gave orders that same evening for two soldiers to evict Bellaard from the Peltzers' property. When the orderly heard this, he remarked that the woman had been given her way much too soon, in his opinion. Was the governor aware of precisely what she had said about him and widow De Cheusses?

When Raye heard the details, his irritation turned to rage. The following morning he despatched a message to the Peltzers, commanding them to appear at the palace without delay, where he treated them to a formidable dressing down for their brutal remarks. When Mr Peltzer tried to interrupt, the governor barked: 'Silence! Clear out, the pair of you. Out of my house this instant or there'll be hell to pay!'[4]

On their way out, Peltzer growled: 'The only one who'll have hell to pay is the one who owes the devil. Who does the fellow think he is? I've said it before and I'll say it again: De Cheusses was a much better governor, a hundred times better!'

Once again, the orderly overheard Peltzer's remark and passed it on to the governor later that day.

The Peltzers had returned home by this time. Their friend Pleger, who had heard that they had been summoned to the palace, was already waiting by the door in the company of Mrs Vos, eager to hear what had happened. Mrs Beyland, who lived opposite, also crossed the street, determined to satisfy her curiosity.

Elisabeth also happened to be standing at the door, having stopped by that same morning to collect her money. Mrs Peltzer let her in but paid her little attention. The conversation centred exclusively on the governor.

'The fellow's nothing but riff-raff!' Peltzer bellowed. 'How he became governor is a mystery to me.'

'I thought he was a kind man, with the best interests of the colony in mind,' said Elisabeth.

'Best interests? Best interests? My dear woman, you have no idea. Let me tell you the truth of the matter and listen carefully: the man does not deserve to be governor. He roared at myself and my wife as if we were slaves. Who does he think he is? And do you know why he's here? Because they wanted rid of him. He might be governor, but at least I don't have to live with his past. The man was forced to resign his commission.[5]

'How do you know that?' Elisabeth asked, taken aback by the seriousness of the accusation.

'I have my sources,' Peltzer growled. Mr Pleger also had a word to say about Raye and Mrs Beyland seemed convinced that the governor had treated the Peltzers abominably.

Elisabeth realised that this was not the appropriate moment to introduce the topic of Mrs Peltzer's debt. She decided to return home. Later that day she opened her ledger and placed three question marks after the name Peltzer.

She stared outside, her chin resting on her hands.

She thought about Carl Otto. She missed him! How long would the expedition last? She hoped he would quickly return and that his company would at least have enjoyed some success this time. It was unpleasant for soldiers to return so often from the front without results.

She also thought about the conversation earlier that afternoon. The Peltzers had said terrible things about the governor, yet she was still convinced he was a decent man who only wanted the best for the colony.

She heard the slaves shifting furniture below and remembered that Masra Frederik was organising a card evening. She thought it best to go downstairs and offer her assistance.

'Make sure there are enough ashtrays and the Jenever rack is well stocked,' said Maria as her sister descended the stairs. The Jenever bottle in the front room turned out to be empty. Elisabeth sent Amos to the cellar to fill it.

The governor was the first guest to arrive. He acted as if he was pleased to see her. 'Ah, Miss Elisabeth, how are you?' he said with a smile. 'Am I too early?'

'No, Excellency, not too early, but I must apologise for Masra Frederik. Masra Keizer was taken ill suddenly and Misi Keizer asked Masra Frederik to take a look at him. He'll be back shortly,' said Elisabeth.

'Please sit down,' said the governor. 'I hear you have a taste for books. What have you been reading lately?'

'*Robinson Crusoe* by Daniel Defoe,' Elisabeth whispered.

Governor Raye nodded approvingly. 'I say, very impressive. Even I haven't read Defoe.' His interest in talking about books quickly passed. 'Who did you say was sick?'

'Masra Keizer. Out of the blue,' said Elisabeth.

'How dreadful! I hope it's nothing serious,' said Governor Raye. 'Keizer is a fine fellow, but of course most of the colonists are fine people and it's such a pleasure to work with them. It's a genuine privilege to be governor of this colony.'

'But some folks are not always as nice as they pretend to be, Excellency. You should be careful.'

'Is that right? Be careful, should I? Of whom?' inquired the governor.

'I mean people in general, Excellency, no one in particular,' Elisabeth answered, but the governor glared at her and said: 'No, Miss Elisabeth, don't pretend. You do mean someone in particular and I would appreciate it if you would tell me who we are talking about?'

'The Peltzers... they... eh... some of the things they said about you weren't very nice,' said Elisabeth hesitatingly.

'The Peltzers? About me? Didn't I just oblige them by ordering their lodger to get out of the house?' said the governor. 'Was it because I didn't act immediately?' he continued. 'My orderlies mentioned something to that effect. I thought I had made it clear to them. Criticising me in my capacity as governor is most unbecoming. Were they on about that again?'

'Yes, something along those lines,' said Elisabeth quietly.

'So what did they say?' the governor insisted.

'I... eh... I don't remember,' said Elisabeth, wishing fervently she hadn't raised the subject in the first place.

'You know exactly what they said, miss, and I order you to tell me everything you heard,' said Governor Raye as he rose to his feet: 'Out with it, this instant!' he commanded

Oh God, what have I started, Elisabeth thought. 'Peltzer said, "The fellow's nothing but riff-raff,"' she blurted almost imperceptibly. '"At least I wasn't forced to resign my commission."'

'What did you say? Did Peltzer say that?' roared the governor. 'Miss, will you repeat what you said?'

Elisabeth repeated what she had just said, her voice quivering.

'Fine! Then it's time for the Peltzers to learn that words have consequences,' the governor bellowed. 'Tell me, miss, was anyone else involved?'

'Yes, neighbours, I think,' said Elisabeth.

'Did you recognise them?' the governor asked, his piercing gaze pinning Elisabeth to the spot.

'Only Mrs Vos,' said Elisabeth softly.

'That bitch as well! Did she have anything to say? Speak up! What did she say?' the governor snarled.

'I didn't hear her say anything,' said Elisabeth.

'Again, miss, tell me again what Peltzer had to say,' the governor commanded sternly, and Elisabeth was obliged to repeat Peltzer's words for the third time. 'Are you sure about this?' the governor barked. 'The man called me riff-raff and claimed I was forced to resign my commission? Is that what you heard, miss?' Elisabeth nodded. 'Tell me again,' Raye commanded, but as fortune would have it Frederik Bosse entered the room at that moment and Elisabeth was able to slip out quickly and unnoticed.

Upstairs in her room she could hear the governor shouting at the top of his voice and Masra Fredrik or one of the other gentlemen trying to calm him. What had she started? If only she had kept her mouth shut!

In the space of a couple of days, the news had spread through the city like wildfire. Governor Raye sent soldiers to escort Mr and Mrs Peltzer from their home to the fort, where they were questioned for hours on end regarding offensive remarks they were alleged to have made about the governor. The Peltzers denied everything, but the governor had the testimony of the free negress Elisabeth. Most of the colonists thought it madness that the governor had behaved in such a fashion, having a white couple dragged from their home as if they were criminals. The furious Peltzers announced to anyone who would listen that Governor Raye had clearly lost his mind. Who would believe the testimony of a negress? Was he still unaware that blacks are not allowed to testify against whites?

During the next council meeting, which the governor chaired by virtue of his office, he informed the assembly of the Peltzers' defamatory remarks and of their denial. The councillors shrugged their shoulders. If the Peltzers were contesting the accusations then they must be false. Did the governor realise he had been at fault having innocent people brought to the fort under military escort? The governor was incensed… he had the testimony of the negress.

'A negress?' Legislative Councillor Van Meel retorted scornfully.

'A free woman who reported of her own free will, and six times no less, that she had clearly heard the Peltzers' insults,' the governor bellowed.

Councillor Lemmers advised the governor not to believe the woman and above all to remain calm.

'But the woman heard them and others must have heard them too!' the governor exclaimed. Councillor Talbot intervened: 'Who? What others? Did they report it? Have they complained? Of course not. A negress! Goodness, Excellency, negroes lie all the time.'

'It's in their nature,' said another councillor. 'They can't distinguish between truth and lies.'

'I demand an inquiry,' roared the governor, hammering the table with the chairman's gavel.

'An inquiry? But surely there were no other witnesses? If others had come forward you would have heard by now,' said Van Meel.

'Fine! If this sort of thing is permissible… if people are free to insult me in public, as chair of this council and governor of this colony, then I no longer consider it an honour to discharge my office. Gentlemen, I am leaving. I shall inform the Directors immediately of my decision,' said the governor in a measured tone. He pushed back his chair and left the council chambers.

The councillors stared at one another in disbelief. Lemmers, the senior among them, broke the silence: 'Call the man back. Let's not saddle ourselves with yet more problems. An inquiry can't do any harm.'

The governor stopped in his tracks and turned.

'You're right, Excellency, the matter requires investigation,' said Van Meel, his hand on the governor's arm.

'Now we're talking,' said the governor and he returned to the council chambers, Van Meel at his side, and took his place once again at the head of the table.

A solemn Councillor Lemmers got to his feet: 'Please don't misunderstand us, Excellency, we hadn't quite seen the matter from that perspective. If it is true, then the most senior functionary of the colony has been insulted and that cannot be tolerated. Let the legislative councillor investigate the affair and report back to you and the council.'

Governor Raye nodded, picked up the gavel, and the meeting resumed.

Van Meel set about his inquiry the following day. He paid a personal visit to the Peltzers, who continued to deny everything. They had so many witnesses. Mr Pleger and Mrs Vos had also been in the house. Pleger confirmed that he had heard nothing; Mrs Vos maintained that she was not at the Peltzers at the time of the incident, but had arrived an hour later. Mrs Beyland, the neighbour opposite, had also been standing on the doorstep at the time. She had heard people talking and shouting, but had been unable to understand much of it and had not been aware of any insulting remarks. Van Meel didn't interrogate the free negress Elisabeth. There was no need, he thought. She would simply lie as before. On top of that, several colonists were willing to swear on oath that the Peltzers were decent people, and that such insults were beyond them.

Van Meel's report was ready in time for the next council meeting. The councillors listened with sombre faces and concluded once again that the governor had been overhasty and perhaps even rash in believing the negress and having the Peltzers fetched from their home. But fine, he was new to the colony and probably unaware that negroes could be such terrible liars. It was now apparent from Van Meel's investigation that the negress had lied.

'But why would she lie?' asked Raye at a loss. A ripple of laughter ran through the council chambers. 'Because they always lie! The woman is probably looking for a favour, trying to get into your good books. That's why she made this whole thing up.'

'She doesn't need any favours from me. She is a free woman. She lives with a decent family in a good house,' the governor observed.

'You still have a lot to learn about the negroes, Excellency. Free or not, lying is second nature to them. You have to admit, nobody would believe the word of a negress against the word of decent white folk, now would they? And don't forget, that Elisabeth, that free negress, is nothing more than a common whore, just like every other free negress!' said Van Meel.[6]

'Surely not,' said the governor. 'I thought she was respectability itself.'

Mirthful laughter filled the council chambers. 'Come, come, Excellency,' Councillor Talbot declared. 'All negresses are whores! The creatures have no sense of sin. They cohabit with men in the most scandalous fashion, and for all to see.'

Van Meel sent soldiers to fetch Elisabeth on 3 August 1736. He roared at her in public that she 'had better provide sufficient evidence within the next forty-eight hours, otherwise you will be punished with lashes, branded and banished as an example to the entire colony'.

Shortly afterwards and lost for words, a very silent Elisabeth made her way home at the side of her brother-in-law Frederik Bosse.

At home, Masra Frederik told his wife what had happened. Elisabeth sat in a corner of the room, hushed and staring into space. 'Van Meel's not in his right mind. The way he turned on Elisabeth, you'd have thought he was mad. Completely out of proportion,' said Bosse. 'Never mind. Witnesses will come forward quickly enough, I'll see to it myself. Mrs Vos, Mrs Beyland, Pleger. I'll speak to them right away.'

He returned a couple of hours later. 'Where is Elisabeth?' he asked his wife.

'In her room, refusing to eat,' she replied.

'It's getting complicated,' said Bosse. 'They refuse to testify. Pleger says he wouldn't dream of giving evidence in defence of a negress. Mrs Vos wants nothing to do with Van Meel, and Mrs Beyland claims she didn't hear what was said.'

'Heavens above! What now?' Maria sobbed.

'Hush, woman, calm yourself. It'll be alright. We'll find witnesses. First, dinner! Boy, gin and bitters, on the double!'

Bosse took a short rest after dinner. When he came downstairs from his room, he was surprised to find his other sisters-in-law Catharina and Nanette, and even mother Mariana – who rarely left the house because she had difficulty walking – on the back porch. News travels fast in Paramaribo and word of Van Meel's threats had reached them before noon. Maria informed them with a sigh that Elisabeth was not the only one to have heard the Peltzers' remarks, but the others were refusing to testify.

'Does Elisabeth know about this?' asked mother Mariana.

'No, we haven't told her.'

'I'm going to fetch her,' said Catharina. She climbed the stairs and returned a few moments later followed by a silent Elisabeth, who eyed the huddle of people staring back at her in unison.

'Those people, the ones who heard what you heard, are refusing to testify,' said Masra Frederik.

'Is that right? Then there's nothing we can do, is there?' Elisabeth answered.

'Have you any idea what you're up against, young lady,' Maria screeched. 'How can you be so calm? You heard the threats yourself. Isn't there anything she can do, Frederik. Can't she say she's sorry?'

'Sorry? Sorry for what?' asked Elisabeth. 'I'm sorry I thought it right to warn the governor, if that's what you mean. But I don't see it making much of a difference.'

'No, I mean, can't you just say… eh, eh… that you made a mistake?' Maria suggested charily.

'That I made a mistake? Not on your life. Never! Listen here: I made no mistake. I told the truth. If others want to lie it's up to them, but I didn't lie!' Elisabeth screamed, her face twisted with rage. 'White people lie. They're liars and hypocrites, the lot of them.'

'They'll whip you and brand you, they might even give you the Spanish Buck. Do you realise that?' Nanette complained.

'Calm down, calm down,' Bosse interrupted, 'it won't come to that. Everyone knows that the governor already had problems with the Peltzers. The orderly at the palace overheard their insults and kept it no secret. Surely it's logical that Raye's public rebuke angered them even more and incited them to further insults? Anyway, Elisabeth is a free woman. Van Meel has no right to carry out his threat without due process and evidence that Elisabeth is guilty of some misdemeanour. He simply has no right! Has speaking become a crime these days? Surely not!'

There was a knock at the door and seconds later the futuboi came to tell Masra Frederik that Heinsius the apothecary wished to have a word. Bosse made his way to the front room and returned a moment later followed by an elderly gentleman. 'Do you see? Everything will be fine,' said Bosse. 'Heinsius has just agreed to give testimony of his own accord. He was at the Couderc' house next door to the Peltzers that afternoon delivering medicine for Mr Couderc who had intestinal problems. Mrs Couderc told him there had been a dreadful row that morning in the neighbouring house. She had overheard Peltzer cursing the governor at the top of his voice.

'Precisely,' Heinsius nodded affirmatively. He was planning to inform Van Meel about it and thought Mrs Couderc would also like to testify, seeing things had come to a head.

Early the following morning, Bosse sipped coffee on the rear gallery. 'I told you it would sort itself out,' he said to his wife. 'The second witness offered to testify yesterday at the café. Bellaard also heard the Peltzers' hysteria. He used to rent rooms above their storehouse and had come to pick up the last of his things. He heard Peltzer and his wife's shrieks and is certain the word "riff-raff" was used. He also saw Elisabeth leave. He'll be giving testimony tomorrow.'

'What a relief,' Maria sighed. 'Elisabeth will be comforted, I'm sure, but I hope she learns from the incident to be more guarded in future.'

But a couple of hours later, Bosse was informed that Van Meel had refused to accept Bellaard's testimony and had followed the advice of the legislative councillor who claimed he was a hostile witness. He had been evicted from the Peltzers' property and had every reason to testify against them. The testimony of the apothecary was also turned down on the grounds that it was second-hand and Mrs Couderc, who had given him his information, had once more refused to have anything to do with the affair.

Everyone in the colony was now talking about the free negress Elisabeth and the difficulties she was facing after telling the governor that the Peltzers had insulted him. The Peltzers themselves spoke little about the matter, although they were overrun with visitors in the days that followed, curious to hear what had happened and to express their incomprehension at the injustice their fellow white colonists had been forced to endure. Friends even travelled from their plantations to the city and the subject of the Sunday sermon turned around coloureds who were unable to deal with the responsibility of freedom and misused it to the disadvantage of their betters.

'You see why slaves shouldn't be granted their freedom. That woman thinks she's equal to us,' Mr Vos exclaimed.

'What an imagination. The hussy simply spoke to the governor as if he were her equal, the bitch. The woman should be punished,' Councillor Lemmers insisted.

On 6 August 1736, Van Meel delivered the final report of his inquiry during the council meeting. He was of the opinion that proceedings should be initiated, not against the Peltzers, who had done nothing wrong, but against the free negress Elisabeth. She was guilty of a serious crime. She was a gossip-monger,[7] and her gossip and lies had endangered people's lives. If her accusations had been believed, the Peltzers might have suffered serious punishment for their alleged insults. They might even have been given the death penalty. The same negress, moreover, had perjured herself when she informed the inquiry that there were people willing to testify that she had spoken the truth. The individuals in question had in fact declared under oath that they had heard nothing.

The council members agreed with Van Meel's suggestion and voted to initiate proceedings against the free negress Elisabeth. Van Meel was given orders to begin immediately. On 30 August 1736, he wrote a letter to the Directors of the Suriname Society informing them about the case. He added that his worthy addressees 'should be aware that the free negress is known throughout the colony as a common whore' and 'I would have burned my fingers had I doubted the testimony of such decent folk against the sole testimony of such an infamous individual, while the people who were present insist they heard nothing.'[8]

September 1736

The platoon to which Creutz belonged returned in triumph, two months after their departure from Paramaribo. This time they had been successful. Although twelve soldiers and two non-commissioned officers had died – ten had been wounded, among them Lieutenant Smeets – they had nevertheless managed to destroy two Maroon villages, burn their houses and supplies and capture eight runaways. The four males among them were immediately beheaded. Three women, one child and the hands of the beheaded men were brought back to the city. On this occasion, one of the soldiers walked ahead of the procession blowing his trumpet loud and proud, and everyone could tell that the spoils of their expedition were worth proclaiming.

People joined the procession and a couple of lanky youngsters shouted: 'Well done! Death to the runaways!' The captured women and the child were handed over at the fort. The soldiers were allowed to rest for a while, were given a cold drink to quench their thirst, and were told they could go home for a week's holiday.

When he returned to the Bosse residence, Creutz was not welcomed by Elisabeth as he had hoped and expected. He found Captain and Mrs Bosse on the rear gallery and could barely believe his ears when Bosse told him what had happened to Elisabeth.

'A court case? What nonsense! She's done nothing wrong!' Carl Otto exclaimed.

'No indeed, she's done nothing wrong, and if she had been aware of the consequences she would of course have kept her mouth shut,' said Masra Frederik. 'She wanted to warn the governor. An act of kindness and nothing else.'

'And now her act of kindness is being rewarded with a court case and perhaps even a guilty verdict,' said Creutz.

'Precisely,' said Bosse.

'So what are you going to do? You can't just leave it at that!' Creutz shouted.

'They say everything's possible in Suriname,' said Bosse. 'There's no avoiding the court case, but I have hired the best lawyer available, Jozef de Cohue.'

'And what does he think?' asked Creutz.

'That the entire matter has been grossly exaggerated, of course, and that we can hope for a positive outcome. He's convinced the case will collapse due to lack of evidence,' Bosse answered.

'Where is Elisabeth?' Carl Otto asked.

'In her room. She refuses to see anyone, has eaten almost nothing and hasn't touched her harpsichord in all of three weeks,' Bosse lamented.

'It's so unfair, and such an injustice,' said Mrs Bosse with a gentle voice. 'Perhaps she'll feel better about it all now that you're back, Carl Otto. Try to cheer her up.'

'It's more important that Creutz uses his influence to persuade the councillors and Van Meel in particular of Elisabeth's innocence,' said Bosse.

'You can be sure of it,' Creutz exclaimed indignantly. 'Goodness, what a farce! This can't continue. I'm off to take a bath then I'll have a word with Elisabeth.'

An hour later, Carl Otto knocked on Elisabeth's door. When she did not respond he shouted: 'Elisabeth, it's me! Open the door!'

The door flew open and he entered the room. Elisabeth fell into his open arms and he embraced her.

'You'll have heard all about it, I'm sure. They're pressing charges against me. I'm a gossip-monger, they say, and deserve to be convicted.'

'What utter nonsense! They'll see reason. They'll never make such ridiculous charges stick,' said Creutz with confidence.

'It's that Van Meel,' said Elisabeth. 'He's after my blood. He'll try anything. What can I do? Nothing! Just sit back and let them make their accusations and spread their lies. I'm black, so I must be a liar! It's all so vile, so wrong. I hate those councillors, the lot of them. They call themselves civilised white folks! They're nothing but riff-raff, scum.'

'Hush, my love, calm yourself. It will settle itself, I promise. It'll all work out for the best. No one will harm you.' He soothed her gently, caressing her head and back. 'Come, sit with me for a moment.' He sat down and pulled her onto his lap.

She rested her cheek against his and said: 'I've missed you so, so much. This is a nightmare. There's no other way to describe it. I keep thinking it's a bad dream and that I'll wake up and everything will be back to normal. But when I wake up I realise it's not a dream after all, but reality. And everyone has something to say about it. Sisa Maria even wanted me to say I was mistaken after all and that I'd heard the Peltzers say nothing, but I flatly refuse. I heard what I heard and I wasn't alone. They're the ones who are lying but no one believes me. Blacks always lie, don't they.'

'The miserable scoundrel. Everyone knows Van Meel!' Carl Otto protested. 'If I get my hands on him...'

'There's nothing you can do. Van Meel was in charge of the inquiry, if you can call it that. They insisted I provide witnesses to support my claim, but Bellaard's testimony was rejected because they said he was biased and Masra Heinsius's testimony was second-hand and unacceptable. And don't forget, one of the directors in the Netherlands is Van Meel's brother,' said Elisabeth.

'I'll make a start by talking to a number of people. I'll make sure everyone understands you had no reason to lie. Has anyone ever caught you lying? How many others have fallen victim to Van Meel's despicable practices? If anyone's lying, it's him. Cheer up, my girl. It'll all work out.' And then he said with a smile: 'Isn't it time you welcomed your dearest Carl Otto with a loving kiss?' and their lips met in an instant.

The free negress Catharina left her house on Keizerstraat to visit her sister Maria Bosse on Waterkant. It was still early. She noticed people at the market as she passed the old Oranjetuin. She also planned to buy some provisions but that would have to wait for the return journey. She first wanted to have a word with her little sister Elisabeth, who had become the subject of every conversation in the last few days. Nanette wept constantly, mother Mariana kept herself to herself but sighed every so often and even Izaak, always an example of levelheaded calm, had worked himself into a flap about the false accusations that had been laid at his little sister's door and the looming court case.

Elisabeth of all people, Catharina thought. Elisabeth was different from her, not only because she had never been a slave like mother Mariana's other children, but because she had enjoyed a completely different upbringing. Elisabeth was proud and haughty, Catharina thought. She had imagination! But the entire family was partly to blame. Instead of putting the young lady in her place they simply went along with her airs and graces. Elisabeth couldn't stand the idea that her mother and sisters wore a pagni at home, for example, because she considered it slave clothing.

Catharina wore a pagni because it was thinner and cooler than the warm clothing her sister insisted she wear. When Elisabeth visited their house and found the women wearing a pagni she would lose her temper and scold everyone as if it were a mortal sin. Fortunately, she didn't visit Keizerstraat very often, and when she did, a futuboi would announce her arrival in advance. Nanette would then run inside and change her pagni for a dress and she, Catharina, and mother Mariana would quickly pull a skirt and jacket over their pagni. Nanette would even put on a wig for her sister, but she refused to do such a thing. Why should she put a blonde wig on her head made from the hair of a dead person, some unknown blonde-haired white? Catharina found her own thick, black curly tresses quite acceptable, thank you very much. She couldn't understand why she should cover them with a stupid blonde wig, which only made things even warmer. Elisabeth by contrast, was always dressed to the nines, European style, with stockings and shoes. And she even wore a wig and a bonnet indoors.

It was time Elisabeth learned her place, Catharina thought. She was black, pure and simple, and black people were treated differently in the colony of Suriname. That's what she wanted to make clear to her sister once and for all.

Catharina entered the property via the negerpoort and found Sisa Maria and Masra Frederik sitting on the rear gallery.

'Ah, Catootje!' Masra Frederik exclaimed cheerfully and Catharina answered with a smile: 'Good thing Elisabeth didn't hear you.'

'Don't worry about Elisabeth. The poor child has other things on her mind,' said Maria with a sigh.

'That's exactly why I'm here,' said Catharina.

'It's terrible that such a thing should happen to Elisabeth of all people, but we have to take some of the blame. We've always let her have her way,' said Catharina and she sipped at the cup of tea Fenisi had placed in front of her.

'What do you mean?' asked Masra Frederik.

'We all let her do whatever she pleases. She acts like a white person and everyone does whatever she says,' said Catharina. 'That's why she doesn't know her place. Is there another negress who would tell the governor that white people had said less than kind things about him? Elisabeth's common sense must have abandoned her. Surely she should have realised that this could have unpleasant consequences.'

'Perhaps. But it's easy to say that now, after the event,' Maria lamented.

'Don't you think the time has come for Elisabeth to offer her apologies, Masra Frederik?' asked Catharina.

'Apologies for what and to whom? She didn't lie!' said Masra Frederik. 'If she offers her apologies it will look as if she did lie after all.'

'What if she spoke directly to the Peltzers? The Dutch are very sensitive when it comes to money. What if she were to waive their debt and tell them she never intended to cause them problems? They would be delighted and she would have the opportunity to ask them to go to the governor and withdraw the charges,' Catharina concluded.

'It's not about the Peltzers anymore. The case is between Van Meel and Elisabeth,' said Masra Frederik.

'But the governor is your friend, isn't he? He plays cards with you in your own house!' Catharina exclaimed.

'Used to,' said Masra Frederik, 'but not any longer.'

'Can't you talk to him and explain that Elisabeth meant nothing bad by what she said. Tell him what kind of person she is. He has to understand!' Catharina suggested.

'Elisabeth would never agree, never!' said Masra Frederik.

'She doesn't have to know!' Catharina insisted.

'Cato's right, man. We should at least try,' said Maria, but her husband shook his head and said: 'If you ask me we're overreacting. Van Meel will never be able to make his charges stick.'

'Frederik might be confident about it, but not me,' Maria groaned.

'Elisabeth will never apologise or ask for an apology, never, and I agree with her. I've hired the best lawyer there is for her and he also thinks it will all blow over,' said Masra Frederik.

'I hope you're right, my dear brother-in-law, and I hope she takes this as a lesson. I would like to have a word with her. Can she come downstairs?' asked Catharina.

'I'm not sure,' said Maria. 'She's been so... eh... so withdrawn these last few days. She just sits in her room and says almost nothing.'

'Fenisi!' Catharina shouted, and when the slave girl arrived she commanded: 'Fetch Elisabeth. Tell her to come downstairs this instant.'

A few moments later, Elisabeth presented herself to her sisters and brother-in-law. 'What's the matter?' she asked curtly. 'Why did I have to come downstairs in such a hurry?'

'Sister, I'm here because I want to help you,' said Catharina.

'Is that right? And how can you help me?' said Elisabeth haughtily, and she turned on her heels and headed for the door.

'Listen to me!' Catharina yelled, and when her brooding sister returned she continued: 'Look, mi gudu, we are negroes! We are negroes! You might be cultivated, you might be good-looking, you might be an astute businesswoman, you might be rich, but this is Suriname and as a black in Suriname you don't have the same rights as the whites. And precisely because you're better than them in so many ways, some whites are jealous of you and want to hurt you. They haven't been able to find anything else against you and are using this to put you in your place. Surely you understand that?'

'Yes, I understand. But what difference does it make?' said Elisabeth calmly.

'So what are you going to do?' Catharina replied.

'Nothing! Wait!' Elisabeth replied.

'What if you were to go to the governor and offer your apologies?' said Catharina.

'What? Apologise? Why should I? Because I thought it right to warn him? The governor should apologise to me!'

'Don't say such things, sister! Someone might hear you?' snapped Catharina, sussing her sister's strident reaction.

'I will never apologise. Never! Is that why you came? Is that what you came to tell me? Well then, you've had your say!' At that Elisabeth turned and headed once again for the door, but Catharina yelled: 'You are black, girl. Take a look in the mirror and you'll see. Whether you like it or not, a black must always be sakafasi.'

'I know I'm black, but I'll never be sakafasi. I'm not a slave. I never have been, you hear, not me. I don't know what sakafasi is, because I've never been a slave,' Elisabeth snapped.

'It's only by accident that you're not a slave, pure accident,' Catharina shouted.

'There's no such thing as accident. People with my character are not born as slaves. I'll never be sakafasi,' Elisabeth screamed.

'If only you *had* been a slave,' said Catharina. 'Then you would know how black people are supposed to behave.'

'Do you envy me? Is that what this is all about?' Elisabeth yelled.

'Don't flatter yourself, girl. There's nothing I envy about you. You should learn to control your tongue. All I'm trying to do is help you realise the way things are in this life. There are white people in Suriname and they are the masters. Even if you're not a slave, the whites expect the blacks to behave in a certain way and you don't meet their expectations. That's why they're out to punish you. Get that into your head, once and for all!' Catharina insisted.

The two sisters stood face to face like a pair of bantam cocks.

'Girls, girls, compose yourselves,' Maria pleaded on the verge of tears, taking hold of Elisabeth's hand.

'Is that why she came? To teach me a lesson?' Elisabeth shouted. 'The nag should learn to button her lip.'

'You should've thought of that yourself when you went gossiping with the granman, then you wouldn't be in such a predicament,' Catharina yelled back.

Elisabeth pulled her hand from Maria's grasp, raced upstairs to her room and slammed the door behind her.

Frederik Bosse shook his head: 'Clearly not the desired effect!'

'Now you've made her even worse,' a vexed Maria scolded her sister. Catharina looked around. She saw her sister and brother-in-law in their comfortable back room. Their slave girls Amarante and Fenisi, who had followed every word of their conversation, sat on the rear steps, pretending they had heard nothing. Maria wiped the tears from her eyes. Catharina took a deep breath and calmly continued: 'Our sister is stubborn. Our mother will have to intervene, make a tapu and hide it near the stairs to the Red Court. Perhaps it will help, Masra Frederik will be proven right, and it will all just blow over. I've done my best, now I'm leaving.'

Three days after his return, Creutz ran into his friend Helling in the café.

'Bloody good expedition, man,' Helling bellowed when he noticed Creutz at the door. 'Come, sit here and have a drink on me. I hear you managed to behead no less than ten of the buggers and burn a couple of villages. Good job! At this rate we'll be rid of the scum in no time!'

'If only you were right, man, but it's going to take more than a few successful expeditions,' said Creutz with a smile. 'And while we're in the middle of the jungle all sorts of things are going on in the city. Van Meel's back in action, I hear.'

'You're telling me! They say that black girlfriend of yours has worked herself into a fine spot of bother,' said Helling.

'Ridiculous! Raye was already up to his neck in problems with the Peltzers. Didn't he have them summoned to the palace to face insult charges? His orderly overheard them. And when a negress tells him more or less the same thing it suddenly ceases to be true. The case is a sham. The woman's done nothing wrong,' said Creutz.

'Van Meel claims she's been telling lies,' Helling continued.

'She never lied. It's out of the question. And even if she did, my friend, is that any reason to start a court case? If a lie is enough to have someone condemned then the entire colony's in dire trouble.'

'Maybe so, maybe so,' Helling chuckled. 'We've all been condemned and that's why we're all sitting here in Suriname prison colony.' He gulped at his Jenever and mused: 'Sometimes it's just like a prison. There's nowhere to go and you keep bumping into the same people.'

After a moment, Creutz said: 'Van Meel's out to get her.'

'We all know Van Meel,' said Helling. 'He likes to attract attention and the best way to go about it is to lash out at someone else. A black's the perfect victim. That way he gets the entire colony on his side. You know the sort! Poor colonists, scraping an existence, living from hand to mouth, the only thing they can pride themselves in is the whiteness of their skin. They'll love every minute of it. She's not going to get off easy, that girl of yours. Van Meel's heading for success.'

'Not if I have anything to do with it. I'll tell everyone to stop this nonsense. Why would she make up such a lie? What would the advantage be?' Creutz exclaimed indignantly, but he soon realised that prejudice can be more powerful than logic. A host of recriminations were thrown at him from every side: he was a fool, he was ignorant, probably under the influence of kroi, hah, negroes know all about that hocus-pocus, of course the negress was guilty. She was nothing but a gossip-monger looking for excitement. Why? Negroes lie, it's in their nature. Creatures like that weren't refined and cultured like white folks. That's why they couldn't tell the difference between a lie and the truth. There was nothing to be done about it. High time they made an example of someone. Free negroes needed to be reminded that gossip-mongering was forbidden. It was also wise to remind slaves that lying wouldn't be tolerated, even if they had won their freedom. Van Meel would take good care of the matter. Anyway, there was more important news doing the rounds: Governor Raye is planning to marry widow De Cheusses. Charlotte Elisabeth Van der Lith had already gone through two governors and now she was consort for the third time. She didn't even have to move out of the palace.

The wedding was planned for the end of November. Little time was wasted importing all sorts of things from the Netherlands and even from France, not the least of which a splendid silk and lace bridal gown. The entire colony was looking forward to the celebration. Creutz was to make sure he didn't spoil everyone's pleasure by droning on about that negress of his. Van Meel still had to finish his inquiries. First the wedding! Perhaps the bride would be blessed with a longer marriage this time round.

Before the wedding, on November 16th, Cadet Carl Otto Creutz received an invitation to an audience with the governor together with Cadets Landsknegt and Meije who had also come to the colony three years earlier. The governor solemnly announced that the cadets had been promoted to the rank of reserve officer for their extraordinary merits and handed each of them a charter that had arrived just two days before. Creutz had made up his mind to speak to the governor about Elisabeth, but the presence of officers and captains during the audience made it impossible. As he was leaving, he whispered to the governor: 'Excellency, may I beg a moment of your time? It's a private matter, you understand.'

'Wait a moment,' said the governor and he shook hands with the rest of the departing guests.

'It's about the free negress Elisabeth, Captain Bosse's sister-in-law,' said Creutz when he was alone with the governor a couple of minutes later.

'I refuse to speak about the woman,' said the governor abruptly. 'She's caused me enough trouble as it is.'

'I realise that... but is it right... all she wanted to do was warn you, nothing else...' Creutz spluttered.

'Let me give you some good advice, young man. Confine yourself to matters you understand, military matters,' said the governor condescendingly. He concluded with a 'Good day, Reserve Officer Creutz', turned and left the room. Creutz made his way to the door, bitterly disappointed.

Captain Bosse and his wife were naturally invited to the wedding celebration at the palace.

'I'm not going,' Maria told her husband. 'I don't want to run into Van Meel or anyone else taking pleasure in my sister's misfortune for that matter.'

'We don't have any option, my dear,' said Bosse. 'If we stay at home it will be interpreted as an insult to the governor. Let's not saddle ourselves with even more problems. Anyway, such occasions are ideal for learning other people's opinions and, who knows, devising potential strategies.

But Maria had a heavy fever on the day of the wedding and Frederik was able to excuse her absence while preserving the usual decorum. When he arrived home, he felt it better not to tell her about the radiant Van Meel he had witnessed, boasting triumphantly about the advances he had made in the case of the gossip-monger, the free negress Elisabeth.

March 1737

'They'll stick needles into her tongue'; 'She'll get the pansboko, a hundred times over'; 'They'll cut off her ears and her tongue'; 'She'll be sentenced to death... they'll torture her and burn her alive.' These predictions came from the slaves as they lingered in the doorway of old Cofi and his wife Nana's room before going to bed. But Fenisi was clear in her mind: 'Eh eh, that's what they do to slaves. Misi Elisabeth isn't a slave. They can't do that to her.'

'Be done with that nonsense about being a slave or not! Elisabeth is black, a negress, just like you and me, and they'll not let her forget it,' said Amos

'But free folks get different punishments from slaves,' Fenisi insisted.

'If it suits bakra, maybe, but this time...? Mark my words; they'll punish her just like any other slave. What has she done? Nothing! Absolutely nothing! But bakra is determined to find her guilty and bakra always gets his way. They'll make something up. If bakra wants you punished and maltreated, there's no avoiding it.'

'Amos is right,' said Cofi, spitting a mouthful of tobacco juice on the ground. 'If she had been a slave they would have taken her to the fort long before now and doled out her punishment. She might even be dead. Because she's free they have to feign a court case. Bakra wants her punished and bakra will have his way. It's one of the worst things bakra can do to negroes. Lord above, how did bakra ever find his way to our part of the world, only to bring us to another country and treat us worse than animals? Is it ever going to end? Never! Look, that woman is free but it makes no difference because she's also black. She has to suffer because she's black, pure and simple. Father in heaven, why have you abandoned us? When are you going to help us? Help that poor woman…!'

'But surely Masra Frederik should be able to help her?' asked Amarante.

'He's powerless. He might want to help but he's only one bakra against all the rest,' said Bruno the coachman.

'I wish all the runaways would come back from the forest and kill the bakras. They're a bad lot, all of them. Look what they do to negroes! We've never done anything to them. They just arrived in our country, stole our people and brought them here to abuse them. They say their god gives them the right, that it's in the book of their god. What can we do? What can we do? Even people who are supposed to be free are not free. The bakra can always get them and charge them with whatever they want! Ke!' Cofi wailed.

The women agreed: 'You're right. That's how it is,' but Amarante interrupted: 'Shush, don't make such a noise. The people in the big house don't need to know we're talking about them.'

Maria Bosse lay in bed but could not sleep. She hadn't slept well in months and frequently got up in the night to sit in her rocking chair in the back room.

She brooded about her past as a slave. She had taken such care to hide it, but it was getting stronger and was threatening to suffocate her. She had done all she could to behave like a white woman, to forget that her mother was a black slave woman and that she herself was born a slave.

She was a mulatta, with as much black blood in her veins as white. As a child, she had been a slave because her mother was a slave. Her mother had never spoken much of her life before coming to Suriname. All Maria knew about it had come from Kwasiba.

Their white father had been good to them, had never hidden them and had always presented them as his children. When he married, Jan Van Susteren had immediately told his white wife that his mulatto children were to live in his house and she had never objected. Maria and Charlo had always lived in the big house, while mother Nanno and the other children lived in slave quarters at the back.

Sometimes Misi Prijna's nieces would stay overnight or her lady friends would pay a visit with their daughters. Then Maria was expected to serve the girls hand and foot and follow them around to be ready for their orders. One of the girls was now the present Mrs Planteau, a kind woman who visited Maria from time to time.

Much to everyone's surprise, when Jan Van Susteren died, his last will and testament stated that his widow was not only to purchase the freedom of the mulatto children but also that of their mother. At the widow's request, Maria and Charlo received the name Jansz at their emancipation instead of Van Susteren, since that, after all, was what they were, Jan's children. The children, who were fourteen and thirteen at the time, inherited a sizeable sum of money with which Charlo was later able to buy a house with grounds and start his carpentry business.

Misi Prijna had kept Maria in the house and considered it her duty to give the girl a good upbringing. Fine clothes and shoes were bought with Maria's personal inheritance. She was sent to catechism classes, was baptised, and she had to learn to behave like a white woman. It didn't take long before a suitor presented himself. She was fifteen when she married widower Pierre Mevila, a man twenty-six years her elder. She wasn't really happy about the marriage, but Misi Prijna had told her to grasp the opportunity with open arms. Mevila was rich, was the owner of a large sugar plantation called Saltzhallen and had no heirs because his four sons and daughters had all died before reaching adulthood.

Maria had done what was expected of her, even during the marriage. At first they lived at Saltzhallen, but the young newlywed wife almost became ill with homesickness, missing her mother, brothers and sisters, and even widow Van Susteren. There was no one to talk to because the other plantation owners in the vicinity were not keen on admitting a young mulatta into their circles. She accommodated her husband in everything, although she detested his fiddling with her body and the puffing and groaning that went with it. She had hoped to have children but they did not come and this only made her homesickness all the more intense. Mevila was aware of his wife's predicament and when he himself fell ill he decided to have a house built in the city and to move to Paramaribo.

Maria and Mevila had just moved into their house in the city when Elisabeth was born and Maria asked her husband if she could raise the child because she was free and was not allowed to live with her brothers and sisters who were all still slaves. Mevila had no objections. Everything was fine as long as she didn't become a nuisance. He didn't want anything to do with black family members. He had married a mulatta and she had to behave like a white woman. He wanted to avoid every memory of her slave past and refused to have black family members in the house. He rarely saw Elisabeth, since she was being looked after by Kwasiba and only came into the house to sleep in a room far removed from that in which Maria and her husband slept.

Mevila died a couple of years later. Five months after his death, Lieutenant Bosse presented himself in search of paid lodgings. But he didn't last long as a lodger. They were soon married and then everything changed.

Bosse insisted that the free negress Elisabeth should be raised as a free child.

She was dressed as a white girl, ate with him at table, learned to read and write and to play the piano. Had they made a mistake in raising Elisabeth in this manner? What had they made of the girl? Shouldn't they have realised that she would start to behave like a white person, and perhaps go too far? But surely that was for the best! Didn't they always insist that free slaves should forget they were black as quickly as possible? Stuff and nonsense! How can a black person forget he's black? Every glance in the mirror would be enough to remind him!

When Charlo bought the freedom of Maria's other brothers and sisters, Bosse, who had been promoted to captain in the meantime, accepted official responsibility and became their civil guardian, a requirement of every emancipation. He cheerfully welcomed the entire family in his house and it then became particularly clear to Maria that Elisabeth was quite different from her brothers and sisters.

And what was the result of Elisabeth's upbringing? She had apparently forgotten that she was black, to such an extent that she considered herself at rights to speak with the governor as if they were equals. This had been her downfall and it was the reason all those whites were making such a fuss. People found it inexcusable that a black woman had thought it appropriate to speak to the governor and to criticise whites. What would become of her now? Bosse was optimistic and continued to insist that she had nothing to fear. Legislative Councillor Van Meel had no evidence to convict her. Maria did not believe him. If a white wanted to bring charges against a black, he would find a way. She had seen examples enough.

They could make neither head nor tail of Elisabeth who kept herself to herself. She even became angry when the matter was raised in conversation and she would scream at anyone who dared to open his mouth. Her own thoughts remained a mystery. She kept silent, continued with Bosse's book-keeping, wrote his requisition letters, but rarely ventured outside. She spent most of her time in her room and Maria had never seen her crying or anxious. She spoke with Creutz and Creutz alone and seemed to be less dejected when he was at home. Sadly, the increasing number of jungle expeditions kept Creutz away much more than she would have wished. He had returned a week earlier, fortune had it, and Maria hoped he would be able to stay in the city for a while and be with Elisabeth on the day of the court case.

No one knew what was going on in Elisabeth's mind, but in her room she gave in to frequent bouts of teeth-grinding rage, cursing Van Meel, the governor and all those who had been out to get her. How could she have thought for one moment that being free meant having rights? Blacks didn't have rights and if evidence were needed she could provide it.

'I hate them… I hate all the whites… wretches to the last of them…' she hissed through her clenched teeth. But they won't get me, she thought. They're out to humiliate me, Van Meel at the forefront, thinking he can get me on my knees begging for clemency. What can I do? she asked herself time and again, knowing all the while that there was only one answer to her question.

She had to end it all, to take her own life.

She knew well enough that she wasn't the type to commit suicide. She wasn't depressive and had enjoyed life so far, but if it came down to it, if she was certain she would have to suffer, to accept public humiliation, then she preferred death. She had to think of a good way to die. It wouldn't be diffi- cult. Black folks knew all sorts of poisons. Slave women were constantly being accused of poisoning their masters, even if the latter had died of some illness or other, or excessive drinking. The negroes knew how to lay their hands on countless toxic plants, but she couldn't come up with a single name. Someone would have to help her find the appropriate plants, but it would have to be in the strictest secrecy, otherwise her plan might be exposed. Who could she ask? Who could keep her secret?

Old Cofi, he would help her, he had come from Africa as an adult, he would understand, he hated all the whites and always spoke about their misdeeds with disgust. She would have him find the best poison to use and make sure she acquired some. She would tell him she planned to take it if all she could expect was torture and humiliation and Cofi would understand. Once she had made her decision she felt more relaxed. She did her work as always, often think- ing to herself: how much longer will I be able to continue? Will I be dead and buried in a couple of months?

Carl Otto had returned sick from his latest expedition to the Cottica region, where his platoon had spent eight unproductive weeks battling fever, malaria and diarrhoea. Several soldiers had died along the way. Creutz had had to bury six of the twenty assigned to his command, and had decided in his capacity as reserve officer that they should stop and return to the city. The runaways weren't worth such terrible human sacrifice.

Emaciated, the corners of his mouth cracked and dry, he had returned to the Bosses, where the entire household was anxiously awaiting the pending court case.

'You're the only one I can talk to about this. I try not to bother Maria about it because I know how much it saddens her. My sisters Catharina and Nanette are here almost every day, but if I talk to them they get so emotional and I can't bear it. When I'm gone, Carl Otto, remember that I loved you. And I loved Masra Frederik like a father, but I hate the other whites. I hate them… I hate their culture… I hate their god… I hate their rules… everything!'

'So much hate, Elisabeth. You shouldn't speak that way. If you really love me, then you don't really hate the whites. What Van Meel and the others are doing is dreadful, but not everyone agrees with them by a long shot. Your brother-in-law told me yesterday that friends had promised their support and Misi Planteau visits your sister every day,' said Creutz as he tried to take her hand, but she fended him off and continued: 'Who cares! They're the exception. Plenty more are taking great pleasure in my misfortune. That crazy negress will get what's coming to her, they're saying.' She paused and then said gently: 'The person I hate the most is myself, yes myself! And do you know why? Because for all that time I thought I belonged, that I was one of them. What a fool I've been!' She collapsed into a chair and covered her face with her hands.

'There, there Elisabeth,' said Creutz gently. 'You're not alone.'

'I truly believe white people are the personification of all that is evil. Look at them rant and rave! They're like animals, like skinned pigs, they even look like skinned pigs,' she concluded calmly.

'And me? Do I look like a skinned pig?' asked Carl Otto.

'Perhaps… but I do enjoy pork now and then,' Elisabeth answered.

Carl Otto took her hand with a smile and said: 'You look wonderful when you're angry. Your eyes sparkle like the stars. And what does "when I'm gone" mean? Don't be afraid. Van Meel will never get the chance to torture and humiliate you in public. Have courage, my love, all will be well. Masra Frederik has contacts everywhere and he thinks so too. Rest assured, Van Meel doesn't have a leg to stand on. Come here, mi gudu,' and he pulled her onto the bed beside him.

He often comforted her with kisses and cuddles but they never took it further than that. When their embraces became too passionate, Elisabeth was usually the first to stand and say: 'No, Carl Otto, you know how I feel. But I might as well forget my wedding plans since I'll never have what I desire.'

'Don't say such things!' Creutz exclaimed. 'I'll see to it that you have what you desire. I promise.'

Creutz visited the café most evenings, where the pending 'court case' had been the main topic of conversation for quite some time. One evening Daniel Pichot put in an appearance. The Pichots were a French Huguenot family who had lived in Suriname since 1690. Marriage and inheritance had brought them considerable wealth and several plantations and they were considered prominent among the colony's planters. Young Daniel liked to impress the officers and reserve officers, aware that they were all newcomers to the colony.

'My brother-in-law has just the right punishment for that negress,' Creutz heard Pichot say to a group that had gathered around him. He moved closer to be sure he could hear what the man had to say, conscious that Van Meel was married to Constance Pichot, Daniel's sister.

'Listen,' said Pichot, visibly enjoying the attention. 'There's an ordinance stating that free folk revert to slavery if they commit a serious crime. Well, my brother-in-law plans to prove that the gossip-monger is guilty of a serious crime. Then she'll revert to the status of a slave and she can expect a slave's punishment. To make sure she stops gossiping they'll cut out her tongue. After she's been whipped and branded he intends to purchase her and send her to his country estate La Solitude where she can tend the cows and the pigs and sweep out the dung from their sheds. He says that's where she belongs, in the cow shit.'

Pichot appeared to find his story particularly funny. He exploded with laughter and those around him laughed along. 'That's a good one – in the cow shit,' one of his spectators cackled. Another insisted: 'Those dainty fingers of hers are used to the harpsichord. She'll need a serious whipping if you ask me.'

Everyone laughed except Creutz, who listened to what the men had to say: 'This'll be an example for all the blacks. Some of them might be free but they need reminding that blacks are always inferior to us, free or not,' one of them exclaimed.

'That riff-raff should never be set free,' an elderly man barked. 'Blacks are meant to be slaves and to stay slaves. Look what granting them freedom has done! They think they're equal to whites. Give them an inch and they'll take a mile. Before you know it, some free negro or other will want to marry a white woman!'

In the commotion that followed, one of the officers shouted: 'Fortunately that's not allowed. It's forbidden by ordinance.' Reserve Officer Helling interjected: 'I'm telling you, those blacks would do anything to get their hands on a white woman, and don't think the free blacks aren't arrogant enough to give it a try.'

'Off with their heads if they dare,' grunted Walraven, an older man who had married Lucie Gabion a couple of months earlier and had the feeling that his young wife wasn't the least bit fond of his company. He also thought she was much too interested in his mulatto futuboi who was frequently seen in her vicinity. Walraven tossed back his Jenever and grunted anew: 'Forget the courts, I say. Rack 'em and behead 'em!'

Creutz left for home after a while. Was that Elisabeth's future? What could he do? How could he help her? He longed to be able to spirit her away from the place, but how and where? Perhaps he should bring her to the interior, let her join the Maroons. Then she would be lost to him forever, but at least she would be alive. But the idea was absurd, he quickly realised. Imagine Elisabeth in a hut in the jungle with a bunch of runaways.

When he arrived home, he noticed that Bosse had not yet retired for the night and was sitting by the window in the front room smoking his pipe.

'I have bad news,' said Creutz. 'Pichot told everyone in the café about Van Meel's plans for Elisabeth.'

'And?' Bosse inquired.

'Apparently there's some ordinance or other that forces a free black to return to slavery if he's committed a crime. Van Meel intends to prove that Elisabeth's tittle-tattle was a serious misdemeanour and that she should be treated as a slave. That means she can be lashed and branded, have her tongue cut out. He then plans to purchase her and set her to work in the animal shed at his country estate La Solitude.'

'But that's excellent! Wonderful news, superb!' said Bosse nodding vigorously.

Lost for words, Creutz stared at Bosse as he puffed on his pipe, his eyes glistening; 'Good!' he said yet again.

'You think it's good? Excellent? Have you lost your mind?' Creutz roared.

'Shush, quiet, come here, sit down and listen?' said Bosse. He got to his feet, shut the window, took another chair and pointed to a chair at his side. He then turned and said to the futuboi nodding off against the wall: 'Apollo, you can go outside now, off to sleep.'

The boy jumped to attention. 'Guneti masra,' he whispered and left the room.

'Pour me a glass of something and help yourself while you're at it,' said Bosse. When Creutz handed him his glass, he said: 'Check if the boy's gone to bed. No one else has to hear what I'm about to say.'

Creutz checked the door and the rear gallery but there was no one to be seen.

'Sit here,' Bosse commanded, 'and remember, this is between you and me.' After a couple of puffs at his pipe, he said: 'That ordinance does indeed exist, but Van Meel isn't aware of its subtleties. It only refers to liberated slaves, after their emancipation. When the ordinance was written, free blacks were always liberated slaves. No one had heard of blacks born free. Elisabeth was born free. Her mother was already free when she was born? Elisabeth was never a slave and can never be forced to return to the status of a slave. If this is what Van Meel is after, then the courts will have to set her free because the punishment does not apply to her. This is excellent news!'

'Are you sure about all this?' asked Creutz.

'Yes, I'm certain. I'll try to find a copy of the ordinance for you, but you can take it from me that that's what it says, word for word, and it's going to save our Elisabeth. What a stroke of luck! What a relief!' Bosse sighed.

'You're telling me,' said Creutz. 'I was on the point of fleeing with her to the interior. I was even ready to let her join the runaways.'

Bosse laughed. 'You've never spoken to me about it, but do you have serious plans for my sister-in-law?'

'Yes, captain. I want to be with her. We've talked about it a great deal. Elisabeth is a magnificent woman. She doesn't want to just move in with me, she wants marriage, a wedding. But marriage between blacks and whites is also forbidden by ordinance. At least that's what everyone tells me.'

Bosse patted him on the back. 'Once we've overcome the present obstacle, the next one will be easier,' he said. 'But we'll sort it out and fulfill Elisabeth's wishes. Don't say a word about our conversation. It's impossible to keep a secret round here, and Van Meel needs to be kept in the dark otherwise he'll change his tactics. He has to believe that his plan will work.'

'But I have to tell Elisabeth… she has to know. If she hears that Van Meel can't touch her she'll be relieved beyond words,' said Creutz.

'No… keep it a secret for now,' said Bosse mulling the situation over in his mind. 'Let Van Meel do what he must… let him delight in his plan.'

After breakfast the following morning, Carl Otto looked in to Elisabeth's room. He found her in silence, staring out of the window. When she saw him she smiled and asked: 'Will you be at my side, when the court case starts?'

He embraced her and whispered: 'Of course I will. It'll all be over before you know it and then we can do whatever we want. Don't be afraid. It'll be fine, believe me. And then we can marry. Will you marry me?'

She looked at him and whispered: 'Oh, Carl Otto. You're so sweet.'

'Answer me,' he insisted, as he kissed her face, her nose, her lips. 'Say you'll marry me… say it!'

'If we can marry and I make it through this alive, yes my love, I will marry you,' Elisabeth sighed.

'We'll show them, eh? Just wait and see!' Carl Otto concluded.

On 18 April 1737 at ten o'clock in the morning, a messenger delivered a letter from the Court of Criminal Justice to the Bosse household on Waterkant.

The free negress Elisabeth was summoned to appear at court on April 23rd. The summons stated that she was guilty of two serious crimes: attempted murder and perjury.

'My God, my God,' Maria screamed as Bosse read her the summons. 'Attempted murder! But when? How?' The woman became hysterical, started to shake and then fainted. Amarante and Fenisi had to use smelling salts to bring her round and they washed her face with cold water.

'Calm yourself, woman, calm yourself. It will all be fine. Don't upset

Elisabeth. Surely this is evidence that Van Meel has lost his mind completely. Everything will be fine. Just stay calm.'

Elisabeth herself listened to the summons with apparent composure, but when the slaves were busy with Maria and she was alone for a moment with Carl Otto and Bosse, she shivered and asked: 'Are you sure everything will work out as you say, Masra Frederik?'

'Put your mind at rest, mi gudu, it will all be fine. We'll be by your side,' said Creutz reassuringly. 'Joseph de Cohue's excellent defence speech is ready,' said Bosse. 'Van Meel is in for a nasty surprise.'

Later, in her room, Elisabeth sat by the table, her chin resting on her hands. Her brother-in-law and Creutz had managed to calm her, and she had set aside her plan to take poison. What if it doesn't turn out as we hoped? What if Van Meel gets his way... what then? She had to speak to Cofi immediately and have him procure poison for her. She had Amarante fetch him. Moments later he was standing on the rear gallery, afraid to come any closer.

'Cofi, you must find poison for me. Make sure there's enough and don't waste any time. Tell no one! Look, take this,' and she gave the man five guilders.

'Please, misi,' said Cofi, but Elisabeth interrupted. 'No pleases! Just make sure I have poison and tell no one. I need it quickly. Tomorrow or the day after.'

'Yes, misi,' said Cofi gently, and he turned and left.

That same evening, the population of Paramaribo was startled by reports that Maroons had attacked Plantations Remoncourt and Reijnsberg in the Upper Suriname region. They had killed the owner and foreman at Remoncourt and had set the sugarmill and the supplies store on fire. At Reijnsberg, they had taken slaves, tools and provisions with them. Two soldiers on guard at Plantation Berg en Dal had managed to beat them back, but they had made it clear they planned to return with reinforcements.

Plantation Berg en Dal was the property of Mrs Raye and she was beside herself. Governor Raye commanded the immediate departure of a military detachment to protect the place. His wife was sick with worry and all this excitement was not good for her, as an expectant mother. Creutz received news that he was to ready himself for a short but forceful attack on the Maroons along the Upper Suriname. They were to leave in two days.

'But then you'll miss the court case,' said Elisabeth when she heard that Creutz had been called up. 'Don't go, Carl Otto, don't go, stay, please, I need you.'

'I would prefer nothing more, my love, but if I refuse to go they'll treat it as desertion, and desertion carries the death penalty. Van Meel would do everything in his power to be sure I'm convicted. Refusing service would only make things worse. Don't be afraid. It'll all be fine. I shouldn't be away for long. We'll be back in three weeks, and this court case nonsense will be over by then. You know our plans. Once this insanity has passed, it'll be our turn to let them see what we're made of. Two days later, Carl Otto and Elisabeth said their farewells with a passionate embrace and fervent kisses. Elisabeth watched from her bedroom window as he left with Rufus in his wake. I wish it were three weeks from now, she thought, and all this misery had passed. Dear Carl Otto, hurry back.

23 April 1737

The chamber of the Court of Criminal Justice was packed to the doors. Everyone appeared to be interested in the case against the free negress Elisabeth. When she entered the room flanked on either side by her brother-in-law and her lawyer Joseph de Cohue, a murmur ran through the assembled crowd. Someone shouted, 'You can't make a silk purse from a sow's ear!' Laughter filled the room.

Trembling with rage, her lips stiff and pinched shut, Elisabeth took her place beside her lawyer. Masra Frederik squeezed her hand firmly, before making his way to the front row. Beyond Bosse, none of her family members were present. They had all remained at home on Elisabeth's explicit request and were waiting with bated breath for information of her appearance.

Legislative Councillor Van Meel read the charges aloud. He spoke for more than half an hour, droning on about vulgar villainous individuals who abused their freedom. He accused the free negress of attempted murder. If people had believed her, Peltzer could have been sentenced to death for insulting the sovereign (lesé majesté).

In Elisabeth's defence, Joseph de Cohue argued that the charges and indeed the entire investigation were absurd and out of proportion. There was no evidence whatsoever that Peltzer would have been given the death penalty if Elisabeth had been believed. Had someone ever been condemned to death for such a thing? Never!

The demands of the legislative councillor followed. He claimed that slaves tended for the most part to be liars. That's why they were slaves. Their masters were aware of this and often paid no attention to their lies because they tried to be understanding. Free individuals had a certain responsibility, however, which they were obliged to use correctly. The accused was a free woman and should be punished with this responsibility in mind.

Like the prey of a snake, hypnotised before it attacks, Elisabeth gazed wide-eyed at the red-robed white man in front of her. His cold penetrating blue eyes nailed her to the spot and she stared motionless at his mouth with its twisting viper's tongue, vaguely aware of the sounds and words it produced. The same mouth demanded the penalty that would apply to any free person found guilty of such a crime: one hundred lashes in public and exile from the colony forever![9]

Only after Van Meel had taken his seat to make way for Joseph de Cohue did Elisabeth dare to turn, breathless from anxiety, to look at her brother-in-law, who was seated in the front row. Bosse made a gesture with his hands, a gesture of powerlessness. This was far from what he had expected. Was Van Meel going to win?

Joseph de Cohue continued his defence, insisting once again that the case was exaggerated and absurd, that his client was completely innocent, that the credibility of the court was at stake when an innocent person could be condemned in such a way. He demanded that Elisabeth be freed immediately.

Elisabeth heard little if anything of his plea. One hundred lashes in public and perpetual exile from the colony continued to resound in her head.

She suddenly realised that it was over and she looked questioningly at her lawyer de Cohue who said: 'Sentencing has been set for tomorrow. You'll be acquitted, of course. It will all be fine!'

Elisabeth left the court in silence at Bosse's side and climbed into a waiting carriage. The people outside jeered and shouted: 'There she goes, the gossipmonger. Just wait, next time you'll be in a different carriage! Liar! Whore!'

The entire family was waiting at home when she arrived. Elisabeth took a seat without saying a word and stared into space. When Masra Frederik reported what had happened, everyone started to speak all at once.

'Perpetual exile from the colony?' Maria wailed. 'But where will she go? She has no other country!'

'A hundred lashes will kill her,' Catharina and Nanette howled. 'She's never been lashed before. She'll never survive it.'

Elisabeth gazed at them in silence from the settee. She felt as if it had nothing to do with her, as if she were standing at a distance watching herself in the middle of her terrified and lamenting family.

'The court will never agree to Van Meel's demands,' said Bosse. 'De Cohue's defence was excellent. He made it clear that she was innocent and that the entire affair was absurd. What a demand! Imagine, exile for a negress!'

'But what if the court gives in to him? Do something, Frederik. Offer them money, a lot of money. Offer Van Meel money. Money can put this right,' Maria exclaimed, and the entire family agreed.

'That's the solution. We should have thought of it earlier. Money can help. We'll give them all we have,' her sisters and their brother Izaak insisted.

Catharina sat beside her sister and embraced her. 'Rest assured, Elisabeth. It will all be fine. They could never banish you from the colony. That's for people from Holland, not for us. Suriname is our home.'

'If that's the case, then they'll come up with a punishment equal to exile,' said Elisabeth resignedly.

In the privacy of her room she decided the time had come to take poison. Cofi would bring it and she would take it. Where was Amarante? She had to fetch Cofi immediately.

Amarante returned and said with hesitation: 'Cofi's nowhere to be found, misi.'

'Where is he then? He must come immediately!' Elisabeth screamed.

'Misi, misi, Cofi is gone. He's gone looking for something for misi. Nana doesn't know when he'll be back?'

Elisabeth did not eat, drink or sleep that night. The following day she was still in a daze. Her only interest was Cofi. Had he returned? What was keeping him? Masra Frederik frequently looked in to see how she was. Each time he would say:

'It will all be fine, my girl, don't be afraid.'

The evening before the court was to issue its ruling, a number of the Bosses' friends came to offer their sympathy. Van Harlingen and Planteau downed one bitters after the other as they sat with Frederik in the front room. They considered the entire affair nonsensical and suspected that the governor and council members were just as guilty of this outrage as Van Meel. Later in the evening, Mr and Mrs Van Daale dropped in. Mrs Van Daale joined Maria in the dining room and shared her suspicion that Van Meel had been encouraged by his in-laws, the Pichots, who considered themselves Suriname's aristocracy, or something of the like.

Elisabeth was awake the entire night. She first sat at her table, then paced up and down her room mumbling quietly to herself every now and then. A hundred lashes. She had never been lashed before. She looked at her arms, lifted her nightdress and looked at her body and her legs. Firm black skin, no sign of a scar. What would it look like this time tomorrow? Lashes were painful. She had seen slaves being lashed often enough, how the whip landed with a crack on their naked back, leaving behind bleeding welts. She had seen slaves stifle the pain and had heard others squeal in agony. What would she do? Squealing was out of the question. Otherwise, she would give the bystanders what they wanted. She hoped she would faint.

Would they remove her clothes first, would she have to be naked? When Amarante came into her room in the morning Elisabeth insisted on taking a bath. Amarante went downstairs to fill the large bathtub in the cubicle next to the botralie with water. After her bath, Elisabeth said gently: 'And now a massage.' Lying on her bed, Amarante's massaging fingers were like sweet caresses and when it was over, she said: 'Bring some rose-scented oil. I want to smell my best. Now my white silk stockings, the pretty ones, my lace underskirt and my red silk dress. When they undress me for those hundred lashes, they must see beautiful clothes, more beautiful than they've ever seen their own wives wear.'

'I want to walk,' she told Bosse. 'I want everyone to see me. I'm no longer afraid. Perhaps it will be the last time… It's time for all to see what the free negress Elisabeth is made of. I want them to remember me, but not as some frightened creature. I want them to remember the real Elisabeth: a defiant woman, who doesn't care a hoot about that riff-raff, that rabble!'

The court delivered its verdict: the free negress Elisabeth was a sham informer. The prosecution's insistence on a hundred lashes in public was considered inadmissible, but permanent exile from the colony was certainly appropriate.

Everyone was upset when they arrived home. Maria was crying, mother Nanno had hobbled over to Waterkant and was now sitting in silence on the rear gallery. All she could say was: 'Ke, ke ba.'

Bosse left almost immediately and returned a couple of hours later with two friends, Jan Van Harlingen and Jacob Van Daale. Elisabeth had to go with them without delay to the Court of Criminal Justice where Joseph de Cohue was already waiting.

In the presence of Van Harlingen and Van Daale, Frederik Bosse pledged all his assets on his sister-in-law, the free negress Elisabeth's behalf. Joseph de Cohue insisted that his client Elisabeth had been seriously prejudiced by the court's sentence and ultimate verdict[10] and had it placed on record that he would be seeking a revision from the States General.

'Requested revision to be submitted to the clerk's office. Offender to await result outside the colony.'

Elisabeth barely had the time to realise what was happening. She heard that she was to leave Suriname on the next available ship. 'Not as a prisoner, but as a passenger. I'll make sure of it,' said Bosse. 'And you can rely on the States General in Holland to give you a fair and honest revision! No demented Van Meel to deal with and no prejudiced colonial Court of Justice.'

'But what do I do when I get there? How do I live? How long will it take? They're sure to find me strange and laugh at me. They've never seen a negress in the flesh before. I've nowhere to go, no one to meet me. Where will I stay? My God, what a punishment! Why? Why this? I refuse to go!' Elisabeth bawled in desperation.

Bosse realised that this was in fact the first time he had seen Elisabeth so upset and distressed and it touched him deeply. 'I know, dear child, but I'll see what I can do,' he sighed. 'I'll give you a letter to take with you for Reijdenius, our merchant. He knows us and he knows you very well. Haven't you corresponded with him regularly all these years? He'll make sure you have a good lawyer and everything will be fine.'

'I want to believe you, dear brother-in-law, but do you remember how many times you've assured me that everything would be fine? What if the unexpected happens and the States General find me guilty? What then? Will I have to stay away forever? Will I never see my family again? What should I do in Holland with all those hypocrites?'

Preparations were made for the journey at a feverish pace. On the advice of a number of white ladies, warm clothing was readied, chests were filled and baggage packed. Elisabeth did not involve herself. She had to pack but she could not concentrate and had no idea what she should take with her.

Would Carl Otto have heard about the verdict, she wondered as she sat in her room, her mind reeling. Had news reached him? Was he on his way back to the city, in time to say farewell, in time to see her depart, perhaps forever?

But Creutz was hunting down runaways along the Upper Suriname, close to Plantation Berg en Dal. He knew nothing of the court's verdict and could never have suspected that his darling had been banished from Suriname and would not be there when he returned.

Two days later, Bosse brought Elisabeth to the ship. She had asked to go alone, but their house on Waterkant was so close to the river that she could see her entire family from the deck watching from the windows and the front stairs. At high tide, the sails were hoisted and the boat departed. People waved from the quay with handkerchiefs and passengers waved and shouted their farewells. Elisabeth remained still, watching as the houses on Waterkant grew smaller and smaller. Once the ship had left the estuary and sailed into open sea, the passengers made their way inside to their cabins. But Elisabeth remained on deck and clasped the handrail with both hands as the Atlantic surge showered her with spray and the droplets merged with the tears on her cheeks. She stared into the distance until Suriname was nothing more than a hazy line on the horizon.

PART TWO

Elisabeth's Diary

Amsterdam, 18 June 1737

Here I sit, in a townhouse on Leidsegracht in Amsterdam. It has been chilly and wet the last few days, but now the sun is shining. It's almost as warm as Suriname. The sky is an intense blue. I'm sitting at an open window in an unfamiliar room. I can see trees, their leaves fluttering in the wind. Particles of dust dance in the rays of sunlight that pierce the air. Do they always dance like that? At home the house is full of sun all day long but I never noticed the dust before. Sunlight here is clearly something unique. Everyone talks about it and Mrs Reijdenius asked if I would like to join her for a walk the other day since the weather was so clement. She said it was better than sitting at home. I usually don't take walks. When I'm outside people stare at me and I'm not in the mood to entertain the public.

But I fear I'll have to get used to it, at least for the duration of my stay here in glorious Holland. I pretend to be in good spirits and I managed to put on a brave face for the journey, but deep down I'm scared. Of course, I'm scared. Who would not be scared in my place? A black woman in Holland! The Hollanders are such horrible people! My family and friends have always insisted that they are truly the most dreadful of the whites, and black people in Suriname know what they're talking about. The Hollanders invent the most awful punishments when their slaves do something wrong, and often when they do nothing wrong but their owners are convinced nevertheless that they've lied, stolen or cheated. Hanging by the ribs on a meat hook, lashings, torture, amputations, cutting off the ears and nose, all of them punishments invented for the most part by the Hollanders. I have always thought we were fortunate that Sisa Maria did not marry a Hollander. Masra Frederik is a genuinely good man. But now I'm in Holland and surrounded by Hollanders. My lawyer Joseph de Cohue and Masra Frederik gave the impression that requesting a revision of my case from the States General was something commonplace, run of the mill. But what is the States General, or should I say who are they? The authorities in Suriname are made up of Hollanders! Van Meel is a Hollander! Surely the States General are also Hollanders? Aren't they likely to support their own people? What if the revision favours Van Meel and the punishment is confirmed? Heaven only knows what they'll do with me. Perhaps they'll invent some extra punishment or at least insist on the punishment Van Meel demanded in Suriname: a hundred lashes and banishment forever! That would mean staying here until the day I die!

'It will all turn out fine,' they told me at home, but I should never have let them convince me with their soothing words. I should have done what I had set my mind to do: take poison and put an end to my misery. But now I'm here and I have no idea what the future holds.

Black people are out of the ordinary here and people stare at them and even mock them. In spite of the riches many here have acquired through the slave trade, blacks are and remain curiosities in these parts. This is Holland, and Holland for the Hollanders stands supreme. For me, Holland is a curse, the place of my exile.

I arrived in Amsterdam a week ago. The ship that carried me into exile, docked at a particularly busy port. The passengers disembarked, but I waited for a while, unsure of what to expect. After all, I am an exile. My official travelling papers listed Mr and Mrs IJver as my guardians. Blacks are unable to travel alone in Holland. Even if they are free, they must always be accompanied by whites. For an exile like me, it's even worse. Fortunately, Masra Frederik arranged for me to travel as if I were accompanying Mr IJver. I'm sure it must have cost him a pretty penny. The day before we arrived, Mr IJver asked if I knew where I was expected to go on arrival and I replied: 'Reijdenius on Leidsegracht.' 'Good,' he said, and he and his wife ignored me for the rest of the journey.

I stood by the handrail and watched as everyone busied themselves dis-embarking, heaving trunks and other baggage back and forth. When all the passengers had left, I asked the captain how to get to Leidsegracht. 'The barge,' he replied and yelled something at a man who boarded a moment later, looked me up and down and asked the captain if I had any baggage. My belongings were brought from my cabin and the captain shook my hand: 'He'll see you to your destination.'

'Where to?' the man asked.

'Reijdenius on Leidsegracht,' I answered. The man looked surprised at first. I had no idea why so I showed him a coin. He then got a move on and took one of my trunks. I followed him down the gangplank onto the dock where a couple of lanky lads were lurking around. One of them shouted, 'Ugh, a black.' The man yelled something I didn't understand and the lads scuttled up the gangplank to fetch the rest of my belongings. We crossed the quay and walked for a while before boarding a small barge. The man pushed the barge from its moorings with a pole and we navigated the moats and canals through the city. The water was green and foul-smelling. Tall stone buildings flanked both sides and I could see people walking along the embankment. I realised we were on Amsterdam's infamous canals and that these were townhouses. It may have been my frame of mind, but everything appeared so grey and sombre: the canals, the houses, the people's clothes. Everything was black or dark grey, drab and colourless.

When we arrived at our destination, I asked the bargeman to wait for a moment since I had no idea how Reijdenius would react at the sight of me and even less what I would do if he refused to receive me. I pounded the door with the heavy brass knocker and it opened immediately. A woman wearing a bulky blue apron and a white bonnet stared at me. She was clearly shocked and started to tremble. Her mouth fell open and remained so as she stared. I showed her the letter addressed to Reijdenius and told her for the second time: 'This letter is for Mr Peter Reijdenius of the firm Reijdenius. Surely I'm in the right place!'

She then covered her mouth with her hand, grabbed the letter and slammed the door in my face. I didn't know what to do except wait. In the meantime, two boys had approached us on the street. They shouted something and ran away, only to appear again later with more children and a couple of adults. They laughed, they pointed, they yelled, but I didn't understand a word. When they came closer, I clearly heard someone say: 'That's muck and no mistake.' I felt intimidated. I had been standing in front of the door all of ten minutes and had started to wonder what I should do if no one let me in when I heard voices and the door opened once again. Wringing her hands, trembling and with a terrified expression on her face, the woman in the blue apron had returned with a man by her side. I'm not sure whether he was also taken by surprise at my appearance, but he certainly didn't let it show. He bowed and said contritely: 'Please accept my apologies, miss, for the ill-mannered behaviour of my maid. She has never seen a... a... someone like you before.' He noticed the horde on the street and said hastily: 'Come inside, please, come inside.'

I pointed to the barge and asked: 'What should I do with my belongings?'

'One of the servants will look after them. He'll pay the bargeman and bring your baggage inside.'

I was brought to an office. Mr Reijdenius, as the man turned out to be, made it clear at great length that it was an honour for him to receive the sister-in-law of his valued friend and business associate and to offer her hospitality. He had quickly read the letter, would study it presently in detail and would, of course, be happy to do whatever was expected of him.

A short while later he brought me to the drawing room where I was invited to take a seat while he fetched his wife. He must have informed her about me in advance because she did not seem surprised when we finally met. She offered me tea, which was brought in by the still trembling maid in blue. Mrs Reijdenius asked if I had a place to stay. When I answered in the negative and informed her that I knew no one in the city, Reijdenius suggested I lodge with them for the time being. They have room enough, and besides, Bosse is an important business partner in Suriname. He's shipped the entire output of Saltzhallen to

Reijdenius for years and he does all the purchasing for the plantation and takes care of Bosse's sales. And after all, I am Miss Elisabeth, with whom he has also done frequent and amicable business over the years.

After tea, the maid led the way to my room, which was on the first floor. My belongings had already been brought upstairs in the meantime. The maid curtsied and sped from the room.

There I was. Alone! Alone in a strange world, with no one to unpack my baggage. Would I have to do it myself? But where would I hang my clothes? I went downstairs and stopped outside the office door. I heard voices. I heard Reijdenius say: 'What can we do? We have to offer her hospitality and the best of care. She must be attended to hand and foot. Her brother-in-law insists on it, and you know how important Suriname is for business. We are Bosse's representatives here and he expects us to do whatever he asks of us.'

I knocked on the door. A young man I had not yet seen opened it, bowed, took my hand and brought me to a chair where he pretended to sit and then said emphatically: 'You sit, chair.'

How strange, I thought to myself, until his father barked: 'The young lady speaks Dutch, Jan, just like you and me.'

Reijdenius' son was taken aback and said: 'Please forgive me.' I nodded and asked his father if it was possible to have someone to help me unpack my belongings. The expression on his face prompted me to add: 'I'd be happy to pay!'

'Fetch your mother,' he said to his son. The latter disappeared and returned followed by his mother.

'Anna can help you for the time being and we'll make sure you have your own biddy by tomorrow,' said Mrs Reijdenius when her husband informed her of my request.

I had no idea what a 'biddy' was, but I would rather have bitten off my tongue than expose my ignorance. Anna would probably be the trembling maid. Not exactly my first choice, so I said it could wait until the morning.

After returning to my room, I wondered what I should do with myself. I sat at the window for a while and looked outside. I then decided to unpack one of my chests after all. Roughly an hour and a half had passed when one of the servants knocked on my door and asked if I would be coming down for dinner. I was introduced to Reijdenius's other son in the dining room and then we took our places at the table. It was so strange to dine at the same time as the men. At home, Masra Frederik and Carl Otto ate alone and I usually ate with Maria or by myself. I had the feeling throughout the meal that all four men – Reijdenius, his two sons, and the servant attending us – were staring at me. I'm more used to slave girls bustling back and forth from the kitchen at the back with plates and dishes. But I had never been at table with a servant constantly presenting me with a plate. I took tiny mouthfuls, mainly because I did not like the food, but also because of the unremitting gaze of my audience.

After dinner we retired to the drawing room for something to drink. Mr Reijdenius informed me that he planned to write a letter the following day to a lawyer in The Hague and send it by mail. I returned to my room. I longed for a bath, but decided to wait until the next day and washed myself from top to toe at the ceramic washbasin on a table by the wall.

The 'biddy' – a young girl of about fourteen – arrived the following morning. She had clearly been informed in advance of her duties and that her mistress was a black woman. Miebetje is a constant source of surprise, but she is kind and full of questions. She unpacked my remaining bags and chests and gasped incessantly: 'Oh miss, what a beautiful dress!' or 'What gorgeous shoes!' and 'Is that real gold?'

When she had finished unpacking, she asked what she should do next. I told her to go downstairs and that I would call her if I needed her. She left the room and it suddenly dawned on me that I had a white servant girl. Imagine: the free negress Elisabeth has a white servant girl. I'll have to get used to the idea, that's for sure. Whites here are ordinary maids and servants: they fetch and carry and have to take orders from their masters and mistresses just like slaves.

The following morning I went downstairs and knocked on the office door. The surprised reaction of both Reijdenius and his son when I entered the room and their even greater surprise when asked if the letter for the lawyer was ready and if I might read it, led me to believe that such things were not done here.

Back in my room, I asked myself what I was going to do the whole day long. I have absolutely nothing to occupy me. I sit in my room without anyone to talk to. Even if I were to go outside, I would not know where to go. It's enough to drive a person mad. And I have only been here for three days! What if I have to stay here for three months or ten months? I would certainly fall ill. How many days do I have to wait? I'll never manage. I needed something to keep me busy, so I made up my mind to keep a diary, to write down everything that happens to me here. It probably won't amount to much, but I can always write about my feelings and thoughts as well. It doesn't matter what, as long as I have something to do!

I made my way downstairs to the office for a second time and asked if someone might purchase paper and ink on my behalf. 'For what purpose,' Reijdenius inquired. 'To write, of course,' I replied. He said he could offer me a sheet of paper to write a letter if that sufficed.

'But I need a lot of paper,' I said. 'I am planning to write a great deal.' At that he ordered the servant to fetch me a couple of sturdy quires of writing paper, some quills and a pot of ink.

Miebetje brought my supplies this afternoon. She must have spread the news by now that 'the negress does nothing but sit in her room and write'. Everyone probably thinks that writing is some kind of abnormality among the blacks.

I started my diary this morning. I've been here four days now. How many multiples of four days will I have to spend here before I can return? I want to write everything down, but I don't know where to begin. So much has happened this last while. So much! So many incomprehensible things, so much injustice and unfairness. It feels as if I am having a nightmare at times and I can hardly believe what's happening, that all those dreadful experiences are my own. Then I dream that the nightmare has passed and everything is as it used to be when I awake, that I can hear the voices of slaves behind the house and carts trundling past on the street. But I'm not dreaming and I don't wake up. This is reality... terrible, cruel, wretched reality... my reality.

I begin with the journey. I did not know what to expect when we left Suriname, but the journey was not unpleasant. On occasion, one of the passengers would condescend to speak to me. But the helmsman was friendly and we chatted frequently. The sea was calm, the wind favourable, and according to the helmsman it promised to be a safe journey: no incidents, no hijackers, no buccaneers. The latter was perhaps a little unfortunate as I had already considered joining a band of buccaneers. I had plenty of time on the ship to reflect on everything that had happened. When the weather was fine, I would often relax on the quarterdeck and gaze out at the mighty and magnificent Atlantic Ocean.

The ocean can be overwhelming. The changing colours of the sea surprised me: first blue, then green and grey. I also spent time on deck in the evening. It was always wonderful. Sometimes dark, with only the stars to light the sky, and sometimes radiant in the moonlight. I had the good fortune to witness a full moon on the journey, an exceptional experience. The ship seemed to be floating on an immense golden circle and I was in the middle. It made me feel so different, so special, like being far from reality, in another world. I sat there for hours, taking in as much as I could, enjoying every second. I appreciated then how much of a privilege it was to experience such a moment. It made me realise I was alive and I wanted to live life to the full. I decided there and then that whatever should happen, I would never let anyone intimidate me. I would take pleasure in whatever suited me, even now, in this strange land. I would refuse to behave like a terrified little mouse and allow myself to be forced into a corner. I would refuse to be afraid!

The ocean makes you realise that human beings are an insignificant part of a greater whole. We blacks have been aware of this for a long time, but the whites still put on airs and graces and act as if they're the masters of everyone and everything. It has to be admitted nevertheless, that the whites succeeded in crossing the mighty ocean, travelling from one continent to the other on a sailboat. And here I was on just such a ship! I was also on my way to a new world. I no longer cared about what stood before me: I was fit for anything and I was determined to succeed!

All the colonists in Suriname, all the whites that is, want the blacks to be subservient. They, the whites, dominate the world, and blacks only exist to do their bidding. That's why blacks must always be sakafasi. They should certainly avoid the idea that they are free to do what they want. They are only allowed to do what whites let them do.

I now realise what my mother was trying to warn me about. She rarely spoke to me and I seldom saw her, but I overheard her say to Sisa Maria more than once: 'Don't raise the child as if she were white. She's not white. She might not be a slave, but she's still a negress and she should know that the blacks are her people, that she belongs among the blacks.' When I grew older, my mother's words bothered and irritated me. From time to time I would think: hush up old woman, mind your own business and stay out of mine. I had to learn the hard way that I was not in charge. But after all, I was always the free negress Elisabeth, raised from birth as a rich young lady in a spacious house on Waterkant. Sisa Maria and Masra Frederik always treated me as the daughter they had longed for. According to my mother, brothers and sisters, I'm spoiled and I behave like a white woman. What complete and utter nonsense. I'm more than well aware that I'm black!

Did Sisa Maria sometimes think back to my mother's words and her warning? My mother may have been uneducated, but her wisdom proved her right. I am black and I behaved as if I were white. That was the source of all my misfortune. I told the governor something about a white person and what happened? I had to take the blame!

I miss Masra Frederik and Sisa Maria, my slave girl Amarante, my brothers and sisters, especially Nanette. I miss them dearly, but above all I miss my friend, my Carl Otto. A white man, perhaps, but a white man with different ideas from the rest, just like my brother-in-law Masra Frederik who has taught me so much.

The proverb says: 'Pride comes before a fall.' Was I proud? Did I go beyond my station? Did I think I had all the answers? I probably did.

The older I became, the more people took it for granted that I knew everything. I had even convinced myself that no one could fool or deceive me. My sisters sought my advice, I had money, I was well dressed, I was a lady; I behaved like a white woman! But I'm not a white woman and that was my downfall. I should have realised that white people in a colony like Suriname would never accept such a thing. I clearly did not know everything.

If only I could turn back the clock, back to that fatal night, a year ago to the day. Carl Otto told me it was a serious affront for an officer to be forced to resign his commission, and riff-raff was such a terrible word.

Van Meel hates me. Van Meel is married to a Pichot and the Pichots are French Huguenots who think Suriname belongs to them because they collectively own more than a third of the plantations. They're immensely wealthy.

The Pichots don't mix with the mulattos, but Van Meel was always around when Masra Frederik gave a reception, simply because the drinks were delicious and plentiful.

That court case! Sometimes I wake from a nightmare in the middle of the night, drenched in sweat, the words of Van Meel echoing in my mind: Gossip endangers lives! This is equal to attempted murder!

If only someone would murder him!

Why did Van Meel change his mind? Why didn't we hear him demand that the free negress be returned to slavery as he must surely have been planning? Someone must have warned him. But who? Who told him I was born free and had never been a slave? Perhaps it was an acquaintance, perhaps even someone I know quite well? Was it to help me or thwart me? I'll probably never know.

Look at me here, alone in a strange land. I left without saying goodbye to Carl Otto. How did he react when he discovered I was gone? Does he miss me? Does he long for me? Or has he forgotten me perhaps and gone in search of another, more befitting woman?

Will I ever have my revenge on that wretched Van Meel?

Mr Reijdenius sent the letter to a particularly well-known lawyer in The Hague. We're waiting for an answer. I may have to visit The Hague in person.

According to Reijdenius, everything will be fine. How many times have I heard that same promise? I am a black woman. Do blacks in Holland have rights? They don't in the colonies, that's for sure, but Masra Frederik insisted that the motherland was different. Is it possible for Holland to be a mother to me also? Oh God, please let it be so, please let it be so.

Will I ever see my family again? Will I ever return to Suriname? How can I live here in Holland? I know no one! I am so alone and miss my loved ones dearly, especially my darling Carl Otto. Will I ever see him again? Will I ever hold him in my arms, kiss him, yield to his embrace?

No one, not a living soul, could ever have imagined this would be my fate. Exile! Vile, infernal exile. The most dreadful fate!

25 June 1737

I have been in Holland two weeks now. So many things are different here. I find the light bothersome. I'm well aware that they have four seasons here, that we are now in the middle of summer and it's sometimes just as warm as it is at home. But the light is new to me. Daylight continues well into the evening. The sun is still shining at eight o'clock and the sunset takes so long it's almost ten before it gets dark. It's already light by four in the morning and the sun is shining again by five. Day and night are much the same at home. The sun rises around six and sets around six-thirty. The wearying daylight makes it hard to get to sleep at night. When Mrs Reijdenius asked me how I was yesterday I told her that everything was fine, but that I was having trouble with the light. I should have said nothing at all. The woman had absolutely no idea what I was talking about. When I told her I found it hard to sleep because of the light she replied: 'Then you'll love the winter when it gets dark around four.' 'How dreadful!' I exclaimed, and she looked at me as if I had lost my mind.

If I sit at my window and look outside, I can see barges go by on the canal. I thought I knew a great deal about Amsterdam, but this was new to me. So many barges plying the canals; they seem to be at least as important here as the streets. Isn't there a city in Italy without streets, where gondolas on the canals are the only form of transport? The occasional coach trundles along the street, but not on wheels, strangely enough. They glide along on beams of wood. When they arrive at the bridge, a boy runs ahead and places an oily rag on the ground to help the horse pull the coach over the ramp. The entire thing is beyond me. 'Surely they have wheels here!' I asked Miebetje why they do it this way, but she just shrugged her shoulders and said: 'Dunno!' I then asked Reijdenius's son Jan and he told me that there was a rule that forbade the use of wheeled vehicles in the city. Very strange!

Two weeks! At first, I thought I would never leave the house, but I had to do something. It was such a nice day yesterday that I decided to take a walk in the neighbourhood. It felt safer to take Miebetje with me, and a good thing too. She knew practically everyone. People stared at us out of curiosity. Miebetje nodded or smiled and shouted something or other and then the passers-by winked back or laughed.

It was a very warm day, and when we returned to the house after an hour's walk I told Miebetje that I would love to have a bath and asked her if it was possible. She didn't really understand my request but was happy to find out. A particularly irritated Mrs Reijdenius appeared shortly afterwards and asked what I had in mind. Did I want to bathe in one or other river? I replied: 'No, in a bathtub, don't you have a bath I can use?'

Mrs Reijdenius said that such things were not done in Holland. I had a pitcher and basin in my room. If I wanted to wash, I should use them. Bathing was an unhealthy pastime and unbecoming to boot. Honestly! I've been washing myself every day from head to toe with a splash of water from the pitcher in my room. The woman has no idea of course how much I long for the bathtub in the scullery at home on Waterkant and Amarante's healthful massages.

I hope the lawyer in The Hague replies soon. What if the man refuses to take on the case? What if he doesn't see the point in it and thinks it will be rejected whatever he does? What then? Will I have to remain here forever? What a frightening thought!

In the evening at dinner, I asked Reijdenius how long he expected the lawyer would take to respond to the letter and if he thought he would take the case. He didn't expect an answer within the month, he replied, but he was certain the lawyer would take the case. 'He'll be well paid for his trouble,' said Reijdenius, 'and he'll have to work hard for it. Try not to worry. It will all be fine.'

30 June 1737

The weather has been magnificent for two weeks in a row. I got it into my head to take a drive in one of those covered sledges. I wanted to see Amsterdam. I asked Mr Reijdenius if it was possible and he replied without taking a breath: 'Yes, of course. Just let me know when and I'll have the coachman collect you.'

I thought Sunday would be fine and, as arranged, there was a covered sledge at the door on Sunday afternoon. I went for a drive; to the Dam, through Kalverstraat towards Leidseplein. I saw the townhouses of the wealthy and the run-down neighbourhoods of the poor. There were people everywhere, but none were alone like me. They walked along in twos and threes, and whoever was on his own must have been on his way somewhere, must have had a goal.

I was back at the house after an hour and a half and I felt lonelier than ever before! All I have is my book, in which I can write down what I think and feel. I've been here three weeks already. How much longer?

Mrs Reijdenius sometimes realises how bored I am and invites me downstairs to join her for tea. She is curious about everything!

The conversation took a strange turn the other day. She thought that I was a slave and said: 'News reaches us here from time to time that slaves are mistreated, but if you are anything to go by such rumours are untrue.'

I didn't understand her and said: 'No, it's quite true, many slaves are subjected to dreadful abuse, lashed for little if any reason and sometimes killed.'

'But you seem to be prosperous, well dressed, able to read and write, travel to the Netherlands.'

I answered indignantly: 'But I am not a slave!'

'No!' she screeched. 'What are you then? You are black after all!'

I was speechless. I looked at the woman and thought to myself: How can I explain such matters to an uninformed Dutch woman?

'Mrs Reijdenius, the majority of black people in my country are indeed slaves, but I am not one of them. As circumstances would have it, my family was liberated from slavery and my mother had become a free woman before I was born,' I said.

'Oh? Is that possible? I see. But you can't change the colour of your skin. Don't people treat you like a slave?'

'No, I can't change the colour of my skin, and some people prefer to treat me like a slave for that reason. That is precisely why I'm here,' I answered curtly, but the woman was unstoppable: 'Oh, so the majority of blacks are indeed slaves. But are the reports about mishandling and abuse genuine or mere gossip?'

I lost my temper and barked: 'Slaves they may be, but do you know the reason why? Because white people, especially Hollanders, sail from Amsterdam to Africa where they buy negroes. They then transport them to the colonies where they set them to work on the plantations, like animals.'

She appeared not to notice my anger and said: 'I suppose someone has to do the work, but it's hardly necessary to mistreat them. There are men here in Amsterdam with dog-drawn carriages. Most of them treat their dogs well because they depend on them, but some treat their animals terribly and forget they provide them with a living. Isn't it stupid, eh? The poor animals are forced to pretend fidelity to their owners!'

I was furious. I thanked her for the tea and made my way upstairs. The woman can't help it, of course. White people are all the same. Negroes exist to work for whites like animals. They even claim that God ordained it so and that it is written in the Bible. I've read a great deal of the Bible and I know you can find whatever you want in it. One day one thing, the opposite the next.

I sent Miebetje downstairs no less than five times yesterday, just for the pleasure of knowing I had a white maid at my service. I finally sent her out to buy perfume for me and told her to hurry back. When she returned an hour later I told her she had been away far too long and that I would dismiss her if she persisted with this kind of behaviour. The poor child was trembling, but I was satisfied.

8 July 1737

I received a package this morning containing letters addressed to me! What bliss, what a joy! I have never been so happy to receive a letter. Miebetje brought them to me. I was shaking so much I could hardly open the seal. Miebetje just stood there and was obviously curious. 'That'll be all,' I said, 'you can go now.'

When I opened the package and realised it contained a letter from Masra Frederik and another from Carl Otto, I could hardly contain myself and it took a few minutes before I was calm enough to read them. I wanted to read the letter from Carl Otto first, but I forced myself to wait until I had read what Masra Frederik had to say.

Dear sister Elisabeth,

Fate has been so terribly unkind to you. We are still bewildered by everything that has happened and it pains us sorely. Everyone here misses you and sends their warmest greetings together with their prayers that you will survive this ordeal. I sincerely hope that Mr Reijdenius was able to find you a good lawyer and that your affairs are now in good hands. I have also sent him a letter urging him to do his best for you and not to worry about the costs.

Your friend Creutz was distressed and dispirited beyond words when he returned and heard what had happened to you in his absence. But I'll let him speak for himself in his own letter.

I heard from the secretary that he had seen a letter from Van Meel to the Directors of the Society asking permission for a period of leave. Perhaps it will help to have him away for a while. It means an alternative legislative councillor will have to correspond with the States General on your case. Keep praying that justice will be done and everything will be fine. In the meantime, many greetings, especially from your sister Maria, from your sisters Catharina and Nanette, your brothers, your mother, all your companions here, and from your brother-in-law,

Frederik Bosse

My thoughts turned to my family and I sighed. Masra Frederik seems to think that Van Meel's absence will serve my case. If only the scoundrel had been on leave a year ago, then none of this would have happened and I would still be at home in Suriname. The man is nothing short of a villain!

I didn't want to be angry and have to read Carl Otto's letter in a bad mood. I opened it slowly, and as I did, I realised that I had never read anything written in his hand. His handwriting was dreadful, but what he wrote was so, so sweet. I miss him terribly.

My dear Elisabeth,

If I had suspected you would not be there on my return I would never have left. If only I had deserted my post and we had been tried and condemned together. At least then we would be together. I miss you beyond words!

Everything is different without you: the house, the people, Paramaribo, life itself. I only realise now how much you mean to me, the important place you have in my life.

But I should not write about my own sadness, although I miss you so much I cannot bear it. In the first place, I should think of you, all alone in a strange land, in strange unfamiliar surroundings, without your beloved family and everything you hold dear. My sweet, what gives you the strength to endure this misery? I am here and can do nothing to help. How are you coping? Do you have decent lodgings? How do you fill your day? Is there someone to talk to? If only I could be with you. Your brother-in-law insists that the States General will make sure that justice prevails. I hope he's right and this wretched situation comes to an end as soon as possible. I am not a writer and I have little to say, but above all, I want to tell you that I long for you from the very bottom of my heart and every hour without you is almost a punishment. I will wait for your return. You fill my thoughts and I can picture you before me and hear your sweet voice. Make no mistake, my love. Whatever happens, I am yours forever,

Carl Otto Creutz

Tears suddenly filled my eyes and I started to sob uncontrollably. I longed for home, for Carl Otto, for my family, for Amarante and Fenisi, for Paramaribo, for everything. But they are in Suriname and I am an exile in this wretched land! I don't remember ever having cried so much. I did not go down to dinner and ate nothing that evening. I simply lay on my bed and wept.

15 July 1737

Miebetje came to tell me this morning that Mr Reijdenius wanted to see me in his office. The long-awaited letter had arrived and Reijdenius read it to me. Mr Hoyer, the lawyer from The Hague, agreed to accept the case, but claimed it would not be easy and asked for an advance of five hundred guilders. It was of vital importance that I visited him in The Hague without delay. He had already inquired about board and lodgings on my behalf and had made arrangements with a respectable landlady who could offer me two rooms and the help of a maid. He asked me to make my way to the address provided on arrival. Mrs Verstegen, the landlady, was expecting me.

I leave by towboat for The Hague in three days' time. Miebetje is sad that I'm leaving and the poor child wants to come with me. I had no difficulty with the idea but Mrs Reijdenius insists that she stay here in Amsterdam with her family and that I take a new maid in The Hague.

I thought a towboat would be something similar to our tent boats, but Reijdenius's son Jan informed me that it was a barge pulled along by a horse on the canal bank. I find it difficult to imagine!

I'm in such a hurry to leave and I hope to make headway with my case.

Mrs Reijdenius just informed me that they are having guests for dinner tomorrow evening. Her brother and his family and Reijdenius's sister and brother-in-law will be coming. I'm convinced she invited them on purpose just to put me on show!

17 July 1737

The dinner was yesterday evening. I was dressed to the nines. If Reijdenius's guests are here to see me, I thought, then I'll give them something to look at! The family also arrived in splendid attire! Mrs Reijdenius's brother and sister-in-law had brought their fifteen-year-old daughter along. The child was dreadfully fat. She was wearing a highly ornate dress with all sorts of frills and bows and she stared at me incessantly with her bulging eyes. During the meal, she slurped noisily at her soup, which dribbled onto her double chin. Reijdenius's sister and brother-in-law wore burnished black. They have a married son who has two sons of his own. They were obviously proud of their grandchildren and they spoke about little else.

I had the impression that the family was planning to marry off Reijdenius's eldest son to his chubby cousin, but Jan appeared completely uninterested. Perhaps that is why he paid exaggerated attention to me. He sat beside me at table and his cousin sat directly opposite. She said nothing to me throughout the meal but did her best to converse with Jan now and then. On each occasion, however, he involved me in the conversation and even pretended that he and I shared secrets with one another, which caused the mother of the fat child to raise her eyebrows. It was an amusing game and I enjoyed myself greatly. The guests asked what it was like in Suriname. The way we live is a complete mystery to them and they have the strangest ideas about it. I told them (and boasted a little) about our house on Waterkant, about our plantation, our carriages and tent boats, our takings when the wine and Jenever flow in abundance, and my own trade in silk, velvet, lace and wigs. They were impressed! Serves them right!

The Hague, 23 July 1737

I've been in The Hague for two days now. The journey itself was quite extraordinary. Jan Reijdenius accompanied me to the towboat. Early in the morning, I said farewell to Mr and Mrs Reijdenius and stepped into the canal barge, which was waiting in front of the door. We first made our way to the Singel and then to the Overtoom where I transferred to the towboat. We left the Overtoom at eleven o'clock sharp and headed towards Haarlem. The boat was indeed pulled along by a horse attached with a rope. The horse gently trotted along and had a man on its back.

There must have been twenty passengers onboard, gathered in a beautiful room with wood-panelled walls, and glass windows providing a view of the outside, but most of them were more interested in me than the passing scenery. The journey took a full two hours. In Haarlem we had to cross the city to board another barge. My cases and trunk were loaded onto a kart together with the other baggage and brought to the following towboat, which left at three o'clock. Those who were travelling first class – Mr Reijdenius had seen to it that I was among them – were served a meal onboard.

We arrived in Leiden at seven o'clock. A barge-hand charged a boy to bring me to an inn where I caused quite a commotion! I heard someone whisper: 'Jolly black, eh!' I was served a meal here also. I could see and feel the other guests looking at me from every side. When I cut my meat into portions, I heard a woman say: 'Here's me thinking she'll rip it apart with her teeth, but she eats like decent folk, with a knife and fork.'

The following morning I boarded the next towboat and we set off for The Hague where we tied up at the Spui at twelve o'clock.

Coaches were waiting to bring the passengers to their destinations. I approached a coachman and showed him the address I had received from Mr Hoyer. The man looked at me and then informed me that the journey would cost three pennies. I produced the money from my purse and handed it to him. 'Three pennies,' I said, 'and two more if you load up my cases and trunk and carry them inside when we arrive.' He immediately jumped from the coach-box and hurried to do what I had asked.

When we arrived, the man jumped down a second time and held open the door of the coach for me. He then went to the door of the house and knocked. The door opened and I was confronted once again by a maid who stared at me in astonishment, her hand in front of her mouth.

'Mrs Verstegen?' I asked.

'Yes, yes,' she yelped and ran inside. I saw someone coming along the corridor and heard the maid say: 'I believe it's the lady from the colony. I've never seen someone so black in all my days.'

Mrs Verstegen also appeared surprised so I quickly asked: 'Are you Mrs Verstegen? Did my lawyer, Mr Hoyer, arrange rooms here on my behalf?'

'Yes indeed, of course, you'll be from… from eh… the colony if I'm not mistaken,' and I answered: 'Yes, I'm from Suriname.'

When my belongings had been brought inside and I had freshened up a little, the maid came to ask if Mrs Verstegen could see me. She was very friendly. She told me that she had once been quite comfortable. Her husband had made a good living trading with the east, but now he was dead. She had two married daughters and she rented rooms: 'Only to decent ladies with a good background,' she said. 'I've given you the room at the front on the first floor as your sitting room and the room at the back as your bedroom. A lady who used to be governess to the children of Baron Van Heesberg occupies the front room on the ground floor. She's old and finds it difficult to get about, that's why I gave her a ground floor room. The room at the back is my salon. We take tea together in the afternoon in the conservatory, which looks out onto the garden.'

'My own room is on the second floor at the back,' she continued, 'and the widow of a clerk who worked at the town hall lives in the large front room. The widow of a church minister lives in the small side room on your floor. She can't pay much, but she helps out by mending clothes.'

The other ladies came downstairs a short while later and I was introduced to them. They all stared at me, surprised and curious. Then tea was served. The former governess pointed out that I spoke very meticulous Dutch and was sure that I had had a good teacher. 'Yes, an excellent teacher,' I replied.

The reverend's widow carefully scrutinised me and asked: 'Are you here for the Captain?' I had no idea what she meant and replied: 'No.' She then said: 'Oh, but you must know him, surely.' The clerk's widow, Mrs Helder, joined her and said: 'Of course you know him. He's from Africa, like you.'

I reiterated: 'I don't know the man and I do not come from Africa. I'm from Suriname.'

'Isn't that in Africa?' inquired the reverend's widow and Mrs Helder interjected: 'You don't know the Captain? How strange! He's also a negro, and as black as you.'

I then became very angry and before I lost my temper I exclaimed: 'Do you know Louis Quinze?'

'Louis Quinze?' inquired the reverend's widow, taken aback.

'Louis Quinze? Who do you mean? Surely not the King of France?' asked Mrs Helder diffidently.

'That's exactly who I mean. Louis Quinze, the French King.'

'Don't be ridiculous, not personally, of course not,' the reverend's widow replied, her lips pinched.

'Oh no?' I replied. 'How strange. He is white just like you and lives somewhere in Europe.'

The women looked at me in astonishment and then looked at each other, but before they had the chance to continue, the former governess coughed and croaked: 'The young lady is right. How could she possibly know the Captain? He lives in The Hague and she comes from Suriname!'

After tea, I went to my room and once again I was confronted with the fact that I had no one to help me unpack. The letter from Hoyer had stated that Mrs Verstegen would place two rooms and a servant girl at my disposal. After a while I made my way downstairs and knocked on the sitting-room door.

'I would like my own maid,' I said, 'a biddy perhaps?'

'But of course,' she hastened to say. 'None of the other ladies has a maid, but if you insist. Is there anything else?'

I hesitated for a moment and then said: 'Yes, there is one thing. We don't know how long my stay will be, but I could be here for quite some time. Is there somewhere I could buy a harpsichord?'

'For yourself?' asked the landlady, surprised.

What nonsense, I thought to myself. Of course it's for me! No wonder she's surprised, a black who can play the harpsichord. I appear to be a source of perpetual surprise. She said she would inquire about availability.

Dinner was brought to my room by the same maid that opened the door. Her name is Marie and she is a housemaid. There is also a scullery maid named Kaatje and a manservant named Huib. Marie prepared a small table in the corner of the room and kept looking over her shoulder as if she were expecting something. In spite of my hunger, I didn't enjoy the meal. The food even looked tasteless.

It was a warm day and I was sitting at the window when Marie arrived to clear the table and take away my tray. She informed me that Mrs Verstegen expected the ladies to join her in the evening for refreshments in the garden.

When I heard voices coming from the garden, I went downstairs.

The other ladies were already fanning themselves and sipping glasses of wine poured by the manservant.

Mrs Verstegen said: 'Miss Elisabeth, Ka will ask her sister tomorrow if she can provide a biddy for you and I'll send Huib for information on the harpsichord you asked about.'

The ladies looked at me and then exchanged meaningful glances with one another. The reverend's widow almost choked. The governess then croaked: 'A harpsichord, indeed! Are you planning to take lessons? Perhaps I can be of assistance. I once taught his lordship's son and the ladies of the manor the principles of music. My fingers are a little stiff nowadays, but I used to be quite good. I taught them the beginnings and then, yes, then a real musician joined us at the castle and we often enjoyed evenings of music.'

I nodded. After my outburst that afternoon, I had decided to be more careful and avoid unpleasant remarks. Who knows how long I will have to share a house with these ladies? I decided to make friends with them. They were well intentioned, if a little ignorant. What does it matter if the old governess thinks she has to teach me the principles of music.

The reverend's widow complained about the heat, adding that I must have been used to it.

Mrs Helder also found it warm, and the governess said: 'The baron would always throw a garden party in this sort of weather. Countless aristocrats would then arrive days in advance with their entourage and personnel. The castle sometimes has to accommodate hundreds of guests, and the prince and princess are usually among them. Such pleasant memories!'

Mrs Helder continued: 'The prince and princess are such fine people, don't you think? I met them once at the city hall.' The reverend's widow added: 'Members of the royal family regularly attended my husband's services.'

I said nothing, but thought to myself: they're all trying to make an impression. Gossip-mongers to the last of them, but no one would dream of sending them into exile!

The Hague, 2 August 1737

More than a week has passed. I have not written much because I have not been in the mood. In addition, I'm still getting used my new environment and want to explore everything.

Two days after my arrival in The Hague, I finally unpacked my own belongings to the best of my ability. It took me half a day. In the afternoon, I asked Mrs Verstegen to order a coach for me for the following day to bring me to my lawyer, Mr Hoyer.

When she saw the address, she said: 'Prinsengracht! A respectable and prominent firm of lawyers.' I took note.

The governess was alone in the salon that afternoon. The other two ladies had gone for a walk and had yet to return. We had tea and biscuits. When Mrs Verstegen left the room for a moment, the governess said: 'Miss, I've been thinking about your reaction to the remark made by Mrs Helder and Mrs Weide (the reverend's widow). While I fully understand your reaction, you must realise that people here are not accustomed to… eh… eh people of your colour.'

'I understand completely,' I said, 'and I don't hold it against them.'

'The Captain is a negro from Africa who lives in The Hague and has made something of an impression because of his intelligence. He became a Christian and was even baptised two years later in Reverend Manger's Kloosterkerk. The event attracted considerable attention and was the talk of the town for several days.'

I simply nodded and said, 'Oh,' not knowing how else to react. After a moment's silence she continued: 'We heard that you're only here for a temporary visit. When will you be going back?'

'I don't know yet,' I said. 'I hope it doesn't take too much longer. I'm here to settle some affairs, you understand.' There wasn't the slightest chance of me telling her why exactly I was in The Hague.

'Wouldn't you think of becoming a Christian while you're here and being baptised like the Captain?' she asked.

I looked at the old lady in her chair and thought to myself: you think I'm a savage ripe for conversion, don't you. Then I said, 'I'm already a Christian and have been for years. I was baptised as a child.'

She was taken aback and blurted: 'Oh yes, well, of course! But that's wonderful. And do you go to church?'

'Yes, every Sunday,' I responded. 'It's the most normal thing in the world.'

'Wonderful, wonderful!' she exclaimed. 'You must be sure to go to the Kloosterkerk. Reverend Manger will be delighted to see you.'

'Why? Does he know me?' I said, although I knew what she meant.

'Perhaps he'll introduce you to the Captain,' she said.

'Only if I have need of it,' I snapped, and immediately regretted my abruptness. I did my best to change the subject and to my relief the ladies returned from their walk at that moment, arriving just before Mrs Verstegen and Marie with the tea trolley.

'Miss Elisabeth has already been baptised and plans to go to the Kloosterkerk on Sundays,' the governess croaked.

'Oh, really? You're Christian?' exclaimed the reverend's wife. 'And do you know anything of the Bible?' In spite of my resolution to avoid being unpleasant, I snapped yet again: 'What would you like to know?'

She looked at me questioningly and I said, 'Fine then! Shall we try something from the first letter of Paul to the Corinthians?: "For just as the body is one and has many members, and every member of the body, though many, form one body, so it is with Christ; for through one Spirit we were all baptised into one body – Jews or Greeks, slaves or free – and we were all made to drink of one Spirit. For the body does not consist of one member, but of many. If the foot should say: because I am not a hand I do not belong to the body, does that make it any less part of the body? And if the ear should say: because I am not an eye I do not belong to the body, does that make it any less part of the body? If the entire body were an eye, where would hearing be? If the entire body were hearing, where would the sense of smell be? But God arranged the members of the body, each according to its place. If they all formed a single member, where would the body be?" That was chapter twelve, verses fourteen to nineteen. Have you heard enough?' and I concluded my performance.

A painful silence descended on the room, and probably intending to break it, Mrs Verstegen said: 'Miss Elisabeth, our Kaatje has found a biddy for you. She'll be here on Saturday. What would be the best time?'

'The time is of no consequence,' I replied, and turning to the other ladies I said: 'Enough Bible for today, I suppose?' The reverend's widow almost choked on her tea and the governess coughed tellingly. Mrs Verstegen started on about the weather and Mrs Helder joined in. The tea party continued without further incident. I held my tongue.

The following day I made my way to my lawyer's office on Prinsengracht. A courier opened the door, looked me up and down and brought me to a waiting room. He returned a moment later and led me with a courteous bow to a large study where Mr Hoyer was already waiting. He was very polite, showed no signs of surprise, inquired whether my lodgings were to my satisfaction, and if I would ever get used to being so alone in a strange land. He then started to explain in some detail what he was planning to do and how he was planning to go about it. He was going to study the documents and submit a request to the States General. I asked if the request would be submitted soon and he replied: 'Certainly, but I may have to procure further information from Paramaribo.' I saw no need. I had brought all the relevant papers with me and if he needed to ask questions I was at his disposal. Mr Hoyer went on to say that the States General would do nothing until they had requested and received the necessary documents from Paramaribo.

'But what if they do not send any documents from Suriname,' I asked.

'Then we'll keep writing until we have what we need,' he answered calmly.

I was stricken with terror and realised that none other than Van Meel would be charged with despatching the requested documents. This would allow him to keep the case open as long as he had a mind to do so, and he could decide not to send certain documents. I was being handed over to Van Meel yet again.

I was almost speechless with anger and all I could manage to say was: 'But what if the documents don't come, what happens then? Is it possible to have a revision without the documents?'

Hoyer thought I had misunderstood, of course: 'Without documents from Suriname, the States General will be unable to begin the revision,' he said, and then did his best to reassure me: 'The documents will come, I'm sure of it.'

'But it might take years,' I shrieked.

'Years? Nothing of the sort. A year perhaps. Such cases can be slow, but don't lose courage, it will all be fine.'

I sighed and said: 'May I see the request before you submit it?'

'In due course, certainly,' the man replied and then turned to the topic of the weather. He found his city, The Hague, particularly beautiful and asked if I had seen much of it, if my lodgings and the neighbourhood were pleasing, if the ladies were friendly, if I was growing accustomed to the food. He suggested I take a tour of the city and other such nonsense. He talked without interruption and didn't listen to a word I said.

I returned to my lodgings dispirited and went straight to my room where I stared into space, downcast. I was in bed by eight o'clock.

I was haunted by the idea that Van Meel would be charged with sending the case documents and would refuse to do so. Masra Frederik had said that the scoundrel had requested leave, but who knows how long it would take for permission to be granted. Wasn't he capable of hiding the documents in such a way that he alone could find them? As legislative councillor, he was even in a position to make documents disappear altogether. Heavens above! The very idea of my fate being in the hands of such a monster was simply dreadful. No matter what I did, I could not be rid of the man.

I felt desperately downhearted. Everything seemed so sombre, so difficult. I avoided the ladies and had no desire to chat, but I couldn't get out of going to church on Sunday. I was escorted by Mrs Helder on my left and Mrs Weide on my right. Everyone turned and stared as the three of us entered the church. I noticed a couple of people at the back standing up to get a better view of me and my two escorts looked around with such pride, as if entering a church arm in arm with a black woman was to their personal credit.

The minister gazed at me explicitly from the pulpit and stated in his word of welcome that he was highly honoured to greet another African soul in his church. God's ways may have been unfathomable, but they were always good nevertheless, and he went on to fill the church with a stream of meaningless platitudes. I wasn't in the mood. If you ask me, the Psalms were off-key and needlessly drawn-out. After the service, the minister shook hands with the congregation as they left the church. I, however, was greeted with both hands. He wanted to know who I was... and he inquired, not unexpectedly, if 'the Captain' had sent me.

'No, reverend,' I said. 'I don't know any Captain and I have no connections with the man whatsoever. I also do not come from Africa.'

I believe I had knocked him off balance and thus prevented him from saying what he was planning to say. 'A fine Sunday, reverend,' I hastened to add and descended the stairs. Mrs Weide and Mrs Helder had wanted to stay longer and enjoy the attention they had attracted on my account. They were disappointed.

The following morning, Monday, my biddy arrived. The child is so unlike Miebetje in Amsterdam. Miebetje was a pleasant, lively girl, full of laughter and cheerful. Zwaantje, on the other hand, is pale and wretched. I think she might be sick. She rarely has a word to say and when she does she whispers shyly. Oh well, she's obedient and that's the main thing.

25 August 1737

I explored The Hague a little, first by coach and then on foot. I even found my way to Sorgvliet where only the very rich live in their magnificent mansions and miniature castles. Fortunately, there were hardly any people on the streets as the few I did encounter stared at me with unconcealed curiosity.

I have been thinking about my situation in the meantime and have decided to write two letters, one to my brother-in-law Masra Frederik:

My honoured brother-in-law Masra Frederik and dear Sisa Maria,
I miss you terribly. I am presently in lodgings in The Hague, procured for me by my lawyer Mr Hoyer. The place is fine. I have decent rooms and a respectable landlady and I share the house with a former governess, a churchman's widow and the widow of a town hall clerk, all of whom are very kind to me.

My lawyer, Mr Hoyer, received me well and explained the procedure he will follow. He first plans to write to Suriname and only then to submit a request for revision to the States General. He will ask for all the relevant documents to be sent and the States General will do the same to allow them to study the case in detail. I realise, dear brother-in-law, that it all sounds very reasonable, but I am anxious nevertheless, since the same legislative councillor, Van Meel, is the one who will have to send the requested documents. If he does not do so and the cooperation of the authorities in Suriname is lacking, the case will slow to a standstill and the entire affair might take years.

I beg you, my dear brother-in-law, to use your influence where possible to ensure that the documents are despatched.

You wrote that Van Meel had requested a leave of absence. Was it granted? Has he already left? If so, who is his replacement? Is it someone you know? Can you rely on the new legislative councillor to send the requested documents?

My spirits are low. Success seems almost beyond my reach. Please keep praying for me and hoping for the best. Much love to you both, and to my brothers and other sisters and the entire household,

with love and affection,

Elisabeth

I longed for home, for everyone I held dear and especially for Carl Otto. He still fills my thoughts and I miss him. If only I could talk to him, touch him, caress his cheek, taste his kisses. How does he busy himself when he is not on an expedition into the jungle? Who does he talk to? I read his sweet letter time after time until I knew it by heart. In spite of the pain, my love for him tells me that I must let him go, set him free. I must write and tell him he has no obligation to me.

The very thought filled me with despair. I spent the entire day in a daze, reflecting, and even forgot to send the letter to my brother-in-law and sister. Reijdenius in Amsterdam had told me to send my letters for Suriname to him and he would send them together with his business communication.

A week after writing to Masra Frederik and Sisa Maria, and with pain in my heart, I faced the inevitable and gathered the courage to write to Carl Otto:

My darling Carl Otto,

I wish it were otherwise, but I must write to say you are under no obligation to me and that I do not hold you to the cherished promise you made when you wrote that I was yours forever and always. My dearest friend, everything appears so sombre. This sickening affair is far from being settled. When I left Suriname, my brother-in-law and De Cohue my lawyer were so encouraging that I believed I would return after six months, ten at the most. Now I know better. My lawyer here has informed me that he first needs all the documents to be sent from Paramaribo before he can study the case. I fear this will take a long time, perhaps a very long time, especially if we are dependent on Van Meel. I also don't know how long it will take for the case to come before the

States General. My darling Carl Otto, if you should meet another woman in the meantime, someone no doubt more fitting, please do not let yourself be guided by any sense of obligation to me. I love you, but if our relationship is doomed to nothing, I must understand and accept the inevitable. You are my best friend, and I hope and pray that we can remain the best of friends forever.

I have been attending church here in Amsterdam. Three visits already and I have become an object of curiosity. The people even stand up to get a better view of me and the minister is elated. He thinks he's saving an African soul and is aglow with pride.

In addition to the landlady, there are three other women in residence: the former governess of a baron – she's so old that she croaks when she speaks; the widow of a church minister who dwells in the past, when her husband was still alive; and the widow of a town hall clerk who thinks she knows everything. All three are convinced it's their duty to civilise me and teach me everything I should know.

I also have a biddy who helps out during the day. She is named after a swan but she looks more like a startled chicken. She's so small and thin and she trembles with fear whenever I speak to her.

Make sure Rufus takes good care of you during your expeditions and above all take care of yourself and be sure to eat and drink enough. I hope you capture plenty of Maroons. As long as they don't get you and you're spared illness I will be happy. I think of you all day and every day. Keep well, dear friend. I love you,

Elisabeth

I folded the letter quickly and sealed it. Was I afraid perhaps that I might not send it?

10 September 1737

I finally sent my letters to Reijdenius and hopefully they are now on their way to Suriname. How will Carl Otto react?

Autumn has arrived. The leaves on the trees are turning gold and brown and the days are getting shorter. Not so long ago it felt like summer, at least that's what everyone said. I went for a walk along the Lange Voorhout. It was truly wonderful to see the sun glimmering through the yellow and russet leaves. A couple of days later it started to rain and didn't stop the entire day. To me it's cold and chilly, but everyone tells me this is nothing. It's also very windy and the ground is covered with leaves. There are chestnuts in some places, similar to ours but covered in a green, spiky shell.

Zwaantje is a little more relaxed. When I ask her something I get more than three words as an answer. She's from a big family. Her mother was blessed with eleven children and six of them are still alive. She coughs a lot, an irritating hack. I asked if she was taking anything for it and she said that her mother gave her onion with sugar. Mrs Verstegen gives her bread and bacon, a necessity, she maintains, with the winter on its way. In any case, she's probably better fed here than at home.

20 September 1737

My harpsichord arrived yesterday. What an experience! What a commotion! But let me go back a couple of days to the moment Mrs Verstegen announced during our customary evening drink in the conservatory that the instrument was soon to be delivered.

The governess asked where I was planning to put it and I answered: 'Why, in my room, naturally.'

She then said: 'Wouldn't it be better to leave it in my room?'

Surprised at her suggestion I answered: 'No, of course not. Why should I?'

'I thought it might be better,' she replied. 'You won't be playing it without my supervision for quite some time. And you're welcome to come to my room whenever you wish.'

'What an extraordinarily friendly gesture,' exclaimed Mrs Helder, echoed by Mrs Weide: 'Yes, very friendly.'

I thought to myself, you've all lost your senses, but I said without turning a hair: 'Thank you kindly for the generous offer, but I think it best to keep the harpsichord in my own room.'

'But what about all the stairs,' the governess inquired, and Mrs Helder chimed in: 'Such things weigh a ton!'

Fortunately Mrs Verstegen came to my rescue: 'The house is equipped with a hook for a pulley.'

The people here have a handy method for getting heavy furniture to the upper floors. A hook on which one can hang a pulley is attached to the front of the house. The chest was smoothly hoisted upstairs by a group of men on the ground, while a second group heaved it into my room where the instrument was unpacked and positioned on my instructions.

Everyone came to watch. Even the governess managed to climb the stairs step by step, with the help of Mrs Verstegen and Marie, the maid. I couldn't get near the harpsichord at first. The governess immediately took her place on the bench, surrounded by Mrs Verstegen, Mrs Helder and Mrs Weide, each trying to outdo the other's jubilation. 'What a magnificent instrument… beautiful… superb!' The governess touched one of the keys and observed: 'A good tone, pure! Happily!'

She then started to move and massage her fingers. I could hear her joints crack as she said: 'As you can see, my fingers are a little stiff, but I think I can still play something.' Falteringly and with the utmost caution, she played something barely recognisable.

'Beautiful, beautiful,' the other ladies exclaimed.

The governess appeared to realise all at once that she was in my room, playing my instrument, and that I was nowhere to be seen. She shouted with her now familiar croaking voice: 'Miss Elisabeth, won't you join me. Look, these are the keys, black and white. You'll be using the white keys for the most part in the beginning. I think we should start by learning musical notation. Come along, touch one of the keys.'

I was watching from a distance.

'Come now, don't be silly, it won't bite,' she insisted.

'Later,' I stammered, 'I'll try it later.'

As the governess stood up and shuffled slowly towards the door, I took my place at the harpsichord. I looked first at the keys and caressed them without playing a note. The governess turned, saw me sitting, and said: 'Press one of the keys'

I did just that and then stared at the old woman in the middle of my room.

'Don't you hear? Beautiful, eh?' she said.

I could no longer contain myself. I started to play, one of Bach's cantatas. I hadn't played for almost six months and my fingers were stiff, but I soon found my rhythm. I sat with my back to the governess, unable to see her, but I'm told she almost fainted from shock. The other ladies stared in amazement, riveted to the spot. Mrs Weide was the first to collect herself and said: 'Heavens, how wonderful,' but the governess said nothing. As I was playing I saw her leave the room out of the corner of my eye, assisted by Mrs Helder and Marie. After a moment or two, Mrs Verstegen and Mrs Weide also left the room. I continued to play, one cantata after the other. I was even surprised I could play so much by heart. In the end, my bony maid Zwaantje was the only one left listening. When I finally stopped, she gasped: 'Oh, miss, that was beautiful. You are such a good player!'

The other ladies have not spoken about the incident since.

26 September 1737

I have not seen the governess for the best part of a week. Before now she came to Mrs Verstegen's salon as soon as she heard my voice, or sent Zwaantje with a message telling me she wanted a word, but since the incident with the harpsichord there has been little evidence of her. I do believe she's angry with me.

The other ladies avoid the subject as well as my musical skills, although they hear me play every day. I decided to raise the matter myself and said just yesterday to Mrs Verstegen: 'I hope you and the other ladies are not bothered by my playing. I asked to be allowed a harpsichord in my room, and I presumed you would have expected me to play it. If you prefer me not to play at certain times I will do my best to oblige.'

'Not at all,' she replied. 'You don't bother me one bit. I enjoy your music and I think the other ladies would agree with me.'

'With the exception of the governess, I imagine.'

'I'm sure you understand. The governess is a proud woman and has taken offence. She feels you made a fool of her,' Mrs Verstegen explained.

'Let's get one thing clear, Mrs Verstegen,' I interrupted. 'I did not make a fool of the governess, she made a fool of herself.'

'What do you mean? You are a skilled harpsichord player, yet you led the governess to believe she had to give you lessons,' said Mrs Verstegen, her voice raised. 'She holds it against you and I'm inclined to agree with her.'

'Is that so? The governess holds it against me?' I snapped, and when she replied: 'Well of course she does!' I continued: 'Then she should blame her own presuppositions. From the first mention of a harpsichord, the governess and all of you presumed I was unable to play it and that I would need lessons. I am black, after all, from the darkest jungles of Africa, and if not Africa then Suriname. I am black and that makes me uncivilised. I still needed to learn the basic principles of polite society and the governess was kind enough to offer her services.'

I became more agitated as I spoke and continued: 'You hold my behaviour against me. Try to put yourself in my situation for once. How would you feel? Oh yes, I forgot: negroes don't have feelings, and since I am a negro there's no need to account for my feelings. That's what the white people think, isn't it? How would you like to be confronted with such an attitude wherever you went?'

Mrs Verstegen was lost for words. Her face had turned red and all she could do was stammer: 'Yes... eh... eh... oh yes.'

I continued calmly: 'I am a negress and I am black, black and proud of it. But I am not stupid or backward. Take a good look at me and be aware of this:

whatever whites can do, I can do, and often better! It's time you realised here in high and mighty Holland that decidedly civilised kingdoms existed in darkest Africa when people in the Low Countries were still running around in animal skins and living in caves!'

My voice must have carried upstairs and attracted Mrs Helder's attention. Mrs Verstegen, who was clearly embarrassed by my outburst, turned to her the moment she entered the room: 'Miss Elisabeth claims that she made a fool of no one and that the governess only has herself to blame for presuming she knew nothing of music and needed lessons.'

'That may well be the case,' said Mrs Helder, 'but Miss Elisabeth made no attempt to correct her misapprehension.'

'What if I had told the governess I could play? Would she have believed me? Dear Mrs Helder, you all thought I was ignorant and unable to do anything. From the moment you set eyes on me, you were ready to convert me and make me a Christian. You probably thought you would have to teach me to read and write. I'm black, therefore I must be stupid! Now you know better. Good, I prefer not to talk about the matter any further. All I want to know is the following: does it bother you when I play or should I look for rooms elsewhere?'

'No, no, you don't bother us in the slightest,' Mrs Verstegen blurted. Turning to Mrs Helder she asked: 'Surely Miss Elisabeth's playing doesn't bother you. I enjoy it, to be honest.'

'No,' said Mrs Helder. 'I listen with pleasure and I'm certain Mrs Weide thinks the same.'

'Then the matter is closed,' I said. 'Good afternoon, ladies, I'm going outside for a walk.' And with that I left the room, leaving my landlady and fellow lodgers behind in the realisation that they now had plenty of material to gossip about.

I walked to the Voorhout and from there along the Noordeinde. People stared at me wherever I went and some of them even followed me for a while. A bunch of rogues shouted something and I had to conceal my unease and pretend not to notice. But if one of those rogues should lay a hand on me, I would give him the clouting of his life. Fortunately, nothing of the sort has ever happened, but I'm ready if it does.

When I returned after a good hour's walk, there was no one in the salon. I was about to go up to my room when Mrs Verstegen appeared with a welcome message.

Mr Hoyer had sent a courier to ask if I would come to his office. My request was ready for submission.

27 September 1737

I visited Mr Hoyer's office this morning. The courier brought me directly to the boss's study. He was very kind, informed me that the request was ready for submission, and hoped it would be to my satisfaction. He rang for the courier and asked him to invite Councillor Landman to join us. I was then introduced to his assistant, Landman, a young lawyer who had been given charge of 'my case'.

'Mr Landman drew up your request, miss, and can explain everything,' said Mr Hoyer. He turned to his young colleague and said: 'Please be kind enough to take Miss Elisabeth with you and go through it.'

Mr Landman brought me to his office. After much shilly-shallying, he finally got round to reading the request. He read slowly, three words at a time, and looked at me expectantly at every pause. I thought to myself: get on with it, man! After five sentences at this tempo I said: 'May I read the document myself? If there is anything I don't understand I will ask.'

The good fellow blushed and stammered: 'Oh, but of course.'

I read the document and everything was clear, but I felt obliged to say something nonetheless: 'I like it, especially the formulation of the opening statement,' and I read it aloud: "That she, the petitioner, had the misfortune to have been brought in front of the Court of Police and the Court of Criminal Justice by the honourable Willem Gerard Van Meel, legislative councillor of the said colony..."[11] And that is precisely what happened: the petitioner had the misfortune! And what a misfortune! It was the legislative councillor who had turned it into a crime!'

I asked Mr Landman what he thought of my chances and he told me he had no idea. Perhaps such answers are characteristic of professional modesty, but it was not to my satisfaction. My lawyer should at least be able to offer an educated guess on the matter. And that's what I said, a little curt I suspect, given his shocked expression and stammering response: 'Yes... eh... yes, we'll do our best and... yes... eh... yes.'

I then said, 'Tell me how you plan to go about your work. The request is ready. You submit it, I imagine? What do you do then? Do you simply wait for a response from the States General? I hardly need a lawyer for that. I could do it myself!'

The man blushed an even deeper red and his stammer turned into a stutter: 'N... no... eh... no, m-m-miss, we study everything with care ourselves first and we consult all sorts of documents and legal collections to determine the best approach to the case.'

I didn't quite understand him and made it even more difficult by asking: 'What exactly do you intend to study?'

'We study various documents to determine whether such a case has appeared before a court before and what its decision was at the time,' he answered.

'I can't imagine that such a case has ever appeared before another court,' I said. 'Have there been other Van Meels in the course of history similarly determined to cause harm to a free negress? And what do you do if you cannot find a similar case?'

Landman hesitated for a moment and then said: 'Miss. Even if a case is not exactly the same as yours, we can always learn about the law from it and about what is generally accepted.'

I then asked: 'May I participate?'

The question surprised him completely. He was so shocked, he knocked a book from the table. He blubbered, dumbfounded: 'I, I don't know. You have no knowledge of the law.'

'No, that's true, and you know everything about the law, by heart?' I inquired.

'Obviously not!' the man exclaimed. 'No one does, but it is our profession. A lawyer's job is to occupy himself with the law and study everything about it at all times.'

'And the States General? What will they do?' I asked.

'Most likely they will charge a jurist with your case and the jurist will follow the same procedure,' said Landman.

'Study everything,' I said. 'But no matter whether the study produces results or not, there is always a next step. What might that be?'

'Then they have to determine whether the accusation is well founded,' said Landman.

'Accusation well founded,' I shouted. 'Of course it's not well founded. It's mean and malicious, that's what it is!'

'Oh miss, pl-please, try to keep ca-calm,' Landman stuttered nervously. He stood and walked towards me. 'Can I offer you something? Tea perhaps?'

'No, no, I'm calm,' I said and continued unruffled: 'How do you and the States General determine whether an accusation is well founded?'

'Hmm, there's no simple answer, I'm afraid,' he replied. 'We have our methods. But you can trust us. We're here to help you and we know what we're doing.'

I suddenly had an excellent idea.

'But of course, lawyers are professional people,' I said. 'It must take a great deal of training to be a lawyer, Mr Landman. How do you go about it?'

'Study, naturally, study at the university,' he replied. He was now on home territory and his stutter had disappeared.

'Is study at the university open to everyone?' I inquired.

'Not everyone, miss. The university only accepts those with a good educational background, and you need to know Latin,' Landman answered.

'I have a good educational background, but sadly I don't know Latin,' I said.

'But, miss, the university is not for women!' Landman quipped.

'You mean, I will never be able to attend the university,' I said. The man was taken aback and shook his head in desperation. I remember having the urge to tease him a little and I said calmly, 'Good then, no university for me. But tell me, how did you study law? Was everything explained to you at the university or did you have to study from books?'

'From books, of course, the university only offers guidance. The student has to do most of it himself. There were books aplenty, hefty tomes to the last,' said Landman pretentiously, pointing at the bookcase. 'We still use them for reference.'

'Everything in Latin?' I asked.

'Most of it, yes, but an important work by the renowned Hugo de Groot is now in Dutch. Look, we have a copy right here.' He pointed to a substantial volume on his desk, picked it up with care and handed it to me.

'*Introduction to Dutch Jurisprudence*,' I read aloud. 'Does it contain all there is to know about the law?' I inquired.

'Almost, but not everything. New cases appear in front of the courts every day,' he said.

'Was my case new?' I asked for a second time and I glared at him intently.

He thought for a moment and then said: 'No… no. To be honest I'd never heard of such a case, but that is what the book is for. I can use it to check if a case such as yours has ever appeared before the courts.'

'And you're going to study the matter,' I concluded.

He nodded.

'Is this book for sale?' I asked.

'Yes, of course, at the university. Legal experts consider it indispensable.'

'I want to buy a copy,' I said.

'But, miss, do you really intend to buy it?' the man asked, a little shaken.

'You said it was for sale,' I exclaimed.

'Yes, the legal experts all have their own copy, but… eh…eh… why would you…' he stuttered. I replied abruptly: 'Or do you think I am incapable of understanding it?'

'No, not at all, I just wondered…' he said hesitatingly. 'Such a suggestion has never been made before. I'm not even sure if it's allowed.'

'Surely my own lawyer would hardly try to prevent me from using my mind and intelligence to study my own case!' I snapped.

'No, of course not,' said Landman, but he didn't sound convinced.

'If you would like to help me, please order a copy of Hugo de Groot's *Introduction* on my behalf and let me know the moment it arrives,' I said. And that was that!

The temperature in the room was on the low side, but the poor fellow still had to wipe the perspiration from his brow.

I resolved to learn as much as I could about the law. If Landman does not purchase the book I shall inform Mr Hoyer that I demand it. I don't imagine it will be so very difficult. I will read everything and study it carefully. No one will ever be able to deceive me about the law again.

20 October 1737

What dreadful weather! Rain, strong winds lashing the leaves from the trees, roof tiles flying about everywhere. You can hear the wind literally howling round the house. But the people here tell me this is nothing and that the real autumn storms have yet to come.

Poor Zwaantje! I hardly dare send her outside on an errand for fear the wind might blow her away. She looks pale, her eyes are sunken, and she has a permanent cough. The fire in my room is kept kindled and the place is cosy and snug. I prefer to leave the lamp burning during the day to keep out the darkness. When I discovered that Zwaantje spent much of her time in the cold scullery, I invented all sorts of chores she could attend to in my room while she sat close to the hearth. I have little doubt that the other women in the house find this strange – personnel don't belong in one's room – but I feel sorry for the poor child and she isn't the slightest trouble. She sits in a corner, quiet as a mouse, listening to me play and busying herself with repairs or cleaning.

While I'm forced to stay inside for days on end, the weather in Suriname is magnificent. The dry season is warm and most people join friends and family on their plantation where the wind blows in the afternoon, October's glorious 'kowru winti'. In the early evening people walk along Waterkant and often drop in for a chat and something to drink. I miss my home! How much longer must I stay here? When can I expect progress?

25 October 1737

I received a batch of letters yesterday, forwarded by Reijdenius. Letters from home, how wonderful! One from Masra Frederik, with a few lines from Maria at the bottom, and one from my dear, sweet Carl Otto!

Paramaribo, 16 August 1737

Dearest sister Elisabeth,
Our house seems so quiet without you. We all miss your cheerful laugh and witty observations. Your friend, poor Carl Otto, is at such a loose end without you. But do not lose courage, dear sister. I have reason to believe we can expect you back among us soon. Read on!

Governor Raye suddenly passed away last week. The man had only been sick for a couple of days and had visited me a week before he died. His sudden death is such a pity, not only for Suriname but also for us. We had finally managed to win the governor over. His own dealings with Van Meel had brought about a change of heart and he came to tell me about it in person. While he did not exactly offer his apologies, his visit was well-intentioned nonetheless. What happened? Van Meel had requested and been granted a period of leave. His wife was very ill and he considered it more advisable to have her treated in Holland. He presented himself to the governor on July 23rd to inform him of his departure. The governor remained calm and wished him a pleasant stay in patria. Imagine Raye's amazement when he heard a commotion on the front terrace a moment later and Van Meel showering him with a deafening torrent of abuse. The man ranted and raved, complaining that Raye hadn't the right to dismiss him from the palace. It was a public place and belonged to all of the colonists.

The governor, who had said farewell to the man in all serenity only moments earlier, was at a complete loss. He made his way outside to see what was going on, only to be confronted by a furious Van Meel, sword in hand, and a mouth full of obscenities. When Raye saw him, he roared: 'Look at him, he's threatening me. Come on then, I'm up to you!'[12]

Infuriated at the man's misconduct, the governor summoned the orderly and insisted he be removed from the terrace. This simply intensified Van Meel's rage. Raye went back inside, but Van Meel continued his abuse all the way to the café where he ranted on about the governor's unwarranted pretensions. Raye was a worthless governor, and Suriname would be better off without him. The insults were endless.

During the governor's visit, he told me he now believed he had done you a great injustice by handing over your case against Peltzer to such an unstable and unreliable legislative councillor.

Raye informed me he had actually reached this conclusion immediately after the case was over and for this reason had written a letter to the Directors in which he asked how the States General might react to the knowledge that Van Meel had not addressed all of the witnesses, especially those who had volunteered to testify. He also informed them of his own experience of Van Meel's ability to lie and to use his lies to create uproar.

Besides the Van Meel affair, Raye had informed the directors that his experience of the council members and some of the colonists had disappointed him greatly and he told me in confidence that he had tendered his resignation because he was incapable of working with them. Upon acceptance of his request, he planned to return to the Netherlands, present his version of your case to the High Council if possible, have Van Meel brought before them and insist on a speedy revision.

Sadly, Governor Raye is no longer with us and no longer able to carry out his plans. To our good fortune, however, he wrote everything down in a letter to the Heren XVII. The secretary told me about it after the funeral. The letter was to be despatched according to the late governor's wishes and could be made available to the States General. With a little luck, it will expedite the revision and free you to return to us.

I heard from Reijdenius that your lawyer, Mr Hoyer, is a well-known expert. Have you been in contact with him? Are you satisfied with his services? What does he think of the case? Are you happy in your new lodgings? We think about you every day and pray for your continued good health and that your temporary stay in Holland will be free of difficulty,

Your devoted brother-in-law Frederik Bosse

Dearest sister,
See! Things have turned out well after all. Raye is dead, but before he passed away, he experienced at first hand what it is to be lied about and falsely accused. Do you remember our maxim 'Lei hati moro soro'? Wel, granman kon sabi fosi a dede.

What luck that he told Frederik all about it and wrote to the big guns in Holland. Everything should now go according to plan and you will soon have your revision.

Your sisters, brothers and mother Nanno send their greetings. Frederik called them together and told them what the governor had said before he died. Your brothers, especially Kwakoe, were outraged that none of this had been made known before the court case, but there's no use crying over spilt milk. Catharina and Nanette say it's a pity they cannot write for themselves, considering they have so much to tell you. Let's pray for a speedy and positive outcome. Stay well, mi gudu, we miss you and think about you often,

Your loving sister Maria

My darling Elisabeth,

Masra Frederik will doubtless have told you all about the governor's death. It's sad that granman had to go to meet his maker, but fortunate that he was decent enough to tell us just in time about what happened with Van Meel. Yes, my dear girl, the consternation in the colony was unbelievable. Everyone was talking about Van Meel ranting and raving on the steps of the governor's palace: 'I don't give a cuss about the governor'.[13] Rayneval witnessed the entire thing and did his best to calm the maniac but to no avail. The governor was so shocked by what had happened he immediately tendered his resignation. Sadly he died before his letter reached its destination. The day after he visited your brother-in-law he took ill and he died within the week.

Yet another elaborate funeral with the council members as pallbearers. Mrs Raye was swathed in ceremonial black for the third time and managed to play the mournful widow again, although she must be getting used to it by now. She'll probably ask to be allowed to stay at the palace, and if the next governor is a bachelor they can marry immediately and avoid any discussion about sleeping arrangements. The name Raye will not disappear altogether from Suriname. Our thrice-over widow is apparently with child.

I cannot wait for your return. Are you managing alright in Holland? It is the height of summer as I write these words, but autumn will be with us soon enough and how will you be faring then? Have you been in touch with your lawyer? What does he think of the case? We have just returned from an expedition. It was scorching and dry and some careless soldiers caused a massive forest fire, which must have warned off the Maroons. We returned empty-handed.

Last week I joined Masra Frederik on a visit to Saltzhallen. I missed you even more at that moment and kept thinking: wouldn't it be wonderful if Elisabeth were here? We visited so often together, everything about the place reminds me of you. I pray and implore that we can put this entire episode behind us and I can hold you in my arms, feel you, smell you, and fondly kiss your darling lips.

Eternally yours,

Carl Otto Creutz

Such sweet letters. I had to be alone with my thoughts, my desires and my sorrow. I gave Zwaantje a couple of pennies and told her to go home. Once she was out of the room I let go and wept.

6 November 1737

The courier from the lawyers' office brought a second invitation. The cold, grey drizzle persuaded me to take a carriage. I thought Hugo de Groot's introduction to Dutch law had arrived and I was being summoned to collect it, but I was mistaken. Landman was already waiting and he escorted me to Mr Hoyer's office. Hoyer came towards me with open arms and welcomed me cordially. He told me to take off my mantle and be seated and instructed Landman to have the courier prepare tea. He prattled on about the weather, urged me to wrap up warmly, not to underestimate the cold and damp *et cetera, et cetera*. The tea arrived with a tray of biscuits. In the meantime, I looked around in search of a package with my book inside, but saw nothing. As Mr Hoyer sipped at his tea I said: 'Were you able to order the book I requested, Mr Landman?'

Landman looked at Hoyer, and Hoyer said: 'That's precisely why we asked you to come to the office, Miss Elisabeth. Landman informed me of your desire to purchase a copy of the *Introduction to Dutch Jurisprudence* and your plan to study it. Excellent, I thought, evidence of your drive, your eagerness to learn, your refusal to admit defeat. But de Groot is for specialists, if you understand my meaning. Much too dry and boring for a lady. That is why we thought…'

I felt insulted and snapped: 'I suppose you think women are stupid and black women even more so!'

'Absolutely not,' Hoyer continued calmly, 'and I'm well aware that you are exceptionally gifted, intelligent and well educated. If that were not the case, the suggestion I am about to make, if I may, would be out of the question.'

I blushed and held my tongue. Mr Hoyer continued: 'As I told you earlier, Landman here has been charged with your case. He is a highly qualified jurist and familiar with the literature. We thought it might be better for you to write down any questions you have on paper and give them to Landman. He will then put together a response, consult the literature where necessary and provide references to the passages related to your respective questions. This will allow you to scrutinise each answer yourself without having to embark on a lengthy and unexciting course of personal study. While I have no doubt that you would succeed in such an endeavour, I fear nevertheless that it would demand a great deal of time. We hope, after all, that your case will soon be resolved and you will be able to hasten back to your family. What do you think of our plan?'

I nodded. 'You're right,' I said and turned to look at Landman, 'but is it fair to burden him with so many questions?'

He blushed and said: 'I'm sure I'll manage. It'll be my pleasure.'

We chatted a little longer and then I accompanied Landman to his office.

'The book is on my desk. It's always at your service. Ask whatever you want and I'll do my best,' he said.

'Am I such a difficult client?' I asked.

'Difficult? No, not difficult,' he replied and added on reflection: 'An interesting client, very interesting.'

For one reason or another, the ice between us seemed to be broken. I remained seated for a moment and asked if I might look at his other books. We walked over to the bookcase and he removed the books one by one, read its Latin title aloud and told me its meaning. We returned to our seats after a while and talked at length. I asked what was going to happen next.

He said that the case would be studied for procedural errors and to determine whether the writ had been properly served. I naturally wanted to know what kinds of errors were possible and he said: 'In the interrogation of witnesses, for example.' He launched into a long list: my name, the place, the circumstances. If one single error had been made, the entire case would have to be repeated.

I asked what would happen if it turned out the accusation was groundless and told him about the letters from Masra Frederik and Carl Otto. 'Before he died, the governor wrote a letter to the Directors about his experiences with Van Meel,' I said. 'Do you think his letter will be considered by the States General?'

'Of course,' said Landman. 'Let's hope it was sent with the other documents. You see, you have reason to be confident. The entire case will probably be declared invalid.'

God grant it so!

I have to admit that Landman has turned out better than expected. I only realised after I left that I had spent almost three hours in his office. He also seemed to find our conversation a pleasant one. We agreed that I would return after two weeks with whatever questions might arise in the meantime and review the results of his research.

21 November 1737

Last Sunday I accompanied Mrs Helder and Mrs Weide to church once again. They wanted to walk, but it was too cold and wet for a walk so I ordered a carriage. I naturally invited them to join me and they were all too pleased to accept. Although the majority of churchgoers are used to me, I still attract attention. I'm not sure if my presence inspired it, but whatever the case, the minister's choice of theme for his sermon was slavery!

His passionate sermon spoke of Noah and his sons, especially Cham. The Bible says that the negroes are descendants of Cham, who ridiculed his father and brought a paternal curse upon himself.

The descendants of Cham were obliged to serve Noah's other sons and that is why they were made slaves. As I listened to the minister's tirade I wondered why service for many was the same as abuse and torture. Was the minister aware of the real situation? Even if it were true that negroes are slaves because of the Bible, shouldn't those who serve be treated humanely, no matter what? Is the theory that negroes are wild, uncivilised and undeveloped also based on the Bible? It is possible, of course, since you can find whatever you want in the Bible. The reality is that white people do not see negroes as human beings, but rather as a sort of animal with the intellectual capacity of a six-year-old white child. That is why the whites are so curious about the negro Captain. According to the minister and his consorts, the Captain is an exception and deserves the community's support. They are now paying for his theological training and have plans for his future. Of course, they will send him to Africa to convert the negroes and part of their conversion will naturally be the acceptance of slavery.

After the service, many of the congregation shook the minister's hand and praised his fine sermon. He radiated contentment and looked at me expectantly. I was walking beside Mrs Helder and quickly slipped outside as she was shaking the minister's hand. Mrs Weide shouted: 'Miss Elisabeth, the minister would like a word,' but I pretended not to hear and climbed into my carriage.

When the ladies joined me in the carriage a while later, Mrs Weide complained: 'You ran off so quickly. The minister wanted to speak with you in person.'

I replied bluntly: 'I can do without the minister, thank you!'

We returned home in silence.

Zwaantje isn't here today. Mrs Verstegen tells me she's ill. I thought she had seemed better that last few days. She had rosy cheeks and her eyes appeared to sparkle. I thought it was because of the good food she received when she was here at work. When I shared my thoughts with Mrs Verstegen, she shook her head and whispered: 'Ah, miss, that's precisely what's so misleading, the rosy cheeks, the sparkling eyes… Dear oh dear, that's how consumption works, you see. The poor child!'

I was taken aback. Was Zwaantje so ill?

'What can we do?' I asked. 'Can't we send her something to build up her strength?'

'Certainly, but it won't help much. The winter is a difficult time for the poor,' Mrs Verstegen sighed.

I pulled out my purse and gave her two silver coins. 'Can we ask Huib to fetch some provisions and bring them to the family?' I asked. 'And let them have this as well, they'll be needing it,' and I gave her a third coin.

It seemed to me that the poor people of Holland had to endure such severe punishment. Poverty here does not only imply hunger, it also implies cold. How dreadful! Zwaantje was in my thoughts the entire day. Poti!

4 December 1737

It's snowing! What a magnificent sight! When I opened the curtains this morning the world was completely white. Pretty as a picture! Huge snowflakes like tufts of cotton are still fluttering to the ground. I wanted to be part of the white world outside my window. I dressed and made my way to the garden. It was truly splendid. I touched the snow, grabbed handfuls from the ground and thought to myself: this is the illustrious snow we hear so much about in Suriname. Huib, the manservant, was watching me and had to laugh at my delight. 'If you were a child, miss, all the other children would have covered you with snow by now,' he said.

'Don't grown-ups play with the snow?' I asked.

'No, miss, it's much too cold for grown-ups,' he replied.

'What a pity. I'd love to make a snowman as the children do,' I said.

'I can give you a helping hand, miss, if you like,' he suggested. 'Let's ask Mrs Verstegen,' I said.

I have an appointment with Landman at Hoyer's office later today, but this time I'm going on foot. I can't wait to walk in all that pretty white powder. Mrs Verstegen had nothing against it, although she advised me to wrap up warm and wear thick woolly socks. I shall do precisely that. I'll wear my new fur cape and keep my hands warm with my new fur hand muff. I caught sight of myself in the mirror and said: 'The free negress Elisabeth in the snow! Wonders will never cease!'

7 December 1737

Walking in the snow was fun at first, but by the time I reached the city it had turned into a filthy black sludge and my feet were freezing cold. When I finally arrived at Prinsengracht, my feet were like blocks of ice and melting snowflakes dripped from my hat onto my face. The sight of me must have startled the courier who opened the door: 'Oh, miss, you must be chilled to the bone.'

Landman appeared and hurried me to his room where there was a warm fire. He told me to take off my wet clothes and not sit close to the hearth right away. When I told him I had walked through the snow he insisted I take off my shoes. He even fetched a towel and got to his knees to dry my feet. I thought to myself in the meantime: what a bizarre situation. Here I am in a lawyers' office in The Hague with a white legal expert on his knees drying my feet, a black woman's feet. I couldn't contain my laughter. Landman asked if it tickled and I feigned a nod. I thanked him, told him it was very kind of him to dry my feet and complemented his thoughtfulness towards me. He blushed!

Our discussion was rather unusual on this occasion. We didn't talk about the law or the court case, but about ourselves. I don't know how it happened but we suddenly became very personal. I told him about home, my family and Carl Otto, and Landman told me about himself and his family. He is married to his second cousin, someone he has known all his life. They have a one-year-old child. Their first child died a couple of weeks after the birth and this is their second. He did not give me the impression that he was very happy at home. Hoyer is his father's cousin. He was very curious about life in the tropics and asked question after question, simply confirming my conviction that the people here have absolutely no idea how we live in a country like Suriname.

20 December 1737

I paid another visit to my lawyers' office three days ago. Landman was busy with another client when I arrived and I was invited to wait in a charming antechamber where I browsed through a local newspaper entitled 's Gravenhaege Courant. It was chock full of interesting columns and I was so busy reading I barely noticed Landman enter the room. I had heard in Suriname that newspapers were a regular feature of daily life in Holland. I understood this was a newspaper and I found it extraordinary. Three editions per week, no less.

'May I continue to read?' I asked Landman.

'But, of course,' he said. 'Perhaps you would like to take it with you?'

'Very much,' I said.

As we were talking in his room I asked what I should do to have the newspaper delivered.

'We'll organise a subscription for you, then you'll receive every edition.' A sound idea, I thought.

'I'll take care of the paperwork,' he said. 'First we need your name and address: Miss Elisabeth... eh... eh... Van Suriname. Dutch style, is that good?'

'I prefer Miss Elisabeth from Suriname, if you don't mind.'

'From?' he asked, clearly surprised at my preference, but I answered resolutely: 'Yes. Miss Elisabeth from Suriname.'

And that was that. I could hardly explain to the man that black people in Suriname were given names beginning with 'Van' as a sign that they were slaves, someone's property. I have never been a slave and have never been someone's property, and I refuse to take a name beginning with 'Van'.

The newspaper was lying on the doormat this morning. Mrs Verstegen inquired excitedly if I had a subscription and if she might read it. It wasn't long before the other women expressed an interest. We agreed that I would read it first then pass it on to Mrs Verstegen and that she would pass it to the governess and then to Mrs Helder. 'May I ask for it to be returned when everyone has read it,' I asked. Everyone agreed and our household became fervent readers of the 's Gravenhaege Courant. I planned to preserve every edition and take them to Suriname when I returned.

28 December 1737

Christmas has come and gone. I wasn't looking forward to it in the least. Christmas should be celebrated at home with family, but I have no home here. It turned out fine in the end. Mrs Helder joined her son's family for the day. The governess, Mrs Weide, Mrs Verstegen and I enjoyed a glass of mulled wine in the salon that evening. The governess suffers terribly from rheumatism and I helped her in and out of her room. I think she appreciated it and is no longer angry with me.

I haven't been outside for the best part of a week because of the dreadful weather. The snow is gone, but the rain and ice-cold wind persist. How can anyone live in this miserable climate? We're so blessed in Suriname!

30 December 1737

Zwaantje is dead. Her brother came to tell us yesterday. I was so upset and wanted to go to her immediately. Mrs Verstegen strongly advised against it, but I felt it was my duty. I wanted to see her family and say farewell to the child in person.

When Mrs Verstegen realised I was determined to go, she insisted that Huib accompany me. I now understand why she was so concerned. It was a terrible neighbourhood, dingy and foul-smelling. The people live in small musty rooms. Everyone stared at me with unconcealed curiosity. A couple of children ran ahead and warned Zwaantje's mother that I was coming. Poor Zwaantje was already buried, her mother told me. She thanked me for the money and wiped the tears from her eyes with the corner of her apron. 'It's a hard, hard life being poor,' she said, and all I could do was nod in agreement.

2 January 1738

Another year has gone. The people here don't celebrate as we do in Suriname with our family get-togethers and dancing into the night. It was a testing time for me and I thought constantly of home. Let's hope I'll be able to return to Suriname in 1738 and be with my own people once again! Mrs Verstegen said she would find me a new biddy. I suggested she look for an older girl this time, someone like Marie.

'If it's possible, I would prefer a proper maid, someone who also sleeps here,' I said. 'I will cover the costs, of course. Would there happen to be room for her in the attic? I won't be using her services all the time so she will also be at your disposal when you need her.' Mrs Verstegen found it an excellent idea and the same afternoon our new maid Ada arrived, a strapping girl with chubby arms and round rosy cheeks. She is clearly not sick.

28 January 1738

It has been below zero for a week and the canals and ponds are frozen over. People everywhere, especially children, have taken to their skates. It's a cheerful picture, skaters sweeping across the ice, laughing and larking around. The weather is beautiful. The sky is clear and blue, the sun is shining and everyone is happy. I tried the ice myself but not with skates. It was extremely slippery and although I was afraid, I was also determined to see what it felt like. I enjoyed a glass of slemp and a biscuit at a stall. A crowd of children gathered round me and I treated each one of them to something tasty.

It's still cold but it does not compare to the wind and the rain. It's also clear that the days are getting longer. Not before time. I hate the darkness.

I visited Landman again this morning. I had nothing new to ask him, but I wanted to check if any documents had arrived from Suriname. Sadly not. It's taking such a long time. Landman was pleased to see me. We talked at length about the weather and everything I had read in the paper. He told me there are books for sale in the Ridderzaal. I plan to go as soon as the weather improves.

He invited me to join him and his wife for tea on Sunday. I was delighted to accept. I'm curious to see what he's like at home with his family.

6 February 1738

I visited the Landmans last Sunday. He seems to have a nice house. All I saw was the salon and that was pleasant enough. His wife is the caring type. She said little, and when she did speak it was about their child or their home. We first took tea from pretty teacups and ate cake, then wine was served. Landman and I did the talking, which ranged over a host of topics. The lady of the house rang a little bell from time to time and had a word with the maid. The boy was allowed to come in accompanied by his nursemaid. He wanted to grab everything in sight and managed to knock over one of the teacups. Landman was angry and snapped at him and the boy started to cry. His mother cuddled him and said that his daddy was 'naughty'. I felt sorry for Landman, who was staring shyly into space, and pretended I had noticed nothing.

Will I ever have children? And if I do, will Carl Otto be the father? I hope so, from the bottom of my heart, I hope so. The longing is sometimes so overwhelming I wish it could happen there and then. How long must I wait? How long before my case begins to show signs of progress? I want to get out of here!

3 March 1738

Something happened today. It was fine weather and I hadn't been outside for two weeks so I decided to take a walk. I walked along the Voorhout. The people of The Hague say it's the most beautiful avenue in Europe. I'm sure they're right. I later crossed Bookhorststraat at the corner of the Lange Beestenmarkt, and you'll never believe who was suddenly standing in front of me: Mrs Van Meel! Yes, the wife of the legislative councillor from Suriname.

The woman almost fainted when she saw me. I was equally surprised, of course, but I didn't let it show. I stood my ground and looked her straight in the eye. She glanced at me for a second and then continued on her way. I watched her walk away and then decided on the spur of the moment to follow her. After a while she looked back and saw me behind her. She increased her pace and so did I. I wanted to laugh out loud. She looked back again and I made a couple of gestures in the air as if I was putting a curse on her and I pointed in her direction. The woman started to run so fast she almost fell over. I ran at the same speed, gloating to myself at her terrified expression. She looked back a third time as she was about to cross the street and turn the corner. I followed and saw her open a garden gate and pull vigorously on the doorbell of a house. I kept my distance and made my way to the opposite side of the street when I saw her go inside. I'm not sure if she lives there, but she had clearly gone inside and I was sure she was watching me through the window behind the curtains. Amarante once told me that the woman was terrified of wisi. She had had months of trouble with swollen legs in Suriname and was convinced that a slave girl had put a curse on her. She naturally imagines that all negroes are experts in the black arts. It's time for you to learn a lesson, I thought. I raised my hand, drew all sorts of circles in the air and blessed myself. I then crossed the street and started to walk up and down in front of the gate, stopping for a moment to stamp up and down a couple of times. I then quickly checked to see if anyone was coming and when I was sure the street was empty I spat on the ground, bent over and pretended to be writing something on the pavement in front of the house. It gave me a certain degree of satisfaction to know that the woman behind the curtains was shaking with fear, terrified that I was putting a hex on her.

Spring has arrived, announced by the appearance of little white flowers they call snowdrops. Tiny green leaves have sprouted on the trees and the sun sometimes feels warm. No one in the house is happier than the governess. She had so much trouble with rheumatism in the winter and was virtually unable to walk for days on end. I honestly felt sorry for her and I visited from time to time. My Ada also helps out now and then and she seems to appreciate it, at least that's what she tells Ada. I haven't been back to church. I believe Mrs Helder and Mrs Weide are unhappy about it, but what should I care. I refuse to listen to that minister and his ridiculous theories. All he does is appease the whites, make them think they're good, God-fearing people and that the world would be so much worse without them. It all leaves me cold.

15 March 1738

Yesterday, I returned to the house into which Mrs Van Meel had disappeared. I walked from one corner of the street and back again three times and then I took my place opposite the house. At a given moment I could clearly make out people watching me from behind the curtains. I was about to cross the street when the door opened and a maid stormed outside: 'Away with you, gollywog, dirty nigger,' she yelled. 'Take that magic of yours elsewhere!' I walked on and pretended to be very surprised. At that moment a gentleman passed by and looked in amazement at the maid and at me. I shrugged my shoulders and the man said to the maid: 'Come now, is there any need for all that? The woman's done nothing.'

'She wants to bewitch us,' the maid screamed. The man looked at me and I shook my head, shrugged my shoulders as if I had no idea what she was talking about and pretended I was just passing by.

The man briefly walked beside me and asked: 'Do you know that woman?'

I shook my head and sighed and the man said: 'Dim-witted illiterates. Perhaps she's never seen someone like you before. You shouldn't hold it against her.'

I decided to stay away from the house for a while. Van Meel is quite capable of dragging me in front of the courts for witchcraft. I had achieved my goal: his wife was afraid of me!

3 April 1738

Hoyer's courier brought a letter yesterday and I had an appointment with Landman this afternoon. A pile of documents from Paramaribo had been delivered to the States General and copies had also been sent to Hoyer. They were sent on January 27th. 'Is Raye's letter among them?' I asked eagerly.

'Several of the documents bear the late governor's signature,' said Landman, 'but we haven't examined all of them yet. That's the following step. You see, we're making progress at last. Everything will be fine in due course.'

He smiled. He has such a charming smile. It makes him look so young and then he reminds me of Carl Otto. Or is it my imagination?

'When do you expect to have completed your study?' I asked.

'Oh, a week at the most,' he replied.

'Do you mind if I come back next week? I am so curious to see your reaction to the governor's letter. I know what it contains. My brother-in-law wrote to me about it. I'm so fortunate the governor put everything down on paper. I'm certain it will help.'

'I'm sure it will, Miss Elisabeth, I'm sure it will. So, as you can see, everything is falling into place. In the meantime, you should make the most of the good weather. Spring is here and it won't be long before you're on your way back to Suriname and your loved ones,' said Landman. I felt like throwing my arms around him. I didn't, of course, but I left his office light-hearted and carefree and was tempted to skip all the way home.

11 April 1738

I visited Landman yesterday as planned. What a disappointment. The documents sent from Suriname contained an extract from Raye's letter dated May 1736 but there was no sign of a letter to the Directors written in July. I wasn't only disappointed, I was furious. The documents also contained a letter from Van Meel addressed to the Directors and dated 30 August 1736. The letter pointed out, among other things: 'The addressees should be aware that the free negress is known by everyone here as a common whore.'[14]

Landman blushed as he read the words to me. I roared from the bottom of my heart: 'That scoundrel!'

'You could press charges against Van Meel,' said Landman gently, 'take him to court for slander.' I sneered and thought to myself: poor Landman has no idea about the way things are in Suriname.

'Even if I was a whore, thank God I'm not *his* whore!' I said, but Landman did not understand.

Masra Frederik had said nothing about Van Meel's replacement, but it made little difference. Surely the secretary would be responsible for despatching the documents. But who is the secretary? Most of those people are against me and want me to be found guilty. I wrote immediately to Masra Frederik and told him what had happened. I begged him to go to the secretary and persuade him to find the letter and send a copy. I also wrote to Carl Otto, but he's probably on an expedition. Perhaps everyone in Suriname has long forgotten me.

All this excitement was for nothing. It is and remains difficult. Will I ever be able to leave here? Am I doomed to spend the rest of my days as an exile in a foreign land, where I know almost no one and where I have no family? And what if I have to stay here after all, what will I do then? Reijdenius pays for my lodgings and legal costs on the instructions of my brother-in-law. I had brought enough money with me to cover my other expenses – at least that's what I thought, but it's running out fast. I had plenty set aside in Suriname, and so many unpaid credits that I thought I could survive here for a year. But I've been here for a year already, and I have no idea how much I have left in Suriname. I can do business in Suriname, but here? What can I do here to earn my living? I can see their faces: a black woman as a merchant! Perhaps I should ask to be Frederik's business representative, to take over Reijdenius's job? I would be up to the task but would they let me? I fear not.

This is misery. Pure, unadulterated misery!

28 May 1738

It has been quite some time since I wrote in my diary. To be honest, I was so angry on the last occasion that I hurled the book across the room and collapsed on my bed in a flood of tears. The book landed behind the couch and Ada found it a couple of days ago and left it on the table where it remained untouched. I was not in the mood for writing. All I did was play the harpsichord. I started with pieces that allowed me to express my anger, but little by little the music changed. These are all my own compositions. When I play it feels as if I'm in another world, and I think about Carl Otto, Suriname, our house on Waterkant, Saltzhallen. I allow my imagination to run wild and picture what it will be like when I return: Carl Otto and I living in our own house, with children. Will I ever have children? My melodies sound charming and cheerful, if I say so myself.

The governess asked me a while ago to visit her in her room. 'I enjoy your music,' she said, 'especially the wonderful melodies of the last few days. As soon as you begin I get up from my chair and open the door so that I can hear you better. So beautiful, so sensitive and sweet. On occasion I think I recognise something, but I can never remember the name of the composer. Who wrote those lovely melodies you've been playing the last few weeks?' I didn't want to tell her I had composed them myself so I answered, 'I can't remember, his name escapes me.'

'But surely it's written on the score,' she remarked.

'I no longer have the score. I just happened to remember a number of pieces, but the composer's name has slipped my mind,' I spluttered. She said nothing, but she had a strange look in her eye.

The weather is beautiful. The sun shines almost every day, the birds sing, and there are flowers everywhere. The streets are alive with children playing and people walking in the sun. Sadly, the beautiful weather does not match my own feelings. I am so sad, so sombre. I can't help thinking about what happened to me a year ago in Suriname. A whole year has passed and how much have I achieved? Nothing, if truth be told. A request has been submitted and nothing more. I'm not in the mood to go outside. All I do is sit in my room and gaze through the window or play my harpsichord. I rarely see my fellow lodgers.

About three weeks ago, Ada knocked on my door one afternoon and came in with a letter from my law firm. 'Leave it on the table, Ada,' I said, without interrupting my play.

She stood still with the letter in her hand and said: 'But the courier's waiting at the door, miss.'

I stood, took the letter from her and recognised Landman's handwriting. He asked why I hadn't been to his office for such a long time and hoped I wasn't ill. I sat and wrote a brief reply. I thanked him for his concern, informed him that I was not ill, that I had no further questions for the time being, and that it made no sense to come to his office if there was nothing new to discuss.

But yesterday Landman appeared in person. I was in my room doing nothing in particular at the time, daydreaming, a little cheerless, when Ada came to inform me that I had a visitor, a gentleman.

I went downstairs and found Landman in the salon.

'I wanted to see for myself, Miss Elisabeth,' he said. 'Mr Hoyer and I are worried about you and concerned about your silence.'

'Dear Mr Landman, what sense is there in me coming to your office and bothering you with all those questions? The case is at a standstill. I'm no further forward than I was this time last year,' I replied. He was about to say something, but I interrupted: 'As a matter of fact, the entire affair has taught me to have no expectations.'

'But surely there's no need to be so pessimistic, miss,' he said.

'Do you have something to tell me, Mr Landman?' I snapped. He looked at me earnestly and said: 'Nothing new, perhaps, but something important nevertheless. I took the liberty of writing to the Directors of the Suriname Society in Amsterdam. I made reference to their correspondence with Governor Raye and asked quite explicitly for a copy of his last letter. And yesterday, Miss Elisabeth, yesterday we received a transcript of the said letter.'

'You have it!' I exclaimed. 'Is it what I expected? Was my brother-in-law correct about its contents?'

'To the letter, miss. Precisely as you had informed us. This document will help us, miss. Rest assured, a little patience and everything will be fine.' His face was aglow with satisfaction.

I gulped and gasped with relief: 'Thank you. Will you be sending the letter to the States General?'

'I'm afraid that won't be possible, but I can submit a new request and ask for it to be treated with urgency. I will make reference to the important passages in the correspondence between Governor Raye and the Directors in Amsterdam,' he answered.

'When?' I asked eagerly.

'As soon as possible,' he said with a smile. 'But I have something else for you.' He handed me a card. It was an invitation from Mr and Mrs Hoyer to attend a garden party on the grounds of an inn on Zeestraat in celebration of their silver wedding anniversary. There was to be a concert followed by dinner and a ball.

'Mr Hoyer has asked me to collect you,' said Landman. 'The celebrations begin at seven o'clock on June 8th. I'll be here with the carriage at six. What do you think?'

I nodded and we walked to the front door where he gave me his hand and said: 'Good afternoon, Miss Elisabeth. See you on the 8th!'

I felt reassured to some degree. I wondered as I climbed the stairs whether Hoyer had invited all his clients to celebrate his silver wedding anniversary.

9 June 1738

The Hoyers' anniversary celebration was yesterday. As agreed, Landman collected me in his carriage at six sharp. I was wearing a new ballgown and looked very elegant, if I may say so myself. I had expected Landman's wife to be with him and was surprised to find him alone. I asked where she was and he told me that she was expecting their second baby in a couple of weeks' time and was unable to attend the festivities in her condition.

The inn on Zeestraat was quite a distance away. The garden was beautifully decorated with garlands and paper lanterns that were lit after dinner had been served. Landman walked at my side and introduced me to so many people, some of whom stared at me out of curiosity while others acted as if a negress at a garden party was an everyday occurrence. Landman sat beside me at table on one side and an older gentleman by the name of Van Zuylen sat on the other. He knew a lot about Suriname because his brother had been a commander in the colony under Governors Temming and De Cheusses. He had corresponded with him and had heard much about the place when his brother was on leave. Sadly he took ill and passed away during his last visit home.

Mr Van Zuylen was a cheerful fellow. He asked all sorts of questions and the humorous stories he told made him laugh so loud on occasion that everyone at the table looked in our direction. I had the most enjoyable time. Landman was also very cheerful and kind. We danced several times and attracted considerable attention on the dance floor. The fireworks were magnificent, although they scared me a little. I must have let it show, since Landman put his arm around me for protection. Or did it have another meaning?

It was already past midnight when we climbed into the carriage but Landman felt it was far too beautiful a night to go home. He instructed the coachman to drive around a little before dropping me off. Out of the blue he took my hand and said gently: 'Life in Holland isn't that bad after all, is it Miss Elisabeth?' I laughed and said: 'No, not that bad.' But as I was undressing for bed, an uncomfortable feeling overcame me. What did Landman mean? Perhaps he doesn't really believe in what he's doing and is convinced I will spend the rest of my days as an exile in Holland.

I must have been very tired, since I fell asleep in spite of my anxiety. But the same thoughts still haunted me this morning. Tomorrow, I intend to go to Landman's office and demand to know the truth. If he has no faith in my success then it's time to put an end to our relationship. I can think of better ways to spend Masra Frederik's money.

30 June 1738

It's the height of summer! Wonderful! I took a walk along Hoogstraat today where I bought a new hat, ordered another, purchased silk for two new dresses and brought it straight away to the costumier. I now have two invitations, one for a garden party next week and one for an afternoon tea party on July 15th. I attended an evening of music yesterday at the home of a very prominent family in Clingendaal. I was quite surprised to receive the invitation a few days ago. At first, I wasn't sure who Commissioner Chardonnier was, but later I remembered I had met him together with his wife at Hoyer's reception.

Mr Van Zuylen must have advised them to invite me. I noticed him the moment I entered the hall, and a place had been reserved for me beside him. He appears to have found out that I play the harpsichord. We talked a great deal about music and during the interval, he introduced me to many of his friends. He treats me as if he's known me for years and calls me 'Miss Elisabeth from Suriname'. He tells everyone I am living for the moment in The Hague and that I am an excellent pianist and composer. If truth be told, he's never heard me play a note.

I visited Landman last week. I was determined to come straight to the point and ask him what sort of game he was playing but I didn't get the chance. He came to meet me with such enthusiasm, insisting that I was the very person he wanted to see. He had put together a new request and planned to submit it the following day. He also included a separate note with the request, pointing out that letters sent by the late Governor Raye in May and June 1737 contained information relevant to the case.

After taking the opportunity to review the documentations, I asked him if he believed in what he was doing and he exclaimed, almost indignantly: 'But of course!'

I then asked what he had meant when he said: 'Life in Holland isn't that bad after all.' He blushed and said coyly that he had enjoyed the evening at the Hoyers, especially my company at table, and he had hoped the feeling was mutual. What could I say?

All at once he exclaimed that the weather was far too pleasant to spend the day in a musty office. 'Let me show you how beautiful The Hague can be. I want you to remember your time here with affection. I'll be with you presently.' He then disappeared only to return a moment later with the announcement: 'This afternoon I'm taking you to a country inn.' And that's precisely what we did. We set out in an open carriage and took afternoon tea.

We attracted a lot of attention. I always do, but that afternoon, with such a cheerful young man by my side, gracefully doffing his hat at just about everyone in sight, all eyes were turned in our direction. Landman is no longer the timid young fellow I met a year ago. Could he be in love? All the signs are there. When he dropped me off at home, he held my hand for a long time and insisted I promise to visit much more often.

'Surely not,' I said. 'I would keep you from your work.'

'On the contrary, you are a tremendous incentive to work,' he exclaimed so loud it made me laugh.

'How often should I come?' I asked teasingly.

'If you ask me, every day,' he said and he lowered his voice: 'I mean what I say. I long for you more and more.'

I felt embarrassed and spluttered: 'And how is your wife?'

'Fine, fine,' he replied.

'Still expecting?' I continued, and he answered:

'A little more than a week now.'

'I hope it all goes well,' I said and rushed inside.

20 July 1738

I visited the Landmans and their new baby yesterday. Mrs Landman gave birth to a strapping seven-pound boy two weeks ago. I gave them a silver teething ring as a gift and they served brandy and buttered crispbakes with sugared aniseed, a custom in Holland.

The garden party and the tea party have come and gone. I had the impression that everyone wanted to talk to me, and on both occasions the infamous Captain was naturally part of the conversation. I've grown accustomed to the fact that people talk about him as soon as they see me. The guests were predominantly women and the hostess was truly most charming. She kept repeating how special it was to have me as her guest and insisted I come more often.

Mr Van Zuylen was not at the tea party, but during the garden party he behaved once again as if I was his personal discovery. He took me by the arm and introduced me to all the other guests. I had already been introduced to most of them on one or other occasion.

I now know why I received all those unexpected invitations. I have apparently become 'bon ton' among The Hague's more reputable families. It's considered chic to have the black lady from Suriname attend your garden party or soirée. I provide an exotic feature, and I play the part with panache. I drink tea from the finest china with my little finger raised, chat about this and that, listen politely to the other invitees' commentary on the music and the musicians, well aware that some of them can't tell one note from another, and smile graciously when they compliment me for my knowledge of the Dutch language. My Dutch skills are a frequent topic of conversation. Everyone is amazed that I picked it up so quickly, completely unaware of course that I have been speaking Dutch all my life.

31 July 1738

The ladies here in the house are very impressed by the invitations I receive and the company I've been keeping lately. An invitation arrived today from Lord and Lady Van Swevelen. I was at the costumier for a fitting when the card was delivered. During our evening drink in the garden, Mrs Verstegen suddenly declared: 'You received a special invitation this afternoon. I saw a coat of arms on the card.'

'An invitation from Lord and Lady Van Swevelen,' I said, 'to a *dîner dansant* at their country house in Voorburg.'

Mrs Weide cooed: 'Oooh!' and Mrs Helder exclaimed: 'How lovely, how wonderful. I take it you know the Van Swevelens?'

'I met them once, at one or other tea party, I believe,' I replied, 'but I can't say I know them.'

'What a privilege nevertheless to receive an invitation from such prominent people,' said Mrs Helder. I held my tongue and thought: if only you knew what

I really think of it all. I'm playing their little game. I go to their soirées and teas and talk and talk, but I do it in the hope that it will help my case and help hasten my return to the place I really belong.

Moments later the governess said: 'You know, dear child (yes, she cossets me these days), you know you're mixing with the upper crust?'

'Is that so?' I asked.

'But of course!' the governess croaked. 'The Van Swevelens aren't just any old family. They're aristocracy, and not just any old aristocracy. Do you realise you'll be mixing with the aristocracy?'

I don't know what inspired me, but I answered: 'I'm not just from any old family either. In Africa my father was king of an enormous kingdom and my mother was a princess. She was dressed in golden robes and was carried around in a sedan chair before the robbers captured her and sold her to the slave traders.'

Everyone was stunned into silence. I looked around at them and chuckled to myself when I realised they didn't know what to say. I broke the silence and said: 'Good night, ladies, I'm off to bed.' I paused for a moment outside the door and heard them whispering. Hah! That'll keep them gossiping for a while.

20 August 1738

I received post today from Suriname. Masra Frederik wrote that Carl Otto was seriously ill after returning from an expedition. The letter was dated June 14th. I felt terrible when I read it and I still can't stop thinking of him and praying for his well-being. He had written a few lines of his own: *Darling, it's not as bad as it seems. I was exhausted, but now I'm getting stronger thanks to the care and concern of your sister and Amarante. I sleep a lot, which is a blessing since in my dreams I am with you. As ever, your Carl Otto.* His handwriting seemed a little unsteady and I realised that these few lines must have cost him considerable effort. He's putting a brave face on it, of course. What has Amarante been doing for him? Not too much I hope. Food and drink, nothing more! Masra Frederik also wrote that he had personally asked the secretary to send copies of Governor Raye's last letters and that the secretary had promised to do so.

31 August 1738

It has been so terribly warm the last couple of weeks I've found it hard to breathe at times. A colossal storm tore the branches from the trees yesterday

and it rained so hard it reminded me of our sibibusi, before the beginning of
the dry season.

It was much cooler and more pleasant weather yesterday. I went for a walk,
and paid a visit to Landman's office on the way.

'Just the person I wanted to see,' Landman exclaimed. 'I was about to send
the courier yesterday but changed my mind because of the dreadful weather.
You'll never guess what we've received.'

'Letters from Suriname!' I shrieked

'Yes, Miss Elisabeth,' said Landman with a smile, 'including the copies we
had requested, which have also been sent to the States General!'

"This is only the beginning,' I said. 'How much longer now?'

'Not long,' Landman answered, brimming with confidence.

We sat and talked for a while and then he suddenly said: 'Have you no
further questions?'

'What do you mean?' I asked.

'You don't write anymore, those pages full of questions you used to send. Is
everything about the law clear to you by now?'

I thought to myself: far from it. There's so much more I want to know. I want
to know about marriage. I want to know if the law forbids marriage between
blacks and whites. But I didn't exactly know how to pose the question since it
was clearly unrelated to my case and I wasn't sure how Landman would react.
'For the time being I have no questions,' I said.

He looked outside and said: 'The summer will be gone soon. Come with me.
Let's enjoy the good weather while we can. Come, let's go out in the carriage.'

Moments later we were riding along in a carriage on our way to the same
inn we had visited the last time. We sat by the pond and looked at the water.
He took my hand and caressed it. I don't know what to do with his advances.
I'm not in love with him. I like him, but nothing more. To cap it all the man is
married. What does he expect of me? To be his concubine? Just like the black
women in Suriname are concubines to white men? No thank you!

On our way home he kissed me. The first time I gave in to it but the second
time I gently pushed him away. Fortunately, we were almost home and I could
quickly leave the carriage.

'Thank you for a wonderful afternoon,' I said when he took my hand as I
was about to step out.

'Thank you, thank you very much,' he whispered. He was about to kiss me
again but I managed to pull my hand free and I ran to the door, which Ada had
opportunely opened.

In bed last night I remembered what I wrote a year ago about the fear I had
of being in Holland and my conviction that the Hollanders are the negroes'

worst enemy. But now I must confess I was mistaken. It's not true. In the last year I have experienced nothing but good things. No one has treated me badly. On the contrary, wherever I go I meet friendly and obliging people. Everyone is so kind to me. Why do the Hollanders in Suriname treat the negroes so badly?

I think I know the answer. I am alone. If there were ten thousand negroes in Holland it would be a different matter. Then it would be just like Suriname where the whites are a minority and the blacks outnumber them massively. That's why the Hollander's are intent on keeping control. That's why they have so many dos and don'ts for the slaves. That's why they are so cruel to the negroes, especially the slaves. Black people shouldn't be encouraged to think they have the same rights as the whites. What a difficult, complicated world.

13 September 1738

Autumn is just round the corner. The trees are starting to shed their yellow and brown leaves. Am I to spend yet another winter here after all? My case seems to have come to a standstill. One of Landman's learned friends assured him that the States General were hard at work on the matter. But now they've asked for more documents to be sent from Suriname. How much longer is it going to take?

I received a bundle of letters from home, a couple of lines from Sisa Maria, a letter from Masra Frederik and a sweet, sweet letter from Carl Otto. Sisa Maria informed me that our brother Izaak is sick. I hope he gets better soon. He is such a gentle and caring brother. I sometimes think good people die long before their time, like our dear brother Charlo. I'm particularly worried about my finances here. When I was forced to leave Suriname, Masra Frederik told me not to worry about money. He would stand as guarantor for me, and take care of all my costs. I told him I would treat his help as a loan, but how will I ever repay him? And what must I do if I am forced to stay here as a result of the revision. How will I live? Everything I have in Suriname will be spent by then. I can't live on my brother-in-law's generosity for the rest of my life. I now realise that a negative decision on the part of the States General would require me to disappear in one way or another, and for good!

28 September 1738

It's raining. Grey, gloomy, miserable rain. Everything has turned grey! What a climate! The governess is sick. She's been confined to bed and I think they're not expecting her to recover. I paid her a visit. Her room was dark and musty, and she could only manage a feeble whisper. Mrs Verstegen informed me yesterday that the governess needed private nursing care. I asked why she didn't arrange it and she looked at me strangely and said: 'Private nursing costs money!'

Naturally, I knew nothing of the financial situation of my fellow lodgers, but Mrs Verstegen explained that the governess had no money of her own and that her board and lodging were paid for by her former employer, the baron.

'Can't you inform the baron that she's sick and needs extra care?' I asked, but it was apparently a stupid question. I told Mrs Verstegen that Ada could help the governess whenever possible and that is precisely what she does.

1 October 1738

Perhaps Mrs Verstegen followed my advice after all. We heard that Baroness Hoogheem Van Oversta, who was raised by the governess as a young lady, is coming to visit her tomorrow. The commotion in the house is enormous, a frenzy of cleaning and polishing in preparation for such a prominent visitor. I asked Ada if the governess was aware that the baroness was coming to visit her and she told me she was sure it had lifted her spirits. In spite of her illness, the elderly lady is seriously concerned about what to wear.

'What to wear?' I asked, 'but surely she's confined to bed?'

'She says all her clothes are worn and threadbare. She wishes she had a new bed jacket since her only jacket is stained and even has holes in it. She asked me to fetch it from her wardrobe and then asked me to wash it, but it's so tattered I'm afraid it won't survive the wash. When I told her she was so upset she started to sob,' said Ada.

'Take a look in my coffer,' I said. 'I have bed jackets enough. Find a new one and give it to the governess.'

Ada did what I asked and came to tell me a while later that the governess was most grateful and that the new bed jacket had set her mind at rest.

2 October 1738

The baroness was here this morning. She didn't stay long, perhaps a half hour. She certainly didn't notice all the polishing and scrubbing that had kept Marie, Huib and Ada busy for three days prior to her visit. Her manservant followed behind with a basket containing two bottles of wine, some eggs, a pound of butter, a bottle of cream and a bed jacket. The governess is thrilled by it all. The baroness's visit clearly did her the world of good and Mrs Weide and Mrs Helder are still talking about it.

They made sure they were downstairs in the salon, and when the baroness was finished with the governess they invited her in to make the acquaintance of the other lodgers. I preferred to stay in my room. The governess was full of herself after having received such an honoured guest, but she doesn't know what the baroness said to the others in the salon. Apparently she thought that the governess was on her last legs and she hoped it wouldn't be a long drawn-out affair.

I just paid a visit to the governess. She was sitting up in bed supported by her cushions and her eyes seemed clearer than before. I asked if she was in pain and she said she felt much better. She pointed with pride to the gifts on the table by the bed.

I later heard from Mrs Verstegen that the baroness had also left a silver coin for some nourishing soup.

12 October 1738

Last Sunday I accompanied Mrs Weide and Mrs Helder to church. I thought it made sense, otherwise they'd likely have proclaimed me heathen because I never go.

The minister saw me sitting in the pews. After his sermon, he announced with a loud voice that Professor Van Honert from the University of Leiden had informed him that their protégé, the Captain, was making excellent progress. 'It won't be long now, my dear brothers and sisters, before you can see and hear it for yourselves. Our worthy African brother will be standing in this very spot, presiding at the services in honour of the Lord our God,' he boomed, and I thought to myself: I'll have to make sure I'm not here that day.

When we arrived back from church, the governess was sitting upright in her chair. She seemed so much better. The baroness had clearly been wrong.

14 October 1748

Landman was here today. He wanted to know why I hadn't been to the office for such a long time.

'Such a long time?' I asked. 'I was there last week.'

'That's a long time,' he lamented. 'Too long for me!'

I laughed and said I had planned to visit today, but had changed my mind because of the bad weather.

'Then it's a good thing I'm here,' he said. 'Do you have a moment for me? May I come in?'

Mrs Helder and Mrs Weide were in the salon so I invited him up to my room. It would have been impossible to talk to him in the presence of the other ladies.

He removed his wet coat in my room and took a seat on the couch. I asked Ada to bring tea.

He told me that there had been some progress in my case. The jurist from the States General had recently sent him a long list of questions, which he had fortunately been able to answer with satisfaction. I believe he actually had nothing new to say, but was just babbling on.

He then asked if I would play for him. I consented and started with a couple of church Psalms followed by a Bach cantata. I was ready to stop at that juncture but he insisted I continue: 'Please don't stop. Keep playing!' As I was playing one of my own compositions, he got up and stood behind me. Before I knew it, he was caressing my neck and back, gently at first but then his hand became firm and forceful. I stopped playing and said, 'You're disturbing my concentration.'

He helped me to my feet and kissed me, but when his kisses became more fervent I pushed him away and said calmly: 'We shouldn't be doing this. This is not right.'

'Oh, Miss Elisabeth! My desire for you is indescribable,' he said trembling.

My answer was composed: 'You mustn't feel this way, it isn't right. It will only hurt us, and many others besides. Let us be good friends and nothing more, Mr Landman, I beg you.'

He appeared to respond to my words and recover his composure: 'You are right, Miss Elisabeth. Forgive me.'

I nodded reassuringly and said: 'I believe it's time for you to go. I'm sure people will be wondering where you are.'

'Yes, of course. I hope you can excuse my behaviour!'

'How can one not excuse a gesture of love?' I replied with a smile. This appeared to cheer him immensely. He kissed my hand and whispered: 'Sweet

Miss Elisabeth, please come and visit me soon. We have so much to talk about, and I treasure our conversations more than anything.'

20 November 1738

Everyone in the house is sick, with the exception of the governess, who is clearly much improved and is crowing her head off as usual. The weather is dreadful: rain, hail, wind, mist. Mrs Verstegen was the first to succumb. She sneezed and sniffled and wandered through the house with a shawl round her neck to keep her warm. She insisted it was just a winter cold but it got worse rather than better and she finally had to spend a couple of days in bed. Mrs Weide was next, followed by Kaatje. Ada spent the entire day running from pillar to post with hot toddies and hot water bottles. Then it was my turn, with Mrs Helder in quick pursuit. When I needed Ada the most, she was unable to help as she herself had been felled by the cold. I'm now feeling much better, although still a little out of sorts. It's dark and grey and miserable outside, and it's beginning to dawn on me that I will have to endure another winter here.

I've visited Landman's office on a couple of occasions, but the last time he was at home with the cold. I scribbled a note wishing him a speedy recovery and asked the courier to deliver it to him. Soon after I was taken ill myself, the courier appeared with a thank-you note. Landman was evidently on the mend. Ada told the courier I was sick in bed and the following day a large basket of fruit arrived from Hoyer and the rest of his staff, together with a very sweet letter from Landman. Do they do this for all their sick clients?

The dreadful weather and my persistent cough continue to keep me housebound.

10 December 1738

Wonderful news! The courier arrived yesterday with a letter telling me to come to my lawyer's offices immediately. Landman met me at the door full of enthusiasm. A letter had been received from the States General fixing the date of my hearing for 5 January 1739.

'At last,' I sighed. 'One and a half years later!'

Even Mr Hoyer made an appearance to assure me my case would soon be settled. I told Landman after he had gone that my case was far from being settled. This was just the beginning.

'But my dear Miss Elisabeth,' he said. 'Have you so little faith in us? In me?'

'It's not that,' I replied. 'I just don't know what to expect from the States General.'

He gazed at me with piercing eyes. The man is in love. I can tell by the way he looks at me. He expects me to reciprocate, give in to his touch, his intimacy, but I don't want to. When he came out from behind his desk, I stood up and grabbed my shawl. Landman is a decent man, but I don't know how to deal with his feelings for me. He is my lawyer and that is what he should stay.

As I made my way home, I wondered to myself how long the hearing would last and I was once again confronted with the persistent question: what do I do if the hearing has a negative outcome. And what about Landman and his feelings? Should I get involved with him to secure my future in the event that my request is rejected? How would I feel being with a man I do not love and what would my status be: his mistress, his concubine, his wife? It would never work. My heart is in Suriname with my family and all those dear to me. I love Carl Otto. He's the man that I want and no other. Only… I hope he still wants me.

10 January 1739

Christmas and New Year have come and gone. I had not been looking forward to the festivities but they turned out to be much better than I had expected. Mrs Verstegen did her best to create a festive atmosphere here in the house, but with all the invitations I had received I was rarely present. On Christmas Day, I attended a sumptuous dinner at the Hoyers' place. Landman sat beside me at table, of course, but this time he was accompanied by his wife and I noticed her frequent glances in our direction. Yesterday I spent the evening with Mr Van Zuylen at the Théatre Français on the corner of Casuarisstraat and Schouwburgstraat. Mr Van Zuylen appeared at the house a couple of weeks ago. I was sitting at the harpsichord when Ada came in and handed me his card. When I asked what it meant, she told me that the man was in the salon and that Mrs Verstegen had asked if I would be coming downstairs. He was indeed in the salon, chatting with the ladies and quite at home. Mrs Helder and Mrs Weide were thrilled by the presence of such a respectable gentleman and they did their utmost to make him comfortable. He talked for a solid hour about this and that and complimented my playing. When he stood to leave he said that he had actually come to ask if I would accompany him to the French opera. He was barely out of the room when Mrs Helder lamented: 'Sad, eh, that poor wife of his.' Mrs Weide concurred: 'He can't have it easy himself, I imagine. What a difficult and heavy cross to bear.'

I had never heard anything about a Mrs Van Zuylen and certainly didn't have the impression that Mr Van Zuylen was weighed down by a heavy cross. I had always thought the man was a widower. The ladies said nothing about his poor wife's circumstances and I refused to reveal my ignorance of the matter. When I was alone with Mrs Verstegen a couple of days later, I asked if there was something wrong with Van Zuylen's wife and she told me that the woman had trouble with her nerves. He didn't want to send her to an infirmary and had someone in service to take care of her needs.

Mr Van Zuylen collected me yesterday evening as planned. He was as cheerful as ever and he informed me politely that it was an honour for him to spend the evening with such a beautiful and elegant lady. Apparently, he found my new hat particularly appealing.

We went to the French opera where they were performing Molière's *Le Malade Imaginair*. Van Zuylen wasn't impressed. Some of the actors were unsure of their lines and lost track now and then, but I enjoyed every minute. People stared, of course, but once the performance was underway they lost interest. What a spectacle: plenty of music, splendid costumes, gunfire right and left and illusions of every kind. I understand a little French, but at times it was incomprehensible. It mattered little, of course, since the opera itself was magnificent. Mr Van Zuylen did not behave like a pitiable old soul with a sick wife at home. He laughed heartily and downed several glasses of wine. After the performance, he wanted to ride around for a while but I insisted he take me home.

Fortunately it was a short journey. Mr Van Zuylen placed his hand on my knee as we were arriving at my lodgings. The coachman assisted me out of the carriage and Van Zuylen accompanied me to the door. I hastily shook his hand, thanked him for a wonderful evening, and disappeared inside.

I asked Landman what I should expect during the hearing and asked if I could attend one, but he was adamant that I stay at home and wait. 'Nothing happens worthy of mention,' he assured me.

I'm still waiting!

20 January 1739

It's freezing. We have had clear weather and crisp blue skies for all of four days now. The temperature is well below zero. The sharp frost is the topic of every conversation. I know it's cold but for some reason I don't mind. At least it's better than the drizzle and the biting wind. I strolled to my lawyer's office this afternoon and stopped for a while on the way to watch the ice-skaters on the Hofvijver. Cheerful people everywhere and lots of children, some of them very young, skating behind a chair; couples hand in hand gliding across the ice and a high-spirited procession of boys and girls holding onto a long pole. I had an overwhelming desire to join them, to be part of their good cheer. I felt so alone and lonely that my self-pity almost had me in tears by the time I finally reached the office.

'The Hofvijver is frozen over,' I said to Landman. 'I was watching the skaters.' My feelings must have been easy to read. The words were still fresh on my lips when Landman exclaimed: 'Miss Elisabeth, you must learn to skate. Let me teach you!'

'Oh... but I'll never manage...' I gasped.

'Why not?' Landman interrupted.

'I'm much too old for skating. Don't you have to start as a child?' I inquired.

'Not at all. Skating is for everyone no matter what their age. It's like walking, you just have to learn.'

'But I don't even have skates,' I protested, but he said he was well aware of that and promised to find me an elegant pair designed especially for ladies. 'I'll collect you tomorrow afternoon at two,' he said and he was gone. It's now one-thirty and I can hardly wait.

22 January 1739

Yesterday we went skating. It was an afternoon to remember. The main pond was busy and overcrowded. The very idea of making a fool of myself in front of all those people scared me and I said, 'I don't dare. Everyone will stare at me and laugh. I don't even know the basics!'

'Let's go to the smaller pond where it's not so busy,' said Landman. He first put on his own skates, asked me to sit on the bank and then attached the blades to my shoes. 'Try to stand up,' he said. 'Don't be afraid. I've got you.'

He took hold of me firmly. 'Now it's time to move,' he commanded. It worked, but only because he was holding me so tightly.

It wasn't as difficult as I thought. I was terrified at the start but after a while I became more and more daring and even managed a couple of strokes on my own. If I lost my balance, Landman's strong arm was there to support me. A little later we crossed arms and he guided me across the ice. I was skating, me... skating! When I realised what I was doing I was so taken aback I almost fell. After a while he brought me to a refreshments stand where I had the chance to sit and enjoy a warm drink. Landman then took to the ice on his own for a moment, whirling around in circles and loops.

He swept across the ice towards my chair, grabbed the armrest and shouted: 'Watch carefully, watch what I write!'

I watched and blushed with embarrassment. His loops and whirls spelled out: I love you!

Neither of us spoke. I sipped my hot drink and we returned to the ice, arms crossed.

It was dark when we stopped and I told him it was time for me to go home. We removed our skates and made our way to a nearby inn where they were selling hot pea soup. Landman insisted on buying me some and while we were waiting he took my hand and said: 'You said nothing when I wrote in the ice. Do you mind if I call you Elisabeth?'

'Of course not,' I replied, 'but what's your first name? You never mentioned it before?'

'Wouter,' he said with a smile, 'a typical Dutch name.'

'Thank you for a wonderful afternoon, Wouter,' I said.

'I should be thanking you,' he said. 'An afternoon I'll never forget.' He looked me in the eyes and continued: 'You did see what I wrote on the ice, didn't you?'

'Yes,' I replied, 'I saw what you wrote, but I don't know what to say. Perhaps it would be better if it were not so. It's not good and nothing good can come of it. It can only bring us… I mean it can only bring me problems and I already have enough of them.'

He nodded and stared into the distance. To conceal my unease I started to blow on the piping hot soup, which the innkeeper had served by this time.

'Do you understand how difficult it is for me?' he said all at once.

'What is difficult about it?' I replied.

'Everything,' he said, 'everything. I am responsible for your case. I want to do everything I can for you. You have to win and you shall win! But your victory is my loss. It means you will leave Amsterdam and disappear from my life forever. I live for every moment with you, for our conversations, for the couple of hours we spend together each week, for the sight of you, the sound of your voice, your eyes, your beautiful mouth, your gleaming smile. Even when you're angry and enraged you're still wonderful. I can talk to you like a man. You know so much, have such a clear understanding of things, and you know how to express yourself. Your knowledge of the law has become so extensive, it's almost as if we are colleagues. But then I look at you and see a magnificent black woman. I could never have imagined that black women could be so beautiful, so different, so desirable.'

My heart melted. What should I say? How should I respond?

'Dearest Wouter, don't do this to yourself,' I said. 'There can be nothing between us. You are a married man with a sweet wife and loving children. What am I? I don't belong here. Do your best for me, help me to win my appeal then I can leave this place. If I had to stay here for the rest of my life I would be thoroughly miserable. Surely you wouldn't want me to be unhappy.'

To soften my words, I rested my hand on his and said: 'Your tokens of love are delightful, believe me. I consider it an honour to be their recipient, but let us end it here. Your help in winning my appeal would be the worthiest token of your love. Believe me, I shall never forget you.'

We finished our soup and he brought me home. Before I went inside he took me in his arms and kissed me passionately. I gave in to him and responded to his kisses.

Have I betrayed you, Carl Otto? Should I feel guilty? No, I don't feel guilty.

28 January 1739

It's still freezing and there is ice everywhere. I was thinking of the afternoon I went skating with Wouter. I haven't seen him since then and haven't been to his office. I would love another opportunity to take to the ice. I told Mrs Verstegen that I almost had the hang of it and would like to try it a second time. She found a pair of skates in the cellar and Huib cleaned them up for me. When he brought them to me I thanked him for his kindness but said I didn't dare go out on the ice on my own. He looked at me for a second and then said coyly that he wouldn't mind accompanying me. Mrs Verstegen agreed to the idea and we headed off to the pond where Landman had given my first skating lessons. Huib did his best. He took hold of me when I was in danger of falling and we skated together, side by side, arms crossed. It wasn't the same as before, with Landman. Anyway, I had learned something new, and that's what it was all about, after all!

31 January 1739

Yesterday it started to thaw and the weather is miserable. The courier arrived with a letter from my lawyer this afternoon. Landman wants me to come to the office. He has something he wishes to discuss with me. I wonder what it's about. It's too late to go today and the weather is far too ugly. I'll go tomorrow. I hope it's good news.

2 February 1739

What a mess! I'm livid, sad and disappointed all at once. Nothing is going as planned, nothing! What a disaster!

I made my way to my lawyer's office yesterday in the best of humour. When I saw Landman, I realised immediately that he had bad news. 'What's wrong?' I asked, and he answered with hesitation that the hearings had been postponed until additional documentation arrived from Paramaribo. I could barely contain myself: 'What kind of a dirty trick is this? Are they trying to delay my appeal on purpose? Surely they had all the documents they needed!'

'I've been thinking of submitting a new request and asking them to treat the matter with urgency,' said Landman.

'What's the point?' I roared. 'I've lost all faith in those requests of yours. How many have you sent already? Has it helped? Not a bit!'

Landman didn't know what to do with himself. He put out his hand to comfort me but I was so angry I declined it and pushed him away. 'Do you have a role to play in all this? Have you been conspiring against me? Is it your fault my case has ground to a standstill?' I snarled.

He wanted to say something but I refused to listen. I charged out of the room in a rage and slammed the door behind me.

I know poor Landman doesn't deserve this, that he's doing his best and genuinely wants my case to succeed, but my anger had the best of me and that is why I said what I did.

I may have ran home in a fit of tears, I can't remember. All I know is that yet another disappointment was awaiting me.

There was post from Suriname, but nothing from Carl Otto. Masra Frederik wrote that Carl Otto had been away on a major expedition and had already been gone for six weeks. He also wrote that Izaak had passed away. Izaak was such a dear brother and I was deeply saddened by the news of his death, but then I read further. Before he died, Izaak had asked Masra Frederik and Sisa Maria to raise his daughter Bettie. She's now staying with them. Masra Frederik even had the nerve to write: 'So now we have a new little girl, playing on the rear gallery and racing along the corridor, and her name is almost the same as yours. Your sister Maria is in her element with such a little one to care for.'

Perhaps I'm being unreasonable, even jealous, but I can't help thinking: they've forgotten me, now they have Bettie. I've never felt so miserable, so alone, so lonely. I keep thinking of home and picturing them with Bettie, the little brat. How old is she now? Five or six? I don't know and I don't care. Here I am stuck in this godforsaken place and they're at home with Bettie. It's an injustice!

I hardly slept a wink last night. My thoughts were focused on one question only: what if the revision is rejected? Even if I win the case it will take an age for the States General to pronounce judgement. Everything takes forever. I've been here two years already and what have I achieved? I'm back at square one, waiting for documents to arrive from Paramaribo. No one informed me how much time the States General would need to pronounce judgement, even with all the documents at their disposal. I insist on knowing and I am determined to find out. I expect Landman to give me a clear and unambiguous answer. Masra Frederik is still my guarantor and Reijdenius is paying my bills, but did they imagine it would take so long? Probably not! What will happen to me if Masra Frederik dies while I am still here? I'm so sick and tired of thinking about it all. Will I have to spend the rest of my life here? How will I live? Perhaps I should find a husband, but how? Should I become Landman's concubine. That would be the best option. At least he loves me. But is that permitted here in Holland? I've seen no evidence of it. People who live together in Holland are all married. Poor, poor Wouter. He says he's in love but I'm sure his intentions are good. It would be wrong of me to put him in an impossible position. But who else is there? Van Zuylen? Should I put Creutz out of my mind because I fear I will never return to Suriname? I don't want to think such thoughts, but I must be realistic. I cannot simply put a stop to them. I keep coming back to the same question. What should I do? What should I do? And if I were to find a husband, would they then say that marriage between blacks and whites is against the law? If it is forbidden in Suriname, it's probably the same here.

Why had I been so unkind to Landman? He was the only person here who truly cared for me and I bit off his nose. I don't know what to think anymore. I'm too tired to think.

9 February 1739

I went to Landman's office and apologised for my discourteous behaviour the week before.

Landman blushed with embarrassment and said that he understood my anger. We had used first names with each other the afternoon we went skating, but in his office I referred to him as Mr Landman. I though it best. He showed me the request he had submitted a few days after my outburst in which he insisted once again that my case be treated with urgency. I asked how long a revision normally took but there was apparently no fixed duration and it all depended on the case in question. Some cases were settled in six months while others took years. Landman maintained that my case should have been settled in six months. 'The distance between The Hague and Paramaribo introduced delays,' he continued. 'It has taken a long time to assemble the necessary documents and there's nothing to be done about it. But I spoke recently to a fellow counsel and he assured me that the case was at an advanced stage. Once the final document is in place, a final verdict should follow without further ado.'

I looked out of the window and said nothing.

'Come, Miss Elisabeth, don't lose courage,' he said gently.

I sighed and said: 'You say the same at every turn, but I still end up waiting. What if it takes them several years more to reach a verdict? What must I do then? How shall I take care of myself if my brother-in-law should die or withdraw his guarantee? It's not impossible, is it?'

He had no answer to my question. After a moment of silence he said: 'You have no need to worry about your future. I'm still here after all. I won't abandon you. Trust me.'

'I have something else to ask,' I said. 'It is not directly related to my case,' I explained, 'it is a question about the law.' I hesitated. Was it not a strange question to ask and would Landman not think I had hidden intentions?

'What would you like to know,' he said in response to my still absent question.

'Are blacks and whites allowed to marry one another here in Holland?' I asked.

'Well naturally, why shouldn't they?' he answered, a little taken aback.

'It's not as natural as you think,' I said. 'It's against the law in Suriname.'

'There's no law in Holland to forbid it. The law makes no mention of blacks and whites. It makes sense when you realise there are few if any black people in Holland. Marriage law alludes only to men and women and says nothing about the colour of their skin. There are laws that forbid marriage between blood relatives, of course, such as a father and his daughter or a brother with his sister, but everything else is possible. Let me show you,' said Landman and he stood up to fetch a book from the bookcase.

'There is an edict in Suriname that forbids marriage between blacks and whites,' I said.

'Look for yourself,' said Landman. 'Here, this is all about marriage and there's not a word about black and white.'

'But those edicts are peculiar to Suriname,' I said.

'I understand that,' he said, 'but I'm not sure whether it's possible for an edict in Suriname to run counter to Dutch law.'

'I wonder how the government would react if a black person and a white person were to marry in Holland and then move to Suriname,' I said.

'They would have no reason to object, not the slightest,' Landman answered vehemently.

'I beg to differ,' I said. 'They would simply refuse them entry. That's their way of avoiding problems. When they don't know how to deal with someone they simply banish them from the colony. Look at me. As far as I know I'm the first black woman to be banished but not the first woman. White women in relationships with negroes have been banished often enough in the past.'

'And what happens in the meantime with the negro partner,' Landman inquired.

'The death penalty every time. Torture or decapitation, it doesn't matter as long as they're dead.'

I stood up to leave. I was content that Landman was not angry at my unpleasant outburst during my last visit. He brought me to the door, took my hand and said: 'Dearest Miss Elisabeth, don't worry too much. Have faith. I'll do my absolute best for you.' I nodded. 'Whatever happens,' he whispered, 'I will always be there for you, always.'

We gazed into each other's eyes for quite some time, then he pressed his lips to my forefinger and ran it carefully over my lips as he softly murmured: 'My dear, dear Elisabeth. I love you now and for always.' I then took his head in my hands and kissed him on the forehead.

20 April 1739

It was fine weather today, the sun shone and it was almost warm. Perfect weather for walking. I went to the Ridderzaal where I bought a couple of books, and then I just wandered around. I passed the local charity school and heard the children rattle off their lessons.

Mr Van Zuylen was waiting when I arrived home. Just like the last time, all the ladies of the house had gathered round him and were listening carefully to his every word. He had yet another invitation for me. 'Something very special,' he said. 'An invitation to a concert given by Mr Francisco Lopes de Liz.'

'Oooh,' yelped Mrs Verstegen and the governess croaked: 'Well I never! Ooh!' Mrs Helder clapped her hands and gasped: 'What a privilege!'

I understood their enthusiasm. I had often heard of Lopes de Liz, but I could never have imagined that I would be attending one of his concerts, which usually attracted only the most prominent guests.

'When is it?' I asked, feverishly trying to decide if I should purchase a new outfit for the occasion.

When Mr Van Zuylen informed me that the concert was the following day I realised a new outfit was out of the question. He apologised for the last-minute invitation. I inspected my wardrobe and decided what to wear. I can't wait!

23 April 1739

The entire house joined in the preparations. Ada helped me get dressed and Mrs Verstegen helped with my wig. I then had to pay my respects in the salon. The other ladies were so excited you would have thought they were coming with me to the concert. They circled around me, touched my dress, my hat, my wig with great delight and advised me on this and that. I was only minutes in the room when Mr Van Zuylen arrived.

The hustle and bustle on the Voorhout, where Lopes de Liz had his residence, was overwhelming. There were so many carriages they had to form a line and deliver their passengers at the entrance one after the other. Gentlemen and ladies in the most magnificent apparel stepped onto the street. Mr Van Zuylen accompanied me into the main concert hall, which is above the coach house in the garden. As we entered the room, everyone turned to look at us and the place fell silent. But then our host came towards us, took me elegantly by the arm, welcomed me with much enthusiasm and announced to the assembled guests: 'Mesdames et messieurs, voici Mademoiselle Elisabeth de Surinam.' The gentlemen bowed and some of the ladies modestly curtsied. It was so wonderful. Fortunately my black skin does not blush, but my cheeks were definitely aglow.

White ladies curtsying for the free negress Elisabeth!

Such a shame they can't see me now in Suriname.

Lopes de Liz accompanied me around the room on his arm for a few moments as Mr Van Zuylen watched and smiled. When the time had come for our host to attend to his other guests, he left me in the company of a group of ladies who immediately started to talk and ask all sorts of questions. They gasped and shrieked every now and then but paid little real attention to what I had to say.

Mr Lopes de Liz has his own orchestra led by the famous violinist Jean Marie de Clair L'Aine, and with a number of prominent musicians in its ranks. The music was beautiful and I was so grateful to Mr Van Zuylen for inviting me and allowing me this pleasure. During the intermezzos and at the end of the concert, liveried servants passed among the guests with snacks and glasses of wine.

I truly enjoyed myself and while I'm quite aware that it was a once in a lifetime experience, no one can ever take this moment away from me.

On our way back to my lodgings Van Zuylen asked what I thought of the concert. 'Wonderful, Mr Van Zuylen. Truly wonderful! I am forever in your debt.'

'Lopes de Liz is not only interested in beautiful music, he is also keen on beautiful ladies,' said Van Zuylen. 'But I suppose he can afford to with his kind of money. He keeps six mistresses, no less. You met some of them at the concert.'

'He must be very rich indeed,' I said, 'and he certainly doesn't keep it a secret. The ladies were dressed in the most expensive outfits. Do they know they share the same lover?'

'I imagine so,' he replied, 'but the man has been the subject of one scandal after the other. Did you know he had to leave Paris in '31 for inciting someone to murder a rival lover?'

'Gracious!' I exclaimed. 'Such a nice man. Is it all true or just mere gossip?'

'I think there's truth in it somewhere. They say he's a very passionate lover,' Mister Van Zuylen concluded. Perhaps he was inspired by his own story, I will never know, but at that moment he threw his arms around me and tried to kiss me. I turned my head and leaned forward to avoid his unwelcome advance and his kiss landed somewhere in mid-air. Then I inquired sweetly: 'How is your wife, Mr Van Zuylen?'

'My wife?' he snapped. 'What do you know about my wife?'

'Nothing,' I said, 'beyond her illness. I was inquiring about her health.'

At first he said nothing and stared into space in silence. After a moment he said: 'She is indeed unwell, quite unwell.'

We had arrived at my lodgings by then. I thanked him for a wonderful evening and stepped down from the carriage. He accompanied me to the door and tapped his hat with his finger: 'Goodnight, Miss Elisabeth.'

I have a feeling he won't be back for some time.

12 May 1739

Landman came by today and asked if I would like to join him for the annual May Fair. 'Are you planning to exhibit me in a tent?' I teased.

'What do you mean,' he said. I could see he hadn't understood.

'My dear Wouter, I'm sure you mean well, but I don't think it would be right for me. Imagine all those people thinking I'm some kind of fairground attraction. I'm black, Wouter, the only black woman in The Hague.'

He looked at me and said: 'But you've been surrounded by people before and it wasn't so bad.'

'True, but the May Fair public is not what I'm used to,' I said, trying to think of a reasonable excuse.

'Shall we go for a walk then?' he asked.

'Where? The Voorhout? Together? You can't be serious. What if your poor wife gets to hear of it?' I said. My question made him blush, although it wasn't my intention. Had his wife already made a remark about me? I don't want to put him in an embarrassing position at home.

'I'm just teasing,' I said with a giggle. 'But a walk is out of the question. The weather is wonderful. Why don't you join me here in the garden for a cup of tea?'

We retired to the garden where he chatted with the ladies who found him a most charming young man. They want to know all about my relationship with Landman, of course, but I'm saying nothing.

'Why don't you come to the office anymore?' Wouter asked as he was leaving.

'I have no more questions,' I replied.

'So you only came to ask questions,' he said hesitatingly.

'I came because I enjoyed talking with you. You took all my questions seriously and our conversations were always such a pleasure,' I said, 'but now...'

'Now what?' he insisted.

'I've made up my mind to wait until you have news for me. It has already taken such a long time, but when I come to the office there is never anything new to be said, never any progress, nothing.' It saddened me to speak to him this way, especially when I saw the look of disappointment on his face. He greeted me and left, downcast and dispirited.

A shame, I know, but it's the truth.

10 August 1739

It's the height of summer, my third in the Netherlands. Can I expect to spend a third winter here? God forbid! Invitations to garden parties, concerts and tea parties have continued the last couple of months, but now I've had enough. Perhaps it's the stifling weather. It's too hot to do anything! Apparently we're having a heatwave. The ladies think we have this kind of oppressive weather at home and I can't get through to them that the heat of the tropics is altogether different.

12 August 1739

It happened. The governess passed away yesterday evening. No one noticed a thing. Marie brought her breakfast this morning and found her dead in bed. She was so taken aback she almost fled the room in tears. Everyone in the house is shocked and saddened. The funeral has to be organised in a hurry because of the warm weather.

13 August 1739

We all attended the funeral. Mrs Weide was inconsolable. She probably thinks she will be next. A small reception was organised in the house after the funeral. The atmosphere in the house is still gloomy. The weather remains warm, but there's a storm on the way. I can hear thunder rumbling in the distance.

5 October 1739

The summer is over and the days are getting shorter. I am stricken with depression. If I had my way I would take to my bed and sleep forever. Even the letters from Suriname leave me cold. They're full of stories about Bettie. I haven't the slightest interest in the child. Let them get on with it. I still receive letters from Carl Otto, but they're nothing but reports of his jungle expeditions and they don't interest me either. I sometimes play the harpsichord. Every morning when I wake I ask myself: How long? How many more mornings must I wake in The Hague? How many?

1 November 1739

The good Lord be praised! The States General has reached its verdict. I am innocent! The words are music to my ears. The verdict of 25 April 1737 has been declared null and void! I am innocent and I can return to Suriname. The stains on the page are from the tears I cannot restrain. I am free again!

The courier arrived this morning with the message that I was expected at Hoyer's office without delay. I told him I would be there the following day but the man just looked at me and said: 'Mr Hoyer and Mr Landman are expecting you immediately.' I understood the seriousness of the situation and was at the office in an hour.

Landman was already waiting by the door. He threw his arms around me and whispered full of emotion: 'You've won, Elisabeth, you've won.' I was too taken aback to respond. At that moment, Hoyer appeared, took both my hands and offered his congratulations as the courier presented me with an enormous bouquet of flowers. I was still completely lost for words when Landman held the letter from the States General in front of my face and pointed to the text: 'Verdict delivered by Van Meel on 25 April 1737 declared null and void.'

I stayed at the office until midday, enjoying the party atmosphere. We first had coffee and cake and then liqueurs were served.

We talked about the next step in the process. I said that I wanted to return home as quickly as possible. Landman promised to write to Reijdenius without delay and have him reserve a place for me on the first ship leaving for Suriname.

I thanked Mr Hoyer, who laughed and said that Landman deserved all the credit. I told him I agreed and thanked Landman for all he had done. I even gave Landman a kiss in front of Mr Hoyer, who watched the poor man's awkward embarrassment with amusement. Landman brought me home and stayed for a while to chat with the ladies, who now realise that I have concluded my business in Holland and will be leaving them in the near future.

Such beautiful words: I'm going home!

5 November 1739

I've calmed down a little after the first flush of victory. I was so lost in my thoughts last night I barely slept a wink. True, I'm going home, but what then? Nothing has changed in Suriname. I'll be the same old free negress Elisabeth again, still expected to be unassuming and subservient because she's black. Van Meel is still there, and others of his sort. Almost every white has it in him to be a Van Meel. How will they receive me, how will they treat me? Isn't there a danger they'll look for some other way to hurt me now that I've won my case? I'm sure of it. They'll find a way without my help. Should I try to blend in, be modest and retiring? If I don't, if I'm not sakafasi, they'll use it against me. In Holland I am an exile, but what am I in Suriname? Officially, I am free, but because I am black, I am not free to be the person I want to be. The colour of my skin makes me a prisoner, imprisoned for being black. I am a prisoner of colour!

Dear God, what must a person do to live a normal life?

How will my family react to my return? Will they be happy? Of course they will, but what will my life be like? Will I live with Sisa Maria and Masra Frederik as before? Will I have to stand and watch day by day as little Bettie becomes a second Elisabeth for them to spoil? I don't even think there will be room for me in the house. I am a grown-up woman with a life of my own. I can't live there any longer. I have to find my own home, live by myself.

How will I find Carl Otto? Is he still waiting for me? Is he expecting me? Does he still want me? Do I still want him?

I once said that I wanted to marry in church before I lived with a man, but I now realise the impossibility of such a dream. Everyone would see it as an act of pride, evidence that the negress does not know her place. I am a negress after all, and in Suriname blacks and whites are not allowed to marry. Would I be allowed a church wedding if I chose a negro husband? But is there a negro I would want to marry?

Good, I'm going back to Suriname but I refuse to be sakafasi to anyone. Money goes a long way among the whites. I will need money. If Masra Frederik's money had not been available I would never had been able to call for a revision. I have to pay him back, which means I will have to earn a great deal. I must set my mind on it, on becoming rich and the talk of Suriname. I'll show those white colonists what I'm worth. The free negress Elisabeth will be a woman of substance, a woman to be reckoned with! Hollanders say: Money counts!

Elisabeth shall have money and Elisabeth shall count!

15 November 1739

I have spent the last week purchasing supplies and arranging for further requisitions to be sent to Suriname on my return. Several suppliers on Hoogstraat have agreed to do business with me. I leave tomorrow for Amsterdam and expect to embark early next week for my return journey to Suriname.

We have been packing for a number of days already. When I say 'we' I mean Ada, assisted from time to time by Huib. I wanted to help but Ada insisted: 'Let me take care of it, miss?' She's right, of course. What do I know about packing?

I'm taking everything with me: my clothes, my hats, my books and other documents purchased over the years at the market in the Ridderzaal, a huge pile of 's Gravenhaege Courant, and naturally my harpsichord. While she was packing, Ada said unexpectedly: 'I'm going to miss you. I had hoped you would stay longer, but now I'll have to look for other work. It's a shame. I was happy here.'

'What about staying in service here with Mrs Verstegen?' I asked.

'With your rooms empty and the governess gone, Mrs Verstegen can't afford to keep me on.'

I spoke to Mrs Verstegen about Ada later that day. She also found it a pity that she had to let her go. I arranged for her to stay until the end of the year. Perhaps Mrs Verstegen will find new lodgers by then. Mrs Verstegen asked if I would like a memento of the governess. Her room had been cleared of the few possessions she had: completely worn-out clothing, a hand mirror Mrs Verstegen intends to keep for herself, a chamber pot, a candlestick and two silver snuffers. I chose a snuffer.

As I look round my room it seems so bare and empty. Everything has been packed and the chests have already been brought to the barge. All I have is a small travelling bag with the things I need for the journey. Tonight will be the last night I sleep in this room. I have to admit my time here was not an unhappy one, but what does the future hold?

Wouter Landman will be collecting me tomorrow morning. Poor Wouter, I shall miss him. I have a gift for him: an elegant silver watch with his name and 'With gratitude, Elisabeth' engraved inside.

I'll give it to him tomorrow when I step onto the barge at the Spui. Farewell room, farewell house, farewell fellow lodgers, farewell land of my exile.

Amsterdam, 19 November 1739

I arrived in Amsterdam two days ago and I embark tomorrow on my journey back to Suriname. I had a long talk with Reijdenius's son, informing him that I plan to order supplies on a regular basis in the future.

My departure from The Hague touched me more than I had expected. In spite of the early hour, Mrs Verstegen and the other lodgers were all present to say goodbye and offer their best wishes.

Wouter Landman collected me. He was agitated and appeared to be shivering although it was far from cold. He was conspicuously silent in the carriage. I was also lost for words, so I took hold of his arm and held it tightly as we made our way across The Hague in the early light of dawn. I said to myself again and again: this is the last time. Just before we arrived at the Spui, I produced the watch and gave it to Landman, but he didn't get the chance to look at it until it was time to get out of the carriage.

We made our way to the first class compartment of the tow barge where he made sure I was settled in and had everything with me. He then took the box from his pocket and opened it.

'Oh, Elisabeth,' he said gently when he saw the watch. The other passengers were wide-eyed with curiosity. People have stared at me since the moment I arrived in Holland and I had grown accustomed to it, but this time I detested their stares. I wanted to be alone if only for a moment with Wouter.

I stood up and said ostentatiously: 'Come, let's go outside,' and I hurried outside with Wouter close behind.

'What are you doing? The barge will be leaving shortly,' he spluttered.

'I don't want to say goodbye with the population of The Hague staring at me,' I whispered. Our carriage was still parked by the quay. 'Do you mind?' Wouter asked the driver. He nodded understandingly and we stepped inside.

The carriage at least provided protection from all those peering eyes. I took the watch from Wouter's hand and removed it from its box.

'Read this,' I said and pointed to the inscription, but it was too dark to read the letters. 'I had your name inscribed, followed by "With gratitude, Elisabeth",' I whispered. 'From the bottom of my heart, dear Wouter, thank you for everything. I shall miss you. I shall think of you always and be forever in your debt.'

'My dear Elisabeth,' he said, and I detected a sniffle in his voice. I couldn't see his face in the dark, but I ran my fingers slowly over his cheeks.

Then we kissed... a long heartfelt kiss. I stepped out of the carriage and hurried back to the barge. He followed me, but with tears in my eyes I shouted: 'No, Wouter, the barge is about to leave.'

As soon as I was onboard, the departure signal was sounded. Wouter Landman stood on the quay. We waved to one another. He stood there for a long time. I went inside and whispered: 'Farewell, dear Wouter, farewell.'

Here ends my diary and the written chronicle of my time in Holland. I no longer need to write. Perhaps I shall start a new diary in Suriname. Time will tell.

Elisabeth Samson

PART THREE

Elisabeth Samson & Carl Otto Creutz

1 December 1750

Elisabeth sat in her carriage as it lumbered, creaked and squeaked its way along Heerenstraat. She inhaled the scent of the orange blossoms planted along both sides of the street and brushed a couple of tiny white flowers from her blue dress.

Men and women, the occasional couple, all of them followed by groups of male and female slaves, were making their way to the Dutch Reformed Church on the other side of Oranjetuin cemetery. All the slaves were well-dressed; the women in starched and colourful baggy dresses, short smock jackets, ankle bands, bracelets and brightly coloured necklaces, the men in trousers and short jackets, the indispensable Sunday hat, but none of them wore shoes. They held parasols on long poles above their masters' and mistresses' heads and carried trays with prayer books wrapped in gold braided velvet on the palms of their hands. A few of the slaves held hands with a white or light brown child or carried such a child on their arm.

Although Elisabeth's house was not far from the church, she always took her carriage. She passed the procession of people and nodded on occasion when someone greeted her. The carriage stopped in front of the church, a large white wooden construction in which the Police Council and the Council of Criminal Justice met during the week on the ground floor and church services were held on the upper floor on Sundays. It was the custom to have services in the morning in Dutch and in the afternoon in French, but on this occasion, the Walloon minister, Duvoisin, was presiding at the morning service because the Reverend IJver was sick in bed.

Elisabeth stepped down from her carriage, assisted by Present and Venis who had followed on foot. Venis made slight adjustments to her mistress's dress and presented her with a silver tray bearing a prayer book wrapped in purple velvet. Venis also tried to brush a lock of hair from her mistress's wig out of sight, but Elisabeth stopped her and muttered: 'Leave it.'

She slowly ascended the stairs and entered the church. A number of heads turned in her direction. Her own head lifted and her back straight, she made her way through the room and took a seat to the right of the pulpit where pews had been reserved for unmarried and free 'housekeepers of colour'.

As she passed the pews reserved for married white women, the wives and/ or widows of council members and rich plantation owners – Audra, Couderc, Cellier, Rayneval, Schipper and so forth – coughed and murmured and she clearly heard someone say: 'Put her in a blond wig and she thinks she's white!'

Elisabeth peered at the woman from the corner of her eye. It was Mrs Audra, of course, who evidently could not stand the idea that the free negress Elisabeth was wearing the latest fashion while her own wig was worn out and constantly shedding blond hairs on her clothing. Elisabeth sat beside her sister Catharina who shifted along the pew a little and said: 'Nanette isn't coming today. She's still at Lankmoedigheid.'

Elisabeth nodded, leaned forward and raised her hand to greet her niece Johanna and the other ladies in the pew. She then whispered in the neck of her niece Bettie sitting in front of her: 'How is little Suusje? Is she better?'

'Yes, thank you,' Bettie whispered back, turning slightly in her place.

Elisabeth looked at her sister Maria who was sitting with the married women and widows on the very back row, next to a few mulattas. They exchanged glances and nodded.

Catharina was about to say something, but she stopped when she heard a kafuffle by the door and men's voices. The governor entered the church followed by the members of both councils and the members of the commission that had arrived from Holland a couple of days earlier, all of them in full regalia. The head of the commission, Baron Von Sporche, scrutinised the assembled congregation before taking his seat on the front row next to the governor.

The minister appeared seconds later and the service started. He raised both his hands and launched into a lengthy prayer, his words resounding through the church. He then wished everyone a warm welcome in French and the congregation sang the first hymn.

Elisabeth's thoughts were elsewhere. Had Venis gone home? She had said nothing on this occasion, but her slaves knew that Misi Elisabeth did not like them hanging around the church and chatting with others during the service. She would also have to speak to Nestor and have him check the carriage. Its creaking and squeaking irritated her.

The minister moved on to the scripture reading, which was about discord. He read from the Bible with a bellowing voice and mispronounced several of the words. It was difficult to understand him. More discord, Elisabeth thought, and she asked herself if the eternal bickering between the governor, the councillors and the planters would ever come to an end. Let them get on with it, she shrugged. The authoritarian Governor Mauricius behaved as if he was the King of Suriname, and according to Creutz he referred to his adversaries – the councillors and rich planters – as 'the cabal'. Everyone knew why the commission, under Baron Von Sporche's leadership, had come to Suriname: the direct result of the three chests of complaints against the governor accompanied to Holland by Salomon Duplessis on the instructions of 'the cabal'. The cabal had presumed that the governor would be withdrawn after Duplessis started court proceedings against him in Holland, but they were mistaken. The Directors of the Suriname Society had now sent a commission to investigate the matter at first hand. Would the commission be able to do their job? They had only been in the colony three days and had already attended enormous parties thrown on their behalf by the Couderc and Audra families and another by Pichot and widow Anna Du Four.

The organ introduced 'The Lord's My Shepherd' and the congregation joined in. The sermon followed, in which the minister continued on the theme of discord. He waxed lyrical in a resonant voice and strong French accent about the magnificence of the colony that had been granted us by God and about our responsibility to maintain its beauty, goodness and above all liveability. Discord should make way for the more superior goal of making use of the riches God had given us and preserving them for generations to come.

Elisabeth had stopped listening. She was thinking of Carl Otto, who had been away for four long weeks. How much longer? she thought. As long as he did not return ill. Suddenly Catharina nudged her in the side.

'Are you listening?' she whispered.

Elisabeth listened carefully. What was the man talking about?

Well, well! He was lamenting the depraved existence of the free coloured population. According to the minister, it was time to put an end to it once and for all. The man had a nerve. Long before he married widow Audra he had been spending five nights out of seven in her bed. It was a public secret! And he dared to stand in the chancel and point the finger!

The Reverend Duvoisin proclaimed that the large number of black people with money, fashionable clothes and fine houses was becoming a threat to the colony. 'They are not afraid to appear in the most expensive silks and velvets, parading the most magnificent wigs and putting on airs and graces of which they are unworthy. Wanton whores, is what they are,' he ranted, 'barred from the sacrament of marriage!'

Elisabeth snorted with indignation. She looked at her sister who looked back at her and mocked: 'Are you paying attention?' The other women were straight-faced and motionless.

'What a hypocrite,' Elisabeth whispered.

"Hush, calm yourself!' Catharina hissed.

True, Elisabeth thought, we don't have access to the sacrament of marriage, but it's only because you forbid it. She saw herself as a young girl insisting to Carl Otto: 'Not yet. I want to marry first, a real marriage, in church.' Her dream had never come true. When she returned from exile, it seemed better not to provoke the authorities. An application to the Commissioners for Marital Affairs for permission to marry would have been provocation. According to the authorities, marriage between blacks and whites was forbidden by edict. And the minister had the gall to preach about wanton behaviour!

The people around her coughed and shuffled. The minister had finished his sermon and the ushers were passing through the church with black velvet bags on long poles. Purses clicked and coins jingled. After the collection, the congregation sang two more hymns and then the minister raised his hands once again, offered the final prayer and blessed the congregation.

The service was over. The governor, the councillors and the members of the commission made their way outside followed by the married ladies. The housekeepers were last. At the bottom of the stairs, a number of the commission members stood in the doorway in conversation with the Reverend Duvoisin. The governor and his wife had immediately stepped into their carriage and were already on their way by the time Elisabeth had left the church.

She noticed that Nestor had been unable to station the carriage close to the church because those of Baron Von Wangenheim, Couderc and Cellier had forced him out of the way. She watched as the Coudercs' slave lifted their son and daughter into the carriage. Their parents were still talking with Duvoisin at the door of the church and the children had to wait. 'Come on, mama!' the boy shouted, while a slave girl popped a sugar comforter into the girl's mouth to stop her whining.

Nestor raised his lash in the distance to indicate where he and the others were waiting. She hesitated: what should she do? Wait or walk over to them? She looked around to see where Catharina had gone and noticed her disappear around the corner of Keizerstraat. Elisabeth made her way over to the carriage. Present and Venis were standing beside it. She placed her prayer book on Venis's tray and took her place inside assisted by Present. She still had to wait, since access to Wagenstraat was blocked by carriages.

'Where is the parasol?' she asked Venis, who confessed with a start that she had forgotten to bring it. 'Send Pietje home to fetch it,' she commanded. Present beckoned the futuboi, who was larking around with another futuboi behind the carriage. 'Hurry home and fetch the parasol and don't dawdle!' he shouted.

By the time Pietje had returned with the parasol ten minutes later, the carriage was already halfway along Wagenstraat.

Elisabeth had Amarante and Dido undress her in her bedroom and ordered Sara to bring a bowl of cold water and sponge down her face and breasts. Dressed in nothing more than a white sleeveless cotton shirt, Elisabeth lay down on her bed. Dido and Sara each took their place on a low bench either side of the bed and wafted cool air over their mistress with huge Indian fans. When their mistress had fallen asleep, the girls quietly left the room.

Elisabeth woke an hour later. She got up, draped herself in a cotton cape and made her way to the dining room. Amarante was sitting on a bench in the gallery and immediately gave a sign to the koekerom. Dido and Sara appeared with plates of meat, vegetables, bananas, sweet potatoes and local relishes. They served their mistress, who exchanged a word now and then with Amarante.

After the meal, Elisabeth sat at her writing desk in the main room. There were lists to inspect but she wasn't in the mood. She stood, made her way to the front room and took her place at the harpsichord. It had been a long time since she had played and her fingers were stiff. She rubbed her hands together, stretched her fingers and hesitatingly started to play. Her fingers loosened after a few moments and she played for the best part of an hour, only to stop, startled by the sudden appearance of Catharina at her side.

Elisabeth closed the harpsichord keyboard and said: 'You were in a hurry this morning. We didn't get the chance to talk.'

'That's why I'm here now,' Catharina replied. 'Have you any idea when the men will be back?'

'No, none at all. But it's about time, don't you think. They've been gone for four weeks already,' said Elisabeth.

'Willem will probably be sick again,' said Catharina. 'Those expeditions! All that fuss, and for nothing!'

'I wouldn't say that,' Elisabeth insisted. 'Carl Otto managed to make his mark. Mauricius awarded him a silver water jug and he was granted land a couple of months ago to set up a plantation.'

'San, granman is generous! And where is the land? Te yanawe, no doubt.'

'No, quite close. Next to Belwaarde, granman's plantation.'

'Rumour has it that granman is furious. He stormed out of church this morning in a rage,' Catharina reported.

'Is that why they left so quickly? And what's making him so angry?' Elisabeth inquired.

'Well, apparently he had been counting on the commission to join him at the palace for a meal after church, but the commissioners went instead with Mrs Audra who had organised something special in their honour.'

Sara and Dido brought refreshments and cake and the sisters indulged themselves and chatted further.

'I'm going to get dressed,' said Elisabeth a while later. She disappeared into her bedroom and instructed Venis to fetch a silk house dress from the wardrobe. She had just finished dressing when she heard Catharina and Amarante talking with someone. She made her way to the main room and realised it was Maria.

'Oh, Sisa Maria, what a pleasant surprise.'

'I've just come from Bettie,' said Maria. 'She's unwell. Mina came to tell me about it, and you know Bettie, she just has to have her Aunt Maria by her side for every little ache and pain.'

'But she seemed fine this morning in church,' said Elisabeth surprised. Amarante asked: 'Misi Maria, what's wrong with Misi Bettie?'

'Oh, it's nothing really, all perfectly normal and healthy,' Maria laughed.

'Is it that already?' said Catharina. 'Our little Loseke doesn't waste any time.'

'What is it then?' Elisabeth asked, unable to understand what her sisters were talking about.

'She's pregnant,' said Maria in a secretive tone.

'What! Already? But Susanna is barely a year old,' Elisabeth exclaimed.

'Anything's possible,' Catharina laughed.

'Ai, that Miss Bettie,' Amarante shrieked. 'But it's a good thing. A woman should have children when she's young and healthy.'

'When is she due?' Catharina asked.

'Oh, it's early days yet,' said Maria. 'But she's already having moments of dizziness and morning sickness.'

'Then it's a boy,' said Amarante.

'That's what they say, but I'm not convinced. Some women have terrible morning sickness and others don't,' said Maria.

'I know women who were dizzy and sick for the entire nine months,' said Catharina, and she told them all about the daughter of a girlfriend who was almost emaciated by the end of her pregnancy.

Elisabeth was lost in thought and was no longer listening.

Catharina and Maria continued to chat for quite some time, with the occasional word from Amarante. Their slaves relaxed on the rear porch with Venis, Dido and Sara. Elisabeth was in a world of her own and did not participate in her sisters' conversation.

'It's getting dark. I'd better be getting home,' said Catharina. She and Maria stood and said farewell to their sister. When the slaves on the rear porch heard this, they quickly finished the leftover cake Sara and Dido had brought from the kitchen.

After her sisters had left, Elisabeth stood by the window and gazed at the sky and the setting sun. She followed a bank of clouds for a while and watched the ever changing colour of the sky. She did not even notice that Firans, the slave in charge of the lamps, had come inside and lit clusters of candles on the wall in the main room and front room. Amarante's voice startled her when she came to ask what her mistress would like to eat

'To eat? Nothing thanks, Amarante, nothing at all,' said Elisabeth

'Nothing?' Amarante asked.

'Nothing,' said Elisabeth. 'I'm not hungry.'

'Something to drink then?' asked Amarante.

'No, nothing to drink,' said Elisabeth, shaking her head.

'Ke misi, drink something,' Amarante persisted.

'Fine then, a cup of cocoa,' Elisabeth sighed.

She looked around the room and thought: why am I so dissatisfied? I have everything I want. 'Sara,' she shouted.

Sara came running. 'Yes, misi?'

'Find Firans and tell him to light the chandeliers.'

'The chandeliers? Is misi expecting a visitor?' asked Sara.

'No, there's no visitor,' Elisabeth replied. Sara wanted to say something but Amarante nudged her and said: 'Don't ask so many questions, child. Do what misi tells you.'

Sara left the room and returned a moment later with Firans.

'Which chandelier, misi?' asked Firans.

'All of them, light them all,' said Elisabeth.

Firans said nothing. He looked sideways at Amarante and fleetingly raised his eyebrow. This was something new. Why did misi want to light the huge crystal chandeliers, each with fifty candles, which were reserved for parties or card evenings?

Half an hour later, the entire house was bathed in light. Elisabeth had finished her cocoa in the meantime and she said to Amarante: 'The girls can go to bed now. I don't need them any more.'

Dido, Sara and Venis stood by the door and shouted: 'Guneti, misi.' Amarante took her usual place on the rear gallery.

Elisabeth sat for some time at the table in the main room. She then got to her feet, made her way over to the window and looked outside. The moon was almost full. 'Waxing moon,' she whispered, shaking her head. She touched the pink silk curtain, tied back and lifted by a red velvet ribbon, and walked to the middle of the room. She paused at length by the table and soothingly caressed its polished wooden surface before making her way to the display cabinet where she gazed at the crystal glasses and Japanese porcelain. There were so many cups and saucers, she lost count every time she tried to tally them. She opened a drawer in the sideboard and looked at the silverware elegantly engraved with an E and an S.

She then made her way to the front room, stood for a while beside the grandfather clock and her harpsichord, and gazed at the paintings on the wall. She sat down on one of the settees with a deep sigh.

'I have everything,' she said out loud. 'Plantation Toevlught, Plantation Welgemoed, Woodland Onverwacht, La Solitude. I have much more than all the others. There's not a single black woman or white woman for that matter who can boast as much as I. I am rich! I shouldn't be dissatisfied, not even slightly. I don't have the right! And Carl Otto. I mustn't forget my darling Carl Otto, who loves me so much.'

Amarante shuffled restlessly from side to side on her bench on the rear gallery. Did misi call her? 'Yes, misi,' she shouted and hurried to the front room. Standing in the doorway, she saw Elisabeth sitting on the settee in a room ablaze with light. What was the matter with misi? Why was she acting so strangely? 'What can I get you, misi?' Amarante asked.

Elisabeth looked up. 'Nothing,' she said.

'Didn't misi call?' Amarante asked.

'No, it's nothing,' Elisabeth answered and Amarante returned to her bench on the rear gallery.

It was nine o'clock when Elisabeth said to Amarante: 'Tell Firans he can put out the chandeliers and the rest of the candles.' She went to her bedroom and could hear Amarante and Firans talking. In a few moments the house was dark. Before retiring to her mat on the rear gallery, Amarante paused at her mistress's bedroom door. 'Does misi need any help?'

Elisabeth answered from behind the door: 'No, Amarante, you can go to sleep now.'

'Guneti, misi,' said Amarante.

'Guneti,' Elisabeth answered gently. She lay on her bed and gazed into the darkness, long into the night.

She had so much, but she didn't have the very thing she wanted the most. A child.

2 January 1751

New Year had come and gone. What a celebration; endless eating and dancing, fireworks everywhere. Carl Otto was asleep.

Elisabeth was not in the best of humour. What a performance! Carl Otto had had too much to drink. Hardly surprising with all the parties at the palace and elsewhere. Everyone had been doing their best to please the commission members, the governor as well as his adversaries, the one trying to outdo the other. On Christmas Day and New Year's Day, the governor organised elaborate dinners for the commission. Mauricius felt the dining room at the palace was too small and used the largest house in the colony for the purpose, which belonged to his son Pieter and was located on Gravenstraat. It was important that the gentlemen of the commission be left with a good impression.

The governor's wealthy adversaries were of a similar mind, organising sumptuous dinners and elegant balls at every opportunity. Mrs Audra gave a New Year ball and invited the entire commission. It lasted into the early hours of the morning. The Scherpings, the Celliers, the Coudercs, the Brouwers, the Reynevals, each of them had organised a dinner followed by a ball at some stage in the preceding weeks or were planning to do so in the weeks ahead.

Who would win the day? The governor or the cabal? Elisabeth was not interested. If she had had her way, however, Carl Otto would not have been involved.

But it appeared that Mauricius could not do without his friends Creutz and Loseke. He sought their advice on everything.

Creutz is in demand once again, Elisabeth grumbled as she looked outside and saw Pedro cleaning and polishing the carriage. I would have seen more of him if he had gone on an expedition into the jungle instead.

Carl Otto called from the bedroom and Elisabeth made her way to the door: 'So you're finally awake!'

'Oh, my head,' the man groaned. 'Water, lots of water.'

Moments later futuboi Pietje brought a pitcher of cold water.

Elisabeth had asked Venis in the meantime to make hot coffee for the master and she and Dido had set the breakfast table. Dressed in thin cotton pyjama trousers and a long shirt, Carl Otto emerged from the bedroom, twisted his moustache, shook his head, ran his fingers through his hair and took his place at the table with a loud yawn. Dido poured his coffee and asked if masra would like eggs and bacon.

'Bring whatever you want,' Carl Otto growled, and he called Elisabeth: 'Babetchen, liebchen, come here.'

'What's all this?' said Elisabeth as she entered the dining room.

'Come sit with me, mi gudu. Don't I at least deserve a good morning kiss?'

She intended to sit on a chair by the table, but he grabbed her and pulled her towards him. 'Come, mi gudu, be nice to me. Ooh, I feel awful. My head!'

'One too many, of course,' said Elisabeth. Standing beside his chair with his arm around her waist, she soothingly stroked his hair. 'Look at the state of you! Nestor will have to give you a shave later. Do you have to go out today?' she asked.

'I don't have to do anything. I'm invited to Bueno de Mesquita's place but I'm not going. I'm tired. All those parties and all that food and drink aren't good for a man. I need a rest.'

He ran his hand over her breasts and smiled at her: 'Let's rest together, just you and me, eh mi gudu? There's only one thing I want and that's to snuggle up next to you in bed. Let's rest together, all day long. What do you say?'

'Foolish boy. Oh alright then,' she said with a smile.

Venis arrived with a covered plate and placed it on the table. Elisabeth pulled herself free of Carl Otto's embrace and said: 'Come, time to eat.'

March 1751

The colony had never before witnessed so many meetings. One discussion followed the other and they were all about the same topic: discord between the governor and the colonists. It became almost impossible for those who wished to remain neutral, since both sides of the debate did their best to win them over.

'Another meeting or another party?' Elisabeth would yell at times when she saw Carl Otto getting ready to go out.

'I'll be happy when this hullabaloo is all over,' Carl Otto grumbled. 'The governor's expecting me later. The man is looking for help wherever he can get it. He doesn't dare speak or act without seeking advice from me or from Loseke. Commandant Crommelin is at the front of it. The governor can't get enough of the man's opinion. He hasn't been to see his family on Plantation Rust en Werk for at least two weeks.'

'Where will it end?' asked Elisabeth.

'I've no idea, but if I were Mauricius, I would have taken the honourable way out and resigned. He had another major argument with Mrs Audra only last week.'

'You mean Mrs Duvoisin,' Elisabeth insisted. The woman had married Reverend Duvoisin three years earlier and this was her fifth marriage, but for some reason people continued to refer to her as Mrs Audra, after her fourth husband.

'Yes, of course, right, you know who I mean,' said Carl Otto impatiently. 'Apparently soldiers have been crossing her plantation. Her watchman fired at them and she made it clear to the governor that she would have their legs shot off if she caught them again.' Granman was furious and ranted that anyone who didn't know better would think that she was the governess and he the minister's wife. It was time he taught the man-eating Samaritan hussy a lesson.[15]

Elisabeth laughed. 'He's right!'

'Do you know what? We have to put up with this drivel day in day out and I'm sick of it. I wonder what it'll be today? And the cabal does nothing but celebrate. They're convinced they're going to win their case against Mauricius and that he'll be forced to leave in disgrace. What a fuss!'

Carl Otto was still grumbling when he climbed into his carriage and drove away as Elisabeth looked on.

Would Mauricius really leave? Elisabeth wondered. Better sooner than later if it were up to her. Not that she favoured the cabal, far from it. She had nothing to do with the cabal, but Mauricius was a terrible man. His own opinion reigned supreme and he was blind to the opinion of others. The nonsense Carl Otto had to put up with about their relationship. And then there was Samuel Loseke. Brought to the colony five years ago because he and Mauricius were 'family'. When the man moved in with her niece Bettie, the governor was livid and took it as a personal affront. So many white men lived with black women that it had become more the exception than the rule for a white bachelor to be alone, but Mauricius refused to tolerate the custom.

A year earlier, the slaves on Plantation Bethlehem attacked and killed the owner, Amand Thoma, because he was sharing his bed with a slave called Eva who was actually the wife of Corridon, one of his slaves. The killers led the other slaves into the jungle, but they were finally caught, and Corridon and his accomplices were brutally punished, hanged by the ribs from a meat hook. Mauricius had triumphantly proclaimed that such instances simply served to prove his point. This was what happened when plantation owners and directors reduced themselves to the level of riff-raff with that black scum, when white men lived in sin with whores, with black and red heathens.[16]

And I'm one of them, Elisabeth thought to herself. He can go to hell for all I care. 'Kis'en moi!' she barked.

1 June 1751

It was raining, and it had been raining for two days. It was as if the house was shrouded by a grey curtain. The little children who normally ran around naked, all had runny noses and coughs. Misi insisted they wear a shirt and ordered Tutuba to prepare calabash syrup. Everyone with a cough had to swallow a spoonful once a day in the koekerom.

Carl Otto was sick and was bothered with a tight chest, a cough and a fever. Hardly a surprise, Elisabeth thought, since he had had to stand for hours in the rain a couple of days ago when Mauricius left the colony. Fortunately, he was now safe in his bed and didn't have to leave for one or other meaningless expedition.

Mauricius's downfall was quite spectacular and he was forced to leave in dishonour. Enough petitions had been lodged with the commission against the governor to fill a couple of chests. They decided that it was better for the governor to leave because the gulf between him and the planters was too wide. They made their decision public in April and Mauricius had listened unmoved.

He later told Creutz and Loseke that the commission had spent too much time being entertained by the cabal to make an objective decision. Mauricius and his family boarded ship a couple of days ago and left the colony. He planned to take his case further in Holland, but according to the cabal, the planters had already won. From the moment the decision became public, a party spirit engulfed the city. A ball was organised somewhere almost every day and the commission members never missed an opportunity to feast. According to Dido and Sara, Mrs Duplessis had given a sumptuous dinner followed by a ball the day before yesterday and Etienne Couderc, the husband of Mrs Audra's daughter Henriette de Cheusses, was planning a celebration that evening. The house in Gravenstraat had been decorated and made ready and all the slave women were busy cooking and baking. Dido talked about a new game that was all the rage at such parties: Mr and Mrs Tyrant. The guests would try to outdo one another impersonating Mauricius and his wife and choke themselves laughing at their own jokes.

Elisabeth was looking forward to a more restful period.

I also hope they put an end to the jungle expeditions, she thought. She wanted to go to Clevia and see what progress had been made on the plantation. Would the director's residence be ready? Carl Otto had to come with her. He may have insisted he wasn't the plantation type and that she should take care of everything as she saw fit, but he still had to come with her. It was also his plantation after all. The thousand acres of land were his contribution. Although she took care of the money and the slaves, Plantation Clevia was registered under the name Carl Otto Creutz. She would try to make it pleasant for him, organise a party with his friends. She would take care of it as soon as he was better; a huge party on Clevia, the new plantation.

'Misi Elisabeth, Misi Elisabeth,' someone shouted by the door.

Amarante rushed into the dining room. 'Come misi! Misi Maria's Afi is here. Bettie's time has come.'

Elisabeth ran to the door where the woman was waiting outside on the stairs surrounded by Dido, Sara and Venis.

'What is it?' Elisabeth asked Afi, who was breathlessly trying to say something to the other slaves.

'I don't know, misi, the baby hasn't been born yet. Misi Maria just sent me to keep misi posted,' said Afi.

'Good, and you've done what she asked. When the child is born come and tell us what it is. Bye Afi,' Elisabeth quipped.

'Bye misi,' said Afi and she descended the stairs, watched by a trio of disappointed slave girls who had wanted to hear the rest of the story.

Elisabeth returned to the main room and sat at her writing desk, but she did not work. She stared into space with a quill in her hand. Bettie is having a baby. A second child. It's so unfair, unjust. Why Bettie and not me? Bettie, Bettie, Bettie. From the moment the girl was born, Elisabeth had had the feeling the child would oust her from her place. And that is precisely what happened. First it was imperative that the child live with Sisa Maria and Masra Frederik when she was in exile in Holland. Just like her Aunt Elisabeth, the girl now had a white companion. But Bettie had been blessed with children and Elisabeth had none.

Elisabeth had done everything in her power to get pregnant. She had been working on it for at least ten years. When she and Carl Otto first set up house together, she thought pregnancy would be a matter of course, but when her thirtieth birthday was closing in and she still wasn't pregnant, Sisa Maria advised her to give nature a helping hand. Elisabeth drank bitters and had her belly massaged for a whole year, because old Za-za was worried her insides might not be sitting as they should. It didn't help. By this time, Amarante got it into her head that her mistress should drink moeroe, but she didn't know anyone who could make it. It later transpired that Tutuba, the cook, had heard of an elderly field negress living on Plantation Saltzhallen who knew all about herbs. While Carl Otto was away on a jungle expedition, Elisabeth spent three weeks at Saltzhallen together with Sisa Maria, Amarante, Venis and Tutuba, and tried everything imaginable. Dressed only in a pagni, an old man gave her three wasis, after which she was brought into the bush where she had to make an offering to mamaisa. Then the moeroe-drinking ritual commenced. Every day at the same time and in the same place, she had to drink a murky concoction of various herbs, molasses and alcohol. It was disgusting! She brought back a stock of ingredients to the city, enough for three months. Starting five days after her period, she drank the same concoction day after day sitting upright in bed while Amarante looked on and called upon mamaisa.

None of it helped.

Elisabeth noticed at one point that Carl Otto had been served fish soup. Fish wasn't his favourite and he grumbled about it, but the next day the same fish soup appeared on the table. Disgruntled, she sent the soup back to the kitchen and summoned Tutuba. Embarrassed and fiddling with her skirt, Tutuba explained that having children wasn't only women's work. The man was just as important, and if something wasn't working as it should, then there would be no children. Fish soup was good, very good, not only for a man's virility but also for the stuff inside the male organ that had to come out to make babies.

What if masra didn't like fish soup? A solution had to be sought. Tutuba first had to make a stock from the fish, strain it through a sieve and then add plenty of smoked meat, herbs, onions and banana.

Carl Otto ate fish soup every day for years on end without knowing it. Tutuba had also said that misi and masra should be together when the moon was waxing. The waxing moon helped everything to blossom and grow.

'We have to make love when the moon is waxing,' Elisabeth told Carl Otto that same evening, and he replied with a smile that he wanted to make love during every phase of the moon. But neither fish soup nor the waxing moon made the slightest difference. Elisabeth could not get pregnant!

One day she burst into tears from the disappointment of it all and Amarante comforted her. The same day Elisabeth heard that Amarante had given birth to two children in short succession while her mistress was in Holland. The first boy had lived for three months and the second was stillborn.

'Oh, how dreadful, I knew nothing about it!' Elisabeth exclaimed. 'Don't you miss them terribly, Amarante?'

Amarante shrugged her shoulders indifferently and sighed: 'I suppose so. But the past is the past.'

'But don't you think it's terrible. You could have had two healthy boys by now,' Elisabeth shouted.

'Two healthy boys maybe, but for what, misi? What did I have to offer them? A life of katibo, a life of hard work, pain and sorrow? No, it's better this way,' said Amarante, and they never spoke about the matter again.

I'm too old for children, Elisabeth thought as she dipped her quill in the inkpot. Come now, she had to pull herself together and stop thinking about it. She started work on her lists of requisitions.

She was still at her writing table two hours later when an enthusiastic Afi appeared at the door and shouted: 'Misi, misi, news!' The slave girls quickly assembled and together with Elisabeth they surrounded Afi on the rear gallery. 'It's a boy,' she said, 'a healthy seven-pound boy.'

'What's his name?' Dido asked.

'What does he look like?' asked Venis.

'Is everything alright with misi?' Amarante inquired.

'Yes, yes, misi is fine. Misi Maria says Misi Bettie is made to have children. Everything went so smoothly. Misi Bettie could be up and about today if she wanted to.'

'What's the child's name?' Dido persisted.

'Masra Loseke mentioned it, but I can't remember,' said Afi. 'I'd better be off. Misi Maria told me to get back right away. Bye Misi Elisabeth.'

Elisabeth went inside, tidied the papers on her writing desk and closed it. She then made her way to the dining room and sat on the settee. Amarante set the table, chancing a peek at her mistress every now and then. Elisabeth sat in silence, a blank stare on her face. 'The table is ready, misi,' said Amarante and

Elisabeth took her place. Amarante lightly touched her hand and said: 'Don't fret too much, gudu misi, don't fret too much. A child can be a blessing, but a mother's greatest sorrow is to have to bury her child. And that happens all too often.'

It was the end of June by the time Carl Otto returned from his jungle expedition. Tired, exhausted and emaciated, he slept for two days in a row. After that he ate six meals a day. Tutuba prepared the most delicious dishes. The kitchen was a hive of activity all day long, while Sara and Venis carried plates of food into the house and brought them back empty.

'We have to go to Clevia,' said Elisabeth.

'Alright, mi gudu, I know that's what you want. Let's invite Willem Herges along for the company.'

'And as soon as we get back, you can take care of that other matter,' said Elisabeth.

'What other matter?' asked Carl Otto.

'You know, our wills,' said Elisabeth.

'Why our wills all of a sudden? Are you sick?' asked Carl Otto

'No, but you don't have to be sick to make your last will and testament, do you? We both have one already, but it's time we made new ones. We have to make it clear that half of our combined property belongs to you and half to me. Wasn't that the plan?' said Elisabeth.

'You know what I think about it. If it were up to me, everything would be in your name. But I know my wife... You won't be happy until you get me into Floto's office. You win, my dear. When we get back I'll arrange for us to pay him a visit.'

They left a few days later for Clevia and Elisabeth was delighted to see such progress. The plantation house was almost finished, the director's residence and the watchmen's houses were already in use. The slaves' houses were exactly as she had wanted: instead of cramped stuffy huts with dirt floors and leaking roofs, there were spacious rooms with wooden floors connected by a flagstone gallery.

'I'll show those bakras that slavery doesn't have to equal abuse,' she remarked as she walked along the gallery and nodded approvingly.

Back in the city, Carl Otto was invited to visit Von Sporche. Several discussions on the question of runaways followed and it was well into the month of August by the time he told Elisabeth one evening that they had an appointment with Floto, the notary public. 'Finally!' she sighed.

22 August 1751

Elisabeth prepared the necessary documents for their visit to the notary's office. The title deeds to Plantations Toevlught and Welgemoed and Woodland Onverwacht were kept in a camphor chest. She would have to show them to the notary, but the main purpose of their visit was to settle matters concerning the property she shared with Carl Otto: Plantation Clevia and their country estate La Solitude.

If only Van Meel could see her now, Elisabeth thought to herself, the same Legislative Councillor Van Meel who had tried to have her condemned in 1737. When the man died in 1742, he was more or less bankrupt. Much of his property had to be sold and she had taken enormous pleasure in casually handing over the money for La Solitude and asking Carl Otto to purchase Van Meel's former possession under a writ of distress. Elisabeth didn't really consider La Solitude a 'country estate' and would have preferred to have called it a farm, in line with its actual function as a supplier of dairy produce with more than one hundred cows. But everyone in Suriname called it a 'country estate'.

At the bottom of the camphor chest she found her diary, a sturdy tome filled with so many memories of her years in Holland. She had almost forgotten she had kept a diary in those days. She started to read. It was such a strange period in her life, alone and lonely in a foreign land. She read about her first weeks in The Hague, in the lodging house with three elderly ladies. Because she was black, and black people were few and far between in Holland, everyone had presumed she had something to do with the Captain, the negro studying to be a minister in the church. She had heard more about him after her return. Carl Otto had told her a couple of years earlier that he had actually become a minister in Leiden and had been sent to Elmina by the West India Company in 1742 to convert the blacks. When he took a black wife, the gentlemen of the West India Company made sure that a Christian woman from Holland was sent to him, the woman he was later to marry. This particularly upset Elisabeth. It was not only legal in Elmina, the man was *obliged* to abandon his black pagan wife and marry a white woman, a deed that would have cost him his life in Suriname. Such a contradiction! Never mind. It was a crazy world, especially when it came to the rules made up by the whites! The Captain must surely have thought so. A couple of years later, the West India Company declared him dead. But no one knew the real truth of the matter. Some said he had taken his own life and others that he had reverted to his old religion and joined in the struggle against the whites who abducted negroes to sell them into slavery.

How would her time in Holland have ended if Masra Frederik had not been there to support her. He had helped her like a true father. He was a good man;

she had known no better. It saddened her greatly that he of all people had to suffer before he died. Poor Masra Frederik! Sisa Maria had also suffered. She was so intensely involved in nursing her husband that she almost fell ill herself. Elisabeth had done what she could for Maria, and Carl Otto had often spent hours at Masra Frederik's sick bed, talking to him and trying to take his mind off the pain. The man was in so much pain it was almost a relief when he died. Such a fine gentleman. If he hadn't helped her as he did, life in exile would have been completely different. What a time it had been in Holland! The free negress Elisabeth, exiled from Suriname. She had made the acquaintance of so many people during her stay. That young lawyer from Hoyer's office, what was his name again? Landman, yes, Wouter Landman. How was he faring after twelve years? My fellow lodgers were already quite elderly when we met and must have passed on by now. It was a stroke of good fortune that she had finally won the case and been declared innocent. As she thought about it, she realised her time in Holland had not been so terribly bad. The uncertainty was the worst part. Living with uncertainty was most unpleasant, and it was a situation she had experienced at first hand.

Happily her life was now completely different. Van Meel, who had made her existence a misery and had her exiled 'for the rest of her days', was long dead. So long, people had difficulty remembering the blackguard.

She had returned to Suriname. Carl Otto was not there to meet her on her arrival in Paramaribo, but when he came back from his jungle expedition and they saw each other again after so long, they spent that first night together. They may not have been married but to all intents and purposes they were husband and wife.

How long had she and Carl Otto lived together in this house? Masra Frederik passed away in 1742 and they had moved to this beautiful home shortly afterwards. Elisabeth had used her own money to have it built. She knew that people liked to talk about 'the fine house' on the corner of Wagenwegstraat and Heerenstraat that belongs to a negress. People also still gossiped about Elisabeth herself: she was a whore, she lived in sin, she practised witchcraft and that was why she was so wealthy. They even said she had used wisi to ensnare Carl Otto, but none of their talk was more than gossip and she paid it no attention. Their tittle-tattle sometimes gave her pleasure. They were simply jealous of everything she had, including her white companion, who never looked at other women. Officially she was a 'housekeeper'. She hated the term. And everyone knew that she was the one with wealth and property. Her property was growing in fact. The following day she had an appointment with the notary public to have it put down in writing that half of their common property belonged to Carl Otto and the other half to her. It had taken all her powers of persuasion to convince Carl Otto to agree to her plan, since he wanted everything to be in her name. After all, she had contributed three quarters of the money to purchase La Solitude and his only contribution to Clevia was the land and the money for the construction of the houses. Money for slaves, planting, and the salaries of the director and watchmen came from her. Her contribution was much more than half, but Elisabeth refused to account for it: they were together, half and half!

It was strange in itself that Carl Otto received the land for a plantation in the first place. He was a military man and not interested in plantations, but Mauricius had given him the property in gratitude for his role in establishing peace with the Maroons. Of all the bakras, Carl Otto was probably the most familiar with the runaways, since he had been pursuing them in the interior for all of fifteen years. It was a genuine peace treaty, sealed with a sort of ceremony. Its ultimate failure had nothing to do with Carl Otto, but rather with the miserliness of the authorities who did not send enough troops to deliver the gifts promised to the Maroons a year later. The contingent was attacked, the gifts stolen, and Adoe and his people, who were waiting in the jungle to collect their gifts, were disappointed. Thinking the bakras in the city had cheated them yet again, they withdrew from the treaty. No more peace!

It was obvious that Mauricius only thought about himself, Elisabeth mused, otherwise he would have known that Carl Otto wasn't the plantation sort. He openly admitted that he wasn't even slightly interested in plantations or their produce and certainly wasn't planning to bother his head about slaves and harvests and yields. He was a military man and jungle expeditions were more his cup of tea than plantations. If he had had his way, he would have rented out the land or sold it, but Elisabeth had insisted: 'It's the perfect place for a splendid plantation.'

Carl Otto had reacted: 'Keep me out of it, mi gudu. You're the businesswoman, do what you want with it.'

Elisabeth thought of her own plantations on Hoer-Helena creek. They both had a name when she bought them: Toevlught and Welgemoed, plantations thriving on the growing demand for coffee. Once again, Masra Frederik had helped her purchase them. The land had already been granted to ex-military men, but the owners had both passed away within months of each other and Elisabeth had asked her brother-in-law to take the plantations over in her name and 'sell' them to her at a later date, for fear they would refuse to sell the land to a black woman. Such fears were a thing of the past and no longer concerned her. Everyone knew she had money and experience. She had become a person to be reckoned with.

In addition to the plantations, she owned a stretch of woodland at

Onverwacht and she had seen to it that her sister Nanette received a similar stretch next to her own. It gave Nanette her own income, although she was naturally not as comfortable as her sister Elisabeth, who also did excellent business in the city selling all sorts of merchandise. She always had the prettiest and the latest... and she had a constant supply of customers. Her earnings were quite substantial.

Prior to her return from Holland, she had stocked up on a variety of things that were virtually unheard of in Suriname and had done very well for herself. It wasn't long before she was able to repay Masra Frederik to the last penny.

Enforced exile in Holland had allowed her to acquaint herself with the latest trends, and Reijdenius was happy to supply whatever she ordered. From the day she returned to Suriname, she made sure her customers came to her for their needs and she no longer delivered as she had done in the past. Mrs Stolkert had once sent her futuboi to ask if Elisabeth would bring over a selection of material and other fancy goods, but she had sent the boy back with a note stating that her stock was so extensive, she preferred her customers to visit in person. And that's the way it continued. Even the women who belonged to the cabal and considered Creutz their enemy were regular patrons. No one deigned to look at her in church, but they were all obliged to buy their material, wigs, porcelain, crystal and other such luxuries from Elisabeth. She watched them stroll wide-eyed and amazed through her house when they needed one thing or another, feigning complete indifference and doing her best to give the hussies the impression she was quite at home with this kind of opulence.

She and Carl Otto had arranged to visit the notary the following day. The new plantation had been registered a year earlier under the name 'Clevia'. When the registrar asked Carl Otto what name he wished to give the plantation, her indifferent companion had told him to choose something appropriate, something with Elisabeth. The man refused and insisted that Carl Otto name the place. It was his land, after all, a gift from the governor. He finally named it Clevia, after Cleve in Germany where he was born. At first he wanted the new plantation to be registered in Elisabeth's name, but she had been able to convince him that this would be a mistake. 'But it all belongs to you, woman,' he had complained, 'the money, the slaves. And you'll be doing all the work. You know there's no sense in asking me for help. Plantations are a mystery to me!'

'No, my dear fellow, the land belongs to you,' Elisabeth had calmly replied.

'Land, land, Suriname is full of land. But without money and slaves the land is nothing more than an impenetrable jungle, worthless!' Carl Otto had grumbled, but he finally gave in and agreed to the idea of dividing everything equally between them and having the registrar record in the deeds that half of their commonly owned property belonged to him and the other half to her.

Elisabeth heard a carriage arrive. Was it Carl Otto? So early?

Dido rushed into the room: 'Misi, misi, two carriages with ladies!' Elisabeth heard them climb the flight of steps up to the front door. A moment later they were in the house: Mrs Duvoisin, her daughter Henriette Couderc-de Cheusses, widow Anna Du Four, widow Lucie Walraven-Gabion, Mrs Duplessis and her daughter Susanna. Amarante invited them to take a seat in the front room.

When Elisabeth appeared, Mrs Duvoisin said she had heard there had been a new delivery and that the ladies were interested in silk and velvet. They would also like to try on the latest hats. Elisabeth brought them to the side room where she stored her stock of material. The ladies could look for themselves and choose what they wanted. Duplessis tried on a purple velvet hat and admired herself in the large mirror. Her daughter clapped her hands with delight: 'Such a splendid hat, mother. You have to wear it when father returns and is made governor.' The girl turned to Elisabeth and said: 'Misi, that hat is for my mother!' Elisabeth said nothing; she didn't particularly like the girl. Twelve at the most, she thought, and the behaviour of a twenty-year-old.

Once they had made their choices, the ladies returned to the front room, where Dido and Sara were already waiting with cups of cacao and trays of cake. The ladies sat and sipped their cacao. They could barely hide their appreciation for Elisabeth's fine Japanese porcelain. They also wanted to purchase silver buttons, bonnet lace, and other fancy goods. Venis and Dido were sent upstairs to fetch the boxes. Elisabeth walked to the stairs with the girls to tell them which boxes to bring. When she returned to the front room she stopped for a moment by the door, out of sight of the ladies. She overheard Susanna Duplessis saying: 'The bitch is stinking rich. Look, she even has a harpsichord.' One of the other women said: 'Probably just for show. Imagine, a negress with a harpsichord.' But widow Walraven whispered: 'Shush, no… they say she can play it.'

Venis and Dido appeared with the boxes. The ladies looked and yelped with delighted and enthusiasm. Elisabeth then had wine served in her finest crystal glasses. After a solid hour of chewing, chattering and choosing, the party left. Venis accompanied them to the door. As they were descending the stairs in front of the house, Elisabeth sat at her harpsichord and played a difficult piece with complicated harmonies. The women look at each other, Susanna exploded with laughter, but Mrs Anna Du Four sighed: 'They appear to be right!'

As darkness fell, Firans appeared to light the lamps. When he was finished Elisabeth told him to fetch Pietje and have him bring the boxes left in the front room upstairs.

Carl Otto arrived a few moments later.

'Plenty of sales today?' he asked when he saw the boxes piled up in the front room.

'Those women,' said Elisabeth, 'and Duplessis' daughter said that her father was going to be governor when he returned.'

'Aha! But that remains to be seen,' said Carl Otto with a grin.

'Everything is ready for tomorrow,' said Elisabeth. 'For Floto.'

'Oh yes, that's tomorrow isn't it,' said Carl Otto, relaxing in a chair.

Amarante grumbled something about Pietje not being there to take off masra's shoes and bring the boxes upstairs. Present came to help Creutz with his shoes and brought the boxes upstairs.

After dinner, Carl Otto reclined on the settee. He shouted 'boi' but Cadet didn't appear so he poured himself another drink. Staring into his glass he said: 'Listen, Babetchen, you know I'm going to die before you, but if it doesn't happen that way, mi gudu, please don't leave me some plantation or other to run.'

'Come on, man, you're surely not planning to spend the rest of your life chasing runaways in the jungle!' Elisabeth retorted. 'Or would you prefer to spend your old age as a beggar?'

'Not possible,' he laughed, 'not with a wife like mine! Come, mi gudu,' he held out his hand. 'Wait, let me take a look outside.' He stood, walked over to the window and stared up at the night sky. 'Perfect, mi gudu. He threw his arms around her, nibbled her earlobe and whispered: 'Let's go to bed. Look, the moon is waxing.'

23 August 1751

The appointment was for eleven-thirty. Floto's office was nearby so they decided to walk. Present walked behind misi and held a parasol over her head.

The slave at Johan Floto's office, who was also his courier, invited them to take a seat. The clerk appeared a moment later: 'Lieutenant Creutz, please go inside.'

'Come, liebchen,' said Carl Otto, but the clerk promptly intervened: 'Your housekeeper can wait here.'

Carl Otto pretended to look around the room and said: 'I don't see any housekeeper. Oh, do you mean my wife? We're both here for the same purpose and we'll be going in together.'

Once they were inside, Carl Otto explained the reason for their visit. Floto behaved as if he had white men and black women submitting their will and testament together every day and prepared the necessary documents.

Elisabeth pointed out that the deeds for Clevia and La Solitude as well as those for Toevlught and Welgemoed had to be registered. Floto prepared the registration documents. Elisabeth insisted that the slaves remained her personal property at all times and were never to be included in the general inventory of the plantation. She had her own reasons for requiring this codicil to be included in the deeds but she did not consider it necessary to share them. Floto added the codicil without question. When the documents were ready, Carl Otto signed them and Elisabeth added her name in graceful letters: Elisabeth Samson

It made sense to employ the surname Samson as did her sister Nanette and her brother Kwakoe. A surname looked so much better than 'the free negress Elisabeth' as she used to be called.

Elisabeth's brothers and sisters agreed on the matter and each of them now had a surname, although Catharina opted for an alternative name and called herself Catharina Opperman.

On their way home, they saw Mrs Benelle on the opposite side of the street. She was in such a hurry that her slave girl almost had to run beside her with the parasol to keep up. She nodded to Carl Otto and he nodded back. Elisabeth thought it strange that the woman was out and about at one in the afternoon, something white women never did for fear they might damage their alabaster skin.

It was warm. Amarante helped her undress while Dido cooled her with the fan. Elisabeth said: 'I saw Mrs Benelle on the way back from the notary. Where would she be going at one o'clock in the afternoon?'

'Perhaps she was on her way to her daughter or one of her friends,' said Amarante, 'to complain about that husband of hers. Masra Benelle has a pretty young mistress, only sixteen, a mulatta beauty. I heard old Masra L'Espinasse was her father. He bought her freedom and that of her mother before he died. Now she's with Masra Benelle, who buys her nice things and is with her every day.'

Elisabeth stood and made her way to the dining room. Carl Otto was already at table being served by Sara and Venis who fetched dish after dish from the koekerom. When he stood to go for his afternoon nap, he said: 'I'm expected at Commander Crommelin's place this evening. He's giving a reception for all the officers.'

'Gracious, that's the first I've heard of a reception,' said Elisabeth.

'Perhaps he's doing it to show his authority. Baron Von Sporche gives so many receptions and other functions. Crommelin is probably trying to keep up with him,' said Carl Otto and he retired to the bedroom.

Elisabeth was about to take a nap herself when Amarante appeared and said: 'Misi… eh, misi doesn't know it yet, but Pietje and Cadet are still not back.'

'What do you mean, they're still not back?' Elisabeth asked. 'Do you mean they've been away since they left for La Solitude yesterday morning?'

'Yes misi, and we have no milk,' said Amarante.

'What's keeping those two? Did they stay the night?' asked Elisabeth.

'I don't think so, misi. Firans clearly told them they had to come back. Hmm, if you ask me they've just wandered off somewhere. Heaven knows what kind of mischief they're up to,' Amarante answered indignantly.

'Does Lucretia know about this?' asked Elisabeth. Lucretia was thirteen-year-old Cadet's mother. Fifteen-year-old Pietje had lost his mother when he was five.

'Yes, misi, but Lucretia has no idea where they are. She told Firans to give them a good hiding when they get back.'

'You can be sure of it,' said Elisabeth, and she disappeared into the bedroom where Carl Otto was lying on his back on their enormous bed, snoring gently.

In the evening, Elisabeth sat at her writing desk examining her papers. She checked to see if everything was up to date and made the occasional note. She noticed that a number of bills were more than six months overdue. She would send Present with a letter of reminder to the ladies in question.

Amarante squatted on a bench on the rear gallery sorting chicken feathers, which Dido, Sara and Venis cut into small pieces by her side to use for stuffing cushions. They whispered to one another about Pietje and Cadet who had still not returned.

'Maybe they've run away,' said Dido.

'If that's true then they can expect a serious beating. Maybe misi will send for a Spanish Buck,' Amarante snapped.

'But if they don't come back there'll be no need for the lash or the Spanish Buck,' said Sara.

'If you ask me they'd better stay away forever,' said Amarante. 'They'll get what's coming to them, just wait and see. Run away? Ha! Do they think it's any easier in the jungle? For zoutwaternegers, maybe. What are those two boys thinking about? Their faya watra is waiting for them every day when they get up and they don't know the meaning of hunger or thirst. Let them try looking for food and drink in the jungle, silly asses.'

'Amarante!' Elisabeth shouted.

'Yes, misi,' Amarante shouted back, scurrying to her feet.

'The girls can go to bed now,' said Elisabeth. Dido, Sara and Venis quickly tidied up and went outside.

'Would misi like a massage?' asked Amarante.

'In a minute, yes, my back,' said Elisabeth. Moments later she was lying on the bed and Amarante was massaging her back with fragrant oil.

'That's enough,' said Elisabeth, 'you can go to bed now. But make sure everything is properly locked first.' Amarante did what her mistress asked before lying down on her mat in the small side room.

An hour later Elisabeth heard a carriage drive onto the property and Nestor the coachman shouting 'Whoa!' She waited in her room for Carl Otto.

As he was getting ready for bed she asked: 'And how was the reception?'

Carl Otto shrugged his shoulders and said: 'The same as ever. Plenty of food, plenty of drink and plenty of nonsense.'

Some time later he said: 'A slave ship arrived this morning. The smell was apparently so awful, the lieutenant at Fort New Amsterdam refused to let it sail any further and insisted it unload its cargo on the spot. He then sent it back to the estuary with orders for the captain to scrub it clean with soap, lemmetje and zuur oranje. The slaves were dowsed with buckets of water and ordered to scrub themselves from head to toe with soap and lemmetje.

'The poor souls,' Elisabeth sighed. 'If black people must be slaves, why add insult to injury with such humiliation? Why abduct them and mistreat them? Why force them to lie in their own excrement and that of others for weeks on end? It's no wonder they die like rats. When will they put an end to this dreadful practice? Everybody has to work, but why does it have to be like this? Ke, ke. If you ask me that's how all those terrible sicknesses get into the country.'

'The slaves were brought to the city today. The sale is probably next week,' said Carl Otto.

'We need a lot of labourers for Clevia,' said Elisabeth.

'I'm aware of that,' said Carl Otto as he took her hand and asked sweetly: 'And tell me, is my darling wife happy with her visit to the notary? Is everything as it should be?'

'Yes, mi boi, everything is as it should be,' she said with a smile.

'Good, now I can die in peace!' he said.

'Are you mad? I'm not quite ready to give up the ghost, nor am I planning on being alone. See, you'll have to live for a long time yet,' Elisabeth replied, and she ran her fingers through his hair.

Suddenly Carl Otto sat bolt upright: 'Babetchen!' he exclaimed. 'Well, my Babetchen, today we were married.'

'Married? What do you mean, married?' asked Elisabeth.

'Yes, my sweet, today we were legally married. You and I did precisely what is required for a marriage. We legally established that we live together and that our property is shared.'

He's right, Elisabeth thought.

'This is our wedding night,' Carl Otto teased, and he slipped her nightshirt upwards with his hand. 'Our wedding night. We must consummate it.' And they did.

Carl Otto quickly fell asleep, but Elisabeth was wide awake. She could never sleep directly after such a moment. A sort of inner excitement kept her awake and it sometimes took a while before it let go of her.

The desire to write something in her diary was overwhelming. She got up and groped her way in the dark to the dressing table. She would have to wake Firans and have him light some candles. Firans was asleep on a mat at the back door. It was the custom for a slave to sleep at the back door in all of the more substantial houses, but Firans was sound asleep and although she prodded his shoulder at least three times she couldn't wake him. He won't be much help in an emergency if he always sleeps so deeply, Elisabeth thought. Ten Maroons could have burgled the place without him being any the wiser. She lit a candle for herself, placed it in a candleholder and sat at her dressing table to write. Every now and then she looked over at Carl Otto who was lying on his belly, naked, taking up most of the bed.

An overgrown child, Elisabeth thought. My sweet child.

The following morning at breakfast Carl Otto said: 'By the way, I'll be leaving on September 1st on a jungle expedition. The ordinary soldiers are already underway with Officer Meije in charge. We're going by boat; three officers and two cadets will be sailing with me. We plan to meet up south of the Upper Commewijne.'

'I'll make sure everything is ready,' said Elisabeth. 'How long do you think you'll be away? And what about the slave sale? We badly need those labourers.'

'I'll arrange it before I leave. How many did you say?' asked Carl Otto as he stood to leave the table.

'A good number. Sixty at least,' Elisabeth answered.

'So many at once is a bad idea. Half now and the other half at the next sale,' said Creutz. 'Come boi, time to go.'

Elisabeth shouted after him by the door: 'No malinkers! Mothers with children. I prefer mothers with children.'

Pietje and Cadet

In the meantime, Pietje and Cadet had taken up with hideaways in Wanica forest and were sleeping in a hut made of branches and leaves. A large number of mostly young runaway slaves had gone into hiding in the Wanica forest, which was on the outskirts of the city. Some of them succeeded in reaching the interior after a while and joining a group of Maroons, but most of them ended up returning to their owners, risking a beating and even the Spanish Buck.

Pietje and Cadet had headed off along Landsweg to fetch milk from La Solitude the day before and they were on their way home with two weighty cans. It was a long, two-hour walk, and when they turned into Weidestraat a mulatta called out to them and begged them to sell her some milk. Although it wasn't allowed, the boys thought that Misi Elisabeth wouldn't notice. A slave woman and a poor white woman appeared on the scene and when they heard that milk was being sold for a penny they also wanted to buy. There was obviously a shortage of milk in the place. Before they knew it, the boys were surrounded by a group of women, all looking for a share. Pietje sold more than half of each can and a while later the boys stopped to count their takings: thirteen pennies in all.

'But what will misi say?' asked Cadet.

'Don't worry. We'll just say someone made us stumble and the cans fell over,' said Pietje.

'Both of us at the same time?' said Cadet, worried about the consequences. 'No one will believe us!'

'Then let's put all the milk in one can and say you fell over,' said Pietje. 'Look, I wanted to help you, put my can down too quickly and some of the milk splashed out. Don't be so afraid. Anyone can stumble. Come, let's go. I know where we can buy biscuits.'

They made their way to a house in Keizerstraat where jars of biscuits and pickles were displayed inside by an open window. While they were tucking into their spoils a couple of moments later, a tall boy wandered up to them and said: 'Hey Pietje, fa yu tan? Give me some,' and he immediately held out his hand. Pietje gave him half a biscuit.

'More, man, more. Don't forget about the tobacco I gave you last week!' said the boy impatiently. Pietje stuffed a whole gherkin into his greedy hand.

'You boys got tobacco?' he said.

Cadet wiped his mouth and said: 'No.'

'Who's he? Your brother?' the boy asked Pietje.

'Eh, yes,' said Pietje

'You got money, I got tobacco. Take a look.' The boy produced a grubby knotted rag from his threadbare trousers and loosened it to reveal a lump of tobacco.

'A halfpenny,' said the boy.

'You're crazy,' said Pietje indignantly. 'Come Cadet, let's go.'

'No, wait,' said the boy. 'Since it's you, a farthing.' Pietje grabbed the tobacco, but as he fished the farthing from his pocket, a halfpenny and a penny fell to the ground. He quickly picked them up and slipped them back into his pocket.

'Where are you heading with all that money? Hmm, she'll be ready with the lash, your misi will,' said the boy. 'Take me, for example,' he said furtively. 'You won't see me with those bakras. I'm living in the forest. Hey, we do what we want, man. Get up when we want, sleep when we want. It's good. Kobi and Agosu are there as well. They're real Maroons, from the real jungle. They've been sent to listen in to the bakras' plans here in the city and report back to the captain. We're all going with them. Then we'll be with the Maroons and we'll teach those bakras a lesson. No more slavery for us, man. Forget the lash and the Spanish Buck. Then we'll be free!' He punched the air with his fist.

'Let's go,' said Cadet, and he pulled at Pietje's hand, but his companion was staring at the boy in admiration. 'Can we come with you?' he asked.

'If you want,' he replied indifferently, 'but I'm not sure if they'll accept you. They don't take everyone. Maybe if I put in a word for you, maybe. I'm off. It'll soon be time for dinner. We can eat our bellies full if we want. We've got everything, man, and we do what we want. Follow me.'

Pietje followed, but Cadet insisted: 'I'm going home.'

'Go away,' the boy yelled at Pietje. 'Go away, don't follow me. Your brother will tell on you and they'll send the soldiers to get us. Go away!'

'He's not my brother and he won't tell,' said Pietje. 'Keep your mouth shut and walk,' he ordered Cadet. 'If you go home they'll send you for a Spanish Buck. Misi might even have you whipped to death. Don't you see? You stole something. You know what they do with slaves who steal! Do you want that to happen to you? You can't go home. Come, we have to follow.'

Cadet would have preferred to go home and make up a bunch of lies to explain the missing milk. He would even have accepted a lashing if need be, but now he didn't dare. He went along with Pietje and the boy.

They reached the edge of Wanica forest and followed a narrow path through the trees. The boy led the way. At a certain point he stopped, looked around carefully and then pushed aside a couple of bushes. He looked back to see if the others were behind him, slipped quickly through the bushes and held them back for Pietje and Cadet. 'Shush!' said the boy, holding his finger to his mouth. They crawled through the bushes, climbed over a fallen tree, passed through a sort of hollow and found themselves in a more or less open plot with two huts made of branches and palm leaves. A small fire was burning next to the huts, with a black cast-iron pot hanging over it on a stick.

'Kobi,' the boy shouted.

'Who's there?' someone shouted back from inside one of the huts.

'It's me, Siko,' the boy shouted.

Cadet was taken aback when he heard the name Siko. Siko was the name of Masra Bedloo's slave. The name was often mentioned in the slave quarters because he stole and ran away and his master sent him to the fort on a regular basis for a Spanish Buck.

'Who else,' another voice shouted from inside the same hut.

'Two other boys. They want to join us and go with us to the Maroons,' said Siko.

'Hmm, not so fast,' said Kobi and he came outside.

As soon as he saw Pietje and Cadet he said: 'Are you mad? They're just kids. We don't need no kids here!'

'They've got money,' said Siko.

'How much money? Let me see,' said Kobi and he held out his hand.

Pietje fished a couple of halfpennies from his pocket and handed them over.

'That's not enough. Give him all of it,' Siko commanded. Pietje was forced to empty his pockets.

'Doesn't that one have any money?' asked a third boy who had emerged from the hut and was pointing at Cadet.

Cadet shook his head, but Pietje yelled, 'He's lying.'

The boy grabbed Cadet by the shoulders. 'Mi na Agosu, I'm the boss round here. Empty your pockets!'

Cadet handed over his money and Agosu said: 'Good, you can join us, but no funny business, understand? If you want to be a real Maroon, you have to do what your boss says. We'll teach those bakras a thing or two. Come, sit down, it's time to eat.'

Siko quickly plucked some large leaves and Kobi served up the food using a hollow calabash and a rusty iron fork. Each of the boys received some banana, cassava and a piece of dried fish. After eating they drank some of the remaining milk and shared out some tobacco. Siko raked the fire while Kobi and Agosu told stories about their adventures in the jungle. If they were to be believed, they had attacked many a plantation, killed directors and white officers and shot any number of soldiers.

It got very late and they could see the stars through the trees. 'See that big star up there,' said Agosu pointing to the sky, 'you have to follow it if you want to reach our group of Maroons in Upper Suriname. Not many people know the way, but I do, I know it well. Come, let's get some sleep.'

Pietje and Cadet were allowed to choose a place in one of the huts. Cadet thought about his mother. Would he ever see her again? What was it like among the Maroons? He was scared.

Two days before Creutz was due to leave, Elisabeth told Amarante to make sure that Rufus packed everything masra needed for the journey. The gallery and the pantry were filled with provisions.

'How much Jenever did you set out?' Elisabeth asked Amarante.

'Two cases, misi, twelve red wine and twelve white wine,' said Amarante.

'But that's not enough,' said Elisabeth. 'Masra said it's likely to be a long expedition. Tell Rufus to fetch another case.'

'Look who's coming,' Sara shouted all of a sudden. Elisabeth looked out of the window and saw Lucretia making her way over from the enclosure on the other side of the street, where the slaves had their quarters behind the stables and the coach house.

Lucretia was holding Cadet by the ear and every so often she gave him a clout on the back of the head. Old Za-za was walking behind them, holding Pietje in precisely the same way.

'Mi Gado,' yelled Amarante, standing by the door. 'Where did those two come from?'

'Where do you think?' Lucretia shouted indignantly. 'They ran away, the scoundrels!' And with that she gave Cadet a few more serious clouts.

'And the smell! They stink to high heaven, the pair of them. A week without a bath of course.' When Lucretia saw Elisabeth by the door she said: 'They're back, misi! Those boys of yours who took six days to fetch some milk! We'll have to teach them a lesson.'

'It was Pietje, ma. I didn't want to but Pietje made me. He sold the milk and wanted us to join the runaways? It was Pietje!' Cadet whined.

'Where have you been all this time?' asked Elisabeth sternly.

'Answer the misi, boy,' Lucretia shouted, yanking hard at Cadet's ear.

'Wai, wai,' Cadet screamed, holding his hand to his ear. 'In Wanica forest, misi,' he continued in a quieter tone. 'It was Pietje's idea.'

'Not just Pietje,' his mother yelled, 'there were two of you.'

'So Pietje, and what happened to the milk?' Elisabeth calmly inquired.

'It fell misi,' said Pietje with his head hung, drawing lines in the sand with his big toe.

'Don't lie,' Lucretia barked. 'You sold the lot. Where is the money?'

Za-za gave Pietje a couple of thumps on the head and commanded: 'Speak up! Where is the money?'

'They took the money, the runaways took it and they kept us prisoner. They didn't want us to leave. Ask Cadet. It's the truth. Tell them Cadet,' Pietje shouted and he started to cry when he saw Firans coming with the lash. 'It's true, they took the money and they didn't want us to leave. I wanted to go home but they wouldn't let us go,' Cadet stammered. 'We escaped! We escaped while they were asleep,' Pietje added.

'Go ahead, Firans, the lash,' said Elisabeth calmly, and she went inside to get on with her work.

Firans grabbed hold of Cadet first, yanked his trousers to his ankles and said: 'Bend over!'

Cadet was already screaming before the lash had touched him. 'It was all Pietje's fault. I didn't want it. I'll never do it again. Wai!'

'You there, trousers down,' Firans yelled at Pietje while he was still lashing Cadet.

'We'll teach you not to lure others into your diabolical schemes,' said Za-za and she yanked on the rope holding Pietje's trousers up.

'Make no mistake! We'll teach you to lure others. So you want to join the Maroons, no? Well go ahead, but you're on your own. Cadet stays here,' Lucretia growled at Pietje and grabbed her son who had just received his final lash.

Pietje was given more lashes than Cadet. By the time Firans was finished, the streaks on his legs and back were bleeding.

'It's time they had a bath,' Amarante shouted as they returned to the enclosure on the other side of the street. 'They stink to high heaven.' Back in the house she said to Elisabeth: 'Misi should keep an eye on that Pietje. He's a bad influence.'

'Don't worry,' said Elisabeth, 'I'll get him when the time's right. I know the perfect punishment.'

Carl Otto Creutz

A couple of days later, a boat belonging to the Society army cruised along the River Commewijne, its broad sails profiting from the strong sea wind. On board were a detachment of officers and non-commissioned officers under the leadership of Lieutenant Creutz. They were on their way to territory south of the Upper Commewijne where new Maroon settlements had been observed and where they had arranged to meet up with the contingent led by Reserve Officer Meije, which had left three weeks earlier on foot.

Meije's group was to take over from Officer Pallack's group and finally allow the men who had been in the area for weeks to return to the city. If they're still there, Creutz thought to himself. How many will have been felled by fever and how many by the Maroons? A jungle patrol never knew for certain what it would find.

Creutz relaxed on deck with his hands behind his head and gazed at the river and the passing plantations. It was early afternoon. Fortune had seen to it that high tide was at two o'clock. Both wind and tide were in their favour and they were making good headway. They had spent the night on Plantation Mon Trésor, where the owner had been delighted with the distraction. His wife had died a year before and they had had no children. He found life on the plantation tedious at the best of times.

The detachment continued on its way after a sturdy breakfast. Creutz was content. If the wind kept up, they might even make it as far as Plantation Vieux Roeland.

'Pipe, boi,' said Creutz to Pietje who was sitting at his feet. Pietje hurried to fill the masra's pipe. Creutz looked at the boy. This was the punishment Elisabeth had devised for Pietje. 'You want to go to the Maroons, no?' she had said, 'then you'll have your wish.' She had said to Creutz: 'Take him with you as a carrier and make sure he has plenty of work. He wanted to get away, didn't he? Well now's his chance to see what it's like in the jungle. I wonder if he'll still want to join the Maroons after this little adventure.'

Creutz smiled at the thought of his resolute wife Elisabeth. The slave sale had taken place on the day he left, but he had been able to arrange to pay a brief visit to the holding quarters before it started and to allocate thirty negroes for purchase, bearing in mind Elisabeth's preference for mothers with children. Elisabeth was to go to Clevia, send the boats to collect the new slaves and wait for their arrival on the plantation. This was the only thing Creutz had to do in all her affairs: go to the sale when new slaves were needed. Women did not generally attend to such matters, and black women were completely out of the question. He knew exactly how Elisabeth would receive the zoutwaternegers when they arrived in Clevia: with plenty of nourishing food. Mothers with children would be given eggs and milk, and the adults sizeable portions of vegetables, meat and fruit. The newcomers would be given several weeks to regain their strength. They would receive new pagnis, pots and pans, knives, calabashes, and other such household items. The negro charged with the health of the household would have to do everything in his power to treat their wounds and ulcers. They would be wormed with green papaya and coconut milk and be given tea made from tamarind leaves to purify their blood. Elisabeth wanted her slaves to be in good condition. If you want them to work hard, you have to feed them well, she would say. And she was right. Her slaves always looked better than other people's slaves. She also made sure they had a decent roof over their heads. Rickety huts with leaf-covered roofs were not her style. Rather, she had wooden huts built with solid roofs and not too many slaves in one room.

'Everyone has the need to be alone sometimes,' she said. 'I'm no exception.' This was why she had not built slave quarters behind her house in the city, but on the opposite side of the street.

Newcomers were housed in pairs with older slaves and were not expected to work at first.

She knew what she was doing, his Elisabeth. In a short ten years, her two small plantations on Hoer-Helena creek had flourished beyond description, and both together generated more profit than one large plantation. But Elisabeth was in complete control and she visited at least once a month for a couple of days to keep an eye on things. No director was going to make a fool of her and she insisted that the slaves be well nourished.

She would certainly do the same at Clevia. Carl Otto had no need to bother himself about that.

He gazed at the magnificent river. What a pleasure and a luxury it was to cruise the river like this. He hadn't regretted a single day of the eighteen years he had been in the colony. It was a magnificent country, so fertile and such a splendid climate although it could get a little too warm at times.

The majority of colonists agreed with him, in spite of their fear of the runaways who attacked the plantations and did endless damage. It didn't occur to them that they should treat their slaves better and give them less reason to run away. And their anger at Mauricius for attempting to make peace with the Maroons was staggering. Carl Otto Creutz had been charged with the task and had succeeded because he knew the Maroons well. They were also well matched. He had learned so many of their customs and practices over time that he knew exactly how to go about persuading them to agree to a peace treaty. It went without saying that he had to offer something in return and he had made promises in the name of the authorities. Those gifts, he thought to himself, those gifts. Everything would have been fine if the authorities hadn't been so miserly. He had warned the governor, the secretary, the legislative council, and anyone else who would listen. 'Do it now and do it right!' he had told them. 'The gifts are an investment and the colony will reap the benefits in the future.' But they had refused to listen. They simply didn't understand the essence of certain matters. Take Mauricius, for example, the governor. The indignation in his face when he saw the list of gifts required by the Maroons was unbelievable.

'Six dolls, finely dressed,' he had exclaimed. 'See what I mean, the diabolical rabble. What kind of haughtiness is this? They agree to peace and before you know it they want their children to play with finely dressed white dolls!' Carl Otto had held his tongue. He knew that the finely dressed dolls were not intended for children, but were to be used by the Maroons in their places of worship and encased in a sort of altar. If he had told the governor the truth, the man would probably have ranted and raved even more and refused to be part of their idolatry. He figured it was better to leave granman with the notion that the dolls were for children.

But the peace was a complete failure. A year later, when the time had come to send the gifts to the Maroons, the governor only sent two soldiers to protect them and their carriers instead of a full detachment. Another group of runaways attacked and killed them and the gifts never made it to their destination. Adoe and his supporters felt betrayed and abused and peace negotiations were back at square one.

Creutz heaved a sigh. Here he was on yet another jungle expedition. It didn't bother him. The work was not hard, at least not for him, and he enjoyed the scenery, the river and the forests.

'How long are you going to chase after Maroons?' Elisabeth had recently asked. He had smiled and said nothing but he knew the answer: the rest of his life.

28 October 1751
Elisabeth

Carl Otto had arrived home a week earlier burning with fever and had spent his time since then in bed, critically ill, under the watchful care of Elisabeth and Amarante. Tutuba concocted drinks from korswuri and prepared bita to reduce his temperature. Old Za-za went to the orange grove to fetch aniseed leaves for a refreshing bath while Elisabeth sat on the bed and dabbed Carl Otto's head with a cool wet cloth. The fever finally broke but not after taking its toll.

'Eat and sleep,' said Elisabeth sternly when he tried to tell her something. Keep your tori for another time. Now you must rest and regain your strength.'

'Misi, where is Pietje?' asked Amarante out of the blue.

'Pietje?' asked Elisabeth, realising only then that she had not seen him. 'Maybe he's still in the jungle. He is a carrier after all. He can't just walk away.' She asked Rufus if he knew anything about Pietje and he answered that he was probably still with the soldiers who had remained in the jungle.

The commander sent Reserve Officer Ranitz to ask after Lieutenant Creutz. Officer Willem Herges, Masra Planteau and Masra Bedloo called at the house to visit their friend, as did a number of young cadets. Baron Von Sporche sent some bottles of wine.

Sisa Maria was also among the visitors. She stood by the bed and shook her head.

'He's much improved,' said Elisabeth. 'He thought he was so used to such expeditions he would never catch fever again. You can see for yourself how wrong he was.'

'The jungle is unpredictable; you never get used to it. Only the Maroons know how to survive there. White people are not up to it,' said Sisa Maria.

She nibbled at the biscuits Elisabeth had had brought and drank lemonade. 'Don't forget it's Suusje's birthday next week,' she said all of a sudden.

'Of course not. Doesn't time fly? She's two already,' Elisabeth replied.

'Two indeed, and such a sensible child. She's a real big sister to little Philip. His first teeth are on the way,' said Maria. 'I'm off to see them now. My best to Carl Otto. Tell him when he wakes that I was here but didn't want to disturb him.'

Maria is truly thrilled with Bettie's children, Elisabeth thought, but they really are sweet. Bettie is so fortunate. First a good husband, Samuel Loseke, a senior civil servant who had come to lodge with Maria a couple of years earlier. He came to Suriname on the request of his good friend Mauricius and acquired the office of 'Inspector of Sugars' shortly after he arrived. Sisa Maria still offered lodgings to officers and civil servants from the Cleve region who had nowhere to stay and Samuel Loseke was delighted with the opportunity. A year later, fifteen-year-old Bettie was pregnant by the man. He took her as his wife and they moved into their own house on Keizerstraat. Seventeen, young, beautiful and mother of two children, Elisabeth thought to herself, and she knew she was jealous. Bettie still had ten children in her. Even if a couple of them died, which often happened, she would still have enough.

Those jungle expeditions are to blame, she thought. Some men are unable to father children when they return to the city. Soldiers are forced to drink so many concoctions to stave off fever. The infertility problem must have something to do with those drinks, she thought, and although she had no proof, she was convinced she was right. Why had Sisa Maria no children? Mevila, her first husband, was too old, but Masra Frederik had also been a military man. He had also been forced to drink those concoctions before and during an expedition, just like Carl Otto and Willem Herges. Her sister Catharina had been living with Reserve Office Willem Herges for years and Catharina was still childless.

Samuel Loseke, on the other hand, was a civil servant and worked for the government. He wasn't expected to go to the jungle, didn't have to drink bita or potions for preventing fever, and he had given Bettie two children in quick succession.

If Carl Otto were to give up the expeditions immediately, would she still be young enough to have a baby? In principle, yes. Her mother was already quite old when Elisabeth was born. She didn't know exactly how old, since she had never known her mother's precise age and she had been dead for years. Perhaps Sisa Maria could tell her how old their mother was when she had her last child.

An overwhelming desire for a child assailed her once again, a child of her union with Carl Otto, a beautiful mulatto child. She had seen him in her mind's eye a thousand times: handsome light brown skin and thick black wavy hair. Just like Bettie's children.

What would she buy as a gift for little Susanna? Should she give her money? Money would be best, a generous amount. Perhaps she could then ask if Suusje might spend the afternoon with her from time to time.

A couple of days later, Carl Otto was so much improved that he was able to walk around the house and even cross over to take a look at the horses stabled opposite.

'Don't forget that we have to decorate the house tomorrow and hang out the flag,' he said to Elisabeth.

'Surely it isn't November 2nd already?' Elisabeth sighed. 'Nestor and Firans will make sure the boys decorate the place. But what about you, man? Are you going?'

'Of course. I have to go to the reception. I think Baron Von Sporche would be upset with me if I didn't appear at his first reception in honour of the princess regent,' Cal Otto replied.

'But you're sick,' Elisabeth exclaimed, 'you can't help being absent if you're sick.'

'The baron will think it's an excuse and interpret my absence as an act of loyalty towards Mauricius,' said Carl Otto. 'Imagine,' he mused, 'Mauricius was still here last year. The man's aggravation at the inhabitants of Paramaribo when they refused to celebrate the princess regent's birthday was simply phenomenal. After all, they had been happy enough to decorate their houses for the wedding of widow Buis!'

'That's right. Anna Buis married her director last year at the end of October. What a celebration, eh? Did granman get wound up about it?' Elisabeth laughed.

'He thought there was something irregular about people decorating their houses for such an occasion and not for November 2nd. "For that mulatta and not for the princess regent!" I heard him complain.'

'What annoyed him most? Decorations for the old mulatta or their absence for the princess?' asked Elisabeth.

'Both, I would imagine, in combination. Mauricius had his own ideas about things. But where did all that fuss get him? A trip back to Holland and court proceedings. And in the meantime we're still here, calmly getting on with life, and free to express our joy by decorating our houses and hanging out flags. It makes no sense to get worked up about futilities in this life.'

'You're right about that, but sometimes it's difficult to distinguish between futilities and more serious matters. What appears to be a meaningless incident can have serious consequences,' said Elisabeth and she rushed out of the room to tell Amarante to have Rufus fetch masra's dress uniform.

The following evening she sat at her writing desk in the main room checking lists of requisitions intended for Reijdenius.

Every now and then she would stop for a moment and stare into space, quill in hand. November 2nd wasn't her favourite day.

An enormous reception was organised each year at the palace on the occasion of the princess regent's birthday and Carl Otto was expected to attend, leaving her alone at home. At moments like this she felt excluded, that she would never become part of the community to which she so desired to belong.

And why?

Because she was black, and nothing else! Not because she didn't speak their language, not because she wasn't cultivated. Cultivated! What a joke! She was the better of more than half the women at the reception and a good many of the men. It wasn't because she did not know how to behave – she could teach most of the women a lesson in etiquette – nor because she couldn't afford to buy new and expensive clothing for the occasion. It was pure and simple: this was Suriname and she was black! Blacks and whites were not permitted to live together, but the rule had been ignored so often by so many that it had come to be tolerated as a matter of necessity. Receptions and other such celebrations were the exception, however, and blacks were not allowed at the palace. Only lawfully wedded women were invited, and since marriage between blacks and whites was forbidden, there were no lawfully wedded black wives. The perfect solution!

Would there ever be an end to it? Would the negroes be forced to be slaves to the whites forever and be treated as inferior beings? How was it possible that white people still refused to believe that black people were truly human because they were said to lack the intelligence of the whites? Everything around them was evidence to the contrary! Black was black forever and always. Even if you wanted to, no money in the world could buy you a new skin. Whites would always see you and treat you as inferior. No matter how intelligent and handsome you were, no matter how much you had demonstrated that you were better in many ways than they, the whites would never change. She heaved a sigh.

What would Carl Otto be doing at this minute? Would he be laughing and talking with the men or would he be showering his attentions on some young white girl? Would widow Walraven approach him cooingly and invite him to take a look at her plantation?

Oh honestly, what was the point in fretting about it. She wasn't welcome at the palace and that was that. She had so many other things. She was rich! The high and mighty ladies at the reception all had to come to her for their pretty outfits. Her income last year was no less than twenty thousand guilders. Once Clevia was in production, her income would increase substantially. Who could boast of such wealth in the colony? No one, not even the governor!

She considered giving her own party, a much bigger party! A party with more decorations than the palace could muster, with much more food and drink, with music and fireworks. When would be the best moment? Carl Otto's birthday, of course, at the end of February. An excellent occasion. She would have Carl Otto invite the guests, all those friends of his with their lawfully wedded wives, to a splendid party she herself would organise. It would have to be a party unlike anything the colony had ever seen before. It was time to let them see just how wealthy she was!

She was already in bed when Carl Otto came home a couple of hours later. She heard him talking to Rufus and she could tell that he had been drinking heavily. She pretended to be asleep and not to notice that he had joined her in bed.

The following morning Carl Otto said: 'Sweet Babetchen, you were already asleep last night and I didn't want to wake you.'

'How was it?' Elisabeth asked.

'Nothing special, although we have a new lieutenant, just arrived. He hails from Bredevoort, which is also in the Duchy of Cleve, not far from Emmerich. I invited them to join us for a meal this afternoon.'

'Them? Who else will be coming?' asked Elisabeth.

'Lieutenant Van Steenberch and his two children. He has a son of eighteen, who is going to be a recorder at the town clerk's office, and a daughter of eleven. His wife has been dead for years. He's alone here with his children.'

A couple of hours later, Lieutenant Van Steenberch arrived at the house with his son Willem and his daughter Philippina.

What a fine young man, Elisabeth thought, when Willem shook her hand and said: 'Good afternoon, ma'am, how kind of you to receive us.'

The girl referred to Elisabeth as 'Mrs Creutz'. She was quiet at the beginning, but after a while she felt more at home, talked nineteen to the dozen and didn't stop asking questions. She walked through the house, was introduced to Venis, Dido and Sara, and sat with them on the rear gallery for a while after the meal.

'What a beautiful home you have, ma'am,' said Philippina, when she had completed her tour and seen all of the rooms. 'Does that doll belong to someone?' she asked, pointing to a finely dressed doll sitting on a chair.

'I keep it for visits from young ladies who like to play with dolls,' said Elisabeth.

'May I?' the child asked, her eyes glistening.

'Pientje, manners!' her brother scolded.

'Of course you may. Now if you wish,' said Elisabeth, and she watched as the girl took the doll in her arms and gleefully examined its clothing and beautifully embroidered underwear.'

'Dido made the clothes,' said Elisabeth. 'She is a wonderful embroiderer, as you can see. Feel free to come and play with the doll whenever you want.'

'Thank you, ma'am, thank you. Father, did you hear? Mrs Creutz says I can come whenever I want,' she exclaimed.

'Mrs Creutz doesn't know what she's started,' said Van Steenberch with a laugh.

'Come at your leisure, young lady,' said Carl Otto. 'My wife loves to have young people about the house.'

5 November 1751
Samuel Loseke

A child's voice shouted: 'Papa,' and Samuel got out of bed to lift his little daughter from her cot.

'It's your birthday, Suusje, your birthday,' he said and he cuddled the cooing child as she threw her arms around his neck.

'It's a bit too early to be getting up,' he said to her gently. 'You need more sleep.'

'Mama?' Suusje asked.

'No, mama's still asleep. Let's not wake her. It's going to be a busy day for both of you, and for the rest of the family,' he said, and he glanced over at the bed where Bettie lay sound asleep with little Philip at her naked breast. He carried his daughter in his arms to the rocking chair in the corner of the room. Suusje popped her thumb into her mouth and snuggled up contentedly to her father's chest.

Samuel rocked back and forth and contemplated his child. Two years old, he thought, a day worth remembering. He saw himself standing in the room with the newborn baby in his arms, his head a whirlwind of thoughts as he gazed at her little pink head and mop of black hair. She blinked and then yawned, and at that moment a strange sensation overwhelmed him: I am a father and this is my child. The words resounded in his head and he promised there and then that he would be a real father to this little creature in his hands.

Who would have thought it would end up like this? It was far from his plans when he arrived in Suriname five years earlier on the invitation of his friend Mauricius. Mauricius's father was a good friend of his own father and was in fact his godfather.

Jan Mauricius was much older than Samuel, more like an older brother or a young uncle. When Mauricius informed his young friend as governor of Suriname that an excellent position awaited him in the colony he did not hesitate to accept his godfather's offer and set sail for a country he knew precious little about, beyond the fact that Mauricius was governor of the place and something approaching a king.

Before long, Samuel was installed as 'Inspector of Sugars', one of the most prestigious functions in the colony. He made his oath of service to the governor himself, although Mauricius had insisted it was not the common practice. For such a close family friend as Loseke, however, he was willing to make an exception.

The governor showered his godson with all sorts of advice, the most important being that he should watch out for those black heathen women, whores the lot of them, who were hell bent on ensnaring white men in their tentacles. This piece of advice was quickly forgotten since the young man had no real intentions in that direction. He did his work correctly and spent his free time reading, studying or playing cards with his friends. He had excellent lodgings in widow Bosse's house, recommended by his friend Creutz who was also from Cleve, as was his landlady's late husband. Widow Bosse had a considerable number of slaves on her property and shared her house with a thirteen-year-old niece. He paid no attention to the child, and could barely make out the difference between her and the slaves until he was given to understand one day that she was a free negress. This explained her European attire. But Bettie was thin and lanky and absolutely not worth a second glance.

Two years later he suddenly noticed a change. She had grown up, had become a young woman with curves in all the right places.

After two years of living in the same house, a degree of intimacy had evolved between them without them being aware of it. He started to have conversations with her, discovered she could read and write and had all sorts of interests. Their conversations became commonplace and he invited her from time to time to join him at table for dinner. He noticed her splendid white teeth and the dimple in her cheeks when she laughed. She was shy with strangers as a rule, but with him it was different. She told him funny stories and jokes. He missed her if she was not there when he got home. He started to long for her, found her beautiful, attractive, and then the moment came when he could no longer control himself and he took her to his room. At first she was shy and didn't dare, but once she had learned how to make love after a little practice, the shy little girl turned out to be a fantastic bed partner who brought him every kind of pleasure.

She fell pregnant. He was taken aback when her aunt told him the news and was suddenly reminded of the advice of his friend the governor. He and Mauricius talked together on a daily basis. He would have to confess. The man was having problems at the time with the Police Council and some of the wealthy colonists. Loseke chose the wrong moment to confess and Mauricius was furious at his protégé's stupidity. The governor ordered him to move out of the house of 'that mulatta, who had succeeded in playing her entire black family into the hands of white men,' as the governor himself put it. Mauricius saw to it personally that his godson found lodgings with a white widow on Gravenstraat.

'Make sure you marry a decent white woman and waste no time about it,' Mauricius had commanded. 'There are women aplenty. What about widow Walraven? She's still single!'

'Not my fancy, I'm afraid, single or not,' Samuel had answered. 'Let me think about it.'

The first evening alone in bed he had felt so desperately lonely. All he could think about was his Bettie, the look of sadness in her face when he told her he was moving and ensured her aunt that he would take care of the child, just like so many other white men who had fathered a child by a black woman.

He was alone in bed in a house that felt so strange. The loneliness he had felt that first night had disturbed him and almost driven him to tears. His longing for Bettie, his remorse at having abandoned her, forced him out of bed, and he spent half the night pacing up and down the room. At first light, he got dressed and made his way to Keizerstraat where he had rented a house. He then hurried to widow Bosse on Waterkant and asked if he could take Bettie as his concubine.

When Mauricius heard that the girl was living in Samuel's house, he flew into a terrible rage, insisted that the negress must have used witchcraft, advised him to talk to the local minister, and told him that the legislative council could have the woman evicted from his house if necessary.

Loseke had stared indignantly at his former friend and responded with carefully chosen words: 'You may be the governor of this country, Mauricius, but you are not the governor of my life. I can make my own decisions. The woman is staying where she is.'

'Do as you please,' said Mauricius. 'Are you planning to give that negro child the name Loseke? You're a disgrace to your family!'

Susanna was born a couple of months later, his Susanna, his sweet little girl.

He was so proud of her. A year later Philip came along. Now he had a son and a daughter. They may not have been white children, but they were beautiful, bright and healthy children. He was happy, he was proud and he was content.

Life was a mystery. Mauricius had brought him to Suriname, but where was the governor now? In Holland, embroiled in a court case. Loseke couldn't understand why such an intelligent man as Mauricius had not been wise enough to approach those old, wealthy French and Jewish families, some of whom had been in the country for three generations, with a little more tact. The man's behaviour had been so arrogant and authoritarian that it wasn't surprising the colonists no longer accepted him and did everything in their power to have him removed. Loseke and Mauricius had not parted company as enemies. Samuel had found it difficult enough for the man, burdened as he was with the painful disappointment of having to leave the colony. He had been like an older brother to him for such a long time, but their friendship was no longer the same.

Samuel gazed at his little daughter and asked himself how anyone could possible be ashamed of such a darling creature. He had decided nevertheless to give his children the name Hanssen, his mother's maiden name, instead of Loseke. He pressed his lips to his daughter's black curls. The girl caressed his face with her tiny hand. 'Suusje hungry?' he said. 'Hungry, papa!' she replied.

He stood and walked to the stairs with the child in his arms: 'Sylvia, little misi wants her milk.'

'Yes, masra,' Sylvia shouted from the botralie.

Samuel returned to the bedroom where Bettie had just opened her eyes. He set Susanna down on the floor.

'Come, sweetie, come to mummy,' said Bettie, holding out her hand. The child ran to her mother and threw herself into her arms.

Samuel looked on, smiling broadly.

The aunts and nieces were expected that afternoon. If Mauricius had witnessed the event he would surely have claimed to have spoken the truth about black women ensnaring white men in their tentacles. The aunts and nieces all had white partners. The first to arrive was Maria, a mulatta, widowed twice over and wealthy.

Nieces La Vallaire and Lucia followed in short succession. La Vallaire lived with Pierre Planteau and had already given him two children. The boys had a great time tearing through the house and La Vallaire frequently had to tell them to calm down. Loseke could clearly remember how surprised he was when the former slave Amimba changed her name to La Vallaire after being granted her freedom. He had never heard of such a name. Bettie assured him that the girl had not chosen it by herself, but had been given it by Pierre Planteau out of respect for his French roots.

Aunt Catharina shared a home with Reserve Officer Willem Herges and Elisabeth was Carl Otto Creutz's concubine. Aunt Nanette was unable to come because she now lived on Plantation Lankmoedigheid as 'housekeeper' to the plantation director Van Herpen.

La Vallaire had brought a cake and all the aunts had gifts for little Susanna. Maria gave her a doll, Catharina a golden bracelet and there was a necklace from Aunt Nanette. Aunt Elisabeth gave her two gold coins in a red velvet box. Elisabeth was the rich one, Samuel thought. The woman was immensely wealthy. Bettie had been named after her but didn't really like her.

'She hates me. I know it, I feel it,' Bettie would say whenever they talked about Aunt Elisabeth. Samuel insisted that his wife was imagining things, but Bettie was convinced of it.

'Watch the way she looks at me,' Bettie had recently remarked. 'You can see it in her face. Revulsion written all over it! I'm certain it's the same when people talk about me in her presence. She doesn't like me. When I was a child, she always made excuses to send me out of the room to fetch this or that or call someone in from the yard. All because she didn't like me being around her.

'I was afraid of her and avoided her whenever I could. It was a relief when she moved into another house with her companion. Think about it. She lives nearby, but does she come to visit? Never! She comes for the children's birthdays, of course, but that's only because the other aunts are here and she's embarrassed to stay away. Well, she can stay away, for all I care, and she can keep her presents.'

Samuel looked at Elisabeth. There wasn't the slightest hint of revulsion. On the contrary! When she asked Maria if she could hold little Philip and took him in her arms, Samuel saw nothing but tenderness and endearment in her eyes.

January 1752
Elisabeth

A couple of days after New Year, the colony was shocked by reports that Maroons had attacked two plantations in Commewijne territory near Hoer-Helena creek. The attack had been planned with precision. By turning on neighbouring plantations simultaneously, neither was in a position to offer assistance to the other. The Maroons were already gone by the time help arrived from plantations further along the creek and their booty of tools, provisions and slaves was substantial. The storehouse on Plantation Hoopwijk had been burned to the ground and the Maroons had thrown burning torches into the loft of the coffee barn on Plantation Toevlught, but the fire had been put out thanks to the bravery of the slaves.

Elisabeth was terribly upset by the news. She wanted to see for herself what had happened to her property, but the tides were against her and she had to wait until the following day.

She went alone. The audacity of the attack had prompted the lieutenants – Creutz among them – to meet and discuss how to respond to the runaways' brutality.

Amarante could not travel with her, since she had to stay and look after the house and Masra Creutz. Elisabeth took Lucretia and Dido instead, together with Abram, Present and Firans from among the male slaves.

The journey by boat seemed endless. All she could think of was her plantation and the state it had been left in by the Maroons. Rumours had reached them about Plantations Hoopwijk and Toevlught, but what about Plantation Welgemoed? Had it also come under attack? She was irritated and angry. Why had those bandits set their sights on Toevlught of all places. Its owner, Elisabeth Samson, was known for treating her slaves correctly. She treated all her workers with respect and she expected her director and the white overseer to do the same. All of the slaves were her people, her own people. They were given plenty to eat, were never overworked, and had decent accommodation. She didn't deserve this! She considered it a humiliation to be the victim of a Maroon attack.

On her regular visits, Elisabeth was in the habit of breaking the journey at Sorgvlied, where the director was a friend of the director of Toevlught and Welgemoed. Sophie, a portly karboegerin and a friend of Catharina and Nanette, was the director's housekeeper. It looked as if they were not going to manage on this occasion, as darkness had already started to set in by the time they arrived at Nooit Gedagt, three plantations before Sorgvlied. But Elisabeth was determined and she ordered the rowers to pick up the pace and had Present and Firans sit up front with burning lamps.

A young futuboi came charging into the house with the news: 'Misi Elisabeth from the city is coming!' prompting Sophie to hurry to the riverbank. She apologised immediately for the director, who had left for the city just two days earlier on account of the attack and its proximity to Sorgvlied. But not to worry, she would organise something to eat in spite of the late hour, and there was plenty of room for the slaves in the slave village. Elisabeth had brought gifts: a bale of cloth for Sophie and a case of Jenever for the director. The stopover was necessary but Elisabeth found the delay unbearable, especially when she was forced to listen to countless stories about Maroon attacks later that evening, which Sophie recounted with gusto and supplemented with all sorts of gory details.

When they arrived at Plantation Toevlught the next day, it became immediately apparent that they had not expected her so quickly. The results of the attack were evident everywhere and little work was being done. Elisabeth understood that the attackers had been well informed about the plantation's day-to-day activities. The director always took a siesta after his midday meal and the white overseer could usually be found dozing off under a tree with his rifle in his hands. It would have been a great deal worse if not for the courageous efforts of the basya, who grabbed the bewildered white overseer's weapon and chased the Maroons off the property, in spite of the fact that he had taken an arrow in his arm and was bleeding badly.

The white overseer and the director both received a vigorous dressing down. Hopeless cases, the pair of them! Sleeping on the job and not worth their wages. She hadn't chosen ex-military men as director and white overseer for nothing. Their lethargic behaviour was an embarrassment to the service and their employer was very unhappy with the situation. Had they checked to see what was missing? Not yet? Then it was high time they got on with it. The misi insisted they submit their report early the next morning.

Basya Isidoor was summoned and appeared with a bandaged arm. Elisabeth asked if the dresneger had taken good care of his wounds and rewarded him for his courage. He was given a new blanket, a hat, and some tobacco. He was also given a rifle and was advised to make good use of it should there be a second attack or should he catch sight of one of the runaways. When she had completed her inspection of Toevlught, Elisabeth made her way to Welgemoed. The bandits had spared the place, but three zoutwaternegers had run away, taking machetes and an old rifle with them.

Elisabeth received her director's report the following day. Damage to the coffee barn could have been a great deal worse, but the disappearance of dozens of machetes, spades, hayforks and even a couple of wheelbarrows was a more serious matter. In addition, six young men had disappeared, four of them zoutwaternegers, together with two female non-native slaves. It was difficult to tell if they had left of their own accord or had been taken under force.

Elisabeth listened straight-faced to the report. When the director had finished his survey she said: 'Good. The stolen goods and the slaves will be replaced. Do your duty in the future and make sure your white overseer does the same. I will be leaving in the morning. The replacement material will be sent as soon as possible. Work must go on. Ask your people if they are willing to put in extra hours. If they agree, be sure to reward them appropriately. But there should be no obligation. Any losses will be deducted from your bonus at the end of the year. I suggest you also stay away from the Jenever. You can run a plantation much better without it.'

When she returned to the city she told Carl Otto that a short but urgent visit to Clevia was essential. They left a week later. She inspected everything herself. Were the negro quarters built according to her specifications? She didn't want poky little cabins, but rather spacious rooms with a decent roof, connected by a gallery. What was the situation with her new employees? Were they used to the work? Were they performing according to expectations? She went out to the fields to inspect the young plantings and to check the condition of the shrubs planted two years earlier. She spoke with the director, Hahn, who had been in service a little less than a year. She insisted that her people should be treated correctly: 'Reward is better than punishment,' she maintained. The lash should be seen as a symbol and not an instrument for keeping order. If there were troublemakers among the slaves, she preferred to be rid of them immediately. She refused to tolerate troublemakers. Elisabeth made it clear to her director that good stewardship would result in a percentage of the profits, although actual profits were still to be registered.

March 1752

Nanette was visiting the city for a couple of days and was staying with Elisabeth. On the first afternoon they went to see their sister Maria on Waterkant. Maria was getting old, they thought, and wasn't looking well.

'So many people sick,' Nanette lamented when she and Elisabeth were together in the dining room later that day. 'I'm worried about Maria. She looks tired and does nothing but cough. And that Masra Wijnand of mine, he's sick all the time. He has trouble with his chest these days and I have to massage him and apply hot compresses.'

'Maybe he's sick all the time because he enjoys your massages,' Elisabeth joked. 'Cut it out,' said Nanette with a tyuri.

'Where is he now?' Elisabeth asked.

'At Masra Benelle's place. He thinks Wijnand should have a doctor take a look at him.'

'Masra Benelle is planning an important feast for this evening,' Elisabeth noted. 'I don't suspect he'll be inviting the doctor to look at Wijnand this afternoon.'

'Did you know Masra Benelle had a new concubine?' Nanette asked a moment later.

'Does he?' said Elisabeth. 'That's news to me!'

Years before, after the revision of her court case in Holland, Elisabeth had made up her mind to avoid offering commentary on white people. It was best to say nothing, she thought, and no matter what she heard or witnessed she held her tongue. From time to time she would say something to Amarante or Carl Otto, but in the presence of others she knew nothing.

'Ha! You live in the city and I live on a plantation, yet I have to bring the foto-tori to you,' Nanette laughed. 'A pretty young mulatta, baya, Planteau's daughter.'

'Do you know her?' Elisabeth inquired.

'No, not really, but I've seen her. Masra Benelle brought her to Lankmoedigheid a while ago. Wijnand was sick at the time and Masra Benelle suggested he come to the city and he would have his doctor take a look at him.'

'Ah! So you've seen them together,' said Elisabeth.

'To tell you the truth, sister, I don't understand why they bothered coming to the plantation. They spent most of their time in the main bedroom upstairs and might just as well have found a room in the city. Masra Benelle wasn't interested in anything and saw nothing of his plantation. She came down to the riverbank some mornings, probably trying to recover after an exhausting night. She didn't make a sound, poti, and she didn't say a word. Tired out from trying to please that man, if you ask me.'

'I don't doubt it. I hope the child has something to look forward to in return!' Elisabeth said.

Two days later, Masra Van Herpen sent a message that Nanette should be by the stone stairs at ten o'clock for the departure of the boat. 'Tell your masra to get well soon, and don't spare the massages,' Elisabeth advised.

The day after Nanette left, Sisa Maria called by.

'I've just been to see Bettie,' she said. 'The poor child is sick.'

'Is she? What's the matter?' asked Elisabeth, expecting to hear that Bettie was pregnant yet again.

'I don't know. I think it might be influenza. She has a temperature and a harrowing cough, poor child. It hurts just to listen to her.'

'You should tell her to bathe in korswuri and drink plenty of calabash syrup,' said Elisabeth.

'I had a full bottle with me. Little Philip can sit up and crawl. He and Suusje have been playing together,' said Maria and she laughed contentedly.

She treats Bettie's children as if they were her own grandchildren, thought Elisabeth jealously.

The following afternoon, Amarante came rushing into the house after stopping briefly at the slave quarters. 'Misi, they're saying Misi Bettie is very sick. They called the doctor yesterday, and he's already been there twice today. Misi Maria is with her,' she said anxiously.

'Heavens, then she must be really sick. Is there anything we can do?' asked Elisabeth.

'Ke baya, the poor girl, ke,' Amarante lamented. 'If it's alright with misi, I'd like to go right away.'

'Yes, good idea. And be sure to ask if there's anything we can do to help,' said Elisabeth. Amarante hurried down the stairs in front of the house and ran along Malebatrumstraat towards Keizerstraat.

But less than half an hour later she had returned.

'Ke misi, ke,' she sighed, 'there's nothing more we can do for her, baya, she's dead.'

'No, surely not!' Elisabeth exclaimed. 'Oh, those children, those poor children.'

'Poor little children. So young and without a mother. Ke baya,' Amarante whimpered.

'Fetch Dido to help me with my shoes, Amarante,' said Elisabeth. 'We're going to see her.'

They arrived at Samuel Loseke's house on Keizerstraat a few moments later and found the place in a terrible commotion. The slave women were crying, Catharina was crying, Sisa Maria was crying. Suusje was sitting on Maria's lap looking around in bewilderment at all those crying grown-ups. Little Philip was asleep. Masra Loseke paced up and down the main room wringing his hands. The body-washers had already been warned and soon arrived to do their work.

Elisabeth made her way home, the words 'Bettie is dead and I was jealous of her' echoing in her head.

The funeral took place the following day. Everyone was heartbroken. The children stayed at home with one of the slave women who hugged them constantly and wailed that they had been left alone without a mother. After the funeral, the family members expected to go to the house of the deceased, as was the custom in Suriname, but Masra Loseke pleaded with them to let him go home alone. He also refused the usual aitdei and preferred not to receive visitors. The family didn't understand. What were they supposed to do? It was the custom. Wouldn't Bettie's spirit be terribly angry? How would her spirit find rest without an aitdei?

'The man is completely crushed, if you ask me. And everyone deals with sorrow in their own way,' said Carl Otto when some of the family commented out loud about the behaviour of Bettie's companion.

Maria had a solution. She would hold the aitdei at her house. After all, Bettie had spent the best part of her short life there and had treated it as her parental home. Eight days long, family friends and acquaintances sat in Maria Bosse's spacious front room. They sang songs, grieved, wept and talked about Bettie, sweet Bettie, who had died so young. Loseke joined them on the last evening, but got so upset Creutz had to take him home.

During the evening sessions, a plan started to evolve in Elisabeth's head. She kept it to herself at first, but the more she thought about it the better it seemed. At home during the day, she paced from one room to the other, stopped now and then to inspect something more closely, talked to herself out loud on occasion and smiled. A week after the aitdei she announced to Carl Otto: 'I have a plan, a good plan. Listen, you must go to your friend Loseke and tell him we will raise his children.'

'What do you mean, we will raise his children?' asked Carl Otto taken aback.

'Simple. He must give his children to us and we will take care of them as if they were our own,' said Elisabeth.

'And Loseke? He is their father after all! He'll want to raise them himself, no doubt. Why would he give up his children?' asked Carl Otto.

'But a man can't raise children on his own. Children need a mother,' said Elisabeth.

'What if he gets married or takes a concubine. Then the children will have a mother,' Carl Otto answered as he searched the table for his pipe.

'A white mother, no doubt, who'll mistreat them because they're mulattos. Nothing of the sort!' said Elisabeth, impatient at Carl Otto's apparent reluctance to see her point of view.

'If you ask me, Loseke's not the type to let any stepmother mistreat his children, no matter what colour she is,' Carl Otto snapped, and it was clear he had had enough.

But Elisabeth wasn't finished. She marched over to him, grabbed him by the shoulder and shouted: 'Don't you understand, man? What about us? We're Bettie's family. Don't we have a say? We don't want the children to end up with a stepmother. I'm her aunt. We, you and me, we can give the children a good home. They'll be better off with us. You have to tell Loseke that. The children have to come here, to live with us. It's for the best.'

'And what if he refuses?' asked Carl Otto.

'He can't refuse. You have to tell him. You have to convince him we're doing it for the children and their best interests,' Elisabeth exclaimed.

'Fine, fine, I'll speak to him,' said Carl Otto. 'Where is Cadet? Boi, bring me my pipe!'

'Yes, masra,' Cadet shouted from the doorway.

'Carl Otto, you have to speak to him,' Elisabeth insisted.

'But I already said I would speak to him, didn't I?' said Carl Otto a little cross.

'You have to do it now,' Elisabeth urged.

'Now?' Carl Otto snapped. 'Have you lost your mind, woman? Now, this evening, impossible. I'll speak to him when the opportunity presents itself but not now.'

'No, no, now, this minute. The sooner the better. Cadet, bring masra's shoes. I want you to go now, Carl Otto. I beg you, please do this one thing for me. I've never asked anything of you before. This is all I ask of you. Go immediately to your friend. Talk to him. Convince him he has no alternative but to give the children to us. We will take good care of them and I will be a mother to them, a real mother. He can visit them whenever he wants, but they have to live here with us. He must decide, now, today. You have to convince him, make him understand. Go, Carl Otto, go now, please!'

Carl Otto stared at his wife with growing amazement. Was this the level-headed Elisabeth he once knew. In all their years together he had never seen her like this. She had never asked something with such urgency, but now she was almost begging. It obviously meant a great deal to her. He could only agree to go.

He stood up and said calmly: 'Good, I'm going, right now.'

While Creutz was away, Elisabeth inspected the side room. Would she let the little ones sleep here or upstairs with a slave girl? Which slave girl? Lucretia? Sara? Venis? She would decide later. In the meantime it would be better to keep them downstairs in the room next to her own. If they cried at night she could be by their side directly. She would have children, they would be her children. Philip was so young he would barely miss his mother and Suusje would be none the wiser after a while. She would be a real mother to them, go walking with them, take them riding in her new carriage. Suusje would be wearing a dress of best lace and Philip a handsome suit of pure white silk. She would buy them toys, a porcelain tea set for Suusje and a doll's house. She would buy Philip a rocking horse for his first birthday. The house would be filled with children's voices and the patter of tiny feet. Finally! Not the way she had planned, but children at last. This was providence. It was meant to be this way, she was sure of it. It was a pity she had thought unkindly of Bettie so often and that she had been jealous of her. Poor Bettie. She was dead, but her children would be Elisabeth's children from now on. I have children, she said, unable to contain herself.

What was keeping Carl Otto? Why was he taking so long? Why hadn't he returned by now? Maybe he would bring the children with him. How silly she was! She should have had him take the carriage. The carriage was essential, of course. How could he make his way home with two little children after dark. Perhaps Loseke would send a slave woman along to carry them. She thought it best not to have any of Loseke's slave women in the house. After all, she had slave women enough, more than thirty. No one in Paramaribo had so many as she. The children could have their own personal nanny. What was keeping the man? He could easily have been back by now. Should she send Nestor to Keizerstraat with the carriage? Yes, that would be the best solution.

'Amarante!' she shouted.

'Yes, misi,' Amarante replied from the rear gallery.

'Have Nestor bring the carriage to Masra Loseke's place,' said Elisabeth.

'Masra Loseke?' asked Amarante.

'Yes, Masra Loseke. Tell Nestor he has to collect Masra Creutz. He'll be bringing the children later,' said Elisabeth.

'Misi Bettie's children?' asked Amarante.

'Yes, masra will be bringing them later,' said Elisabeth. Amarante went outside. She had overheard a good deal of the discussion between misi and masra and wondered what Misi Elisabeth was planning.

Nestor was still harnessing the horse when he saw Masra Creutz climb the steps up to the house.

'What did he say? When are the children coming?' asked Elisabeth at the door. Carl Otto said nothing, walked into the front room and poured himself a Jenever.

'Why are you silent? Did you speak to Loseke?' asked Elisabeth.

'Yes, I spoke to Loseke,' he replied, holding his glass up to the light and taking a drink.

'Well then, what did he say? Why didn't you bring the children with you?' Elisabeth asked impatiently.

'The children were asleep, naturally. Boi!' he shouted.

Cadet came into the room, got to his knees, and started removing his masra's shoes.

'When can we expect them? Tomorrow? Will he bring them or should I collect them myself?' Elisabeth spluttered.

'Boi, take my shoes to Firans and tell him to give them a good polishing. You can go to bed after that,' said Carl Otto calmly. He then turned to Elisabeth: 'Come and sit, mi gudu.'

But she stayed where she was and shouted: 'Tell me this instant. When are they coming?'

'They're not coming,' said Creutz.

'What did you say? Why not? Did you tell Loseke what I told you to say? Did you explain it to him?' she asked, thumping her hand with her fist and fidgeting nervously.

'No, no, I said nothing,' said Creutz calmly.

'You said nothing!' Elisabeth screamed. 'You said nothing! Why? Why couldn't you do that one thing for me? It's all that I ask and you refuse to do it.' She thrashed at his head with her fists. The Jenever glass tinkled across the floor. 'You went to see him, but you said nothing! What kind of man are you? Well then, I'll go myself! I'll ask Loseke myself!'

'No, you won't. You're not going anywhere. I forbid it!' Creutz shouted, grabbing hold of her hand.

'Let me go! Let me go! You forbid it? You? You have nothing to forbid! I make my own decisions,' Elisabeth screamed and struggled to free herself.

'Calm yourself, woman, calm yourself!' said Carl Otto soothingly. 'What in heaven's name is wrong with you? This is not my Elisabeth. Look at yourself. You're so upset you're shaking!' He took both her hands and held them firmly. He looked her in the eyes and said: 'Calm yourself and listen to me for a moment, Elisabeth. Surely you understand that my friend Loseke is crippled with grief. When he saw me he thought I had come to comfort him. He misses his wife desperately and the thought that his children are without a mother only makes it worse. He talked about nothing else: "Ai, my sweet little Suusje and Philip. So young to be without a mother. I have to be father and mother to them at one and the same time. But I'm determined to fulfill my obligations. For the rest of my life, they will have pride of place. I promised their mother. The last thing Bettie said to me was: take good care of my children, and she was conscious of my answer: I'll do everything in my power and take good care of our children." Surely you understand, Elisabeth. When I heard his words, I could hardly tell him about our own cherished plans. Samuel will take care of his own children and that's good. He is their father.'

Carl Otto looked at his wife, at the sadness that had come over her, at her morose expression. 'Come darling girl,' he said softly, 'try not to take it so badly. Be happy for those children, that they have a father who loves them so much.'

She said nothing, turned away from him. He pulled her onto the settee beside him and held her close. He caressed her cheek and said: 'My darling, my Babetchen. Is the pain so great? The longing so immense? Do you yearn so much to have a child? Then I've let you down. I have been unable to give you the one thing you wanted. Alas, alas, my poor girl. You wanted to get married in the church and in that too I have failed you. We've been together for a long time, but our union has not been blessed with children. And that immense longing still overwhelms you. Poor girl, my darling, mi gudu.'

Elisabeth wept against his chest. She tried to swallow her tears but they flowed uncontrollably. She felt so heartbroken, so empty. She searched for Carl Otto's hand and held it tightly. At least she still had her companion, her lover, the only one who knew and understood her.

Amarante had not heard everything on the rear gallery but she had understood what had happened. She shuffled restlessly back and forth on her bench and mumbled: 'Ke, ke!'

August 1752
Carl Otto Creutz

Runaways had been at work again. Brutal attacks on three plantations in succession, made worse by the two days it took the soldiers to come to their assistance. The results were serious, people were dead. A large number of the slaves on Plantation Belle Vue had joined the runaways and the director had been murdered. The overseer on Selden Rust had been fatally wounded, the cane fields torched, a galley and a storeroom burned to the ground.

The people of Paramaribo were exceedingly concerned. The runaways were becoming more and more daring. There was talk that they were planning a large-scale attack on the city itself. Imagine it was true and the city negroes were to side with the runaways. It would spell the end of the colony. After all, there were many more blacks than whites. All the slaves would seek revenge for the suffering they had endured. The Society's soldiers were here in substantial numbers, yet the attacks continued unbridled!

Many women advised their husbands to stop donating money to the runaway fund. The country was full of soldiers, but they had done nothing to stem the activities of the diabolical rabble in the jungle.

Baron Von Sporche had a long discussion with Lieutenant Creutz. Something had to be done, and quickly, to put the fear of God into those Maroons. Creutz was given command of a major jungle expedition. He was to set off in pursuit of the runaways with a band of officers and soldiers and immediately execute each one they captured without mercy.

Creutz left in two boats with the officers, non-commissioned officers and crew. A smaller group set off on foot. They planned to set up camp at Fort Sommelsdijck. Part of the company was to follow the Upper Commewijne and the other part the Cottica, coming together in a sort of human net to trap the runaways in the middle.

The camp had only been set up for a couple of days when a number of the carriers disappeared. Creutz called the officers together for a talk.

'The defectors will betray our plans,' he said. 'We have to change our strategy and say nothing to the crew. The carriers must be kept ignorant. The group under Officer Pallack's command received orders to continue in a south-easterly direction. After a couple of days, a smaller group was despatched with orders to continue behind the plantations on the banks of the Cottica. A small number of men remained in the camp under Creutz's command. The scheme worked. The runaways concentrated themselves on the two groups. When Creutz's group set off, they encountered two Maroon villages, the first of which was completely taken by surprise at their arrival. There were three women, two children and an old man. The soldiers killed the man and one of the women who offered resistance and took the others prisoner. The inhabitants of the second village had had some advance warning. There was no one to be seen, but it was clear that they had departed in a hurry since they had left almost everything behind, including their chickens.

'Wring their necks and add them to the supplies,' one of the officers ordered.

After three days, Creutz's group met up with the group under Pallack's command. They had captured and killed six runaways. They had brought their severed hands as a trophy, which they could exchange for a bonus back in the city. They also had two old women and a younger woman in tow. One of the old women threw herself on the ground and shouted: 'Ke Masra Kroisi, help me, help me. It's me, Akuba from Toevlught. I didn't run away. The Maroons forced me to go with them. Ke Masra Kroisi, help me.'

The young woman kicked the old woman in the side as she lay on the ground and shouted: 'Get up! Keep your mouth shut!'

Two weeks later, Creutz and his command made their way back to Paramaribo by boat. Their mission had been a success. Eight executed runaways, five women and two children. The women and children were locked up in Fort Zeelandia. Cross-examination would determine whether they were to be executed or handed back to their owners after an appropriate punishing.

The people of Paramaribo and the plantation owners were impatient. What was happening with their case against Mauricius? When could they finally expect some results? What was causing all the delay in Amsterdam? Baron Von Sporche, who had been given authority over the colony on Mauricius's departure, did his best to be a decent governor, but there were so many disputes and arguments between the colonists that they had something to keep them busy on a more or less monthly basis. The Jewish community – especially the Carilhos versus the Da Costas – was also plagued with internal conflict, and the members of the Orphans' Court were accusing one another of unsound management. To top it all, the Maroon attacks were becoming more barefaced by the day.

Creutz's group had returned to the city. It was fortunate that their mission had succeeded. The soldiers were happy with the bonuses they received for every dead runaway. The governor intended to distribute the bonuses in person and say a few words of praise and encouragement, but before he had the chance, Baron Von Sporche died. He passed away on September 7th after a short illness that lasted only two days.

It was only after the governor's funeral that Carl Otto remembered the incident with the runaway woman.

'One of the prisoners we took was Akuba from Toevlught,' Creutz told Elisabeth.

'Akuba, Akuba, oh yes, I remember, we used to have an Akuba there. A negress from overseas, a sturdy woman with incisions in her face,' said Elisabeth.

'She begged for mercy and said she had been captured by the Maroons,' Creutz continued.

'Hmm, do you believe her?' Elisabeth asked.

'You never know,' said Creutz, 'although…'

'Although what?' Elisabeth was determined to know.

'Do you think the Maroons are interested in capturing old women like her. Akuba's not among the youngest anymore and the attack on Toevlught wasn't so long ago. If you want her back just let me know and I'll take care of it.'

'Want her back? No thank you. I don't want runaways on my plantation. She has to be punished.'

'So she has to die?' Creutz asked.

'That's not what I said. They could sell her. Maybe she'll do better on another plantation,' Elisabeth answered.

'If they don't believe her story, she'll be put to death,' Creutz declared. Elisabeth looked at him and answered: 'Then put her to death!'

Immediately after the death of Von Sporche, Commander Crommelin called the council members together for an extraordinary meeting. He showed them a letter, which Mauricius had left with him on his departure. It contained a resolution from the Directors of the Society stating that the commander should take over the running of the colony's affairs *ad interim* on the death of the governor. The councillors accepted the resolution.

A few days later, Creutz was in the officers' club having a drink. He had only been there a couple of minutes when Secretary Nepveu appeared and announced that a major conflict had erupted between the commander and the council members. During one of the council meetings, a letter written by Baron Van Verscheur was produced out of nowhere in which the man declared his willingness to become interim governor.

'You know what's behind this, don't you,' said Nepveu. The commander was on Mauricius's side. They don't want anyone interfering in their affairs and don't want a repeat of the past.'

'But surely there are rules to be followed,' said Creutz.

The following morning, six drummers passed through the city informing its inhabitants to the beat of the drum that Commander Crommelin had taken over the colony's administration and had been appointed interim governor. But Baron Van Verscheur had the drummers arrested. In the afternoon, a second group of drummers passed through the city under military escort, informing its inhabitants that Baron Van Verscheur had taken over.

People everywhere gathered outside their houses, offering commentary on the situation for all to hear. When Van Verscheur's drummers entered Heerenstraat, Creutz emerged from his house and saw his neighbours, the De Mirandas, standing on the stairs at the front of their house. 'What do you think?' Jacob de Miranda shouted over to Creutz.

'Unheard of,' Creutz shouted back. 'Nestor, get the carriage ready, we're going to hear what the secretary has to say about all this.' Jacob de Miranda joined him in the carriage and the men headed off in the direction of the palace.

Mrs De Miranda paced up and down in front of her house. When she saw Elisabeth appear on the steps she said: 'Misi Elisabeth, what a situation! Before you know it Mrs Duvoisin will be declaring herself governor. Yes, why not!'

Elisabeth laughed and said: 'It'll sort itself out, wait and see.' She refused to be enticed into making a comment.

The wrangling continued. Van Verscheur based his claim on Crommelin's missive, which spoke of 'a provision in the event that Mauricius should die'. Mauricius was alive and well in Holland, while Baron Von Sporche was dead and his wishes deserved to be respected. Crommelin refused to take part in an assembly he considered to be illegal and left in a rage for his plantation, Rust en Werk.

The cabal still seemed to be active! Mrs Duvoisin organised an extravagant ball on the occasion of Van Verscheur's acceptance of his new position. Opponents such as Creutz and Nepveu were not invited. Several families in Gravenstraat, Heerenstraat and along Waterkant put out flags. Dancing, singing and drinking were the order of the day.

Crommelin remained on his plantation. He did not come to Paramaribo for the reception in honour of the princess regent's birthday on November 2nd, nor did he attend the New Year reception.

Creutz was walking along Gravenstraat one day when Mrs Couderc shouted: 'Mix black and white together and you get a zebra!'

One Sunday, as Elisabeth was taking her place in church, she overheard Mrs Duvoisin say to Mrs Scherping: 'Can't you smell it? That stench?' And she answered, 'You mean the stench of a black whore.'

On 31 January 1753, news arrived from the princess regent and from the Directors of the Society. Van Verscheur and his supporters were severely reprimanded for their behaviour and he was instructed to hand over the reins of power to Commander Crommelin without delay.

Secretary Jean Nepveu rushed to tell Creutz and almost collided with Elisabeth in his haste. Trying to catch his breath he said: 'Good day, Misi Elisabeth. Where is the masra? I have excellent news.'

Creutz had heard Nepveu's voice and appeared in an instant.

'Letters from Holland!' Nepveu exclaimed. 'The Society is furious at Baron Van Verscheur. Crommelin's their man. He is to take over as interim governor.'

'D'you see! It turned out well after all!' said Creutz. 'We must go to Rust en Werk, Nepveu, the commander should be informed immediately.'

'Right away,' said Nepveu. 'The commander will be more than content with the news.'

They headed off together for Rust en Werk on the River Commewijne. When they arrived, they realised that Crommelin's family seemed particularly concerned and sad. Johanna Margaretha, their thirteen-year-old daughter, was seriously ill and they feared for her life. To make matters worse, their eldest daughter Catharina Elisabeth had passed away on precisely the same day – January 31st – two years earlier.[17] The family were huddled together in their grief and were not much interested in what Nepveu had to say. But in spite of the sad circumstances, the news gave the interim governor a sparkle of hope, and when his daughter's condition improved that evening he was able to give his full attention to Nepveu's report.

Two days later, Crommelin came to Paramaribo to take over as interim governor. A number of council members were not present in the assembly, nor did they appear at the simple reception offered at the palace. The Scherpings and the Duvoisins had spread the word among the merchant captains that anyone showing the slightest sign of joy would no longer receive supplies of coffee or sugar.[18]

March 1753
Elisabeth

'Amarante, where is Dido? She promised to braid my hair,' said Elisabeth.

'Dido's not here misi, she's gone to the market,' Amarante replied. 'Shall I send Sara or Venis?'

'No, I'll wait for Dido to return,' said Elisabeth and she continued with her work. She checked the figures in the statements she had received from the director of Clevia. After the best part of two hours she looked up from her papers. It was eleven o'clock. What was keeping Dido?

'Amarante? Is Dido back yet?' Elisabeth asked.

'No, misi, I haven't seen her,' Amarante answered.

'What on earth is keeping her? Since when has she been going to the market, anyway? Surely that's Lucretia's job. And where is Lucretia?' asked a slightly irritated Elisabeth. Things were not running according to plan.

'Hmm, Lucretia also went to the market,' said Amarante quietly.

'No, Lucretia is already back,' said Sara who was dusting the furniture.

'So they were both at the market and Lucretia came back alone. Where then is Dido? I'll have to teach that girl a lesson one of these days,' Elisabeth exclaimed.

'No misi, please,' Amarante pleaded guardedly.

'Do you know where she is then?' asked Elisabeth.

'Ke misi, don't be angry with Dido, ba, ke! I think she's with her friend. If misi doesn't mind, I can braid misi's hair, or Sara,' said Amarante contritely.

'With her friend? Does she have a friend?' asked Elisabeth.

'Yes misi and she's ever so in love,' said Amarante.

'And who is her friend?' asked Elisabeth.

'Well misi, it's Adam, one of Misi Audra's boys, eh-eh Mrs Duvoisin,' Amarante answered.

'That woman!' Elisabeth roared. 'Heavens above, I hope she doesn't make trouble. Does she know about it?'

'Misi Audra knows nothing. Fortunately! Adam comes to Dido sometimes, but his misi doesn't know about it,' said Sara who had been following the conversation from the dining room and had appeared at the door with a duster in her hand.

'Is he kind to her?' Elisabeth asked.

'Ehe misi, very kind. He loves her. He always brings something for her, something sweet to eat,' said Sara.

'And where does he find sweet things to eat?' asked Amarante with a worried expression on her face.

'Maybe he buys it. He works three days a week for a carpenter in Hogestraat,' said Sara.

'You seem to know all about it!' said Amarante sternly. Sara said nothing and returned to the dining room where she continued with her dusting.

'And where is Dido at this minute?' asked Elisabeth.

'I really don't know, misi,' said Amarante.

'Oh well, let the child enjoy herself while she can. We're only young once! As long as she's careful. Send Dido to me when she gets back and tell Venis to come and braid my hair,' said Elisabeth.

Dido arrived back at two o'clock. Elisabeth was about to go to her room for her afternoon nap. 'Misi asked to see me?' said Dido.

Elisabeth looked at the girl. Doesn't she look radiant, she thought. She must be very much in love.

'And your friend, how is he?' asked Elisabeth.

Dido smiled. 'Good, misi,' she said shyly.

'Where do you see each other?' asked Elisabeth.

The girl shrugged her shoulders and mumbled softly: 'Hmm, here and there.'

'Does he treat you as he should? Is he kind to you?'

'Yes, misi, yes, he's kind, yes,' Dido answered with a smile.

'Tell him to meet you here. I think that's better than "here and there",' Elisabeth insisted. 'As long as neither of you neglects your duties.'

'No misi, thank you misi,' Dido exclaimed, her face radiant with delight. 'Is there anything I can do for misi?'

'Not for the moment. Go off now and enjoy yourself,' said Elisabeth with a laugh and Dido hurried outside, exclaiming a second time: 'Thank you misi, thank you.'

Elisabeth saw little of Dido the following week, but then she noticed her in the house with a broom and as she walked past Dido whispered: 'Good day, misi.'

'What's the matter? Where's that smile of yours?' said Elisabeth.

Dido hung her head and said nothing, but Elisabeth noticed a tear run down her cheek.

'Are you ill?' Elisabeth asked, but Dido shook her head in silence.

'Has she broken up with her friend?' Elisabeth asked Amarante a moment or two later. 'Did he leave her?'

'No, misi, that's not it,' said Amarante.

'His misi found out he wasn't sleeping at home, that he was here all the time with Dido. His misi waited for him and had him lashed. One of the futubois sneaked out to tell Dido. Misi Duvoisin has locked Adam up and plans to send him to her plantation. He's leaving tomorrow for Berg en Dal.'

'Dear oh dear! Poor Dido, and that poor boy. We have to do something,' said Elisabeth.

'There's nothing misi can do, he's locked up,' said Amarante. 'And misi knows what Misi Duvoisin is like. She'll treat him badly, that's for sure.'

'Ke poti, that poor boy. And what about Dido?' asked Elisabeth.

'Ja baya! Ke, that's what happens when you're katibo. You're not even allowed to love someone because you don't belong to yourself and the one you love belongs to another. Katibo, a fate worse than death!' Amarante lamented.

'Wait a minute! I could buy him, then he'll be one of us,' said Elisabeth.

'What is misi thinking?' said Amarante with a tyuri. 'Misi Duvoisin will never sell Adam to misi. If she hears misi wants to buy him she'll punish him even more.'

'You're right,' said Elisabeth pondering the situation. 'We have to find another way. We have to buy him without letting her know who we are. I'll have to speak to the masra about it. Perhaps he can suggest something.'

She told Carl Otto all about it.

'And what do you want me to do?' he asked. 'The woman's hair stands on end the moment she sees me or hears my name.'

'That's not a problem,' said Elisabeth. 'She doesn't have much hair left under that wig of hers! But can't you send someone else? She doesn't have to know that the boy is coming to us.'

'Good idea. I'll send someone to make the purchase. But who would be best?' Carl Otto wondered aloud.

'Lieutenant Van Steenberch,' said Elisabeth.

'Yes, not a bad suggestion. Perhaps his son would be better. He can pretend he's making the purchase on behalf of the government,' said Carl Otto.

'Here's the money, man. How much do you think they'll ask? Never mind! As long as the boy doesn't end up on her plantation. Look, here's six hundred guilders… no eight hundred… wait, take a thousand,' said Elisabeth as she fetched the money from the drawer of her writing desk.

'That's generous,' Carl Otto chuckled. 'Why are you doing this anyway?'

'For Dido, of course,' Elisabeth replied.

A couple of hours later, Willem Van Steenberch knocked on Mrs Duvoisin's door. 'The government has a mind to purchase a couple of hale and hearty young negroes,' he said. 'They're needed for the fort prison and perhaps the occasional jungle expedition. We're looking for the rough and ready sort, up to a good lashing and other punishments if they need it. The type you'd be happy to see the back of, if you get my drift. I've been asked to inquire with various owners.'

'I've just what you need,' said Mrs Duvoisin. 'I was planning to send him to my plantation, but this is better. Work him hard there at the fort, he needs to be taught a thing or two about what happens when negroes misbehave. How much are you offering?'

'Eh… four hundred guilders if he's up to the mark,' answered Willem Van Steenberch.

'Four hundred? Are you mad? He's worth every bit of eight hundred,' the reverend's wife exclaimed.

'Is that your best offer?' Van Steenberch bargained.

Mrs Duvoisin refused to go lower than six hundred guilders.

Van Steenberch agreed to return that evening with the paperwork and to fetch the young slave.

Adam was released from confinement around eight and handed over to Van Steenberch, his hands bound and an iron ball and chain around each ankle.

The same evening, Creutz handed his wife four hundred guilders and said: 'Success! Van Steenberch bought the young man for six hundred guilders. What next?'

'Have Van Steenberch bring him here early tomorrow morning. Make sure the slaves know nothing about it. Tell Van Steenberch to knock on our bedroom window,' Elisabeth said with a smile, delighted at the idea that her plan was working.

Adam arrived as planned the following morning. She had Nestor remove the manacles from his ankles and the rope from his wrists. 'Hush,' said Elisabeth with her finger at her lips. 'Say nothing, Nestor!' Adam was hurried inside and Elisabeth sized him up in the gallery.

'So, you're Adam,' she said.

'Yes, misi,' the man replied respectfully.

'And you love Dido?' asked Elisabeth.

Adam didn't know what to say. He loved Dido but didn't want to get her into trouble so he held his tongue.

'Answer, boy, answer,' said Amarante.

'Misi here paid a tidy sum for you and she has a right to know everything,' said Nestor.

Then Adam realised that the misi had purchased him. He didn't know what she was planning, but whatever it was she would have her way. She was his new mistress and there was no way out of it. 'Yes, misi, I love Dido.'

'Good. Then you are free to be with her. But remember, Dido is one of my girls. Treat her well, be kind to her, and don't even think about cheating on her.'

'No, misi, of course not, thank you, misi,' said Adam and he looked at his new mistress full of expectation.

'You can see Dido later. Amarante, bring him upstairs to the back room. Tell him to stand behind the cupboard and only show himself when Dido comes up to fetch something,' said Elisabeth.

Dido came into the house two hours later, summoned by Amarante. She sauntered listlessly into the room and said in a low voice: 'Misi called?'

'Yes, I called. Why such a glum face?' said Elisabeth. 'Are you hungry?'

'No, misi,' said the girl quietly.

'Have you been getting enough sleep?' Elisabeth inquired.

'Yes, misi,' Dido whispered.

'Are you ill?' Elisabeth persisted.

The girl shook her head, her eyes downcast.

'Come on then, Dido, be off with you upstairs to the back room and fetch two blue towels from the cupboard,' said Elisabeth.

The girl slowly climbed the stairs. Elisabeth, Carl Otto, Amarante, Sara, Venis and Nestor waited excitedly at the bottom of the stairs. At first they heard nothing, then a thud, then a shriek.

'Mi Gado!' they heard Dido exclaim, followed by laughs and screams. A blissfully happy Adam and Dido came running down the stairs.

'Mi Gado, misi! It's Adam! What happened? How come he's here?' spluttered Dido as she held her friend tightly and looked elatedly at her mistress.

'Adam will be living with us from now on,' said Elisabeth.

The two lovers threw themselves into each other's arms. Adam kissed Dido without paying the slightest attention to the people around them.

'Aren't you going to thank misi?' Amarante interrupted, yanking Dido's arm.

Dido let Adam go. She fell to her knees, threw her arms round Elisabeth's waist and sobbed: 'Thank you, misi, thank you, I'll do whatever you ask of me. Anything, anything, now and forever.'

'Be off with you,' said Elisabeth, a little embarrassed at the situation. 'Today you are free, today and tomorrow. Go and enjoy your love for one another.'

Adam and Dido rushed hand in hand down the steps at the side of the house.

'Where are they going?' asked Carl Otto with a smile.

'I have no idea,' said Elisabeth. 'They'll probably look for a quiet spot somewhere.' She took Carl Otto's hand and said: 'Such a beautiful thing to be young and free to love one another undisturbed, isn't it.'

Carl Otto put his arm around Elisabeth's shoulder and they walked side by side to the dining room where he pulled her onto the settee beside him. 'It pleases me to see that my wife is more than a hard-headed business woman,' he said.

'And I thought that was just what you wanted, because business isn't your cup of tea,' Elisabeth chuckled.

'I suppose you're right. But I also love the gentle and caring Elisabeth, the one you sometimes hide deep inside. Don't hide it from me, gudu,' was his answer.

Willem Van Steenberch and his younger sister Philippina had been invited to spend Sunday at the home of Elisabeth and Captain Creutz. With their father away so often at Fort New Amsterdam and their mother long dead, Elisabeth felt sorry for them and felt they deserved more. Willem had also earned a special treat, she thought, so she had Tutuba put together all sorts of delights. Masra Creutz retired to his room for a nap after lunch. Elisabeth produced a small box from the sideboard and placed it on the table in front of Willem: 'A small token of my gratitude, Masra Willem. Come along Philippina, let's see what Venis has prepared for you in the main room.' Bristling with impatience, the girl ran after her into the other room where seamstress Venis was standing next to a chair with a splendid gold-braided, blue silk dress draped over the back. 'Try it on for size,' said Elisabeth.

'Oh! For me? How wonderful!' Philippina cheered. 'Oh my! For no reason? Such a beautiful dress!' Venis helped her into the dress and Philippina twirled with glee in front of the full-length mirror, clapped her hands and kissed Elisabeth on both cheeks. 'It's beautiful, Miss Elisabeth. Venis, the perfect fit. Sara, Amarante, look, isn't it beautiful!' She rushed into the dining room: 'Willem, Willem, look, a gift from Misi Elisabeth.'

Willem looked up from the blade he had been admiring. 'Misi Elisabeth is spoiling us. What a splendid dress. Look, she gave me this wonderful blade,' and he held up a dagger with a skilfully carved ivory grip.

'Dido, where is Dido, miss. I haven't seen her since this morning. I want to show her my dress,' Philippina exclaimed.

'Dido is in love, mi gudu,' Elisabeth said with a smile. 'And you know how lovers always want to be together. She'll likely be in the stables with Adam.' Amarante ordered one of the futubois sitting on the stairs to the rear gallery to go and fetch her.

In the meantime, Philippina had returned to Venis and Sara in the main room. Willem looked at Elisabeth, stood up and held out his hand: 'My heartfelt thanks for the wonderful gift, Miss Elisabeth.' He lifted the dagger. 'It's so beautiful. Why such generosity?'

'To thank you for what you did for us, especially for Dido,' said Elisabeth.

'You're genuinely happy for Dido, aren't you,' said Willem.

'Yes, of course. Have you seen how radiant she is? I hope from the bottom of my heart that Adam is worthy of all that love and consideration,' Elisabeth answered. 'I've never seen Dido so content, so happy.'

Willem looked at her and pondered. After a moment or two he asked: 'Do you love Dido?'

'Of course I love Dido,' Elisabeth laughed, a little taken aback by the question. 'She's one of us!'

'I realise that,' said Willem, 'but she's your slave. Please don't think ill of me. I don't mean to be eh… eh, unkind… but eh… eh, isn't it a little strange?' he asked cautiously.

'Strange? What do you mean?' asked Elisabeth.

'I'm not sure how to put it. You treat your slaves well, I know, but they are still slaves and eh… you… eh…' Willem continued, unable to find the words to say what he wanted to say.

'I'm black, you mean,' said Elisabeth calmly.

'Yes... eh... yes, that's what I don't understand,' Willem quipped.

'My dear boy, what can I say? I didn't create the world, I didn't invent slavery and I certainly didn't decide that black people should be slaves to white people. The world is the way I found it, but I did discover something else, something very important. If you want to count in this world of ours, you have to have money. But money doesn't grow on trees. You have to earn it in one way or another, and in Suriname you need slaves to earn money. If it had been possible I would have had white slaves as well, but alas... I want to earn money, so I need slaves. But my slaves are my own people and I don't abuse them. I give them everything they need, even a sweetheart on occasion, as you will have noticed.'

'Everything but their freedom,' said Willem.

'Indeed, everything but their freedom,' Elisabeth concurred. 'But imagine I had spent all my money granting my slaves their freedom. Would I have done them a service? Not in the least. Then I would have no one to work for me. And worst of all, my people might have been free but they would have lost their sense of security. They would be homeless, without a roof over their heads, without food, without care. They would have nothing. Before long they would return to slavery, and probably to atrocious conditions and maltreatment. That's the way life is in Suriname. What kind of choice do I have?'

'But aren't you being hypocritical?' asked Willem.

'Perhaps, but what else can I do? Am I the only hypocrite? I think not. Take a look at those Hollanders for one,' Elisabeth answered.

'The Hollanders? Which Hollanders?' asked Willem.

'Just take a look at the way those Hollanders and white people everywhere earn their money and how they defend their practices,' said Elisabeth.

'Some people in Holland earn a great deal of money, but there's no slavery. In Africa perhaps, but not Holland,' said Willem.

'I know that, Willem, but I also know that the Hollanders keep slavery alive here in Suriname. They bring slaves from Africa and are delighted to tell whoever will listen that slavery has been around in Africa for a long, long time. I'm aware that slavery has been part of many civilisations and still exists in some places. The Greeks and the Romans kept slaves. In Africa, a person becomes a slave when his tribe is defeated by another. But slaves in Africa become members of the family and male slaves are even free to marry their master's daughter if they wish. And if a defeated tribe reclaims victory, the roles are reversed, as long as the slaves haven't been bought up by slave traders and deported of course. Your slavery, or should I say the slavery that the whites introduced, is different. Your slavery is dreadful, degrading, because it is based on race. Negroes are forced to be slaves of white people simply because they are negroes. And in order to defend their behaviour the whites come up with theories that proclaim negroes to be less than human, that they have no brains and cannot think, that they have no feelings, that they're some kind of animal made for work. They use God and the Bible to demonstrate that the Christian European perspective is right.

'Whites, Christians, claim the right to load their ships with negroes and transport them as if they were animals from Africa to America where they're forced to spend the rest of their days, cut off from their families, worked to the bone. Why don't whites do that with their own people? They don't do it with whites because they consider whites to be the superior race. Superior, hmm, you could fool me! Many of them are nothing more than villains. No, the whites use negroes to do their dirty work because negroes are not really human, and if they are they're of a much inferior race. Black people will never recover from this humiliation. Never! You've been here long enough to know that many of the whites in Paramaribo can't stand the sight of me, Elisabeth Samson. Have I done them any wrong? Of course not! I am a negress and in their books I should be a slave, but I'm not a slave. I can read and write and have a successful business. Evidence enough that their reasoning is flawed. That's why they hate me.

'There is nothing more hypocritical and contradictory than the laws and regulations binding in Suriname. They abhor the pagan ways of the slaves but refuse to allow them to become Christian. And if a slave is granted his freedom, he is obliged to become Christian without delay.

'How many white men live with black women? They refer to them as their housekeepers, if they want to be polite, but otherwise she's a whore. Take note, *she's* a whore, a sinful woman, but nothing untoward is said of him. But a white man cannot marry a black woman. That's the way it is. Mark my words, if the possibility existed to purchase white slaves, I would have plenty of them and enough work to keep them busy.'

Elisabeth fell silent. She realised that her words had been too intense for Willem. He was a foreigner after all, a white man. She looked at him. He too was silent.

'My dear young man, forgive my frankness,' said Elisabeth. 'I spoke openly because I trust you and I hope we can keep what I said between us.'

'But you're right, what you said is right,' Willem exclaimed.

'Perhaps, but the truth need not always be made public. Keep what I said to yourself,' said Elisabeth flatly.

'Naturally,' said Willem. A few moments later he asked: 'Do you think slavery will ever be abolished?'

'I don't think so, no. Perhaps one day, in the far distant future, but not in our day. And if it does happen, then, then…'

'What then?' asked Willem, curious to hear what she would say next. 'Then Suriname will cease to exist. Or rather, Suriname as I know it will cease to exist. I can't imagine it otherwise, since the country and everything in it exists in and through slavery,' said Elisabeth. She wanted to continue but held her tongue when she heard laughter and people talking in the other room. Philippina appeared at the door followed by Dido, Venis and Sara, and everyone's attention returned to the blue silk dress.

July 1753

Interim governor Crommelin and the Police Council were at odds with one another. Crommelin even had the feeling that 'the cabal', as Mauricius had called them, were back at work in an extraordinary fashion. When the governor proposed a major offensive against the runaways who had renewed their attacks on the plantations, he was accused of 'abusing his authority'. According to Crommelin, too many of the military were idle and causing too much boisterousness in the city where they frequently got up to all sorts of mischief.

On July 11th, however, news arrived from the Netherlands: Mauricius had won his case!

A blissfully happy Jean Nepveu appeared at the house: 'Misi Elisabeth, where is Masra Creutz? There's a letter from Holland. Mauricius has won his case. Ha ha! Some folks are in for a nasty surprise.'

Creutz heard Nepveu's voice and came to the door. 'What did I hear?'

'It's true, man. Mauricius has won. A resolution of the States General acquitted him of every accusation on May 13th. Duplessis has to pay the costs and Mauricius is free to take him to court for slander!'

'Excellent, excellent!' said Creutz. 'This calls for a drink! Come inside, man. Rufus, where is Rufus?' The little futuboi ran off to fetch Rufus who was ordered to hurry over to Keizerstraat and tell Masra Loseke he was expected without delay. The men relaxed in the front room and drank more than a few glasses to the success of their friend Mauricius.

The following morning, Elisabeth received a visit from her neighbour Mrs De Miranda. 'Whatever will happen next!' said Misi De Miranda. 'Did you hear that Misi Duvoisin was so angry at the news from Holland that it made her ill?'

'No, I hadn't heard!' said Elisabeth in all honesty.

'And Misi Duplessis burst into tears. She had been counting on her husband returning as governor. That daughter of hers, that Susanna, was so angry she started to throw things all over the house. She even had three slaves given a thorough hiding because she claimed they laughed when they saw her so angry.'

'What a world!' Elisabeth answered.

Throughout the colony, everyone was talking about the letter from Holland and Mrs Duvoisin's illness.

'Has misi not heard? She's at death's door. She had a stroke and can no longer speak or walk. Her slaves have to carry her around and she just lies there. If she wants to say something, she mumbles, hmm, hmm, hmm,' said Amarante.

Legislative Councillor Curtius, who had sided with Verscheur, was dismissed, and Secretary Jean Nepveu was appointed *ad interim* in his place. Crommelin, encouraged by the words of praise he had received from the Directors of the Society, was free to proceed with his plans and he invited Creutz to organise a major offensive against the runaways.

Carl Otto was not in Paramaribo when Mrs Duvoisin died on August 6th. Her daughter Henrietta Couderc-de Cheusses told her neighbours that Mauricius was to blame for her mother's death.

Carl Otto Creutz

Creutz, in the meantime, was at the start of 'a major and effective expedition' as Crommelin had put it. Carl Otto hoped that the horde of soldiers assigned to the expedition would include enough useable forces to teach the Saramaccans in the Upper Suriname region a success. They set off at the end of July. Too early in Creutz's mind, since the main dry season had not yet started. A couple of heavy showers proved him right, soaking the soldiers to the skin and bringing a few of them down with coughs and fever. They made little progress and encountered no Maroon villages, only a few patches of kostgrond that had already been cleared. Creutz also fell ill after being jabbed in the foot by a thin, razor-sharp wooden spike, which was sticking out of the ground near an abandoned Maroon settlement. The spike was sharp enough to penetrate the sole of his shoe and make a tiny yet deep wound in his foot, which became infected and unbearably painful. The fact that he could barely walk annoyed him no end and left him with the feeling that he had lost command of the situation. The expedition finally had to leave its captain behind with a high fever. He and Rufus set up camp and Rufus did his best to heal his foot with dram, while filling the masra with copious amounts of Jenever.

Kwami

He had been with the runaways for two years now and still had no regrets. On the contrary! When he got up in the morning he praised the day a Maroon had whispered to him: 'If you want to escape, bearer, then sneak out of the camp tonight. We'll be waiting to help you.'

According to Misi Elisabeth, this was to be his punishment: Pietje had to learn how difficult it was to be a bearer in the jungle. He had learned how difficult it was all right, but he had also escaped. What had Rufus thought when he didn't come back, and Masra Creutz? Probably roared with that booming voice of his: 'Pietje!'

Pietje! What a stupid name. He had changed it from the first moment. He didn't remember much about his mother, but she had once told him that his name would have been Kwami if it had not been for Misi Elisabeth and her ridiculous Pietje. He was now a free man and Misi Elisabeth could call one of her other slaves Pietje. He wasn't her slave anymore. He was no one's slave. He was free!

Life in the jungle was far from easy. The work was hard and they had to be on their guard at all times since the war with the whites was still being waged. Soldiers could appear at any moment intent on killing them. They had to stay one step ahead, but most of the time they succeeded.

Kwami was part of a small group headed by Codjo. When they brought him to their village for the first time, the men explained that he not only needed to be courageous but he also had to swear he would never betray the group. He swore the oath. If they were to capture him, he would endure their torture to the death, but he would never betray his group. He had learned a great deal in the two years that had passed. He could find his way through the jungle, paddle, steer a boat through rapids with a koelastok, was handy with a bow and arrow, could fish, hunt, and best of all: pass through the jungle without detection. He loved his new life. It was full of adventure and to cap it all, he was free. If there were no soldiers about, the women would work the kostgrond and take care of the meals while the men went hunting and fishing. In the evening, everyone settled round a large campfire and told stories, mostly about the hardships they had endured and the way they had been taken from their homes in Africa. The stories were often so stirring that Kwami almost felt ashamed of his own past, born in a house on someone's property in the city where he had lived all his life without maltreatment or terrible punishments. Codjo, on the other hand, had told the story of his capture and the journey from Africa.

His group, which included two women nursing infants, had been chained together and driven without rest along the African coast. When it was time to board the ship, the sailors grabbed the babies and threw them overboard. One woman jumped into the water after her baby and both drowned together. The other woman was in chains and unable to jump, but she started to fight with the sailors, scratching and biting wherever she could. When she stuck her fingers in one of the sailors' eyes, another man hit her on the head with the butt of his rifle. She fell to the ground unconscious, was pushed into the hold and suffocated under the weight of the remaining slaves who were forced in on top of her. They found her dead the next day and had to throw her overboard. Dandilo, one of the other men, spoke of the sharks that relentlessly followed the slave ships, knowing there would be plenty of negro meat to feast on.

'Those sharks knew where their next meal was coming from, and no mistake!' a couple of the others had chuckled, but Kwami didn't understand how anyone could laugh at such a story. When he mentioned it to Nana, the oldest woman of the tribe, she looked at him long and hard and said: 'Let them laugh. If all we could do was weep for our fate, our tears would have dried up long ago.'

The group had recently attacked one of the plantations in search of guns and especially bullets and gunpowder. As ever, a platoon of soldiers was despatched from the city. 'Na kapten Kroisi e kon!' the men would say, aware that Lieutenant Creutz knew the jungle and the Maroons like the back of his hand. But this time Masra Creutz was out of luck. He had stepped on one of the sharp spikes Codjo had buried in the ground near an abandoned village and now he was sick and had been forced to strike camp. The soldiers he had with him were inexperienced, recent arrivals from Europe. Many of them were also sick and hoping they could lie in their hammocks undisturbed.

Kwami had helped clear the lijn to fool the soldiers into thinking they were following the Maroon tracks. In reality it lead to a biri-biri. The Maroons had concealed themselves in the jungle and watched as the soldiers nervously encircled the biri-biri. The officer finally gave the order to cross the biri-biri and the soldiers waded in waist deep, holding their rifles above their heads to keep them dry. At that moment Codjo gave the signal. Kwami and three of Codjo's men broke cover and fired. The soldiers panicked. Two of them took direct hits and disappeared into the marsh, three managed to reach the side of the marsh in spite of their wounds but collapsed on the spot, and the others ran along the banks shooting in every direction, but to no avail. The Maroons were already gone. After the soldiers had continued on their way, a few of the Maroons returned to the scene, dragged two corpses out of the marsh and hid them in the bushes where Codjo and Kwami collected them later for preparation. Kwami was allowed to help. While they were readying the various herbs,

Codjo told him all about the plans for that evening. They were going to invade the soldiers' camp. Kwami had a gift for imitating voices and was to have an important role to play in the attack.

Codjo's men had surrounded the camp around midnight. The soldiers were asleep and noticed nothing. Two soldiers were on watch and were nodding off by the campfire. Without making a sound, Kwami and Codjo dragged the prepared corpses into the camp. Then Codjo fired a shot, which startled the sleeping soldiers. The voice of Lieutenant Creutz resounded through the camp: 'Run, men, run! Take nothing with you! Run! Run for your lives!' The still dazed soldiers scattered in every direction, saw two of their comrades already dead on the ground and tried to save themselves without knowing where to run in the darkness.

In the midst of the confusion, ten Maroons ran into the camp, grabbed rifles, bullets and gunpowder and disappeared unnoticed into the jungle. When the soldiers had recovered from their initial panic, they looked around in shock. Who had passed through the camp? Had the bearers come to save the ammunition? Where was Lieutenant Creutz? Was he in the camp? Surely they had left him behind three days earlier. But they had heard his voice, clear as day!

Codjo's men were already long on their way to their hiding place. They laughed and passed around their booty, praising Kwami for his excellent imitation of Kapten Kroisi's voice.

October 1753
Elisabeth

Carl Otto had returned from yet another expedition a sick man. His company were still positioned in the Upper Suriname region, but when Rufus realised how sick his masra had become he went for help. After following a creek for four hours he finally arrived at a small plantation. The owner was a mulatto. They fetched Creutz in a dug-out boat and tried to make him as comfortable as possible. They brought him first to station Gelderland and from there they boarded a tent boat, which carried him to the city, a two-day journey. Elisabeth was appalled and immediately summoned the surgeon who quickly realised the man was seriously ill. The infection had worsened and gangrene had set in. The only way to save Creutz's life was to amputate his foot, but Elisabeth wouldn't hear of it. She ordered Rufus to stay at his masra's side and sent Nestor and Firans to fetch Kwasi from Timotibo without delay. Everybody knew that Kwasi was the best negro doctor available. Two days passed before Kwasi arrived, two days in which Carlo Otto's life hung in the balance. Jean

Nepveu, father and son Van Steenberch, Masras Planteau, Saffin, Strube, and other friends came to ask after the lieutenant captain's health. They gathered in the front room and asked themselves if it would not be better to intervene and have Creutz's foot amputated. That black woman was waiting for Kwasi, and while everyone believed the man could work miracles, they were afraid his arrival might be too late.

Kwasi treated Carl Otto's foot with herbs, liniments, oils and hot and cold poultices. Slowly but surely his temperature normalised and he stepped back from death's door. It took the best part of a week before there was any sign of improvement, although he continued to be feeble and seriously ill for a considerable period of time. In spite of Tutuba's best efforts and massages from Rufus and Venis, it took months before he could get to his feet and walk.

In the same week that Creutz's life was hanging on a thread, one of Maria's slaves came to fetch Elisabeth. Her sister was dying and she had to go to her without delay. Elisabeth was at a complete loss. She did not want to leave Creutz alone, but Maria was more than a sister to her. She had raised her as a mother. Nestor drove her to Waterkant just in time. Maria died half an hour later.

Elisabeth returned home, feeling stifled by death, especially after news arrived that former officer Van Steenberch had died of a heart attack. During the aitdei for Maria, Elisabeth sat in the front room of her old home listening to the laments of the mourners. Nanette nudged her gently and asked in a whisper how it was with Masra Creutz: 'Not bad, but it's a slow process; he's not out of the woods yet. We still don't know what will happen to his foot.'

'Surely you remember that Carl Otto is the executor of Maria's will?' Catharina asked. Elisabeth had completely forgotten.

'Perhaps we should find someone else to do the job. Carl Otto is still too weak,' she answered.

'Let's leave it until he gets better. Our sister knew what she was doing when she made him executor. There's no great rush,' Catharina suggested.

Creutz improved at a snail's pace. His friends visited faithfully and when they were in the house Elisabeth would complain: Why did Creutz have to spend half his life chasing those runaways in the jungle? Wasn't it time for someone younger to take over? He'd been on the job for twenty years! Was it his fault that the Maroons were becoming more and more violent? No, he had nothing to do with it. He had done what he could and he was staying at home from now on and that was that.

On October 29th, a beaming Jean Nepveu rushed up the front steps and shouted: 'Misi Elisabeth, your wish has come true!' Carl Otto was sitting in one armchair with his ailing foot resting on another.

'There's been a missive from Holland!' Jean exclaimed. 'The princess regent has dismissed the councils without loss of honour or dignity. Nine new council members have been appointed, and Strube is the only remnant of the old administration. You'll never guess who has been appointed as one of the new council members!'

Carl Otto looked at the messenger and laughed: 'Go on, tell me!'

'Carl Otto Creutz, of course!' Nepveu exclaimed.

He then told them in detail about the assembly that morning and how Crommelin had informed the councillors of the princess regent's decision. They had responded with their usual hypocrisy, delighted as they were that it had pleased her majesty to discharge them from such an onerous office, which had brought them so many difficulties. The same afternoon, the drummer passed through the city, publicly proclaiming the dismissals and the new appointments.

On November 2nd, the new councils were installed. It was the princess regent's birthday and flags fluttered above many of the buildings. The governor hosted a sumptuous ball at the palace, which was decorated and illuminated for the occasion. Creutz was unable to attend. He was at home with his foot on a chair and still found it difficult to walk. Elisabeth remembered how November 2nd had always been an occasion of sadness for her, but now she wished her companion had been able to attend the festivities. This time, an evening alone would have been easy to put up with.

It took until November 17th before Creutz was able to take the Police Council oath,[19] leaning on a stick and supported by Rufus. Elisabeth had not given the expected feast. She thought it inappropriate after the recent death of her sister Maria.

She made sure nevertheless that Carl Otto's friends were invited to an excellent dinner and an agreeable game of cards at their home, during which the Jenever flowed in considerable quantities.

December 1760

Elisabeth was sitting at her writing desk surrounded by ledgers and bills. She refused to allow anyone else to take care of her accounts and correspondence and set aside two mornings a week to see to it herself. According to the figures, she had earned fifty thousand in the past year. Coffee was much sought after in Europe and the harvests at Clevia and her other plantations had been excellent. She had rented out Toevlught six years earlier to her young nephew Pieter Planteau, the son of her cousin La Vallaire and Masra Pierre Planteau. His father wanted him to learn the plantation business at first hand and had not accepted Elisabeth's offer to make him director of the place. The young man was to be responsible for the entire plantation and his father was happy to pay the required rent. He probably thinks I'll sell it to him one day, she thought, but then he would be in for an unpleasant surprise. The woodland at Onverwacht had also done well. There was money in Suriname and people were building!

In spite of her own prosperity, life in Suriname had been difficult for many in recent years. Ill-health and death were rife, especially among the children. Jean Nepveu had buried three of his own and the Coudercs had lost a son and a daughter on the same day a couple of weeks earlier. Catharina's partner, Pieter Courvlught, had also died. Almost every family was mourning the death of a loved one.

'Misi, Masra Braband is here to see you,' said Sara, who was busy in the dining room and had heard a knock at the door.

'Ask Masra Braband to wait. I'll be there in a moment,' said Elisabeth.

She already had a good idea why Braband had come to visit. Christoph Polycarpus Braband, verger and organist at the Reformed Church, had been one of her tenants for two years and was living in a couple of rooms above the stables and the coach house. Three years earlier she had had a substantial building constructed on the opposite side of the street in front of the slaves quarters, with the stables for her three horses and a coach house for two coaches.

Braband was not only her tenant, he had also borrowed money from her for a country estate or piece of woodland in Onverwacht. She had told him a year earlier that she and Nanette both owned woodland in Onverwacht, but he had no money to start such a venture so she gave him a loan. Perhaps he was here to pay his first instalment.

'Masra Braband, what can I do for you?' said Elisabeth. Braband got to his feet as she entered the room. He stood there coyly with his hat in his hand, rubbing its rim with his fingers.

'It's about the instalment, misi,' he whispered. 'I've come to ask for a deferment.'

'Oh well, if there's no alternative,' said Elisabeth. 'When do you think you can pay?'

'I'm certain I can make the first instalment in three months' time,' said Braband. 'There have been delays, you see.'

'Fine, then I won't charge extra interest,' said Elisabeth.

'Thank you, misi,' said the man. 'Eh... dare I ask... I'm running a little short at the moment... eh could I borrow a candle and candlestick.'

'I think we can manage that,' said Elisabeth, 'but you will have to ask Firans, he's in charge of the candles and candlesticks.'

'I will misi, thank you, misi,' said the man as he descended the stairs in front of the house.

Elisabeth watched him leave and smiled. She felt a sense of satisfaction when a bakra had to ask for something and behave submissively towards her. She was a woman of substance. In spite of the colour of her skin, many a man raised his hat to her in the street or saluted her as she passed in her new calash. Many of the same men owed her money, since she had been lending to small businesses run by whites, coloureds and blacks for a couple of years. She charged them interest, but not as much as many of the other moneylenders. Her debtors appreciated her generosity. She had money and she was a woman to be reckoned with in Suriname.

She had many white people among her friends and acquaintances, but she was only invited to parties and other get-togethers by free coloureds and mixed couples where the man was white and his partner was a coloured concubine. She frequently gave her own dinner parties and receptions at which no expense was spared and the guests were treated to exclusive dishes, the most expensive wines. On most occasions, the women, both white and black, would praise her fashionable clothing and her beautifully furnished home. Heads turned when she went to church, everyone wanting to see if she was wearing something new. When she and Carl Otto were invited to one or other festivity, she would always arrive with a substantial gift for her host. Willem Van Steenberch, for example, received a magnificent grandfather clock on his wedding day and his sister Philippina Van Steenberch a canteen of silver cutlery when she married Jacques Saffin two years earlier. She also gave their daughter Jacoba a golden rattle to celebrate the day of her birth and a gold chain with rubies for her first birthday.

Elisabeth was never invited to the palace, however, and she was well aware that the married white women who were invited always belittled her and dark-skinned concubines. Elisabeth sighed. Just one invitation to the palace, she thought, just one.

She made her way to the front room and looked around. Braband must be spending his nights in the dark. He had asked for a candlestick. She had presumed he meant a simple candlestick and candle and not one of the many crystal candelabras that decorated the walls of her house.

She heard the coach pull up in front of the house and Carl Otto appeared moments later. His infirmity seemed to be worse, Elisabeth thought. Since the accident with his foot, Carl Otto had walked with a limp and when he was tired, as he now was, it became more pronounced. At least he can sit in comfort, she thought, now we have the calash. She was content that she had insisted on buying a magnificent new coach a couple of years earlier, in spite of his opposition. No one in the colony had a coach like it, with its canvas fold-open roof. Even the governor's coach was more modest and he looked at theirs with jealousy. Creutz had room in it to stretch his bad leg.

Leaning on Rufus's shoulder and with little Otje, Adam and Dido's son, behind him, Carl Otto made his way to the front room. Elisabeth heard a thud followed by loud curses and grumbling. Little Otje screamed: 'Mi Gado,' and Elisabeth rushed to the source of the commotion and found Carl Otto leaning against the table and two chairs lying on the ground.

'Masra hurt himself on the sideboard,' said Rufus as he helped Creutz into an armchair.

'There's too much furniture in this room,' Carl Otto complained. 'Worthless junk! A man can't even move around properly in his own home,' he grunted, swiping at a small side table with his stick. Two Jenever glasses smashed to pieces on the floor. 'Mi gai!' Otje exclaimed.

Elisabeth was already at her husband's side. 'Calm yourself, man, calm yourself,' she said, thinking he must be in a great deal of pain.

Venis appeared and tidied away the broken glass. A few moments later, Rufus poured his master a glass of beer while Otje crouched and loosened his shoe buckles.

'People would be forgiven for thinking that councillors in Suriname are destined to have an argument with the governor,' Carl Otto murmured after a couple of gulps of beer. Elisabeth was given to understand that he had just left a difficult council assembly. The members had been at odds with the governor for more than a year now. The Society wanted to send six hundred men from Europe to reinforce the troops already present and defend the colonists from further Maroon attacks. Crommelin defended the proposal, but the council members disagreed because it meant that the colonists would have to make a larger contribution to the runaway fund.

'What's the point in getting angry, man,' said Elisabeth. 'Just be happy you're not the verger-cum-organist.'

'What are you on about?' asked Carl Otto.

'Braband,' Elisabeth replied. 'He's having a difficult time these days and can't even afford to buy a candle.' She laughed. 'Perhaps you should ask the church council to increase his salary.'

'Braband can see to his own affairs,' Creutz muttered. After a moment or two he said: 'Ah, I forgot to mention. The *Maria Hendrina* is in port.'

'Wonderful! Then we can expect a visit from Captain Hoofd,' replied Elisabeth contentedly.

As expected, the captain arrived a few hours later to pay his respects. A substantial part of his cargo was destined for Clevia – paving stones, bricks and roofing tiles – and he was to return with four hundred drums of coffee.

'And what have you brought for me?' Elisabeth asked.

'Reijdenius sent silk, bonnet lace, new wigs and mother-of-pearl,' Christiaan Hoofd replied, much to Elisabeth's satisfaction.

After speaking with Elisabeth for more than an hour on matters of business, the captain joined Carl Otto at table for dinner and told him about the problems he had encountered on the journey: a long period of calm and even privateers who ultimately left him alone, preferring to hijack ships on their way back to Europe with more substantial cargoes.

Elisabeth inspected the front room the following day. Carl Otto was right: the room had too much furniture. She would move some of it out and make it easier for him to get around. But what should she remove? Amarante, Dido, Sara and Venis also had a look round and Adam and Cadet were at the ready to carry the selected furniture. Elisabeth had two gueridons and four wicker chairs brought upstairs, but it made little difference.

'The harpsichord?' Venis inquired.

'Absolutely not! Why the harpsichord?' Elisabeth snapped.

'Oh, I thought… well, misi doesn't play it anymore,' said Venis, taken aback by her vigorous reaction.

'What about Misi Maria's china cabinet?' Amarante suggested.

'Yes, the china cabinet can go into the side room,' said Elisabeth. 'Can you manage, or should we empty it first,' she asked the men.

The men decided to try it as it was, but Amarante felt it better to remove some of the more delicate pieces first. As they went about their business, Elisabeth was reminded of a minor drama associated with the cabinet.

Carl Otto had been the executor of Sisa Maria's will when she passed away at the end of 1753, but he was still terribly ill at the time and, there being little hurry, not much was said about it. Six months later, however, Maria's house was rented out to tenants. The place had to be emptied and accommodation found for the slaves. Elisabeth, Nanette and Catharina divided the contents between them. Elisabeth was only interested in the china cabinet and a few gueridons, so the remainder went to her sisters. Elisabeth was shocked when Mr Cors appeared at the house ten months later, accusing Carl Otto of unfairness and claiming that Maria had bequeathed the china cabinet to his niece Susanna Nepveu. When Creutz examined the will Cors turned out to be in the right, but Elisabeth insisted that the china cabinet stay exactly where it was. Sisa Maria's house was her parental home and she had an emotional attachment to all the objects in the cabinet. They couldn't possibly mean anything to Nepveu's child. Creutz found the whole business rather sordid, especially when Cors threatened to take the matter to court.

'Oh, give the man his china cabinet, woman,' Carl Otto had grunted. 'You've enough money to buy ten of them and fill them at the same time. As a council member, I can't permit myself any accusations of dishonesty. And certainly not of the theft of a china cabinet. Imagine!'

Elisabeth was stubborn, however, and stuck to her guns. She asked herself why Maria would have done such a thing. Of course, her sister had been friends with the mother, but that was surely not enough reason to leave the child her china cabinet. 'Maria bequeathed so many things to so many people. She set aside money to purchase the freedom of distant family members. Why didn't she leave the child money?' Elisabeth had grumbled.

Carl Otto had an idea. He had a word with Cors and they finally agreed to have the cabinet and its contents valued. The valuation amounted to five hundred guilders. Elisabeth added an extra hundred and handed over six hundred guilders to Mrs Nepveu who deposited the money in an interest account on her daughter's behalf.

Now the china cabinet had to be moved to the side room. But what difference did it all make, she thought. She had her own china cabinet in the main room and she never used anything from Maria's cabinet. When did she even look at its contents? Perhaps Carl Otto was right. Perhaps it was all junk.

February 1762

It was the time of the great bean feast[20] on Plantation Clevia. Dozens of guests were invited and given accommodation in the main house. The festivities lasted three days, three days of sumptuous lunches and dinners, copious amounts of alcohol, hunting parties for the men, juicy gossip for the ladies, card evenings, music and dance.

Carl Otto's health was not getting any better. He was finding it more and more difficult to walk, had pains in his chest and had lost weight. Even though he was sick, however, he attended the weekly meetings of the council whenever possible. As its oldest member he occasionally had to preside in the absence of the governor.

Creutz had developed a tendency of late to lapse into silence and stare into space for hours on end. 'Suriname has changed!' he would say, and he was right. It was clear for all to see. It was no longer a colony of plantations with a small capital as before. Paramaribo had grown, streets and houses had been added in large numbers and many of the plantation owners also had a house in the city. There was a great deal of money to be earned: coffee and sugar were in continuous demand in Europe. Colonists, civil servants, soldiers and a multitude of free mulattos and negroes populated the city. There were frequent disagreements and conflicts, which kept the Red Court busy. One council assembly per week was often not enough. Creutz was of the opinion that many of the problems were due to newcomers who arrived expecting to get rich without delay. They brought new ideas with them and thought that life in Paramaribo would be just the same as they were used to in Utrecht or The Hague. There were even traces of anti-Semitism in the colony.

'The newcomers are unaware that the Jews have been here for a long time, some families for a century or more. Their rights are among the oldest,' said Creutz in discussion with Nepveu and the young Van Steenberch.

It had been Carl Otto's suggestion to organise a bean feast on Plantation Clevia. 'Everyone has to be there,' he told his wife, 'since it will likely be my last.' Elisabeth pretended she had not heard his words. The Van Steenberchs, the Saffins, the Losekes, the Planteaus, the Nepveus and a host of officers were brought to the plantation in well-stocked tent boats.

Elisabeth had done her best and the guests were treated to the most delicious food and the most expensive drinks. Elisabeth brought twenty slaves with her from the city to help prepare the rooms and serve the visitors. She also took the opportunity to show off the beauty of Clevia to her guests. Some of them lodged in the main house, which had a splendid front room on the ground floor with the finest furniture, luxurious curtains and elegant brasses. The dining room boasted a table large enough to seat sixteen and a sideboard. There was a side room with furniture and cupboards, a room looking onto the rear gallery, a scullery, and four large bedrooms upstairs. Other guests lodged in the director's house and the bachelors with the foreman.

A couple of months before the feast, Samuel Loseke had married Geertruida Bleij, the widow of Charles Icard, although they had separated five years before his death. She was wealthy, part owner of two plantations – Bleijenhoop and Bleijenrust – and had a daughter from her first marriage. Mrs Bleij had never lodged in a house in which her hostess was a black woman. She had to admit that everything was exactly as it should be. She had made Elisabeth's acquaintance some time before and had already visited her house. After all, her husband was a close friend and her stepchildren were Elisabeth's relatives.

Haven't Bettie's children grown, their great-aunt Elisabeth thought to herself. She didn't see much of them, far too little in fact. They had turned out to be intelligent and independent children. Their father taught them at home and Philip studied Latin with the Reverend Doesburg. Elisabeth listened to the way eleven-year-old Philip conversed with his older Planteau cousins and was convinced that twelve-year-old Susanna had already become a real lady. The sight of her playing with her younger stepsister and her little cousin Nanette, La Vallaire's daughter, was a joy to behold.

Every effort had been made to ensure the guests would enjoy their stay. The most delicious food was served at every meal. Musicians had been brought in to fill the evenings with dance and music. Card evenings were organised to which the owners and directors of nearby plantations were also invited. Naturally, there was plenty of gossip. Stories had been doing the rounds about Mrs Grande, Susanna Duplessis, who had married François Grande a number of years before and now appeared to have her husband completely under her thumb.

'A dreadful creature,' said Geertruida Bleij. 'She quarrels with just about everyone. Last year she insisted her husband change the name of their plantation from "Grande Plasir" to "Neyd en Speyt", just because she was convinced everyone envied her as mistress of such a beautiful plantation.'

'She makes all the decisions,' Creutz added. 'The poor man has nothing to say.'

'I've never seen someone so jealous!' La Vallaire exclaimed. 'She's even jealous of her slave girls.'

'She's still young,' said Loseke. 'There's plenty of time for her to mellow.'

'If you ask me, the child will never change. She's so spoiled, even her mother found her hard to handle,' said Elisabeth in a moment of weakness, deciding there and then to say nothing more about the matter.

At the end of their stay, Samuel Loseke said to his children: 'I hope you all had a good look around. You won't be seeing the place for a while.'

'Why not, they can come whenever they want,' said Elisabeth.

'That won't be easy. Go on, Philip, tell your great-aunt why it won't be easy,' said Loseke and Philip said: 'Susanna and I will be leaving shortly for Holland.'

'Exactly,' said Loseke when he saw the questioning expressions surrounding him. 'It's a fact. I'll surely miss them, but I'm sending my children to Holland for the rest of their education. Philip is going to the Latin grammar school and Susanna to a boarding school for respectable young ladies. As coloured children they must have the best of the best. In Suriname they will always be second-class citizens, but at least with their background and education they'll be able to hold their own in this colour obsessed society of ours.'

November 1762

Creutz had been sick for the best part of two weeks. In spite of Kwasi's medicines and the best of care, his health had shown no signs of improvement. The pain in his chest and shortness of breath were the most difficult. It made Elisabeth nervous, especially when she noticed that Carl Otto himself seemed to have given up hope.

The room was sometimes dreadfully silent. When she tiptoed past his bed

Carl Otto said: 'Come Babetchen, come here and sit with me. We don't have much time left, my girl.'

She sat beside his bed and caressed his hands. 'Babetchen, mi gudu. We were never able to marry. Perhaps I should have tried since you longed so much for a wedding. Ke, the very thing you wanted most was the one thing I couldn't give you.'

'Gudu, you gave me everything. You were the dearest companion a woman could have,' she whispered in his ear as she rested her head on the pillow next to his. 'Try not to exert yourself, sweetheart. Drink something.' His silence of the last couple of days had only been broken by the occasional coughing fit, which always left him exhausted.

'His fever is getting worse. What should we do?' Elisabeth asked Willem Van Steenberch, who visited almost every day to see how Creutz was progressing. Van Steenberch shook his head despondently, but Carl Otto opened his eyes at that moment and said resignedly: 'People get sick, people die, mi gudu.'

The situation went from bad to worse. On November 5th, Creutz's temperature was so high that he slowly lost consciousness. Elisabeth stayed by his side. She wanted to help her beloved herself, wash his face with cold water, moisten his lips. Now and again he would open his eyes: 'Babetchen, my Babetchen. Where are you? Stay with me,' he would mutter.

'I'm here, mi p'pa, I'm with you,' she answered and caressed his hand. She stayed with him throughout the night. As morning approached she was so sleepy she drifted off from time to time. At one point she woke with a start from a short nap and saw Carl Otto staring at her with a smile on his lips. She was about to say something but when she looked closer she realised he was dead. She continued to stare at him for a long time.

'Mi gudu, you had so much pain, but now it's gone. Thank you for everything you were to me. You're going home, mi p'pa. Waka nanga mi lobi na yu sei.'

She took both his hands, caressed and kissed them one by one.

She then crossed them carefully on his chest, kissed his forehead and left the room. She turned at the door and whispered one last time: 'Adyosi, Carl Otto Creutz.'

PART FOUR

The Wedding

5 February 1764

'It'll never work. I can't do it. Look, another broken quill and ooh, a blot, an ink blot.' Nanette stared at the huge ink blot on the white paper in front of her and at the quill in her hand.

'Quickly, throw sand on it,' Elisabeth exclaimed as she rushed to the table and watched as Nanette scattered sand over the blot, her fingers trembling.

'You're far too tense. Hold the quill loosely between your index finger and your middle finger, support it gently with your thumb and try not to press so hard. Look, let me show you.' Elisabeth demonstrated. 'I'll make you a new quill.' She took a new goose feather and cut a segment off with a sharp knife.

'I can't do it,' Nanette lamented.

'Stop behaving like a child! Of course you can do it. Here, take the pen,' Elisabeth snapped, and when Nanette refused to take it she snarled: 'Every little child can learn to write. Aren't you ashamed of yourself? You're more than fifty!'

'I know, but children have supple fingers. I'm an old woman. Anyway, why must I learn to write at my age? I've managed without it so far,' Nanette grumbled.

'I've already explained. You're a plantation owner now. You'll have to sign documents, that's why you have to learn to write,' said Elisabeth.

'But up to know I've signed everything with my mark and that was enough,' Nanette whimpered.

'Not any more. You have to be able to sign your name,' Elisabeth insisted.

'But sister, I thought we had decided that you would take care of everything and that I would keep out of it. Surely your signature will be enough. And if I really have to sign something, you can do it for me,' Nanette groaned.

'Are you mad? Do you want to put me in jail. Forging someone's signature is a crime,' said Elisabeth.

'No one will be any the wiser,' said Nanette, but Elisabeth was getting irritated: 'Stop this nonsense here and now and keep practising. You must learn to write your name, matter closed. If you can't sign documents as part owner of a plantation then we will have to divide Catharina's inheritance differently. Instead of each of us taking half of Catharinasburg and half of Vlaardingen, let me register one plantation in your name and the other in mine. Then you can get on with your business without any interference from me!'

Elisabeth turned briskly and walked away. Nanette took the quill, dipped it in the inkpot and tried to write to the best of her ability: Nanette Samson. The letters were crooked and uneven, and by the time she had reached the m of Samson there were two fresh ink blots on the paper and the tips of her fingers were black with ink.

Elisabeth sat at her writing desk. Nanette could be unbelievably stupid at times. She knew she could not abandon her to her fate, although there were moments when she wanted to.

Catharina had died a couple of weeks earlier after a short illness and Elisabeth and Nanette were the only surviving siblings. They were sole heirs to Plantation Vlaardingen, which Catharina had originally inherited from Kwakoe, and Plantation Catharinasburg on the River Cottica, which Catharina and Pieter Courvlught had established. Her money was set aside to purchase the freedom of her slaves Premier, Akoeba, Betje, Blanka, Willem and Sander. Elisabeth was to submit the necessary emancipation papers to the Police Council.

When the contents of the will were made public, Elisabeth had immediately suggested that Vlaardingen, as the larger of the plantations, should go to Nanette, but her sister did not agree. She preferred to share both plantations equally with Elisabeth and to let Elisabeth take care of business on both of them. They both owned half of Saltzhallen, left to them by their sister Maria, but Elisabeth took care of its affairs on her own.

'I'm not up to it, Elisabeth,' Nanette had pleaded. 'You are a businesswoman, you know how it all works. Please!' Elisabeth had agreed under one condition: Nanette had to learn to write. Whenever it was necessary she should be able to sign her name.

Dido appeared: 'Misi Elisabeth, Masra Braband is here. He says you sent for him.'

'That's correct,' said Elisabeth. 'Show him into the front room.'

Braband entered the room and said timidly: 'Good afternoon, misi.'

'Please take a seat, Mr Braband,' said Elisabeth. 'I'll be with you in a moment.' She walked over to the dining table where Nanette was still struggling to write her name.

'Let me see,' she said and she picked up the sheet of paper. 'Not bad, not bad, but you still need a lot of practice. Do you know what? Why don't you take the quill and the inkpot home with you. Take some paper as well. Go and practise at home when you feel up to it, then you'll have a better chance of success.'

'Well of course, how else!' said Nanette relieved and delighted that she had managed to get off so lightly.

'Dido, go and fetch Silvie. Misi Nanette is going home,' said Elisabeth and she whispered to her sister: 'I have to speak in private to Braband. He has fallen behind terribly with his instalments.'

'Fine, fine, I understand,' whispered Nanette, now fully aware of Elisabeth's reasons for getting her out of the house.

A few moments later, Nanette made her way down the stairs at the front of the house followed by Silvie, who was carrying her writing materials in a basket.

Elisabeth went to the front room, took a seat and said calmly: 'So, Mr Braband. You and I have something to talk about.'

'Absolutely, misi,' said Braband nervously. 'I was planning to come and see you even before you sent for me.'

'You have missed several instalments. Can you explain?' Elisabeth inquired in a friendly tone.

'My country estate Nuda hasn't been doing well lately and I'm no longer director of the lumber mill. It was losing too much money. I've also had some bad luck with my slaves. Three of my field negroes have died and two of my men ran away,' Braband lamented.

'Are they well nourished? Do you have a good dresneger? You should be more attentive to such matters,' Elisabeth replied. 'But that is for the future and this is now. How do you plan to make your payments?' she continued, looking Braband sternly in the face.

'I don't know, I… I… have nothing at the moment,' Braband stammered.

'Then you will have to put your country estate Nuda up for auction,' said Elisabeth calmly. 'I'm sure you understand that I cannot wait for my money forever. You now owe me more than fifteen hundred guilders. Can you pay me from your salary as verger or doesn't that bring you much?'

'No, not much, misi, five hundred guilders per year,' said Braband.

'Not much at all,' said Elisabeth, 'that's not going to help us. So, what do you suggest?'

'I don't have a suggestion,' said Braband. 'The situation is hopeless. An auction! How much would an auction earn me? Not enough to pay off my debts. Oh God, help me, what should I do?' the man groaned, his hands clasped together and his eyes gazing upwards.

Elisabeth also looked upwards for a second and then said: 'Don't be expecting God to throw down a bag of money.' She looked at him searchingly and said: 'Perhaps I have a solution.'

'Oh misi, if you can help in any way,' Braband sighed.

'Hmm, well… what would you say if all your debts were cancelled?' asked Elisabeth.

'But how? It's not possible,' said Braband quivering.

'It's possible. Everything is possible. Under certain preconditions, of course.'

'Yes misi,' said Braband bursting with expectation.

'You can marry me,' said Elisabeth.

Braband said nothing at first, but simply gaped at the woman in front of him with his mouth hanging open. Then he said: 'Do you mean marry, eh... me as your husband? An actual wedding?'

'That's exactly what I mean, a wedding,' said Elisabeth.

'But how can misi possibly want to marry me? I have no money, no property, yet you have everything. Misi is making a fool of me,' said the man.

'If you marry me, it will all belong to you as well,' said Elisabeth.

'Yes, yes, naturally, but... but... I don't understand. Why do you want to marry me? I can offer you nothing, and... and... I'm not even sure if it's allowed,' said Braband, shaking his head in despair.

'Do you think it would not be allowed? And why not?' asked Elisabeth.

'I heard... eh... I heard such marriages were forbidden,' said Braband hesitatingly.

'What exactly did you hear?' Elisabeth asked.

'That a white man is not allowed to marry a negress. Apparently there's some kind of edict or other,' said Braband.

'Correct, an edict, so they say. But the edict in question, Mr Braband, is from the time of Van Sommelsdijck. In those days all the blacks were slaves. Marriage with a slave is forbidden. Do you think I am a slave, Mr Braband?' asked Elisabeth.

'No, no, misi, certainly not, you're not a slave,' Braband spluttered.

'And I have never been a slave, Mr Braband. I was born free just like you,' said Elisabeth slowly.

'Yes misi, of course misi,' Braband stammered.

'Or am I perhaps some kind of down-and-out, someone who lives on the charity of others?' Elisabeth continued.

'No, misi, not you. You are a woman... eh... a woman of substance and standing, a propertied woman, I mean more propertied than many of the other colonists,' Braband hastened to add.

'Fine, then,' said Elisabeth. 'Am I allowed to marry or not?'

'I'm sure misi will be allowed to marry,' said Braband.

'Good, I'm glad you understand. Now we have to turn to the next question: are you willing to be the bridegroom? You don't have to make your decision right away. Think about it for a while and let me know what you decide. Bear this in mind, if you do it you will be free of debt and, as I say, you will share my possessions. I will continue to see to business matters, of course, but everything I own will also belong to you. Go home and take some time to think about it. Oh, and another thing, if we marry you will come to live here with me and you will no longer have any rent to pay.'

'Yes, misi, I'll consider it, misi, good day, misi,' said Braband. He stood, left the house and shook his head as he crossed the street.

Christoph Polycarpus Braband

Braband sat in his room with his head in his hands and his elbows on the table. What was the woman up to? Why such an absurd suggestion? If he married her, his debts would disappear!

He had to do it, of course he did. But then he would be married, with a wife, an elderly black wife. How old was she? Fifty at least. And he had just turned thirty. She could easily be his mother. And she was black, very black. A negress.

Would he have to sleep with her? The idea wasn't very attractive. Not because she was black; he had slept with plenty of pretty black slave girls who knew how to please a man, but an old black woman... Would that be his bed mate?

He was completely at a loss. Why did the woman want to marry?

He had to do it; he could only benefit from a marriage. She had said that all her possessions would also be his. She had plantations, a country estate, woodland, businesses, houses in the city, slaves. How many did she have here in the city alone? He wasn't sure but it had to be more than thirty. Would they become his servants? Some of them were quite attractive. Linda and Diana, for example, and that Bethseba, pretty young girls not more than fifteen years old. If he were their master, would he be able to order them into his bed? But the misi might not like it, of course she wouldn't.

He still found Elisabeth's proposal hard to understand. Why did she want to marry? Why me? She had lived with Masra Creutz for so many years. Why didn't she marry him? Masra Creutz had a senior function in the colony. Why me all of a sudden and not him? I'm just a poor verger! The time had come to make a decision. He should just do it. Hadn't he prayed to God for help? This was certainly God's doing. He would do it, tell her he accepted her offer and marry her.

Elisabeth

At ten o'clock the following morning, Sara informed Elisabeth that Masra Braband was waiting on the porch. 'He must be on his way to a party, misi, he looks so different,' she whispered. He was indeed clean-shaven, his hair trimmed, and dressed in his Sunday best. He was also carrying a bouquet of flowers.

Standing in front of Elisabeth in the front room he gulped and said firmly: 'Misi, I have come to say I accept your offer. May I in all humility ask for your hand? Will you marry me?'

'Thank you,' Elisabeth replied with a smile. 'Please sit down. If we're going to be married we should be on first name terms. Christoph, isn't it?'

'Yes, misi, eh… of course… Elisabeth,' Braband replied and Elisabeth burst into a fit of laughter. The man was quite startled.

'Don't mind me,' she chuckled, 'it was the look on your face. You look as if you're about to start some disagreeable chore.'

Brabant smiled wryly.

'Venis,' Elisabeth shouted, and when the woman appeared she said: 'Put Masra Braband's flowers in a pretty vase and fetch Abram.'

'Let's discuss business first,' said Elisabeth, 'and when we're done, you can make an appointment with the Commissioners for Marital Affairs so that we can register our intention to marry and fix a date.'

A moment later, Elisabeth's slave Abram appeared on the porch. 'Misi called?'

'Yes Abram, take the key and fetch a bottle of Rhine wine from the cellar. No, on second thoughts, fetch three bottles. How many bottles are there? More than twenty, surely.'

'Certainly, misi, plenty, three dozen,' said Abram.

'Good, bring three bottles, no five. Bring enough for everyone,' said Elisabeth.

Moments later Abram placed five bottles of wine on the table in the room looking out onto the rear gallery. Elisabeth was in the front room talking to Christoph Braband, who was doing his best to contain his astonishment. He kept asking himself if he was doing the right thing, then he thought about his fifteen hundred guilder debt, which he could never repay. He gritted his teeth, heaved a sigh and said to himself: 'Stiff upper lip, man. There's no alternative.'

'What a sigh, Christoph,' said Elisabeth. 'Is it such a daunting task?'

'No, misi, eh… Elisabeth, it was a sigh of relief, I think,' said Braband. She looked at him sternly and he averted his eyes.

'Take a look around you, Christoph,' said Elisabeth. 'You'll have to get used to it all without delay. You've already seen the front room. This is the dining room or main room as we call it and my bedroom is there. There is an additional side room here on the ground floor and there are rooms upstairs. If you marry me, you will become the masra, but don't be messing around with my slave girls, do you hear? You'll be given an allowance, of course, but I will continue to take care of financial matters until I die. After that it's all yours and you can do what you want with it. What do you think? Are we agreed?'

'Yes, misi, yes, agreed,' said Braband. He produced a red handkerchief from his pocked and wiped the drops of sweat from his forehead.

'Amarante, Venis, Diana, Dido, Sara, come here!' Elisabeth shouted.

The women and girls filed into the room. They had been keeping an eye on things and knew more or less what to expect.

'Masra Braband and I are going to marry. You are the first to hear about it,' said Elisabeth.

'Oh, misi, a wedding! Will there be a feast? Will there be dancing?' asked Diana, Venis's daughter.

'Hold your tongue when adults are talking,' her mother snapped.

'There will be a feast when the time comes, Diana, but better say nothing for the time being. We're going to register our plans as soon as possible with the Commissioners for Marital Affairs. Then we can make it public. Help your-selves to a glass of wine. Come Abram, open a bottle...'

Dido laughed: 'Oh, misi is getting married!' and Sara couldn't contain herself: 'Misi is getting married!' Venis and Amarante stared in silence at Elisa-beth and Masra Braband, who drummed the table nervously with his fingers. Abram filled the glasses and everyone drank their wine. After a while Braband said: 'Fine, misi, I'll be on my way.'

'Show Masra Braband out, girls,' said Elisabeth. The girls and the women looked at each other. Who did misi mean? Then Elisabeth laughed and said: 'Dido, Venis and Sara, bring the masra to the door.' They followed Masra Braband from the room and waited on the porch as he crossed the street.

Sara looked at the others and whispered: 'San de fu du nanga misi?'

Dido said: 'She's losing her mind!'

Venis sighed: 'Na bun e drun'en.'

Inside the house, Elisabeth asked Amarante for her thoughts. Amarante shrugged her shoulders. What could she say?

'Speak up,' Elisabeth insisted. 'You must have an opinion. Come Amarante, tell me what you think. Would you marry if you were in my place?'

'Ke misi, me?' exclaimed Amarante. 'I'm katibo, how could I even think about getting married?'

'But do you understand why I'm doing this, why this is what I want?' asked Elisabeth.

'Well, misi, if misi want's my opinion... I don't understand, perhaps I need time to think about it,' said Amarante hesitatingly. 'But, misi, it's none of my business, but if you'll permit me... When misi is married, where... hmm... where is the man going to sleep?'

'Sleep? To be honest, I hadn't thought about it. In the bedroom, I suppose,' said Elisabeth.

'Surely not in misi's room, eh?' asked Amarante, grimacing from disgust.

'No? What do you mean, not in my room?' asked Elisabeth carefully, since Amarante appeared doubtful.

'Listen, mi gudu misi. Misi is a grown-up woman and misi knows what's best, but let me say this one thing to misi. If misi marries that man, he must never lose his respect for misi. He is young, still very young. Misi could easily be his mother. He shouldn't be allowed to see misi's body. He shouldn't be allowed to see misi without clothes. Don't let him sleep with misi. Give him his own bed in another room. Ke, don't misunderstand me, misi. It's out of respect for my misi that I say these things.'

Elisabeth looked at her. Amarante was right. Amarante was almost always right. 'Thank you, Amarante, you know what's best. When the time comes, make sure masra has his own room, one of the rooms upstairs.'

'Yes, misi. He can sleep upstairs,' said Amarante and she left the room.

The Commissioners for Marital Affairs

Masra Braband, the verger-cum-organist at the Reformed Church, had made an appointment to register an intended marriage. Reverend Doesburg and two elders, the three commissioners, were getting ready to receive the husband and wife to be. The elderly minister expressed his delight that the verger had finally decided to tie the knot. While it came as something of a surprise – he had never seen him with a woman before – marriage was always a healthy affair and he was content when people in the service of the church gave a good example. Doesburg was already retired, but when one of the other commissioners was detained, he would take his place. At eleven o'clock sharp, the gentlemen heard footsteps on the stairs leading up to the small meeting room. Probably the verger and his bride to be, they thought. The door opened and the verger entered the room followed by... Doesburg was so taken aback he almost fainted and the other commissioners were completely flabbergasted. Commissioner Pallack was first to pull himself together and he understood the situation immediately: the black negress could not possible be the verger's intended. She was probably here as a witness, possibly as a witness on behalf of one of her mulatta nieces.

'Misi is here as a witness, I suppose,' he whispered.

'A warm welcome, Mr Braband,' said Reverend Doesburg when he had recovered his senses. 'And where is the bride? The witness is only necessary at the wedding itself.'

The verger gulped a couple of times and said: 'Reverend Doesburg, respected gentlemen. We, my bride to be and myself, are here to register an intended marriage.'

'The bride,' said commissioner Pallack, 'couldn't the bride be with you?'

'Yes, the bride to be is here. I am Mr Braband's intended,' said Elisabeth. 'How are you, reverend? How are you, gentlemen?'

Reverend Doesburg coughed pointedly twice in a row. Mr Pallack whispered: 'Fine miss, how are you?' He had to be polite since he had borrowed money from the woman and had yet to repay her.

'Do you mean that you desire to marry one another?' Reverend Doesburg inquired, pointing at Braband and then at Elisabeth.

'That's precisely what we want,' said Elisabeth. Braband nodded. His tongue appeared to be so badly swollen he could not speak.

'Well… but there must be some misunderstanding,' said Reverend Doesburg. 'Marriage is a very serious matter and should not be mocked.'

'The reverend is right,' said Mr Pallack, and the others agreed: 'As the reverend says…'

Elisabeth sat calmly in her chair and looked at the gentlemen questioningly. Braband fidgeted nervously with his fingers.

'I said that marriage was not to be mocked,' Reverend Doesburg exclaimed, raising his voice slightly.

'But who is mocking marriage, reverend?' Elisabeth inquired amiably.

Reverend Doesburg pretended he had not heard her and said: 'Verger Braband, you know the law, don't you?'

'Eh… yes!' Braband mumbled.

'Then you are aware that marriage between blacks and whites is forbidden,' the reverend bellowed.

'May I?' said Elisabeth. Doesburg turned to her, unable to disguise his curiosity and Elisabeth continued: 'May I explain the situation?'

'Please do,' said Reverend Doesburg.

'You are of course referring to the edict, which states that marriage between blacks and whites is forbidden,' said Elisabeth.

'You've heard of it,' Doesburg grumped.

'I've heard of it, reverend, but I have never seen it. I have heard that such an edict exists, but I have also heard that it stems from the time of Governor Van Sommelsdijck. That was in 1684, if I'm not mistaken. This is 1764, eighty years later. In Van Sommelsdijck's day there were no free negroes. Since all the negroes were slaves at that time, it is clear that the edict refers to slaves and not free negroes, since the latter did not exist. I am not a slave, reverend. I am a baptised Christian, I have made my confession of faith. Are you at liberty to refuse to marry a member of the church? I have property, Reverend Doesburg.

I own plantations, houses, slaves. I am led to believe that I am wealthier than many of the colonists. I pay for my place in the church with silver. Can you refuse to marry a confessing member of the church, and such a generous member at that?'

The Reverend Doesburg said nothing. He looked at the woman and then at the verger who mumbled: 'It's all true, reverend.'

Doesburg looked at the other commissioners. Pallack shrugged his shoulders and the other commissioner joined his hands and seemed to be praying.

'Perhaps you are right, miss,' said the reverend, 'but it is not for us to decide. The matter will have to be raised with the colonial authorities, with the Police Council, you understand. The council will have to decide on the interpretation of the edict. Please grant us the time to seek the council's advice.'

'Granted, Reverend Doesburg, but don't take too long. We are also seeking advice on the matter, but not from the council. We're going directly to the highest instance, the Directors of the Society in Amsterdam.'

Doesburg turned crimson. He hadn't had anything to eat or drink that day but he started to cough and choke and Pallack had to thump his back.

'And how do you intend to go about it? You can't simply approach the Heren XVII without introduction,' said the reverend, having calmed himself a little.

'Oh, reverend, money can do wonders,' Elisabeth laughed. 'I have a financial expert and business representative in Amsterdam who takes care of all of my affairs. It will be his pleasure to file a petition of appeal on my behalf with the Directors. Come Braband, we're going. Good morning, gentlemen.' She took Braband's hand and they left the room, leaving the Reverend Doesburg and the other commissioners in complete confusion.

Elisabeth and Nanette

Two days later, Nanette appeared at Elisabeth's house in a terrible state.

'Mi Gado, Elisabeth, what's the matter with you? What are you doing? The entire colony's talking about you,' she lamented as she approached the door.

'Good day, Nanette. Have you been practising? Did you bring your homework with you,' asked Elisabeth.

'Never mind my homework! What's going on here? Are you looking for trouble? Everyone is talking about you,' Nanette exclaimed.

'They're always talking about me, you know that, and I don't have to do anything to warrant it. And what kind of trouble am I looking for? Join me, mi gudu. Would you like a fried egg and some fresh bread?' Elisabeth asked and she continued with her breakfast.

'Everyone's talking about it. They say you went to the church with Braband to register your intent to marry,' said Nanette.

'Yes, that is true,' said Elisabeth.

Nanette gasped for breath: 'How can you sit there calmly and say it's true? Have you lost your senses, woman? Haven't you learned your lesson? Do you want another court case?' she screamed.

'A court case? No, I want a wedding. They can't take me to court because I want to marry. I am an unmarried woman. If I were already married and wanted to marry again there would be reason for a court case. Everyone knows a person cannot be married to two people at the same time,' Elisabeth replied unruffled.

'Stop that nonsense,' Nanette yelled. 'You know fine and well what I mean. We negroes aren't allowed to marry, even if we want to.'

'You see, Nanette, that's where you're wrong, you and all the others. It's a mistake to think that free negroes cannot marry,' said Elisabeth. 'We're free, aren't we?'

'But... but everyone says there is an edict that forbids marriage between blacks and whites!' said Nanette, grabbing her sister by the shoulders. 'My dear sister. You always know everything. You can't tell me that you didn't know it was forbidden!'

'That's what they say, indeed, but they're mistaken. The edict they talk about is eighty years old. It was written for slaves and only applies to slaves. Slaves are not allowed to marry. Goodness, the prohibitions devised by the whites for their slaves are beyond number. They do it to keep them in their place. But why should I not marry? I'm baptised and have made my confession of faith. Don't I pay my dues at the church? I pay more than my dues, and more than the rest of the congregation, if you ask me. Why then should I not be allowed to marry? If they want my money then they have to accept me as I am, including my desire to get married, don't you think?' said Elisabeth with an affectionate smile.

'Oh, Elisabeth, why are you doing this? Why provoke people so? Why do things you know will make people hate you and want to punish you? What if they have you flogged or sent to prison? Why are you doing this? Stop this nonsense now,' Nanette pleaded.

'To prison? Have I committed a crime?' said Elisabeth.

'They say you threatened Reverend Doesburg, that you said you would appeal to the Directors in Holland, that he almost fainted because of the way you dared to speak to him. They're sure to punish you,' Nanette whimpered.

'Calm yourself, woman, calm yourself. None of what they say is true. I may indeed have informed the reverend that I was planning to write to the Directors, but I certainly didn't threaten him. Braband was with me and he can testify. You shouldn't believe everything you hear,' said Elisabeth. 'Come, sit with me. Amarante, tell Venis to bring a plate for misi and have Tutuba fry her an egg.'

Nanette sat down. 'Elisabeth, why are you doing this?' she said almost in tears. 'Why make problems for yourself?'

'My dear sister, it's not as bad as you think. Amarante here knew all about it. Didn't you, Amarante? She, Sara, Venis, Dido and Abram. They were the first to know and we celebrated the news together with a glass of wine,' said Elisabeth.

'What?' Nanette snapped. 'Did you know about this, Amarante? And what did you have to say about it? Didn't you warn your misi?'

'Ke mi, Misi Nanette, how could I warn my misi? Misi called us together and told us she was planning to marry Masra Braband. But ke misi, what was there to say?' said Amarante.

'But surely you know it's not allowed, Amarante. Everyone in the colony knows it. Don't you think your misi is planning something crazy?' Nanette exclaimed.

Amarante looked back and forth at the two sisters, her eyebrows raised, and said: 'Misi is a grown-up woman. She knows what she's doing.'

Venis appeared with a covered plate, which she set in front of Nanette.

'Eat, hold your tongue and listen,' said Elisabeth firmly.

Nanette propped a forkful of egg into her mouth and stared at her sister as she chewed. 'Have you ever known me to act rashly?' said Elisabeth. 'Don't I take good care of my plantations and my other possessions? Masra Braband has a country estate called Nuda, which is not doing well at all, but do you have any reason to complain? What makes you think I'm crazy? Nothing! Didn't you ask me recently to take care of business at Vlaardingen and Catharinasburg? Well, you didn't seem to think I was crazy then, did you? I am fully aware of what I am doing!'

'Whatever you say,' Nanette groaned. 'Fine, I'm the slow one and I don't always understand. So tell me sister, why? You have everything! A beautiful house, plenty of slaves, the best clothes and jewellery money can buy, investments, plantations, everything. Why this?'

'You said it yourself. I don't have everything. I don't have this!' said Elisabeth calmly.

'What! A man! What about all those years with Carl Otto?' Nanette exclaimed.

'This is different. I'm talking about a husband. I want to marry, to be a married woman, do you understand?' said Elisabeth calmly.

'So that's what this is about,' Nanette concluded.

'Nothing more,' said Elisabeth.

'But why Braband? Didn't you say he owed you a lot of money? Why marry one of your debtors?' Nanette asked, glaring at her sister and shaking her head.

'Well, what can I say. Then he will be my husband instead of my debtor,' said Elisabeth with a smile.

Nanette got to her feet. 'Listen, sister,' she said angrily. 'I came here to talk to you, but all you do is mock me. Do whatever you want. I'm leaving.'

'Don't be angry, Nanette,' said Elisabeth and she took hold of her sister's hand. 'We mustn't argue like this. I'm not mocking you, I'm simply telling you the facts of the matter. Yes, I intend to marry, and yes, Braband is my husband to be. I shall free him of his debts, nothing more. The commissioners have told me it's not permitted but I want to hear it from Suriname's real bosses, from the Directors in Holland. If they say no, then there will be no marriage, Braband will be my tenant as before and I will remain an unmarried woman. It's as simple as that!'

Nanette stood by the table and looked at her sister who had spoken to her with such composure. 'Fine, then,' she said. 'Fine. But before I go I want to know one more thing. You were with Creutz for so many years. You lived together as husband and wife. The man was mad about you. Why didn't you marry him?'

After a moment's silence, Elisabeth looked at her sister and said: 'Yes, you're right. But do you know why I didn't marry Creutz? Because I loved him!'

Nanette stared at her and said deliberately: 'This is beyond me. I truly do not understand!'

'It's not difficult,' said Elisabeth softly. 'I loved Carl Otto with all my heart, with everything that was in me. I loved him so much I didn't want him to risk his career for me. That is why I could not marry Carl Otto Creutz.'

Assembly Meeting: Governor and the colony of Suriname's Councils of Police and Criminal Justice, 23 February 1764

A number of the councillors were pacing up and down the assembly room, others sat in groups around the table. The discussion turned around one thing: the negress and her insane plan to marry a white man.

'And our verger, no less,' said Councillor Felbinger with disdain.

'We've allowed that woman to have her way far too long. We should have called a halt to her extreme behaviour ages ago. She seems to think she is white. Look at the carriage she rides in,' said Governor Crommelin.

'The carriage belonged to Creutz,' said Councillor Vieira.

'But she bought it for him, to allow him to stretch his bad leg,' said Willem Van Steenberch, the youngest councillor who had taken the place of Creutz.

'On no account can the marriage be allowed to take place. Imagine the consequences! Before you know it, all those negresses living like whores will want to get married. Then their children will become the legal heirs of plantations and other property,' said Councillor Aubin Nepveu.

'Plenty of mulattos inherit from their white fathers,' said Van Steenberch

'But that's not the same. If we allow a negress to marry then her negro children will become her legal heirs,' Vieira argued.

'The law forbids it and that's that!' exclaimed Councillor Planteau.

'The letter to her business representative has already been presented for delivery in the next mailbag. She has asked Reijdenius to submit a request on her behalf to the Directors,' said Felbinger.

'Your concerns are unfounded. The law forbids such marriages. She can submit as many requests as she likes, the Directors can do nothing but respect the law. That's the answer she'll get,' said Aubin Nepveu.

'Perhaps we should study the edict in detail, just to make sure we know where we stand,' Van Steenberch proposed.

'The edict's nowhere to be found,' Secretary Felbinger lamented. 'I'm afraid the cockroaches or the wood lice must have eaten it. But it did exist, I'm certain of it.'

'The Heren xvii in Holland will surely have a copy. We should write to them about the matter and ask for a copy to be sent by return. Once we have it, we can proclaim it anew to prevent other free negresses from getting foolish ideas,' Crommelin insisted and he announced with a loud voice: 'Gentlemen, the meeting is in progress! You have been invited to this emergency session to deal with one matter only, the request submitted by the free negress Elisabeth Samson and the verger-organist Christoph Polycarpus Braband to the Commissioners for Marital Affairs to be permitted to register their intention to marry.'

Letter from the Governor and Councils to the Directors of the Suriname Society in Amsterdam

According to the laws and customs of the colony, Christoph Polycarpus Braband, organist of the local Reformed Church, and the free negress Elisabeth Samson, have given notice of their intention to marry to the Commissioners for Marital Affairs. Braband is a young man in the prime of his life and his chosen bride is in her fifties. Considering the matter to be somewhat unique, the commissioners decided to refer it to us. Our concern with respect to certain aspects of the case prompted us to refuse the issue of a marriage license for the time being and to seek your advice, respected Directors of the Society. We trust that you, respected gentlemen, will be able to judge what is best and most advantageous in the matter. The question is thus: do we permit such marriages for the entire colony or forbid them?

Allow us to summarise the arguments for and against and to await your salutary decision.

Arguments for

Black people normally live a life of debauchery with each other or with whites, karboegers, mulattos and other combinations that arise from such illegitimate liaisons. In so doing they avoid the church council's godly inspection as well as that of the judiciary and we are inclined to believe that the individuals in question will resort to the same. In this specific instance, the young man would be particularly happy because the said Elisabeth Samson is enormously wealthy and, given what she can expect to inherit from sisters and other family members, is likely to add to her wealth in the future. Her properties would thus find their way into white hands over the course of time, a positive evolution since excessive power and wealth among the negroes gives the impression to our slaves that they can achieve the same status as whites.

If Elisabeth Samson is allowed to leave her possessions to her family, they will remain in the hands of negroes and negresses.

The marriage also has it legal advantages. When there is an element of doubt, the law requires a case-by-case decision to be made. From the biological perspective, blacks are the same as whites, although their hair, skin colour and natural inclinations differ. From the theological perspective, they are all our brothers and sisters. We are all Adam's children, flesh from one flesh, bone from one bone.

Arguments against

Because it is repugnant and loathsome. It is scandalous that a white person should enter into such a marriage for the sake of personal profit or misplaced lust, especially when liaisons of this ilk have always been despised in the colony. We are also convinced that white people are a cut above negroes and that our nature is superior and more noble. How can we otherwise maintain our superiority to these exotic people than by the exercise of our fundamental authority? They would cease to believe in the excellence of our nature if they were free to enter into our marriage bonds. Should their children be considered the equal of ours? Do we not a have certain duty to maintain the superiority and purity of our race?

Reference should be made in this regard to the work of Herlein, published in Leeuwarden in 1718, in which the author makes explicit mention on page 31 of the rulings established by the first governor of Suriname, Cornelis Van Aerssen Van Sommelsdijck, rulings intended to secure the growth and prosperity of the colony

Here we find the following statement: No one in the colony is permitted henceforth to marry a negro or live in debauchery therewith. This edict is no longer present in our archives, but it is a matter of public knowledge that an entire book of minutes together with several legal rulings from the period are missing.

Whatever the case, respected gentlemen, it is clear that the extraordinary intermingling of blacks with true-born Europeans has been considered abhorrent from the early days of the colony.

The very idea of granting permission for this marriage, respected gentlemen, is a source of great concern. Lascivious white women might otherwise be tempted to free negroes in order to marry them. Would they not also be inclined to marry negroes already born into freedom? Thank God we are not witness to the same infamy that forced Governor De Goyer to forbid unmarried white women to engage in such deeds under threat of the lash. Where a married woman disgraced herself in such fashion, however, she was to be branded and the negro in question put to death (see edict of 28 January 1711 in our register of edicts, an authenticated copy of which we have taken the liberty to submit to you, respected gentlemen, herewith).

It should also be noted that the colony not only prohibits by order all marriages considered to be sinful and incestuous by God's law, but also marriages that are considered harmful to society as a whole, regardless of whether they be considered incestuous under God's law or according to the colony's customs.

We have no doubt, respected gentleman, that we have the authority to establish a new law forbidding such marriages or to revive the original edict. In questions related to the sensitive yet serious matter of marriage, however, we consider it wise to seek your advice, respected gentlemen, and we are convinced that you will be kind enough to inform us in due course how best to proceed.

In the meantime, it is clear that our good intentions would be left devoid of significance if people were to be allowed to marry outside the colony. We humbly request, therefore, that you consider prohibiting future access to the colony to all those who enter into marriage with negroes outside Suriname.

Should this marriage be permitted in spite of our desire to the contrary, we would also like to insist on the punishment of whites who humiliate themselves in such a fashion by the withdrawal of their honour and their exclusion from positions of authority in the colony in order to preserve such functions for pure Europeans and not for people of whatever colour.

We would also like to take this occasion, respected gentlemen, to ask you to send us a copy of the minutes and resolutions of this council from the beginning of January 1681 to the end of December 1685, to allow us to complete the secretary's archive.

Having recommended you, respected gentlemen, together with your loved ones, to the sacred and salutary protection of the Almighty, we remain yours respectfully,[21]

Given at Paramaribo, 23 February 1764, signed by W. Crommelin, governor, and councillors J. Roux, J. Vieira, J. Planteau, D. Gallerman, P. Ferang, A. Nepveu, C. de Beauveser, J. Marlin, W. v. Steenberch, J. Felbinger.

Petition submitted by C.P. Braband and Elisabeth Samson via their business representative in Amsterdam Pieter Reijdenius:

Pieter Reijdenius, resident of Amsterdam, has received specific instructions from the petitioners C.P. Braband and Elisabeth Samson, both residents of Paramaribo in colonial Suriname. They request that the Society direct the Commissioners for Marital Affairs in Suriname to register their intention to marry in the appropriate manner and allow said marriage to take place with due ceremony.

The commissioner of the petition is a freeborn negress and has confessed her faith in the Reformed Church. In addition, the said Elisabeth Samson has also been blessed by the Providence of the Lord with earthly goods, to such an extent that she can boast a degree of prominence among the inhabitants of the colony.

The petitioners had determined to enter into a legal and Christian marriage with one another and had presented themselves to this end to the Commissioners for Marital Affairs in Paramaribo to register their intent to marry. To their surprise, they were informed that the said commissioners objected to their plans without asking the advice of the respected members of the Councils of Police and Criminal Justice. The councils in question declared in turn that they were obliged to present the matter to the Society. For this reason, the petitioners decided to address the gentlemen presently assembled in their own name and to ask with the utmost respect that no objection be raised to prohibit this marriage.

Elisabeth Samson is a freeborn negress with considerable wealth in the colony. The prohibition against marriage with persons in a condition of servitude (slaves), which pertains in the colony, cannot be applied to her.

The petitioners also request that the gentlemen of the commission be legally required to allow them to register their intent to marry and that the ceremony be allowed to take place according to the style and custom of the place. The said Elisabeth Samson likewise requests complete freedom and permission to enter into this matrimonial bond without obstacle of any kind and to celebrate it without the involvement of external instances. She hopes that the gentlemen here assembled will not leave the decision to the colony's Governor, Councils and Commissioners for Marital Affairs, in the presupposition that the requested permission is beyond their competence.[22]

A few days after the governor and council despatched their letter, Willem Van Steenberch visited Elisabeth.

'The court has sent a letter to the Directors,' he said.

'Not unexpected,' said Elisabeth, 'but the Directors can also expect a petition from my business representative in Amsterdam. We shall wait and see. Only time will tell, Masra Van Steenberch, don't you think?' asked Elisabeth.

'Of course,' he replied. He really wanted to ask what lay behind the petition and the request to marry but didn't quite dare.

'And how are you, otherwise?' he inquired. 'Is there news from Clevia and La Solitude? What about Toevlught and Welgemoed? I hear you have acquired other plantations.'

'They're making good progress. The coffee price has been rising. I rented Toevlught to a young nephew of mine but he died sadly last year. I don't rent the plantations anymore. I prefer to use a respectable director. Clevia is doing extremely well. The younger trees are already bearing fruit and they have planted more acreage. I'm thinking of making a substantial extension behind the present site.'

'Enlarge Clevia? Is that possible?' asked Van Steenberch

'Why not?' said Elisabeth.

'I don't want to interfere in your affairs, but you know that you only have usufruct on the portion of Clevia that once belonged to Creutz. I think you need permission from the actual heirs, his brothers in Cleve, if you want to enlarge the plantation,' said Van Steenberch.

'That would be most unusual,' said Elisabeth. 'Look, Mr Van Steenberch, all my life I have done whatever I pleased with my possessions, whenever I wanted and however I desired. Do you think Creutz ever interfered? Never! It was never his intention and it was also beyond his ability. Imagine me having to ask someone else's permission now that Creutz is no longer with us! Plain foolishness!'

'I understand your objections, but…' said Van Steenberch.

'No buts, Mr Van Steenberch. Do you know what? I'll just buy up the portion due to Creutz's heirs,' Elisabeth decided.

'Buy it? But there's no need. Half of the property belongs to you and you have usufruct on the other half. You can do whatever you see fit with it. Why would you want to buy it?' Van Steenberch exclaimed.

'You yourself said I would require the permission of the heirs,' said Elisabeth. 'Mr Van Steenberch, take a good look at me. This woman, me. I am Elisabeth. I *refuse* to ask permission for anything. I have to own the property outright, so I must buy it from the Creutz brothers. I imagine you have their address in Cleve. Please be so kind as to provide me with it and I'll have my business representative inform them that I would like to purchase Creutz's half.'

'But madam, it might cost a considerable sum,' said Van Steenberch, fearing he had interfered too much.

'If it costs a lot of money then it must be worth a lot of money, eh?' laughed Elisabeth. 'We shall see. And don't worry, I have money enough. Shall I have someone pour you a glass of wine, Mr Van Steenberch?' She rang a bell and Venis appeared moments later with a steaming pie on a serving tray.

'Well look at that, my Tutuba hasn't forgotten how much Masra Van Steenberch loves chicken pie,' laughed Elisabeth. 'Please sit at the table and eat, Masra Van Steenberch, and let's talk about something else, shall we? How are your wife and child, and your sister Mrs Saffin? Poor Misi Philippina! Has she recovered from her sad misfortune? My heart went out to her when she was forced to bury her little son. But I hear she's pregnant again. We can only hope it will compensate for the loss of little Laurens.'

There was a knock at the door in the afternoon and Diana announced with a giggle that Masra Braband had come to speak with misi.

Braband came into the room and said shyly that he had come to ask if misi had any news. 'No, and you?' Elisabeth inquired. 'No misi, but I noticed Mr Van Steenberch had visited this morning and I thought he might have brought a report from the Red Court,' said Braband.

'A letter has been sent to the Directors, which means they will be receiving two letters, one from the governor and his councillors and another from my business representative containing my request. Their answer might take a long time,' said Elisabeth.

'But what do we do in the meantime?' Braband asked.

'Nothing! We wait!' was Elisabeth's laconic reply.

'I mean, what… what about the debt?' asked Braband, his face bright red, tugging on his moustache.

'Oh, is that it?' said Elisabeth. 'Well Braband, we'll just have to give that time also. For the moment you need pay nothing. Once we receive an answer, we'll know where we stand.'

'Do you think it will take long?' asked Braband.

'Sometimes it takes years to get an answer from the Directors,' said Elisabeth.

'Years! Oh misi, I hope not,' said Braband. 'You're not eh… eh… getting any younger, if you don't mind me saying. I hope we receive an answer on time.'

'By on time, you mean before I die?' asked Elisabeth?

'Indeed!'

'In your case, dear Braband, it would indeed be better if the answer should get here before I die. You surely don't want to marry a dead woman, do you? Then you would be a widower before you were a husband.' Elisabeth laughed: 'Yes, it would be a real shame for you if I were to die before we receive news. A genuine misfortune.'

Elisabeth instructed her business representative in Amsterdam to inform the brothers Wilhelm Creutz and Jan Caspar Creutz in Emmerich in the Duchy of Cleve that she was interested in purchasing half of Plantation Clevia and half of Plantation La Solitude, the same half to which she could claim usufruct and stewardship in perpetuity. The brothers agreed to the sale. The deed of conveyance was legalised on 9 May 1764.[23] The price was still to be determined on the basis of an inventory and valuation.

October 1764

A certain Mr Pottendorf was charged with making an inventory of Clevia and La Solitude, in the presence of the notary Pieter Berkhoff.[24] Elisabeth also invited Willem Van Steenberch to attend. He had made a similar inventory as executor of Creutz's will two years earlier in the presence of two witnesses: Saffin and Bedloo. The same witnesses were to attend the new inventory, but Bedloo was unable to come due to illness and the elderly Mr Boomen took his place.

'Amarante, make sure we don't forget anything. We have to be sure that the gentlemen are well looked after. There should be no shortage of drink, but I am not sure how much I have left at Clevia. You can pack my blue silk dress, the red skirt and the lace blouse. We'll be leaving on the fifteenth. Make sure you're ready, Venis and Diana likewise. Who else should come? Sara? And you of course, Amarante.'

'Ke misi, not me bah. I don't feel well and my leg hurts. It's badly swollen, look!' said Amarante and she lifted her skirt to show Elisabeth her leg.

'Goodness, Amarante, that doesn't look good. What happened?' asked Elisabeth. 'Are you doing anything about it?'

'Oh misi, it's burning hot. I've been wrapping it in banana leaves and dram to cool it down, but it hasn't helped,' Amarante groaned. 'It's difficult to walk.'

'You don't look good at all, poor girl. You'd better stay home and rest. Don't worry, Diana and Tutuba can make sure everything is ready. Tell Venis to organise things. I'll take Linda with me to keep Diana company,' said Elisabeth.

Amarante really did not look well, Elisabeth thought as she climbed into her carriage on October 15th to leave for Clevia and La Solitude. 'Take good care of Amarante, Dido. Make sure she gets plenty of rest and doesn't strain that leg of hers.'

The slaves had already made their way to the Platte Brug, where everyone, including the auditors, was waiting in the tent boat ready to depart for Clevia.

The following day, Elisabeth had the director, Hahn, show the gentlemen around the property. She considered it too warm to have to stand around while they counted the trees, and apart from that, everything had already been registered in writing. When the gentlemen reappeared thirsty and covered with sweat after a couple of hours, their hostess was awaiting them with plenty of refreshing drinks and food in abundance. After the midday nap, Elisabeth presented the auditors with an array of documents and ledgers, told them about the plantation, its maintenance, coffee sales, the kostgrond for the slaves and so forth. Mr Pottendorf was extremely impressed by the black woman's familiarity with her property and everything related to it.

He asked if he might see the list of slaves. 'Certainly,' she replied, 'here it is. But please bear in mind that the slaves are not part of the plantation's inventory. All the slaves here are my own private property. Take a look, it's clearly documented.'

Pottendorf nodded. It was indeed documented, but he observed nevertheless that this was quite unusual. 'Quite unusual for you, sir, but quite intentional on my part,' said Elisabeth.

The evenings were filled with cheerful card games and plenty of drink. Elisabeth retired to her room early, enjoyed a refreshing bath and a massage from Sara, and nibbled at the tray of food Venis had brought.

Diana, Linda and two slave women from Clevia were to serve the gentlemen in the evenings under the guidance of Lena, Masra Hahn's housekeeper. Diana groused and made comments about everything. The plantation was not for her. She preferred the city, where there was plenty to do and see: finely dressed bakras passing in their carriages, beautiful houses inside and out. The city was full of soldiers who were attracted to young slave girls. Diana thought she would lose her mind if she were forced to live on a plantation and spend the entire day working the soil with her hands. Definitely not for her, bah!

'Keep your mouth shut, you,' said her mother. 'Who do you think you are, eh? You're no better than the other people here. You're katibo, pure and simple, so don't forget it.'

Diana longed to be back in the city and wished misi hadn't picked her to accompany her to Clevia. With misi away from home she would have been free to do what she wanted. More importantly, the absence of her mother Venis and Sara would have allowed her to finally spend some time alone in their room with her friend Jean. She missed Jean and wanted to be with him, her handsome friend, a mulatto and slave to their neighbour De Miranda.

Diana wasn't interested in spending the entire evening at the beck and call of a bunch of old men. She was tired and wanted to go to sleep, but it was not allowed. She had to keep up the supply of hors d'oeuvres, and when dinner was finally ready, she had to serve the gentlemen at table. Every time she came close to the dining table one of the gentlemen pinched her buttocks. At one point, the same man poked his hand unobserved under the front of her pagni and brutally penetrated her private parts with his finger. He then laughed and whispered something to his neighbour who also laughed.

When the time had come to clear up after dinner, Lena was called away by Masra Hahn. 'Can I go to bed now, ma, I'm so tired,' Diana asked her mother Venis. 'Off you go then,' she replied.

But just before Diana had the chance to sneak off, Lena returned and said: 'Diana is to bring a glass of water to Masra Boomen's room.'

Diana was afraid. Masra Boomen was the old man who had touched her under her pagni. She knew what 'a glass of water' meant. 'No,' she said. 'I'm not going.'

'Don't be a fool, girl, you must,' said Lena.

'You can't make me. Ma, tell her she can't make me,' Diana pleaded.

'Child, I would love to tell you you don't have to go, but ke, I can't,' said Venis.

'I'll ask misi then,' said Diana. 'Misi won't make me go,' but Sara stopped her: 'Misi's been asleep for hours. You mustn't wake her.'

'Diana,' Hahn bellowed from the front room.

'I won't go,' Diana cried in the botralie.

'Ke girl, it's not up to us. Your mother just told you not to forget you're katibo, didn't she?' said Sara.

'Ke baya, she's katibo alright, but it breaks my heart that she has to learn about it this way, my poor child,' Venis sighed.

Masra Hahn roared for a second time: 'Diana? Where are you? Do I have to come and fetch you with the lash?' The women in the kitchen heard him coming towards the botralie. 'Quick girl, be off with you,' said Lena.

'Mama!' Diana begged, but the women pushed her outside with a tray in her hand. Her eyes downcast and barely able to contain her tears, she made her way along the gallery, wondering whether there was any possibility of escape. But at that moment she ran into Masra Hahn who said sternly: 'No nonsense, do you hear? Come with me!'

He followed her upstairs and knocked on Masra Boomen's door. When the man answered from within, he opened the door and pushed the girl inside.

It was long after midnight when Diana returned to her room, sobbing quietly, and lay down on the floor next to her mother. 'My child, come to your mother,' said Venis softly, and she pulled her daughter close to her, put her arms around her and whispered: 'This is katibo. This is our lot, we poor katibo, ke ke.'

Elisabeth sensed something was wrong as she made her way home a couple of days later, but she had no idea why. All she knew was that there was something amiss at home. She almost breathed a sigh of relief as the carriage turned into Wagenwegstraat and she saw that her house was still standing.

Dido appeared on the porch and Elisabeth saw it in her face. 'What's the matter, Dido,' she asked before getting out of the carriage.

'Oh misi, Amarante...' Dido spluttered.

'What's wrong with Amarante? Is she very sick?' Elisabeth interrupted. Fretfully. Dido shook her head.

'What's the matter then?' Elisabeth insisted.

'She's dead,' Dido sobbed.

'Dead! No, she can't be, she can't be dead?' Elisabeth yelled, and she hurried inside to the little side room where Amarante slept. The room was empty.

'Where is she? Where is Amarante?' she shouted.

'Ke misi, she's already buried,' Dido wailed.

'Buried? Are you mad? How could you bury her without me? You should have waited. How could you?' Elisabeth screamed.

'We had to misi, she died the day before yesterday and we couldn't wait any longer. Rufus went to fetch Misi Nanette and she agreed we should bury her,' said Dido.

Elisabeth sat down in a complete dither. 'Amarante can't be gone. It's not possible! I want to talk to her. I still have so many things to discuss with her. Dido, how was she? Was she in pain? Did she say anything? Did she ask for me?'

Dido told her about what had happened. Amarante had terrible pain and a fever. Tutuba made korsuwiri. Old Jusu tried to rub something into her leg, but the pain was too much and her leg was on fire. It was over quickly. The next day Amarante got weaker and weaker and soon lost consciousness. She slipped away quietly in her sleep.

'I can't manage without her,' Elisabeth lamented. 'So quickly, so quickly. I didn't even get the chance to say farewell. Amarante, she was like a sister to me. Oh Amarante!' she repeated time after time.

Dido and Venis helped her to undress. Dinner was already on the table, but Elisabeth was unable to eat. She sat in silence with a vacant stare.

'Eat something, misi,' said Dido. 'Amarante was sick, she was old, she's gone to her rest.'

'Yes, you're right, of course,' Elisabeth sighed. 'Where is she buried, Dido?'

'On the savannah,' Dido answered. A strange question, she thought. Misi knew that slaves were always buried on the savannah.

'Were you there?' Elisabeth asked. 'Yes, all the women were there. Adam, Jusu and Cadet as well. All of us. Only the children stayed away, together with Za-za and Abram who can hardly walk,' said Dido.

Elisabeth left the table and lay down on her bed in her room. Amarante was dead. She would never see her or be able to talk to her again. The person closest to her, the person she knew most, she would never hear or see her again. She had depended so much on her. Amarante had been familiar with every inch of her body, had massaged her whenever misi asked. She had always asked Amarante's opinion in everything she did. How could she continue without her? How could she manage without Amarante?

Did you ever show her how much she meant to you? Elisabeth asked herself. No, Amarante was never aware of it, because she, misi, had never told her. Amarante was always there and her misi had taken her for granted. Why hadn't she done more for her, why hadn't she shown her more of her love, told her she was like a sister, no... more than a sister.

Elisabeth felt ill at ease, restless, unable to settle. She stood up to go to the rear gallery. What was that she heard? Was that Amarante? Those shuffling footsteps could only be Amarante's. She opened the door of her room and looked along the gallery. There was no one.

In the evening, Venis came to ask if she would like something to eat.

'No, nothing, there's no need,' said Elisabeth. 'I miss her, Venis. I understand why you had to bury her, but I know there's something not right. I didn't say farewell. My sister Amarante is gone and I was not there to say goodbye. It's not right!'

'Yes misi, it's not right. I didn't have the chance to say goodbye either. Sara and I, we miss her terribly,' said Venis. She ruffled the pillow and said: 'Misi should try to get some sleep.'

'Stay here, Venis. Stay here in the room. Don't leave me!' Elisabeth pleaded, overcome all at once by an irrational fear of being alone.

Venis spread out a blanket on the floor and misi gave her a pillow. She lay down and quickly fell asleep, but Elisabeth was wide awake. She heard all sorts of noises and sometimes thought she could hear Amarante talking.

Elisabeth lay awake the entire night. As morning approached, she grew tired of lying in bed, got up and left the room. As she made her way towards the gallery she stopped in her tracks: there was Amarante, sitting on her usual bench. Elisabeth screamed and then burst into a fit of tears.

'Mi Gado, misi, what's the matter?' Venis shouted with a start.

'I saw Amarante,' Elisabeth pointed at the bench on the rear gallery. 'There... there...'

Venis looked. There was no one.

Old Jusu appeared a couple of hours later and said: 'Misi, you must go and say your farewells, otherwise you'll never be at rest.'

'But how? She's dead, you buried her. Why didn't you wait? Couldn't you have waited?'

'No, misi knows we couldn't wait. But I can bring misi to the grave?' said Jusu.

They went to the grave, Elisabeth in her carriage, Sara, Venis and Diana on foot. When the carriage reached Rust en Vredestraat and could go no further, Elisabeth was forced to continue on foot along a small narrow path.

The savannah was littered with piles of sand, the graves of slaves. None of the graves had a name. How would Jusu know where Amarante was buried? But Jusu knew exactly where to go. He stopped and pointed: 'Here it is. You women can go first, then misi can talk to her sister alone and in peace.'

And that's what happened. After the other women had said their farewells, Elisabeth stood by the grave alone. Here lay Amarante, nameless as she had been all her life. 'Hello my sister. Hello Amarante, the most important woman in my life. I never told you how much you meant to me. But what would I have been without you? You were part of me! Rest in peace, mi gudu. Enjoy the rest I never gave you. I can't manage without you! Oh, my Amarante, what will I do without you? I wish I had done so much more for you, that I had shown you how much I loved you.

Farewell Amarante. You remain with me in my thoughts. I'll always honour your memory. Goodbye Amarante, goodbye mi gudu.

The tiny procession slowly left the savannah. Other slaves not occupied with a burial, looked on in surprise at the handsomely dressed black woman and the slave women who had buried no one yet they were there all the same.

When they arrived home Jusu said, 'Misi should take a bath and go to bed. Misi can sleep now.'

January 1766

There was great commotion in the colony. Maroons had been attacking plantations at every turn. The difficult peace that had been negotiated a few years before with the Aucans and the Saramaccans was now being ignored by the Boni Maroons.

They had attacked Plantation Jukemombo at the very moment its director, Biertempel, was in Paramaribo. When the man returned in great haste to his plantation, he encountered chaos and confusion, his wife dead and his little children weeping over the body of their deceased mother. The runaways had also become increasingly daring and were drawing closer to the city. Plantations Tout Lui Faut and Altona had been attacked and pillaged. All the plantation owners were troubled about the situation and the attacks were the talk of Paramaribo.

Elisabeth was also worried, especially about Saltzhallen, Catharinasburg and Vlaardingen, the plantations that were still under her supervision. She insisted that her directors treat the slaves well, to be sure they could count on their loyalty when those miserable Maroons got it into their heads to attack one of her plantations.

'I've prepared the annual report. It was a good year for coffee, Nanette. Vlaardingen has a credit balance of 15,000 and Catharinasburg of 10,000. 12,500 is for you, and I've yet to receive the statements from Saltzhallen,' said Elisabeth.

'Do you mean I get 12,500 guilders just like that?' asked Nanette in complete amazement.

'No, not in cash, you have to reinvest part of it but the rest is for you. How much would you like to take now?' asked Elisabeth.

'All that money, Elisabeth, all that money. But is it right?' said Nanette.

'Right? Are you mad? Of course it's right. And by the way, Nanette, it's about time you started to behave like a person with money. Stop being so mean and pitiable. Spend some of your money. Buy new clothes and get rid of some of these rags,' griped Elisabeth. 'Look, sign here.'

'Today? Must I sign now?' asked Nanette.

'Yes, Nanette, here is the pen.' She gave her sister the pen and stood to let her sit in her place. With enormous care, she wrote in large letters: Nanette Samson.

'Do you know what else you should do? You should extend your house and reorganise the entire place. New curtains, furniture, everything. I'll help you,' said Elisabeth.

'You're right, of course, that's exactly what I should do,' Nanette replied.

'And you should take in more slaves. How many do you have?' Elisabeth continued.

'Six, no seven,' said Nanette.

'Nowhere near enough,' Elisabeth resolved. 'There are house slaves for sale from the estate of Samuel Pichot and the widow of Pieter Mauricius. The latter will certainly be happy with a new owner.'

When Nanette left, Elisabeth continued with her paperwork. She looked at the documents she had received a couple of months earlier from her business representative in Amsterdam in which the Creutz brothers agreed to the sale of their half of Clevia and La Solitude. Jean Nepveu had been appointed as their representative.

She had a long discussion with Nepveu who asked why in heaven's name she was determined to buy out the brothers Creutz. 'You have usufruct on the property and have absolutely no need to purchase Creutz's half of the planta- tions. You can do whatever you want with them and whatever income they produce is for you as long as you live. All you're doing is handing over a pile of money for nothing to those people in Emmerich. Have you too much money?' Nepveu exclaimed almost indignantly.

'Not too much, no. If I buy their half, the plantations will belong to me alone. And perhaps I might take a degree of satisfaction in making the Creutz family a little richer. They had to do without their brother for such a long time. I, on the other hand, was able to enjoy him for many years. It's time the Creutz family had something to be cheerful about and I think Carl Otto would agree.' The discussion was at an end. The deed of payment was prepared. Elisabeth paid 52,500 guilders in cash; 15,000 guilders to be paid by Reijdenius in Amsterdam, 35,000 with a bill of exchange through the bank in Amsterdam with a further 22,000 guilders still to be paid. She waited for notice from Reijdenius that the last of the money had been handed over, after which the property transfer became legally binding.

'May I come in, misi?' asked Venis.

'Yes, Venis, what is it?' said Elisabeth without looking up.

'It's about Masra Braband. The man is seriously ill, misi,' said Venis. Dido joined her and confirmed that he had a terrible cough. 'Adam says he coughs so much he almost chokes to death and then he has to gasp for air.'

'Ask Tutuba to make him some calabash syrup,' Elisabeth advised.

'But he's very sick, misi. I think he's dying,' Dido insisted.

'Is he dying? Hmm, I don't think he wants to die. We should have the doctor come and take a look at him, although it's really none of our business. Tell Rufus to inform the minister,' Elisabeth advised.

'The minister? But misi was planning to marry him,' said Venis.

'True, yes, but right now I am still unmarried,' Elisabeth answered. 'Braband is the verger, he works for the church. Let the church take care of him!'

Braband died that same night.

The minister and the members of the church council took care of the funeral, which Elisabeth also attended. Shortly afterwards, his possessions were removed from the rooms he had rented.

'Well sister, no more wedding plans? All that commotion for nothing! Now half the colony is angry with you for no reason. Don't do this again, please,' said Nanette.

'And poor Braband was afraid I would die before we received an answer from the Directors!' said Elisabeth.

'Fate clearly didn't want you to marry, so put all that marriage nonsense out of your head,' Nanette insisted.

The Commissioners for Marital Affairs were relieved and said to one another: 'All that fretting for nothing. The good Lord took care of it for us. Proof, if proof be needed, that we were in the right. God does not want such abominable intermingling. Let this be a lesson to anyone who wants to transgress the laws of the Lord.'

The following Sunday, the minister's sermon was about the will of God. Elisabeth sat in her highly-priced pew and stared at him. She sensed the governor, the councillors and all the members of the church council turn to look at her when the minister bellowed: 'Man proposes, God disposes. Amen.'

March 1766

The merchant ship *De Vrouw Hermina* had arrived in port and Captain Christiaan Hoofd had presented himself to Miss Elisabeth Samson and Company, since his entire cargo was intended for her. Wine, Jenever, crockery, cloth, and five thousand grey bricks destined for Plantation Clevia. The ship was to return with twelve drums of coffee beans from Clevia, eight drums from Vlaardingen and eight from Catharinasburg.

As ever, a sumptuous meal was awaiting the captain, which he enjoyed to the full.

'I had expected you much sooner,' said Elisabeth as she sat by the table and watched while the captain devoured a bowl of okra soup with tomtom followed by an enormous pie.

'Damage, misi, three weeks in the Azores waiting for repairs,' said Hoofd.

'But there was damage on the last trip as well,' Elisabeth observed.

'*De Vrouw Hermina* is like an old woman, and she's not getting better with age,' Hoofd laughed.

'Wouldn't you prefer to sail in a new ship?' asked Elisabeth.

'Wanting and having are not the same,' said Hoofd. 'I think the boss intends us to sail *De Vrouw Hermina* until she sinks or falls apart!'

'Tell me, captain,' said Elisabeth, getting down to business. She had an excellent idea. 'What would you say if I had my own ship, I mean a ship sailing from Suriname to Amsterdam with my cargo on board? Would such a thing be possible?'

'Of course, miss. Anyone who has enough money can have a ship built, and as you know, the Hollanders are expert shipbuilders. Realen Island in Amsterdam has huge shipyards where vessels are built to order for ship-owners worldwide,' Captain Hoofd replied.

'And if I were to commission such a ship, my own ship, would you agree to be its captain?' asked Elisabeth.

'With the greatest of pleasure, that would be excellent,' Captain Hoofd exulted and he set about explaining what kind of ship he would need. Elisabeth had to laugh: 'There's no point in telling me such things, captain. Save them for the shipbuilders. I shall inform Pieter Reijdenius of my plans and you can discuss the details further with him.'

When Elisabeth told Nanette a few days later that she had ordered a ship, she was taken aback for a moment but didn't dare say anything. It was impossible to contradict Elisabeth. Nanette had to admit that her sister was always correct when it came to business. A ship wasn't quite the same as a plantation, but she was sure Elisabeth would acquire the necessary knowledge to take responsibility for it. Her sister was a success. Nanette experienced it every day. Now she too was wealthy and had money to buy pretty clothes and jewellery. She had fourteen slaves in her house and often didn't know what to do with them. Then she would have them clean the place from top to bottom yet again and bake all sorts of cakes and pastries. She would often invite her nieces and nephew to eat with her. She dressed her godchild Nanette, the daughter of her cousin La Vallaire, in the most beautiful clothes and gradually acquired the habits of the rich.

A few months later, Plantation Belwaarde came up for sale and Elisabeth bought it for herself and her sister without a second thought. The purchase had already been settled before Nanette got news of it, although she had to co-sign the deeds. 'Who would ever have thought that I, Nanette, would be part owner of a granman plantation,' she said, as Elisabeth pointed out where she should place her signature.

Elisabeth received notification from her business representative that the purchase of Clevia and La Solitude had been finalised. The deed of purchase was signed in Paramaribo on 16 June 1767, in the presence of the notary public Jean Vieira. Jean Nepveu also signed the document in the name of the brothers Creutz. Messrs Rhijn and Pinkernel served as witnesses. The deed ended with the words: 'Collated and agreed for the full title of her properties and the entire estate and inheritance in perpetuity...'[25]

The following evening, after the signing, Elisabeth invited the gentlemen and their wives to a sumptuous dinner at her home. Jean Nepveu attended with his wife to be, Elisabeth Buys or widow Stolkert. In a few weeks' time she was to become Nepveu's second wife, his first having died in 1764. Elisabeth also invited his future wife's son to the dinner. Frederick Stolkert attended with his wife to be, Susanna Duplessis. Willem Van Steenberch and his wife also accepted Elisabeth's invitation, together with Jacques Saffin and his wife Philippina Van Steenberch, Pieter Berkhoff and his wife, and Samuel Loseke and his wife Geertruida. All of them had been involved in one way or another with the inventory, evaluation and purchase of Carl Otto's portion of Clevia and La Solitude. Elisabeth had her house decorated beyond compare for the occasion. The guests were seated at the dining table in the main room; crystal chandeliers illuminated the entire house and the table was decked with the finest porcelain and glistening silver cutlery. Musicians played violin and harpsichord in the front room while the slaves scurried back and forth with one dish after another. Only the most expensive wines were served.

When the party made its way home late in the evening, everyone was convinced that Misi Elisabeth was not only extremely rich, but she knew how to comport herself as if she were aristocracy. When Elisabeth heard this she smiled. She was content; she belonged. She would achieve her goal unobtrusively and become a full member of the white elite. It was a shame that Braband had died, since marriage was the only thing she lacked, the status of 'Mrs'. Her ultimate dream was to be invited to the governor's receptions.

Two months after the festivities, Elisabeth received a visit from Willem Van Steenberch. His visits had been less frequent after Carl Otto's death, but they had remained friends nevertheless and she thought he was simply paying his respects.

'Please take a seat, Masra Van Steenberch. Delightful of you to drop in on the elderly,' she said.

'I've come to tell you something, misi, important news from the Directors of the Society. They have replied to the letter sent by the governor and the councils in February and to your own petition.

'The Heren xvii considered the matter a difficult one and passed it on to the States General for their judgement.'

'Ah, I see. So my petition ended up in The Hague. How pleasant!' Elisabeth interrupted.

'Yes, the States General. After studying the documents, they informed the Directors that the existence of an edict forbidding marriage between blacks and whites in Suriname did not make the place any less a Dutch colony. The crucial point is that Dutch law pertains in Holland and there is no Dutch law forbidding such marriages.' Van Steenberch stopped and looked at the woman in front of him.

She smiled and said: 'I thought that was the case. Thank you, Masra Van Steenberch.'

'I'm not the one to thank,' said Van Steenberch.

'Thank you for coming to tell me. You could easily have decided it wasn't necessary, bearing in mind that my prospective bridegroom is dead,' said Elisabeth.

Van Steenberch nodded. He decided not to tell her that the councillors had determined in reality that there was absolutely no need whatsoever to inform 'that black woman' that she would have been free to marry. 'Let sleeping dogs lie,' the governor had said. Fortunately they did not bar speaking about the matter.

They continued their conversation, discussing the colony, the Maroon attacks, his sister and her children.

After he had gone, Elisabeth remained at her table for several hours. She finally got up and said: 'Braband, my foolish boy, you died much too soon.'

Hermanus Daniel Zobre

Hermanus Daniel Zobre was born in The Hague and emigrated to Suriname as a young man of eighteen. When he was a child, his father had told him a great deal of the time he had spent as a soldier in the colony with his brother, Jacques Rudolph Zobre. The latter had stayed and was the owner of Plantation Guilgal. He had served as a captain in the Society's army and had known Creutz well.

Hermanus first served as an officer in the army and then as white overseer on a variety of plantations. In 1766, Zobre bought Plantation Klein Perou. But the mortgage on the plantation was considerable and by the time a year had passed it looked as if the acquisition was doomed to failure. His debts were on the increase and he needed money to invest. He remembered that his father had known Creutz well and had heard that Masra Creutz's former housekeeper was enormously wealthy and was known to lend money. Perhaps she would help him.

Elisabeth was pleasantly surprised when young Zobre called on her unexpectedly, claiming he was a friend of Carl Otto. She remembered the name well enough, and Plantation Guilgal, but she had heard nothing of a brother. She found Herman delightful and their conversation ranged from the Maroon attacks to the good work Carl Otto had done when he was alive. When Elisabeth heard that Zobre owned Klein Perou on the Upper Suriname, she asked whether he had experienced problems with the Maroons, being so far from Paramaribo.

'It's a small timber plantation with the usual tools and materials, but hardly worth a raid,' said Zobre.

He told her about Guilgal, his uncle's plantation, about his mother, his brother and sister in The Hague. Diana and Linda served cake and savoury biscuits. Elisabeth wanted to pour him a glass of wine, but Herman preferred to do the honours himself. Pouring wine was for gentlemen and not for ladies, he said with a laugh. He clearly relished the various treats and told Elisabeth how much he enjoyed the colony's food. Elisabeth wasted no time in inviting him to join her for a meal after church the following Sunday. He cordially took his leave and was given a bottle of wine and a large slice of cake to take with him. There was no mention of money.

The same evening, Zobre went to the officers café, on a side street close to the Square. He bumped into his friend Gossekij who was planning to marry Johanna Van der Wegge in a couple of weeks' time. Johanna was a great-niece of Elisabeth Samson. 'I paid a call to your future wife's great-aunt this afternoon,' said Zobre. 'A kind lady.'

'Which great-aunt?' asked Gossekij.

'The wealthy one,' said Zobre, 'Elisabeth.'

'Ah, Elisabeth. She's rich alright, and still looking for a husband,' said Gossekij with a laugh. He looked his friend up and down and said: 'Maybe she wants you…'

'Who knows,' said Zobre with a smile. He said it as joke, but from then on the idea never left him.

Elisabeth

It was the first Sunday in November. The service was unusually long because one of Governor Crommelin's grandchildren was being baptised. All the prominent churchgoers were invited to a celebration at the palace after the ceremony and Elisabeth thus appreciated it all the more that Herman Zobre was standing beside her on the porch and about to join her for a meal as they had agreed. He had brought a gift, a fine lace handkerchief. Elisabeth found it charming. She had dozens of handkerchiefs in the cupboard, but the idea that the young man had bought something especially for her was flattering. Herman drank a glass of bitters before the meal and told Elisabeth about his urgent need of money. The plantation he had bought was heavily mortgaged and there had been little in the way of profit from his initial investment. Would Misi Elisabeth be interested in giving him a loan?

'Of course I'll give you a loan,' said Elisabeth. 'We can talk about it later. You shouldn't let business worries ruin your appetite.'

Elisabeth asked if he was married or had a lady friend, perhaps a housekeeper?

Herman laughed at her questions. No, he had no attachments. Not because he did not believe in marriage, but simply because the opportunity had never presented itself.

After the meal, while Zobre was enjoying a liqueur and his pipe in the front room, Elisabeth said: 'Masra Zobre, you would like me to lend you money, but I have another suggestion. Would you have any serious objection to marrying me?'

Zobre fell silent for a moment, placed his pipe on the table and said: 'No, Misi Elisabeth, I have no objections. On the contrary, I would consider it a great honour.'

Elisabeth was impressed with Zobre's swift answer. All at once she was betrothed. Zobre had agreed to marry her. She started to tell him about her properties and how she would appreciate being allowed to take care of her own business affairs. 'But of course, misi. You've been renowned for your business acumen for so long. No one can equal you, certainly not me.'

They decided to say nothing about their intention to marry for the time being. They would first go to the Commissioners for Marital Affairs to see if there were still problems with registration.

On 11 December 1767, Hermanus Daniel Zobre and the free negress Elisabeth presented themselves to the commissioners and registered their intention to marry. The commissioners did not protest, but immediately informed the governor and the council members. The secretary considered the matter important enough to take note of it in the governor's journal: 'Today, publication of the banns of Elisabeth Samson, former housekeeper to Carl Otto Creutz.'[26] Apparently he did not consider the name of the groom to be important enough to mention.

The Red Court gave instructions for the registration to be accepted and insisted that no obstacles should be allowed to hinder the spouses in their intention to marry.

It immediately became the sole topic of conversation.

Nanette visited her sister, shook her head and said: 'So you're doing it after all. Where did you find this Zobre?'

'From nowhere, really. Yes sister, the celebration promises to be splendid,' Elisabeth laughed.

On 21 December 1767, Elisabeth Samson and Hermanus Daniel Zobre married. She was fifty-two years old and he was thirty. The marriage ceremony took place at home. Such weddings were expensive and only the wealthy could afford them, which was precisely why the bride insisted on it. A large portion of the coloured population and a number of poor whites who had not been invited, crowded round the newly-weds home in Wagenwegstraat. Inside, the guests ate and drank to their heart's content, and the wealthy bride gave instructions to include the spectators on the street in the festivities. Music played and the people danced. A display of fireworks concluded the celebration. The guests were numerous: family and friends of the bride, friends of the groom. But Elisabeth was disappointed by the absence of those she would have preferred to see at the wedding, those who stayed away. Willem Van Steenberch was present but not his wife. There were no Saffins, no Jean Nepveu and his wife, no Stolkert, no Berkhoff, in short none of the white elite.

Elisabeth withdrew to her bedroom at the end of the evening. Venis and Sara who were helping her wondered anxiously what would happen next. Would the new masra sleep in misi's bedroom? Should they stay out of the room or on the mat inside where they had slept since Amarante died?

But Elisabeth had not forgotten Amarante's advice: he is a young man, he mustn't see misi's body.

Venis was instructed to ready masra's room upstairs. When all her husband's friends had gone and the slaves were clearing up, Elisabeth asked Herman to join her for a moment in her room. He was not exactly sober, tried to throw his arm around her, and slurred: 'Now it's time for us to have some fun, dearest wife.'

Elisabeth pushed him away and snapped: 'Get a hold of yourself, Masra Zobre. Ours is a paper marriage, one that will bring you considerable financial advantage as I am sure you are aware. But I think it best that you have your own room and I mine. Your room is upstairs. We'll talk further tomorrow. Goodnight. Venis! Call Rufus and have him bring the masra upstairs.'

Rufus helped the masra climb the stairs. Elisabeth was unaware that Herman had said to Rufus: 'That misi of yours is a wise woman.'

The following day was set aside for the slaves to celebrate on the property opposite the house. Diana, who had been so looking forward to the wedding, was heavily pregnant and should not have been dancing, but she didn't let her condition hold her back and danced until late in the evening. The following morning her daughter was born and misi named her 'Marry'.

Then it was Christmas.

Together with her young husband, Elisabeth went to church in her calash and the couple took their seat in Elisabeth's usual place among the housekeepers. They passed the pews reserved for married women and saw them whispering to one another. Elisabeth sat beside her grand-niece Johanna Van der Wegge, Gossekij's wife.

Friends of Zobre had been invited for Christmas dinner. They arrived after the service, all of them young men, and heartily enjoyed the food and drink. Elisabeth did not join them. She sat in the front room and listened to the bouts of raucous laughter coming from the dining room where they were seated at table. She had an uncomfortable feeling that she was the butt of their jokes.

After Christmas, Elisabeth awaited the invitation, the important invitation to the New Year reception at the governor's palace. They couldn't leave her out this time. She was a married woman, she was married to a white man. She should have been invited, but the card or letter never appeared.

Hermanus Zobre was a cheerful young man who didn't make life difficult for those around him. He was always polite to Elisabeth and friendly towards the slaves. He demanded nothing, and what he received he accepted with a grateful smile.

He accompanied her on her visits to the Plantations Welgemoed, Catharinasburg, Vlaardingen, Saltzhallen and Clevia. Elisabeth had the directors show him round. She did not consider it necessary to join them. Her visits were tiring enough and she had been feeling her age in recent months. She would then invite Herman to tell her what he thought of the plantations. He complimented her and told her that many a plantation owner could learn from her. He was particularly drawn to Clevia. 'It's an idyllic spot, Misi Elisabeth. Make it a paradise!'

'And how should I go about it,' asked Elisabeth, flattered by the enthusiasm.

'Make the gardens extra pretty, like an English garden with green hedges pruned into figures, flowers and a tea house by the waterside. What a joy it would be! Then it wouldn't only be a plantation, it would become a true country estate, somewhere we can come regularly to refresh ourselves,' Herman exclaimed with fervour.

He's right, Elisabeth thought.

'Don't you need a specialist for such matters,' she asked.

'Yes, of course. You would have to bring a gardener over from Holland, but that shouldn't be difficult,' Herman said.

'Certainly not. My business representative in Amsterdam is sure to know a good gardener who can create a splendid English garden for us,' said Elisabeth. When they returned to Paramaribo, she wrote without delay to Reijdenius and a couple of months later, Daniel Weischer arrived from Amsterdam as gardener in the service of Mrs Elisabeth Zobre-Samson.

Elisabeth was unaware of the fact that her husband was also active in business matters. He had purchased Plantation De Goede Vrede and signed an obligation for 84,845 guilders without her knowledge.

On 23 July 1768, Elisabeth and Herman paid a visit to the notary Berkhoff and both partners submitted a sealed will and testament. Elisabeth had not informed Herman of the content of her will but he had understood it nevertheless. When they married, half of her property became his. What she did with the other half was her business, he thought. He was enjoying life, revelled in being a wealthy man and not having to count every penny. He spent a lot of his time at the café and regularly treated his friends to a round of drinks.

The coffee harvest of 1768 was particularly successful and hundreds of drums of coffee were shipped for a good price. The merchant frigate Elisabeth had commissioned was delivered in November of the same year. Reijdenius paid cash for the vessel, which turned out to be larger, more handsome, and more expensive than any other ship that sailed to Suriname. Elisabeth had made it known that the ship belonged to herself and her sister. At its launch, the vessel was appropriately named *Miss Nanette and Miss Elisabeth*.

While the harvests were exceptional, the coffee prices outstanding and good money was being earned, the atmosphere in the colony was still unsettled. The Maroons had been making life particularly difficult for the colonists. After the peace accord with the Aucans in 1760, the government established peace with the Saramaccans in 1762 with the help of the Aucan chief Araby, and with the Matawi, a branch of the Saramaccans, in 1767.

The primary source of aggression and fear was now the group led by Boni. The Bonis did not stand for any nonsense. They attacked plantations right and left and their increasing rashness left the impression that the entire Cottica region was riddled with them. They were certainly not afraid of the forces sent to rout them.

The Bonis provoked the soldiers, lured them into ambushes, ridiculed them and ran off with their rifles and supplies. The government had no idea of their numbers, but they were known to have villages with hundreds of houses. Even the names of the villages were confrontational: Nomerimi, Misalasi.

The situation was discussed during the council meeting of 1 December 1768. Governor Crommelin was at the end of his tether. An article had been included in all three peace accords stipulating that Maroon communities were to turn over slaves that had escaped and joined them after the peace. But had they met their obligations? No! Slaves continued to escape and swell their numbers.

The governor suggested with a degree of hesitation that the government should seek to make peace with the Boni tribe, but the members protested with vigour. Did the governor realise what he was saying? Was there not evidence enough to show that peace accords were a pointless waste of money? Councillor Aubin Nepveu insisted that a further treaty would spell suicide for the white colonists. It would mean that the entire plantation territory would be surrounded by 'pacified' Maroons. If the slaves were ever to revolt en masse – and the chance was a real one given the events in Berbice – then the colonists would be like rats in a trap. There would be no way out since the unreliable 'pacified' Maroons would naturally come to their assistance.

Councillor Jean Planteau exclaimed: 'We must eliminate the Bonis, get rid of them once and for all, kill the lot of them, the miserable vermin!'

The governor insisted that the colony could not afford a war. Combating the Maroons was enormously expensive and would bankrupt the government if it could not be contained. Once again, the governor and the council members were completely at odds with one another.

Governor Crommelin had had enough. He had been governor of Suriname for more than twenty years and he longed for retirement. He sent a letter to the Directors of the Society asking permission to travel with his family to the Netherlands. Permission was granted at the end of the year but he did not leave immediately. In the meantime, Jean Nepveu had been appointed interim governor, but since Crommelin was still in the palace, he left him to organise the New Year reception of 1 January 1769. Crommelin fervently hoped it would be his last.

Elisabeth had waited anxiously. Would she receive an invitation to the New Year reception? She had not been invited the year before, but she presumed it had been too late to add her to the list of guests. After all, she had only married the week prior to the reception. But now there was no excuse.

The invitation did not appear. Had Zobre been invited on his own perhaps? She had kept an eye out, but had not seen a card or a letter and she refused to ask.

Zobre organised a drinking party for his friends on New Year's Eve. Copious amounts of food and drink, not a woman in sight, jokes and raucous laughter. The revellers headed home in the early hours and Zobre collapsed into his bed.

The following morning at nine o'clock he asked for black coffee and plenty of cold water. A futuboi attended to his request. An hour later, a smartly dressed Zobre left the house.

'Where are you going?' asked Elisabeth.

'For a bit of a walk. I need to clear my head after last night,' her husband replied and he was gone.

Elisabeth was certain he was going to the palace alone.

When he returned she did not ask whether he had been to the reception. He had no need to know how terrible she felt about not being invited. I have a white husband. I have money. I am rich. Why do they refuse to invite me, she kept asking herself. But she knew the answer: they hate me, they're jealous, they don't want me around because I am living proof that their theory about negroes is mistaken. They think negroes are stupid and useless but they're wrong.

The merchant frigate *Miss Nanette and Miss Elisabeth* was handed over on 5 October 1768 and paid for in cash by Reijdenius.[27] The ship made its first trip to Suriname in January 1769. Captain Christiaan Hoofd was particularly proud of his handsome new command and he gave the owners and their guests a guided tour. The ladies gave him permission to organise a full-scale reception for the captains and officers of ships anchored in the harbour. Three weeks later the ship set sail for Amsterdam, loaded with drums of coffee from Clevia, Belwaarde, Catharinasburg, Vlaardingen, Toevlught and Welgemoed, and sugar from Saltzhallen.

Interim governor, Jean Nepveu, was continually at odds with Crommelin and had regular words with the man's elderly wife when he was working at the palace. He complained that everything was too much trouble for her, even a glass of water was refused him. Jean Nepveu had been building his own house for years and it was widely know that it promised to be the most beautiful house in the colony. It wasn't far from the palace, which allowed him to walk home for a glass of water whenever necessary.

In mid-1769, Pieter Mauricius's former residence came up for sale unexpectedly. Up to that point in time, his house was the largest in the colony.

'I want it,' said Elisabeth. 'Herman, I'm going to buy that house and we are going to live there. I'll show them a thing or two. The free negress Elisabeth will own the largest house in the colony. Be off with you, man. Go and tell them immediately that we plan to buy the house, otherwise someone else will snap it up before us.'

Zobre left and returned an hour later. 'Too late,' he announced. 'Mordechay de la Parra, the richest man in Suriname, has already bought it.'

'What a pity, are you sure?' Elisabeth exclaimed.

'Certain. I passed the house and saw de la Parra with notary Berkhoff. The deeds had already been signed. The man is so rich and powerful that they call him King de la Parra! He got there before we did.'

'Damnation,' Elisabeth grumbled.

'But there's nothing wrong with this house, my dearest. Such a splendid building, in such good condition. I'm glad we don't have to move, to be honest. I'm happy to stay right here with my darling wife,' said Zobre, and he kissed Elisabeth's cheek.

Zobre was not a difficult man to live with. He had few demands and he tended to agree with everything his wife suggested. He was kind to Nanette and took the time to explain things to her when she did not understand. He often went to the kitchen after dinner to tell Tutuba and Flora how much he had enjoyed the meal. It wasn't long before the young man had charmed all the women in the house.

Elisabeth appreciated his behaviour at first, but after a while she began to worry that he was being a little too free with her slave girls. Linda in particular seemed to have captured his interest, and Linda was well aware that masra favoured her. She hurried to bring him drinks, to bring things to his room before he had the chance to ask, and she always laughed exaggeratedly at his jokes.

One afternoon, Elisabeth noticed Linda going upstairs with a glass of zuurwater on a tray.

'Where are you going?' she asked.

'Masra asked if I would bring this up to his room,' said Linda.

'When? I don't remember him asking,' said Elisabeth.

'Masra asked me a long time ago to bring him zuurwater every afternoon,' Linda answered abruptly.

'So? Does masra want zuurwater? Venis, take the tray and bring it upstairs to masra,' Elisabeth snapped.

Venis took the tray from Linda who turned to walk away with an indignant tyuri.

'What was that? Was that you!' Elisabeth shouted. 'Come here, girl. Was that tyuri intended for me? Come here, I tell you.'

'No, misi, it wasn't for misi,' said Linda, but Elisabeth screamed: 'Come here!' and she slapped Linda twice across the face. 'I'll teach you to tyuri, young lady, I'll teach you. Now get out of my sight!'

Linda made her way to the slave quarters, sobbing and trembling with fear. What was misi going to do?

She didn't have long to wait. A couple of days later, the boat from Catharinasburg arrived in the city. When the director was ready to return, Elisabeth said to Diana: 'Go find your friend Linda and tell her to come here immediately.'

Elisabeth said to Linda: 'Well Linda, I think it would be better if you went to the plantation. Run off and collect your things and go with Masra Ranting.'

'Ke misi, no misi, please misi, let me stay. I don't know anyone on the plantation,' she begged.

'You'll make new friends in due course. I'm not sure if Masra Ranting wants to use you in the fields. Perhaps not, you're not really up to it. But masra will find appropriate work for you, be sure of that. Hurry along, girl. Sara, go with her and make sure you come straight back.'

Sara walked with Linda to the slave quarters and did her best to comfort her sobbing friend: 'Perhaps she will let you come back after a while.'

'It's not my fault that Masra Herman prefers me to her, dirty old goat that she is,' Linda railed, but she knew that she was leaving for good and that she could do nothing about it.

That evening, Elisabeth overheard Herman ask Venis what had happened to Linda. Before Venis had the chance to answer, Elisabeth said: 'Masra Zobre, would you come here please?'

'Linda is on her way to Catharinasburg. It's for the best. And listen good, mi boi. I'm the boss in this house, and nothing happens here unless I say so. Stay away from my slave girls.'

'But of course, Misi Elisabeth,' Zobre blurted. 'I haven't touched any of your slave girls. Not one!'

'Fine, then make sure it stays that way. I sent Linda to Catharinasburg to help you keep your promises. Do you understand?'

Herman nodded disconcertedly. He had understood.

The situation in the colony continued to be tense, and Boni attacks became more frequent and more violent by the day. There seemed to be thousands of them, and their success tempted many slaves to run away from their plantations and join them in the jungle.

Although Crommelin had already received permission to travel to the Netherlands, he and his family were still in Suriname. He was now an ordinary citizen and had turned into a bad-tempered and grouchy old man. He decided that the time had come to leave the colony for good and he wrote to the Directors for permission. To avoid potential squabbles with his successor, he withdrew to his Plantation Rust en Werk and stayed there out of harm's way.

The colony had also been stricken by an epidemic of throat infections that took the lives of many, especially the young. Four of Elisabeth's slave children succumbed to the dreadful illness, one of them Dido's youngest daughter. Elisabeth also received the unpleasant news that Philippina Saffin's youngest son had died. She felt particularly sorry for the poor woman and wanted to visit her, but before she had the chance she heard from Venis that the Saffins' oldest daughter had also died. Elisabeth went to them without delay. One of the many women she encountered on arrival told her that Mrs Saffin was not ready to receive guests. Mr Saffin recognised Elisabeth's voice and hurried out to say that his wife's good friend Elisabeth was always welcome. Elisabeth was brought to the bedroom where she found the young mother lying in bed looking more dead than alive. Without hesitation, the older black woman took Philippina in her arms. The poor child had been half conscious up to then with a blank stare on her face, but when she felt the maternal caresses of the woman she had known for so long, she burst into a flood of tears: 'Why has God done this to me?' was the only question Philippina could ask. Elisabeth had no answer to her question, but she comforted the young woman to the best of her ability. In the days that followed, Elisabeth was a regular visitor at the Saffin household, and after several weeks she finally managed to get Mrs Saffin to show some interest in Jacques, the only surviving child of four.

The coffee harvest in 1769 was also exceptional. Elisabeth's ship arrived in Paramaribo in June and departed soon afterwards with a full cargo. Captain Hoofd repeated the journey in November of the same year, once again with a fully laden ship.

After Christmas, Elisabeth waited impatiently as usual for an invitation to the New Year reception, but none arrived. If truth be told, she no longer counted on a change of heart from the palace. Why should this year be any different from other years, she thought.

In January 1790, she received alarming news. *Miss Nanette and Miss Elisabeth* had been shipwrecked off the coast of North Carolina and the entire cargo had been lost. The crew had been saved by an American ship and had later set sail for the Netherlands from Baltimore.

Nanette was particularly shaken by the news. 'Perhaps pride got the better of us, perhaps impudence lead us to want our own ship?' she lamented.

'Don't be ridiculous,' Elisabeth snarled. 'Impudence? Where's the impudence? We bought the ship with our own money. Did we ask anyone a favour? I thought you had put that submissive attitude behind you, but I see I was mistaken. Fortunately the insurance should cover our losses, and mark my words, there will be a new ship. If you don't want to be part of it, I'll do it alone, but a *Lady Elisabeth* will sail the seas, come what may.'

The Directors of the Society agreed to Crommelin's request. He was granted an honourable discharge and was free to enjoy his well-earned retirement.

Jean Nepveu was appointed governor. His inauguration was celebrated in splendour on March 8th and 9th. A sumptuous dinner was given on the evening of the 8th. The two upper chambers of the palace were used for two hundred guests and a further eighty were accommodated on the ground floor. A separate room was provided for the Jewish invitees who were served kosher dishes they had prepared themselves according to their dietary laws. An additional one hundred and fifty guests, officers and merchant skippers in port on the occasion, dined outside in an enormous pavilion constructed especially for the celebration.

The festivities continued the following day. Although the interior of Jean Nepveu's house on Gravenstraat, which promised to be something of a palace in itself, was still unfinished, it was used nevertheless for a splendid ladies' reception, after which the guests made their way to the governor's palace where they joined their husbands for the great ball. The rest of the colony was left outside to gape in admiration at the opulence and luxury of it all. Captain Hoogwerf of the warship *Castor*, which was in the harbour at the time, wrote in his log that he had never seen such luxury and magnificence anywhere else in the West Indies and that he would never have believed it if he hadn't seen it with his own eyes.[28]

Elisabeth waited once again for an invitation. She found it difficult to imagine that she wouldn't be invited. Jean Nepveu had known Carl Otto for years, had visited them on countless occasions, had dined at their table. To add insult to injury, Zobre was a regular guest at all the receptions. When she asked him if he had received an invitation and he answered in the affirmative, she said: 'And what about your wife?' Her husband shrugged his shoulders and said: 'I've no idea. Do you want me to ask?' But Elisabeth declined his offer.

The Jewish community was delighted with Nepveu's appointment, and they invited him to be present at a tribute in the specially decorated synagogue on the Saturday following the inauguration.

Former governor Crommelin was still in the colony and at a given moment his family suddenly became the focus of attention and gossip. The Fredericis, friends of the ex-governor, had come to Suriname from the Cape of Good Hope on his advice in 1762. Shortly after their arrival, the couple died, leaving their ten- and eleven-year-old sons without parents. Governor Crommelin took the boys into his family. His own children were much older, but in April 1770, the by then eighteen-year-old Juriaan Frederici asked for the hand of Crommelin's daughter, who was easily ten years his elder. The governor was angered by the request, refused permission and even expelled Juriaan from his house. Everything was readied in haste for departure to the Netherlands and the family left on May 11th never to return. The entire colony was talking about the matter.

'I don't understand,' said Nanette. 'If granman raised the boy in his own household then surely he knows the girl as if she were his sister. Why did the boy's request to marry his daughter anger him so?'

'Precisely that,' said Elisabeth. 'Granman thought they saw one another as brother and sister, but the request faced him with the possibility that they had already been husband and wife, so to speak, for quite some time. They probably did more than hold hands at Rust en Werk.'

'Oh! I thought it had to do with the age difference,' said Nanette. 'Think about it. If she is so much older than Juriaan, then there must have been a time when she saw him as a little boy and treated him as such.'

Zobre, who was also present, wanted to make a remark about the impossibility of a marriage between a younger man and an older woman but changed his mind just in time and said instead that age was no argument.

'Perhaps Crommelin's afraid the young man will not be able to take care of his daughter. Perhaps she needs a firm hand and he thinks Juriaan is too young to provide it. Their marriage would end up like that poti Masra Stolkert and that Misi Susanna,' said Nanette. 'They say it's a dreadful situation and that Susanna Duplessis has her husband completely under her thumb. They fight like cat and dog, and the whole street gets to share in the amusement.'

'You're right, even as a child she was difficult,' said Elisabeth.

Nanette had heard more. 'They had an argument just recently, because he didn't want to go with her to her Plantation Neyd en Speyt,' she continued. 'She doesn't like him being home alone, afraid he'll get up to no good with her slave girls. Now she takes all the pretty ones with her to the plantation.'

'After giving them a good hiding,' said Venis, who had been following the conversation. 'And misi hasn't heard all of it,' she said. 'When Misi Susanna is really angry, she starts throwing things around. Pots and pans, whatever she can lay her hands on. Masra Stolkert was hit in the forehead just the other day and there was blood everywhere. He fled to his mother in the palace and spent the night there. The following day, Granman Nepveu had a word with his stepdaughter-in-law and the couple made up.'

'Well, I'm also married to an older woman, but fortune was on my side,' laughed Zobre. 'My wife would never do such crazy things.'

'And you behave as you should?' asked Elisabeth sweetly.

'But of course, why shouldn't I?' said Zobre. 'I'm the happiest man in the world!'

Nanette sided with Herman. He was different, a true member of the family, kind and helpful. He had been indispensable when it came to the purchase of Van Geerke's house next door. She was most grateful to him, because she had been afraid of looking silly if someone had asked a question she couldn't answer or if she had been asked to write something. She had paid him well for his services, of course, but Elisabeth didn't need to know.

The 1770 coffee harvest was a failure. No one had imagined it possible, nor did they understand what had gone wrong. Previous harvests had been good and those of '68 and '69 had even been exceptional. Zobre was worried, but Elisabeth could see no reason for concern. She had so many plantations, even a meagre harvest amounted to double the output of a normal plantation. The harvest was shipped out in October.

Beracha Ve Shalom, the synagogue on the Jewish Savannah, was celebrating its eighty-fifth anniversary in those days. All the Jewish families in the colony assembled for the occasion and Governor Jean Nepveu was invited as guest of honour.

On October 3rd, ten days before the start of the festivities, Zobre announced that the governor was planning to spend the night at their Plantation De Goede Vrede on his way to the Jewish Savannah. He also planned to inspect the civil guard at the plantation, seeing Hermanus Zobre was the captain of its Thorarica division.

Elisabeth was exited beyond compare. She had to leave for De Goede Vrede without delay. The governor was to spend the night at her plantation. Wonderful news!

But Zobre saw no need for her to go. He would see to the formalities. After all, it was his plantation and he was captain of its civil guard.

Elisabeth's response was biting and to the point. She agreed that De Goede Vrede had been purchased without her knowledge, but reminded him that the money had come from her. She was the real owner and she was going to the plantation to receive the governor and show him she was the best in the colony when it came to receiving guests.

They travelled to the plantation a couple of days later. Elisabeth had insisted that no less than ten slaves should accompany them, which Zobre found unnecessary, given the number of slaves already working on De Goede Vrede. But Elisabeth had her way. Sara and Dido supervised cleaning operations, while Flora, Lucretia and the director's housekeeper worked into the night baking cakes. Zobre asked himself whether Elisabeth was planning to welcome the governor or an entire legion.

Elisabeth's orders were strict. No one, not even the slaves, was to address her as 'misi' in the vicinity of the governor. Everyone had to call her 'Mrs Zobre'.

The governor arrived on October 12th. The civil militia formed a double row of honour from the jetty to the house. A twenty-one gun salute welcomed His Excellency. He passed slowly along the row of honour, after which the men assembled in a circle in front of the house and the civilian officers were presented to him one by one. Jean Nepveu gave a speech and watched the parade that followed. The other ranks concluded the parade with three musket salvos.

The governor turned and climbed the steps to the front porch and was met by the lady of the house dressed in costly attire.

The midday meal was served and Elisabeth's presence at table was little less than ostentatious. She was not a housekeeper, but a married woman. This was her place! She had planned to spend the afternoon chatting with the governor on the front porch but His Excellency did not feel well and decided to extend his siesta.

He came downstairs in the evening, but only the gentlemen kept him company and Elisabeth had to wait until the following morning before she saw him again and he took his leave to continue his journey to the Jewish Savannah.

Zobre accompanied the governor for the remainder of his journey and only came home after two weeks. In the meantime, his wife had heard all about the Jewish festivities and the silver wedding anniversary of the Del Castillos, which had been celebrated on the Savannah with a theatrical performance and an evening of dancing.

December arrived and the situation with the Bonis worsened. The entire colony was living in terror of them. Their attacks had become so violent that the colonists feared for their lives. The names of the chiefs were on everyone's lips – Boni, Baron and Joli-Coeur – spoken with fear and trembling. Hundreds of soldiers were sent to chase them down, but without success. The Maroons had set up an impregnable fort, which they used as the base for their attacks. They called the place 'Buku', because they would rather be reduced to dust than capitulate. They celebrated in the fort at night and mocked the soldiers on their way to the slaughter. The remaining owners of remote plantations had already moved to the city, leaving their property in the care of a director. Jean Nepveu wrote to the Directors of the Society about the worrisome situation and asked for more soldiers. He also suggested that the local inhabitants should be enlisted to fight, and he set up the Free Negro Corps, a sort of obligatory military service for men between fourteen and sixty, culled from the free coloured population.

Elisabeth's niece La Vallaire, who had eighteen- and twenty-four-year-old sons, came to tell her aunt how dreadful it was that her boys were now being forced into the jungle to fight the Maroons.

'I don't know what's going to happen,' she lamented. 'My Simon refuses to fight. He says the Maroons are right and he's on their side.'

Elisabeth listened dutifully to her niece's tale of woe, but her thoughts were elsewhere. She hadn't felt well in recent weeks and had been suffering from frequent stomach pains.

Venis and Sara told her to drink warm milk and Tutuba prepared porridge.

Sometimes it helped, but there were also times that the nagging pain lasted for days on end.

After La Vallaire had left, Elisabeth decided to go to her room. Dido came to tell her that a letter had arrived for the masra. 'Leave it on the table,' she said as she ate from a bowl of porridge Venis had brought her. When she got up, her attention was drawn to the card on the table. She opened it and read to her surprise: His Excellency Governor Jean Nepveu and the Honourable Mrs Elisabeth Nepveu-Buys are honoured to invite the Honourable Mr Hermanus Zobre and his wife Mrs Elisabeth Zobre-Samson to the traditional New Year reception.

Elisabeth stared at the card. She felt her heart skip a beat with delight. She had been invited to the palace. She had been invited!

She stared at the card in her hand for a long time, as if its content was difficult to comprehend. A couple of hours later, Nanette came by for a visit. Elisabeth showed her the card and said: 'Look, the invitation to the New Year reception. Herman and I are invited.'

'Heavens!' said Nanette taken aback. 'Are you going?'

'Well of course I'm going,' said Elisabeth with a laugh. 'Can you see me turning down such an invitation?'

'Hmm, not for me, I'm afraid. With all those people? Never!' said Nanette and she pinched her lips as if she had just thought of something ghastly.

'Oh, Nanette, you really don't understand, do you?' said Elisabeth and she started to describe what she planned to wear.

When Herman arrived home he found his wife in a state of excitement and no longer complaining of stomach pains. She showed him the invitation.

Her primary concern was what to wear. She had to look wonderful on New Year's Day. Her wig, dress and jewellery had to outshine the rest.

On New Year's morning, Elisabeth had terrible stomach pains. She sipped milk, ate porridge and did her level best to ignore it. The calash had been repainted for the occasion in pink with a gold border and two horses stood at the ready. Coachman Nestor was dressed in black trousers and a red jacket. Adam walked beside the calash, likewise dressed in red and black, and two smart futubois followed up the rear. When the coach stopped in front of the palace, Zobre stepped out first, then he and Adam helped Elisabeth. She was dressed in a dark-blue silk outfit embroidered with gilded flowers and with a lace collar. She wore a pure white bouffant wig, a thick gold chain and a ruby necklace around her neck, and ample bracelets with diamonds and emeralds on her wrists. A gold hairpin with a red ruby the size of a marble held her wig in place. Her face was powdered white, but two trickles of sweat ran down her forehead and over her eyes, leaving a trail of black in their wake.

Everyone turned to look when the couple entered the palace and joined the line to shake hands with the governor. White women near the front bowed to one another, whispered and laughed, men coughed meaningfully. Once the governor had greeted his guests, the reception got underway. Zobre joined his friends and the women stood in groups talking and laughing. Elisabeth was alone. No one looked at her. Mrs Nepveu spoke to her briefly as did Willem Van Steenberch and his wife. Jacques Saffin was also alone as his wife was sick. Elisabeth made her way towards a pair of loudly chattering women, but their conversation ended when she approached. She was the only black woman at the reception. Numerous coloured women were present, but they likewise pretended not to know her. Even women who had visited their home or one of their plantations, Geertruida Loseke among them, turned their backs on her. At a given moment, she found herself close to Susanna Duplessis and a cluster of other women. She walked past them and clearly heard Susanna say: 'She looks just like her frigate.'

A slave in livery passed with a tray of hors d'oeuvres. Elisabeth took a plate, but at that very moment she was assailed by a violent stabbing pain. She dropped the plate and grasped her stomach. The boy with the tray was startled and stepped out of the way. A few of the guests looked up at the clatter, but returned to their conversations when they realised that the black woman had dropped a plate. Another slave arrived and quickly cleared the broken pieces of china. Elisabeth leaned forward and held on to a table for support, waiting for the pain to subside. She then stood upright and looked around the room. She had the feeling she was looking at the reception room from a distance and could see all the assembled guests, including herself.

What am I doing here, she thought. Why did I come? Was this the company I so wanted to keep, featherbrained and conceited to the last of them? She saw the governor acting important, Mrs Nepveu surrounded by her lady friends, Hermanus Zobre preoccupied with his companions and not even remotely interested in his wife. She could see them all: Coudercs, De La Croixs, Lemmers, Van Steenberchs, Pichots, Felbingers, Planteaus, and the Jewish families standing a little to the side: Robles de Medina, De Miranda, De la Parra, Bueno de Mesquita, Jessurun, Moron.

Why had she sought to be one of them? Was this what she had desired for so long? Why had she so longed to be invited to the palace? Why did she have to prove to these people that she was their equal? Why had she copied them in everything? Why? This performance, the entire reception was nothing short of ridiculous, and she was the most ridiculous part of it. A grotesque, aging black woman who had made herself look a fright just to be accepted.

She didn't belong here... she had to get out... immediately. She couldn't bear it for another second. She raced outside, her hand pressed to her stomach. She saw the futubois sitting under a tree, but her carriage was out of sight. She held up her hand and one of her futubois came running.

'My carriage… quickly… fetch Nestor!' Elisabeth wheezed. The boy scuttled off and the carriage appeared round the corner a moment later and stopped in front of her.

Adam was missing, but Nestor jumped from the box to help her to her seat.

'Home, quickly!' Elisabeth commanded.

'But the masra…' said Nestor.

'Never mind the masra! Get going, now!' she gasped.

The carriage departed. When they drove up to the house, Venis, Sara and Dido came out to meet misi. Nestor helped her out of the carriage and the women took her inside. Before she had crossed the threshold, Elisabeth tore the wig from her head and tossed it to the ground. Venis helped her undress in her room. 'Will misi be taking a bath?' she asked. Elisabeth shook her head.

'Would misi like some porridge?' asked Sara, but misi refused this also. 'Leave me alone,' she said, 'I want to be alone, leave me.' She then turned to Venis: 'Tell Nestor to return to the reception and wait for the masra.'

Zobre appeared a couple of hours later. 'Where is misi?' he asked. Venis pointed to Elisabeth's bedroom. He knocked and pounded the door open.

'Were you sick? Is that why you left in such a hurry? You didn't say goodbye to anyone,' he said, and then he noticed that Elisabeth was in bed.

She said nothing, but gestured with her hand to be left alone. She heard him leave the house shortly afterwards.

Elisabeth stayed in bed. The women were worried about her and came in the evening to see how she was. 'Is misi in pain?' asked Sara.

'No… now and then, but it could be worse,' Elisabeth groaned.

Later that evening, just before going to bed, the women assembled as if by arrangement around their misi. 'Did something happen, misi?' asked Venis cautiously.

'No, nothing happened,' she answered.

'Did someone die?' asked Sara.

'No, no one died. Why do you ask?' said Elisabeth.

'Misi looks so… so…' said Sara. 'As if misi is sad, very sad. As if someone misi loved is dead,' Dido interrupted.

'No,' Elisabeth sighed. 'It's sweet of you to be so concerned, but there's nothing to worry about.'

The women left the room and she watched them as they went. How could she explain her feelings? How do you explain to others that you're disappointed, that you feel your life has been a waste of time, a lie from beginning to end. Why did an invitation to the palace mean so much to her? Something so ridiculous as an invitation? What had made her feel this way? Why had she thought that living like a white woman would make her happy?

Nanette heard that her sister was sick and came to find her hushed and listless, lying I bed.

'Are you in pain?' Nanette asked.

'I'm fine,' Elisabeth answered.

'Did you go to the reception? How was it?' asked Nanette, but she didn't understand her sister's indifferent answer.

Zobre looked in on his wife from time to time. He had to talk to her about money, but the businesswoman in her seemed to be so apathetic since she had taken to her bed. He tried nevertheless: 'The coffee prices have fallen sharply. Last year's stocks don't need to be replenished. Everyone's saying the price is lower than ever.'

Elisabeth answered: 'It can happen.'

Zobre had problems. He still had to pay for the plantation he had bought and the creditor, Nepveu, was looking for his money. His other creditors seemed to be conspiring against him at one and the same time. He no longer dared to go to the café, because the owner had asked him on his last visit when his rich negro wife was going to give him some money to pay his drink bills.

'I was talking to Jan Malmberg,' he said one evening in February, during one of his visits to Elisabeth's room.

'Who is Malmberg?' Elisabeth asked.

'An agent for the firm Coopstadt and Rochussen. He's been in the colony for a couple of weeks now. He tells me Reijdenius is refusing to pay your bills.'

'I'm sure he has his reasons,' Elisabeth answered calmly.

'Malmberg says that Coopstadt and Rochussen always pay for whatever they trade,' Zobre continued, but Elisabeth was no longer listening.

The pain got worse. She had difficulty admitting it, but there were times when the pain was so intense, all she could do was moan and clench her fists. Zobre sent for the doctor, who said there was little he could do. The best treatment was the milk and porridge misi had already been taking.

Dido, Sara and Venis feared that misi was getting worse by the day. She had grown thin, her skin was dull and her hair had been falling out. But the most painful thing was her lack of interest. She would spend the entire day staring into space and saying little if anything. Dido sent her husband Adam to fetch the negro doctor Kwasi.

Kwasi observed Elisabeth in bed for quite a while and occasionally asked her questions. Her answers were brief. He prescribed a herbal drink, but before he left he shook his head and said that the problem was more in misi's mind than in her stomach.

A message arrived from Reijdenius. He confirmed rumours that the coffee price had fallen sharply. Mrs Zobre-Samson had no need to be concerned, he wrote. She was in the red, but the coffee harvest promised to be good the following year and she could easily rectify matters.

Elisabeth read the letter and said: 'I suppose we'll have to cut back a little.'

Zobre was troubled by the letter? How were they going to live without spending money? They needed so much, not only in the city but also on the plantations.

'We have ample stocks of just about everything,' said Elisabeth. He wanted to say they needed money for a doctor, but she had closed her eyes and no longer wanted to talk. He left the room without making a sound. The situation worried him. His wife had talked about money and business for as long as he had known her, but now she had lost interest and said nothing. He needed money, but how was he to get it?

He decided to come to the point and ask.

That same evening, he peered cautiously around the door of his wife's bedroom and asked if he might sit with her for a while. When she nodded, he sat beside her on the bed and took her hand. 'My dear wife, it pains me to have to ask, especially now, you understand, but I am in urgent need of money.'

'What for?' she asked.

'Oh, you know... the café...' he said.

'Why go looking for something in a café that you have in abundance at home,' she said, 'it's so foolish! But take a look in my writing table. If I'm not mistaken there's still three hundred guilders in the drawer.'

'Thank you,' said Zobre. He wondered how to tell her that he had already used up two of the three hundred guilders. Anyway, he needed a couple of thousand guilders, not three hundred. He had spoken to Malmberg a couple of days earlier and learned that the firm for which he worked as an agent regularly lent money to planters. Malmberg knew that Zobre was worth more than a guilder or two and was prepared to lend him a couple of thousand, but only if he pledged one of the plantations as security. The only solution was to make an inventory of one of the plantations and mortgage it.

Elisabeth was ill. Why didn't she let him take care of business? How long would her illness last? Was she going to die? It was not unthinkable and would be very much to his advantage. She used to be so generous, but now the situation was untenable. He had to be strong, stand up to her. When they married, she had agreed to joint ownership of everything. Wasn't he the head of the household? He needed money and his only option was to take out a mortgage on one of their many plantations. He thought about writing to her business representative in Amsterdam, but he knew that Reijdenius would do nothing unless the request came from Elisabeth in person. How was he going to arrange things?

Nanette came by for a visit the following day around noon. She came to talk to him in the dining room and to tell him how worried she was about her sister.

'Elisabeth is seriously ill,' she lamented. 'She's lost interest in everything, even her plantations.'

Zobre had an idea. He would try to involve Nanette. She was part owner of a few plantations after all. 'Her illness is poorly timed,' he said. 'I've just heard that Belwaarde has to be valued.'

'Why now?' Nanette asked.

'The government is drawing up a list with the value of each plantation,' said Zobre. 'If we ignore them they'll make their own assessment, but it will certainly be far below its actual value. All the plantation owners are organising their own evaluation. They're following alphabetical order and Belwaarde is next in line.'

'Oh, then we'd better waste no time and have the place valued ourselves. Isn't that a good idea?' Nanette exclaimed.

'Yes, if you ask me. But your sister has to request it, Misi Nanette, both you and your sister. I would be happy to make the necessary arrangements, but the request has to come from you. And to be honest, I don't want to tire my dear Elisabeth with business talk,' said Zobre, proud of his lie.

'If that's the case, then I will submit a request immediately and tell my sister not to concern herself. How fortunate she is to have a husband who can take care of this on her behalf,' said Nanette.

'Belwaarde has to be valued,' Nanette told her sister a couple of days later. 'Your husband is going to take care of everything.'

Elisabeth did not ask why there was a need to value the plantation and take an inventory of its stock. It simply did not interest her.

In the weeks that followed, Elisabeth's physical condition gravely deteriorated. She found it difficult to eat and was subject to frequent bouts of vomiting, which often contained traces of blood.

The slave women kept vigil by her bed and did what they could to help her and alleviate her pain. One morning Elisabeth asked for paper and a pen. She sat up in bed as best she could and wrote a letter. When the letter was finished she had Sara, Venis and Dido place their mark under their name.

The misi sealed the letter and had Adam bring it to the notary public Pieter Berkhoff.

Nanette called for Doctor Kwasi a second time. Elisabeth insisted she had no need for medication, only something to relieve the pain. Would that be possible?

Her condition became grave on April 20th. The pain was unbearable and she was drifting in and out of consciousness.

Why are they all standing here, she thought. Why are they crying? She moaned from the pain. She had so much money. Wasn't there anything she could buy to relieve the pain. Why couldn't she make it go away with money? She felt a little better that evening. She looked at the women surrounding her bed and said feebly that there was no need for them to cry or grieve. 'Go to bed, Sara, go to bed, Venis. Dido, go to your man and your children, take good care of them. Thank you for being so kind to me.'

Venis and Sara lay down on the mat beside her bed. Dido went to her room in the slave quarters.

Zobre looked in around eleven. A candle was burning in the corner and everything was silent.

'Are you asleep?' he whispered, but there was no response so he closed the door as quietly as he could.

Elisabeth woke from her slumber an hour later. The pain was intense but she was clear-headed and lucid. Thoughts of every kind filled her head. She was thirsty and tried to call Venis, but she was too weak to make a sound. She thought it bizarre that she had a husband and forty slaves, but at the moment of her death there was no one to give her a little water.

What they say is true, she thought: all of us die alone, all alone. And she drifted into eternity.

Epilogue

Elisabeth Samson died in the night of 20–21 April 1771 and was buried in the Nieuwe Oranjetuin cemetery in Paramaribo. Since her husband did not have her grave marked with a stone, its location is now unknown. In 1763, Elisabeth had a magnificent marble stone erected on the grave of Carl Otto Creutz. The stone can still be admired in the Nieuwe Oranjetuin cemetery.

What happened to Elisabeth's property?

Zobre was sole heir to Elisabeth's estate, although she had set aside the sum of twenty-three thousand guilders as a bequest to a number of family members and for the liberation of a few slaves, each of whom received between five hundred and one thousand guilders to start out on their own.

Her bequest purchased the freedom of the following slaves:

Dido, Adam and their children; Venis, Diana and her children; Sara; Nestor and his family; Rufus, Firans, Present and Cadet.

Jusu, Abram, Tutuba and Lucretia were not freed, but were granted support and allowed to remain on her property without having to work until they died.

Elisabeth Samson's inheritance consisted of the following (f = guilders):

Plantation Clevia	f 200,000
Country Estate La Solitude	f 110,000
Plantation De Goede Vrede	f 85,000
Plantation Toevlught	f 55,000
Plantation Welgemoed	f 55,000
Half of Plantation Belwaarde	f 215,000
Half of Plantation Vlaardingen	f 140,000
Half of Plantation Catharinasburg	f 35,000
A quarter of Plantation Saltzhallen	f 70,000
Half of Woodland Onverwacht	f 50,000
Twelve houses of various sizes in Paramaribo	+/- f 125,000
Total	+/- f 1,140,000

In May 1771, almost immediately after Elisabeth's death, Hermanus Zobre and

Nanette Samson, now the official owners of Belwaarde, requested a mortgage loan with the said plantation as security. The plantation had already been assessed in February 1771, and was valued at 429,813 guilders.

The loan itself amounted to 200,000 guilders, with an interest of six per cent per year. The total sum together with the interest was to be repaid in four years. The money was made available in Paramaribo in August 1771.

Jan Malmberg, captain of a slave trafficking vessel and agent to the firm Coopstadt and Rochussen, was known to have been in Suriname in January 1771. In three of the four letters he wrote to his employer while in Paramaribo, mention is made of H.D. Zobre.

It is clear from his first letter, dated 24 January 1771, that one of his tasks was to convince Zobre that Reijdenius was not promoting his interests as he should. He was also to present Coopstadt and Rochussen to Zobre in a favourable light.

'I showed Mr Zobre the respected gentlemen's letter, referring to the disputed invoices. Mr Zobre had not been aware of the problem and was very upset at Mr Reijdenius. He thanked the authors of the letter for their concern and declared that he would write to them should the response to his own recent letter to Reijdenius prove unsatisfactory. Should Mr Zobre seek to change his business representatives, I am certain that all of his friends will follow suit. I fear, however, that a considerable sum of money will be required to persuade him to do so…'

In his second letter, dated 4 May 1771, Malmberg makes reference to the death of Elisabeth Samson.

'In addition, I can inform the respected gentlemen that Mrs Zobre died a few days ago. Although she left roughly 23,000 guilders to a variety of beneficiaries, her husband remains sole heir to the remainder of her property. For someone who married a black woman only four years ago, he has thus become a man of considerable wealth and is worth more than a million. I visited Mr Zobre's plantation yesterday and took the opportunity to ask whether relations with Reijdenius had been restored. Mr Zobre informed me that Reijdenius had indeed disputed some invoices, but had honoured them after a time. He even declared that future disputed invoices should first be referred to you. I can assure the respected gentlemen that such disputed invoices are inevitable.'

Malmberg's last letter, dated June 27th, returns to the topic of Zobre.

'With respect to Mr Zobre, concerning whom I informed the respected gentlemen that a million would be necessary to persuade him to change his business representatives, I would also like to inform the respected gentlemen that this sum includes a number of individuals who are dependent on him, for whom he serves in part as guarantor, and whose affairs are now in the hands of Reijdenius: Messrs Goskij with two plantations, Esser with one, Kreemer with one, Raadekens with one, and Landsknegt with two. I was able to examine registers of Mr Zobre's coffee plantations and personal receipts at New Year. His debts amounted to a total of 185,000 Dutch guilders. In addition, however, the income from roughly five hundred drums of coffee – between fifteen and sixteen tons – which had already been dispatched prior to his wife's death, still has to be accounted for.'

It is clear that Zobre's marriage to Elisabeth Samson had made him a man of esteem and financial substance. Although he was listed as guarantor for a number of plantation owners and had a personal debt of 185,000 guilders, the fact that he was ultimately worth a total of one and a half million permitted Malmberg to dismiss his obligations as trifling.

In the latter part of 1771, the financial situation of several plantation owners was far from good. There was hope that the market would recover, but in reality the opposite occurred. The Amsterdam stock exchange crashed in 1773, with serious consequences for many of Suriname's planters.

Hermanus Daniel Zobre

Zobre applied for a mortgage on Plantation Clevia on 23 January 1773. The request was dealt with by the Council of Civil Justice in Paramaribo. The Paramaribo representative of the Amsterdam firm Harman Van den Poll & Co. provided a provisional mortgage of 53,000 guilders and sent the initial request to Amsterdam where the mortgage was refused. Zobre was thus obliged to return the provisional payment.[29] The Amsterdam stock exchange crash had already taken place at this juncture. Zobre made up his last will and testament on 25 April 1773, submitted it to notary public Johan Friedrich Haysen Andrex in Paramaribo and left for Amsterdam where he found the firm of J. & M. Marselis prepared to do business with him. Zobre's properties served as security for a single loan agreement with the said firm, which settled his debt to Harman Van den Poll & Co. of 55,000 guilders and an additional debt of roughly 18,000 guilders. Zobre returned to Paramaribo having taken out an enormous mortgage to the value of 800,000 guilders on his combined assets, Plantation Belwaarde, which had already been mortgaged in 1771, excluded.

Zobre owned Plantations Clevia, Goede Vreede, Klein Perou, country estate La Solitude, half of Onverwacht, half of Vlaardingen, half of Catharinasburg, six houses in Paramaribo and half of a further six houses in the same city. His assets totalled 1,872,486 guilders.[30] Plantations Toevlught and Welgemoed are not included. It is possible that Nanette retained usufruct of the properties in question after Elisabeth's death.

Zobre returned to Suriname in 1774. In October of the same year, the owners of Belwaarde received a writ demanding payment of the sum they had borrowed against the property in May 1771. Repayment of the loan with interest had been spread over a period of four years and was to be settled in May 1775. None of the loan payments had been made up to that point. Zobre ignored the writ. In 1776, he bought an additional plantation – Zoelen – but seems to have been unable to put together the sum agreed for the purchase. Zoelen's original owner, widow Koenen, requested foreclosure in 1778 and the Court of Civil Justice authorised the sale of Zoelen to Jean Nepveu for 181,000 guilders.

Zobre did not remarry. He died in October 1784, having lived the rest of his life as a man of wealth and substance in Suriname. He was also administrator of Plantation Reijnmond on behalf of Coopstadt and Rochussen.

Nothing of the 800,000 guilder mortgage he had taken out against his assets in 1773 had been repaid on his death.

A request submitted by the former slave Saartje Van Sober to the Police Council in February 1795 is of some interest in relation to Zobre. The request states that Hermanus Daniel Zobre had purchased her freedom and that he had also intended to do the same for her daughter Francina (a mulatta and most likely Zobre's child). The necessary money had been given to his brother Johan Zobre. Hermanus had died in the meantime, but his brother had not honoured the agreement to purchase Francina's freedom. On the contrary, she and her daughters were poorly treated and regularly beaten by Johan Zobre's wife.

Johan Anthoine Zobre was heir to his brother's estate but refused to accept his inheritance on account of the enormous debt.[31]

The plantations and houses that once belonged to Elisabeth Samson ultimately became the property of the Amsterdam merchants Jan and Theodore Marselis. The hope expressed by the governor and his councillors in 1764 had been realised: Elisabeth's wealth was now in white hands.

Nanette Samson

Nanette must have trusted her brother-in-law Zobre, since she authorised him to purchase the house of her former neighbour Van Geerke in her name in 1770.

At the end of 1774, the owners of Belwaarde received an arrears demand, insisting that they make a start on the repayment of the mortgage they had taken out on the property. Nanette had Hendrick Schouten, her nephew by marriage, write a letter of protest in which she claimed that her part of the plantation had not been mortgaged. Reijdenius's firm replied by pointing out that she had no reason to protest because both halves of the plantation had been mortgaged

It seems likely, therefore, that she knew nothing of the mortgage of 200,000 guilders taken out on Belwaarde in the name of both its owners. From then onwards, Hendrick Schouten, the husband of her niece Susanna Hanssen, became her authorised representative and Zobre faded from view. There is also some possibility that Schouten did not advise her in matters of business, but only wrote and signed letters on her behalf.

In 1774, Nanette bought Plantations Toevlught and Welgemoed from her brother-in-law where she may already have enjoyed usufruct. She took out a mortgage of 115,000 guilders for the purpose from Reijdenius, with whom she still did business.

Her purchase of Zobre's half of Plantation Belwaarde was particularly unwise. The deed of purchase was registered on 24 March 1775, shortly after the arrival of the arrears demand. She thus took the entire mortgage owed on the property upon herself. An inventory of Belwaarde was organised yet again in February 1776 and the place was valued at 237,377 guilders. The mortgage was granted, but given the small difference between the mortgage sum and the evaluation, the lender insisted that other elements be included in the security bond, namely one quarter of Saltzhallen.

Nanette's financial situation deteriorated dramatically. She was unable to pay her debts and was forced into mortgage after mortgage. In 1776, she was granted a mortgage of 100,000 guilders on her half of Vlaardingen and Catharinasburg. The mortgage was provided by the Amsterdam firm Chomel & Jordan.

Unable to make her repayments, Nanette was declared bankrupt in 1778. The Court of Criminal Justice placed her under receivership in 1782. In spite of this, she continued to be known as the 'wealthy and free Nanette Samson' in the latter part of the 1770s and the early 1780s.

John Gabriel Stedman notes in his *Journey to Suriname* and elsewhere that he spent a delightful day at the house of a rich black woman named Samson between January 6th and 21st 1776. He seems, nevertheless, not to have been accurately informed of the situation, since he claims that the woman had been married to a certain Zubli and had recently been widowed. It is more likely that he had information on a rich black woman named Samson whose husband's name was Zobre and he presumed the woman in question was Nanette. Nanette, however, never married, and Zobre was still alive at that juncture. At the time of her death in 1793, Nanette was sharing her home with her niece Nanette Suzanna Peterse, widow of the Reverend Sporon. The following people were listed as heirs to her property: her nephew Philip Samuel Hanssen, her niece Susanna Johanna Hanssen and her children, and her nieces and nephews Planteau and Sporon.

She had lost everything and the inventory of her house was barely enough to cover a couple of pages. She was buried in Nieuwe Oranjetuin, but there is no record of the erection of a gravestone and the grave can no longer be located.

The children of Bettie and Samuel Loseke

Susanna Johanna Hanssen returned to Suriname in 1771 where she married Hendrick Schouten on March 2nd of the following year at the age of twenty-two. The witnesses were her father Samuel Loseke and his wife Geertruida Bleij.

Hendrick Schouten was a civil servant. He is remembered for his mainly satirical poems, four collections of which were published by the *Surinaamsche Lettervrinden* (1785–1787). Schouten was one of the founders of the society. He also founded and financed a drama society under the name Pro Extollenda Eloquenta in 1772. Jews were not allowed to attend their productions.

Mr and Mrs Schouten-Hanssen had five children: Hillegonda Nanette, Christina Elisabeth (with Nanette as godmother), Gerrit Carl François, Hendrik Samuel and Martinus. The youngest child died in infancy.[32]

Gerrit Schouten is remembered as an artist and his panoramas are to be found, among other places, in the Royal Tropical Institute in Amsterdam. An exhibition of his work was organised in Fort Zeelandia Museum in Paramaribo in 1999–2000.

Philip Samuel Hanssen defended his doctoral dissertation at the University of Leiden in 1776 (Knappert 1930: 290) and aquired the title 'Doctor of Both Laws'. When he returned to Suriname, he became a well-known jurist and senior government official. He had children by a negro woman, who was probably still a slave at the time, and the first two were baptised on 17 September 1790. The register reads: Baptised Samuel Hanssen and Jacob Hanssen; father Philip Samuel Hanssen, mother Amimba Van de Valke. The register for the following baptism on 3 March 1791 reads: Baptised Johan Lodewijk Hanssen; father Philip Samuel Hanssen, mother the free negress Amimba Van Hanssen.[33] Susanna Catharina Hanssen, born on 17 December 1789 was baptised on the same day.

Samuel Loseke's wife Geertruida Bleij died in 1774 and Samuel inherited her plantations (Bleijenrust and Bleijenhoop). On 15 February 1780, Samuel Loseke submitted a request to Governor Bernard Texier and the Police Council, asking to recognise his illegitimate children. The petitioner states that he had no other blood relatives and that the children in question were to become his heirs. He writes: 'I humbly request to be purified of the blemish and stain of illegitimacy, to recognise them without qualification, and to grant them all the benefits and privileges of legitimate children...'[34]

The request was granted.

The children of La Vallaire (daughter of Kwakoe Samson) and Pieter Planteau

La Vallaire and Planteau had four children, three sons – Pieter (died in 1763), Jan Simon and Hendrik Petrus – and one daughter, Nanette Susanna Peterse. The poet Paul François Roos, who was a close friend of Hendrik Schouten, composed an ode to Nanette Susanna Pieterse in 1782. The poem was published in the *Surinaamsche Mengel Poezy* in 1804.

Nanette Pieterse married Johan Samuel Donkermans in 1784. He died shortly after the wedding while his wife was expecting their first baby. She remarried two years later, on this occasion with the Reverend Appolonius Adrianus Sporon. He also died while she was expecting their son Adrianus Appolonius Sporon, baptised 17 March 1790. The latter studied medicine at the University of Groningen (Knappert: 1930: 290).

Gravestones

Philippina Maria Saffin-Van Steenberch died in August 1771. Her grave and those of her three children can still be found in the Oranjetuin in Paramaribo.

The gravestone of Carl Otto Creutz is to be found next to that of his niece Helena Bellier-Creutz. The gravestones of Willem Gerard Van Meel's son Johan Willem, Aubin Nepveu and his wife Susanna Cors, and Samuel Pichot can still be found in Oranjetuin. The gravestones of several others referred to in this book are located in the Dutch Reformed Church on Kerkplein in Paramaribo. Maria Jansz's gravestone is located in front of the flight of steps leading up to the door on the north side of the same church.

Elisabeth's house

The house was located on the corner of Heerenstraat and Wagenwegstraat, presently Wagenwegstraat 22.

Hermanus Zobre remained there until he died, after which it became the property of Elisabeth's nephew Philip Samuel Hanssen. It is probable that Philip Samuel enlarged the first floor and added a second. His initials are still to be found on the fanlight above the side entrance: P.S.H.

The building is also known to have been inhabited by Pieter Heidoorn, after which it became the property of the government. It housed the Van Sypesteyn School for a number of years at the beginning of the twentieth century and later became the Colonial Library and the Registry Office.

From 1960 onwards, the building was used to house a succession of government ministries: Social Affairs, Labour and Social Affairs, and Labour and Public Housing. It presently houses the Ministry of Labour.

Relationship between the author and Elisabeth Samson

Elisabeth Samson is not a distant relative and I do not believe myself to be her reincarnation as some have claimed. Why then the irresistible urge, the passion to research the life and person of Elisabeth Samson?

I can only confirm that the passion was genuine. Years before I started, reading historical documents made me wonder what she was like, how she became so wealthy, why she was so determined to marry.

The opportunity to pursue research on Elisabeth Samson arose when my husband was appointed ambassador in Brussels for the second time in 1988. My late husband had plenty to say about my long absences and the amount of time I spent digging through archives in the Netherlands. 'An ambassador's wife should stay at her post,' he said, and he was, of course, right. I responded by saying that my research into Elisabeth Samson had become an obligation.

My husband did not live to see the end of my project. He died in 1991 and I was only able to confirm with certainty in 1994 that the Ministry of Labour in Paramaribo was Elisabeth's former home.

Was it providence or mere coincidence? My husband started work in Surname in 1961 after completing his studies at the University of Leiden. He entered service at the Ministry of Social Affairs and Public Housing, accommodated in the building on Wagenwegstraat 22. A few years later, he became assistant director and was appointed director in 1970. He thus spent seventeen years of his working life in Suriname in Elisabeth's former home, eleven of them in the office of the director above what used to be Elisabeth's bedroom.

Did her spirit come to me longing for rectification in the historical documents that made reference to her? I have no idea. I only sensed the obligation to find out who she was and that I owed this to the people of Suriname.

The results of my research prove that the historians were wrong. Elisabeth Samson's wealth was not the result of an inheritance from a white man who had purchased her freedom and left her his possessions. On the contrary, she was indirectly responsible for the wealth of many white families, including Creutz's family in Cleve and Hermanus Daniel Zobre. Her property finally passed into the hands of creditors in the Netherlands.

Contemporary Surinamese women frequently remark: 'Why did she have to leave her wealth to white people? She could have done something for the poor, for her own people!' But she made her choice as a woman of her day, a choice that would probably be different had she lived today. But Surinamese women still have something to learn from her: you can achieve what you want if you believe in it and persevere. She married, something unheard of in her time! And who knows, perhaps further impossibilities can be achieved, perhaps something of Elisabeth's wealth will find its way back to Suriname one fine day.

Cynthia Mc Leod

Glossary of Terms

Aboma: giant constrictor

Adyosi: farewell

Aitdei: from the Dutch 'acht dagen' or 'eight days'. Memorial gathering held on seven evenings immediately after a funeral. The eighth gathering lasts the entire night. A time to sing, tell stories and enjoy typical snacks and refreshments

Ba: interjection. Approximate meaning: please

Bakra: white man

Basya: black plantation supervisor. Although himself a slave, he was often charged with the punishment of other slaves

Baya: term used in conversation between female peers

Biri-biri: marshland with a grassy surface

Bita: literally 'bitter', also used for all sorts of bitter-tasting herbal drinks

Blankofficier: white sentry, mostly ex-military

Botralie: kitchen scullery used for storing plates, dishes etc.; not used for cooking

Buku: dust or mould

Caiman: giant constrictor

Dram: drink with high alcohol content

Dresneger: a slave appointed to make medicinal potions and treat wounds

Eh, eh: guttural sound signifying negation

Faya watra: warm drink

Fa yu tan?: how are things?

Foto-tori: city gossip

Futuboi: message boy or runner

Granman: governor

Guneti: good night

Karboeger (m.) / *karboegerin* (f.): child of a negro and a mulatto

Katibo: slavery

Ke & *Ke baya*: expression of sympathy

Ke poti: poor soul

Kis'en moi: serves him right

Koekerom: yard kitchen

Koelastok: long pole used by the Maroons to steer their dug-outs

Korswuri: leaves of a specific shrub used to make an infusion that helped
   relieve a sick person's fever; the same leaves were also used for herbal baths
Kostgrond: field planted with cassava, bananas, taro etc.
Kowru winti: refreshing wind
Krasi-krasi: skin rash
Kroi: witchcraft
'*Lei hati moro soro*'? *Wel, granman kon sabi fosi a dede*: 'Lies hurt more than
   wounds'. The governor realised that before he died
Lemmetje: lemon
Lijn: narrow jungle path
Mamaisa: primal mother or mother earth
Malinker: a lame or infirm person
Maroons: runaway slaves who formed new tribes in the interior of Suriname
   and attacked the plantations
Masra: master or mister
Mi Gado: my God
Mi gai: exclamation of shock
Mi gudu: pet name: 'my dear'; also 'my sweetheart', 'my darling'
Mi na Agosu: I'm Agosu
Mi p'pa: pet name for males
Misalasi: I shall lose
Misi: missus or mistress
Moeroe: herbal drink to combat female infertility
Na bun e drun'en: she's delirious with joy
Na kapten Kroisi e kon: Captain Creutz is coming
Negerpoort: a narrow lane at the side of a house connecting the property with
   the street and secured on the street side by a door. Slaves lived on their
   master's property, and were obliged to use the negerpoort only and never
   the front door
Nene: an elderly lady with a nursing function
Nengre: Negro English
No: interjection with a variety of possible meanings
Nomerimi: don't tempt me
Odi: good day
Oranjetuin: literally Orange Grove, now a cemetery
Pagni: wrap worn over one shoulder, sometimes tied above the breasts,
   sometimes under the breasts in the form of a skirt
Pindak: roof made from the leaves of the pina palm
Pondos: large flat raft
Poti: poor soul

Sakafasi: subservient

San: exclamation of surprise or irritation: what!

San de fu du nanga misi?: what's wrong with misi?

Sibibusi: literally 'broom of the forest'. A heavy rainstorm with powerful gusts of wind

Sidon: be seated

Sisa: sister. The custom in early Creole culture was for younger children to avoid direct usage of the first name and address their much older brothers and sisters as *brada* (brother) or *sisa* as a sign of respect

Slemp: milk with sugar and saffron

Spanish Buck: a cruel form of slave punishment

Tapu: literally 'covering', here used for ritual protection

Te yanawe: very far away

Tomtom: dish made from crushed banana and served with soup

Tori: story

Tyuri: chirping sound made with the lips to indicate disapproval or indignation; only used by women.

Wai: exclamation of pain or fear

Waka nanga mi lobi na yu sei: go and may my love go with you

Wasi: ritual bath

Wisi: black magic

Zoutwaterneger: negro born in Africa and not native to Suriname

Zuur oranje: fragrant yet bitter citrus fruit

Zuurwater: lemonade

Notes

1 Bronnen voor de studie van Afro-Suriname [Sources for the Study of Afro-Suriname], vol. 15; trade editions were published in 1994 by Vaco in Paramaribo and Conserve in Schoor.

2 ARA/OPR (Office of Public Records), ONAS (Old Notarial Archives Suriname) Inv. nr.7 folio 82.

3 SS 164 Letter Governor Raye to Directors of the Society.

4 SS 164 Letter Governor Raye to Directors of the Society.

5 ARA/OPR Court of Police 17.

6 ARA/OPR Court of Police 17.

7 ARA/OPR Court of Police 17.

8 ARA/OPR Court of Police 18.

9 ARA/OPR Archives States General LIAS W.I.C. 55781.

10 ARA/OPR SS incoming correspondence and documents 164.

11 ARA/OPR Archive States General LIAS W.I.C. 77771.

12 ARA/OPR SS 264 Letter Governor Raye to the Directors of the Society, July 1737.

13 ARA/OPR SS 264 Letter Governor Raye to the Directors of the Society, July 1737.

14 ARA/OPR Archive States General LIAS W.I.C. 55781.

15 ARA/OPR OAS/GS Inv. nr. 5 Diary Governor Mauricius.

16 ARA/OPR OAS/GS Inv. nr. 5 Diary Governor Mauricius.

17 The gravestone of Catharina Elisabeth Crommelin can be found on plantation Rust en Werk.

18 J. Wolbers, *Geschiedenis van Suriname*, S. Emmering: Amsterdam, 1970, p. 242.

19 ARA/OPR OAS/GS Inv. nr. 8, Diary Governor Crommelin.

20 When the planter decided that the first haricot beans of the year had been harvested he would give 'bean feast'.

21 The original Dutch text was adapted for the modern reader by the author.

22 The original Dutch text was adapted for the modern reader by the author.

23 ARA/OPR ONAS Inv. nr. 218.

24 ARA/OPR ONAS Inv. nr. 123.

25 ARA/OPR ONAS Inv. nr. 123.

26 ARA/OPR OAS/GS Inv. nr. 9. Diary Governor Crommelin.

27 Municipal archive, Amsterdam; Notarial archive 12875/792.

28 J. Wolbers, *Geschiedenis van Suriname*, S. Emmering: Amsterdam, 1970, p.299.
29 ARA/OPR ONAS, Inv. nr 378.
30 Municipal archive, Amsterdam; Notarial archive, 12737/42.
31 ARA/OPR ONAS 52, folio 51.
32 ARA/OPR OAS Reformed Church Register, 1.06.11.16.
33 ARA/OPR OAS Reformed Church Register, section baptisms.
34 ARA/OPR Police Council microfilm 423, folio 84.